PRAISE

The Secret Spice Café Trilogy
BY PATRICIA V. DAVIS

"With incredible plot twists and fabulous, poignant ending, this final volume by author Patricia V. Davis is the finest of them all. The ship itself truly comes alive, with the same detailed and magical description that Davis always incorporates, but there are more far-flung locations to discover through the visionary and clever narrative techniques at play. *Demons, Well-Seasoned* is an absolute must-read that will not disappoint fans of the epic series."

—*Readers' Favorite*

"This intriguing and intense novel is a multi-layered story...a tale of magical realism, mystery, paranormal activity, and suspense. At the same time, it is, at its core, a story of love. Well written, fun, atmospheric. Five out of five stars."

–**Eric Guignard, Bram Stoker Award winner of** *That Which Grows Wild*

"Davis has a deft touch when it comes to blending the very real and relatable personal stories with the paranormal, supernatural, and thriller elements. Added bonus for me, the *Queen Mary* isn't just the setting; she's fully one of Davis' well-drawn, satisfying, and complex characters."

—**Mark B. Perry, Emmy award-winning writer of**
Picket Fences and Ghost Whisperer

"I was so drawn in by the storytelling, the history, and the women, that I could not put down the book until I had completed it from cover to cover. There is something for everyone: history, food, mystery, magic, ghosts, and romance. It is going on my favorites' shelf. I highly recommend it."

—*Mac's Books*

"The writing is beautiful, the story engaging, the ending satisfying. This novel is the kind that sticks with you, lingering for days, making you miss the characters and most certainly the setting. Wonderful book."

—*The Fictional Housewife*

"What impresses me about Davis is the volume of research she does and the subject matter experts she consults as she develops her stories…"

—**Jo Murray,** *On the Water* **columnist**

"The trilogy, bubbling with spirits, sizzling with adventure, and a dash of romance, is set aboard the great ocean liner, the *RMS Queen Mary*. The true history of the ship and her illustrious passengers is mixed into these delicious stories. Don't skip the Author's Note at the end of each one."

—*Fencepost*

"A beautifully-structured novel that builds layer upon layer of meaning, held together with gossamer threads and magic."

–*Huffington Post*

"A fast paced and intriguing read. Loved the setting of the *Queen Mary*, and tying in history and lore. Thoroughly enjoyed this book."

—Susan Schild, *USA Today* Bestselling author

"Smart and sassy—great for fans of Liane Moriarty."

—Book Club Cheerleader

"Davis throws in well-developed secondary characters and many engaging details about food, magicians, psychics and the stately ship herself, all without sacrificing the compelling pace; in fact, these details are equally as engrossing as the heart-racing suspense. ...Perfect for readers who enjoy both the supernatural psychological suspense of Jennifer McMahon and those who love Nora Roberts' storytelling prowess across many genres."

—IndiePicks Magazine

"Complex, rich, and satisfying...especially recommended for mystery enthusiasts looking for something different by way of setting, feisty and strong female characters...and a story line brimming with revelations and intrigue that aren't easily predictable."

–Midwest Book Review

"...Completely amazing."

—RT Book Reviews

"Davis's patient hand at storytelling threads itself into a perfect and suspenseful character of its own in this wonderfully dark and moody tale brimming with beautiful juxtapositions: modern technology with old world tastes and scents, surface interactions with deep, ghostly otherworldliness, and the common narratives around women and friendships with the ethereal, the intuitive and the feminine."

—**Amy Guth, President,** *Association for Women Journalists Chicago*

"So imaginative and so much fun, you won't want to put it down. I love a good ghost story, but a ghost story that has more than thrills within its pages makes a very rich ghost story, indeed."

—**Ann Garvin,** *USA Today* **bestselling author**

"Patricia V. Davis captures the essence of grand magic performance in this haunting novel."

—**David Copperfield, magician**

"A perfect read for when you are cruising, especially if you are crossing the Atlantic or travelling over Halloween. It should definitely go on your cruising shortlist."

—*Whitterings of a Cruise Ship Reader*

"Ghosts, romance, friendship, and food…what a great combination. From the very first page, I was drawn to the characters and their lives aboard the Queen. A bit of history, woven through a newly formed partnership, wrapped in mystery and intrigue. A wonderfully delightful story."

—*Books or Books*

"…An exceptional, uniquely gratifying novel. Make yourself something tasty to eat, put your feet up. You're going to be reading for a while.

—David Corbett, award-winning author of *The Mercy of the Night*

DEMONS, WELL-SEASONED

BOOK THREE

THE SECRET SPICE CAFÉ

ISBN 13: 978-1-7320649-6-6

Published by HD Media Press Inc.

THIS IS A WORK OF FICTION. Names, characters, places, dates, and incidents are either the product of the author's imagination or are used fictitiously.

Names: Davis, Patricia V. (Patricia Volonakis), 1956- author. Title: Demons, well-seasoned / Patricia V. Davis. Description: Albertson, NY: HD Media Press Inc., [2019] ǀ Series: The Secret Spice Café trilogy; book III. Identifiers: ISBN: 978-1-7320649-1-1 (hardback)ǀ978-1-7320649-6-6(paperback) ǀ 978-1-7320649-7-3 (Kindle) ǀ LCCN: 2019947580 Subjects: LCSH: Mambos(Vodou)--Fiction.ǀWomenpsychics--Fiction.ǀAfricanAmerican women-- Fiction. ǀ Female friendship--Fiction. ǀ Family secrets--Fiction. ǀ Demonology-- Fiction. ǀ Ghosts--Fiction.ǀSupernatural--Fiction.ǀ Parapsychology--Fiction.ǀMetaphysics--Fiction.ǀ Redemption--Fiction.ǀ QueenMary(Steamship)--Fiction.ǀRestaurants--California--Long Beach-- Fiction. ǀLCGFT: Historical fiction. ǀ Magic realist fiction.ǀ BISAC: FICTION / Occult & Supernatural. ǀ FICTION / Visionary & Metaphysical. ǀ FICTION /AfricanAmerican/ Women Classification: LCC: PS3604.A97269 D46 2019 ǀ DDC: 813/.6--dc23

Cover design and typeset by Tanya Quinlan

Interior design inspired by burl wood panels aboard the RMS Queen Mary

Printed in the United States of America

DEMONS, WELL-SEASONED

BOOK THREE

THE SECRET SPICE CAFÉ

PATRICIA V. DAVIS

HD Media Press Inc.

For
June Allen, Angela Parks, Kathy L. Murphy,
and all the other brave warrior women in my life. And to all women
who find their courage in the eleventh hour of their lives, as I did,
this one is for you.

ACKNOWLEDGEMENTS

If you're a reader who has stuck with me and this trio of novels until the end, then you're the first I wish to acknowledge. I thank you three times, once for each novel. My publisher thanks you, my agent thanks you, my characters are flattered, and my critics think you're too easily pleased. They might be right, but thank you just the same.

If you're a reader who wrote to tell me how much you enjoyed my work, or if you actually took the time out of your busy day to post a favorable review, then you need to know you inspired me to keep going. You were there, right next to me, on the night I wrestled with my work to the point where I was sure I had no business being a writer. I remembered the things you said, and they helped me try again.

If you're a reader who has become a friend, (and you know who you are) you've enriched my world by your presence in my life. Be certain that you sparked an idea in one of my stories. Be certain I thought of you while I was writing this series, and smiled. I may have even named a character after you. If you're one among these, I'm thankful to you and pleased in a way I can't describe that the work I started doing so late in life brought you to me. You're a gift, and I treasure you.

If you're another author who has helped me in any way, I will always remember that you did a good deed for me when I needed one, and I hope I can return the favor one day.

If you're an old friend or a family member who has supported my dream all these long years, and you're still here cheering me on, I love you.

I'd also like to shout a loud, long thank you to the following:

Houngan Toby Tarantino of Voodoo Authentica, New Orleans, and Priestess Miriam of the Voodoo Spiritual Temple, New Orleans. Thank you for seeing me, thank you for talking to us, thank you for your guidance, your patience, and for sharing your history with me. I hope I've done justice to the rich and beautiful practice of Vodou.

Angela Parks Papadopoulos, my beautiful, supportive friend who helped steer me in the right direction so I could immerse myself in the splendor of Louisiana and the fascinating history of the Creole people.

The ship aficionados, *Queen Mary* experts and authors who never made fun of my ignorant questions, corrected me kindly when I got things wrong, and praised me more than I deserved when I got things right. Your expertise had been invaluable, and I thank you for sharing it so generously: Colin Green, Christopher Rossetti, Dave Smith, David Lee, Derek Hollowday, Fran Hirsh, Jacob Larese-Callahan, Jimmy Kidd, Keith McIntyre, Laura Hirsh, Les Pickstock, Mervin Clarke, Michael Ryan, Mike Morin, Nicole Strickland, Ralph Rushton, Ramon Meneses, Jr., Richard Hunt, Rob O'Brian, Robbie Phillips, Robert Nigro, Tyler Joshua Frederick, Vinny Frittatta, Jay Braiman. Special thanks goes to Commodore Everette Hoard, whose knowledge of the *RMS Queen Mary* history and love for her is unsurpassed.

To Barrie Getz, James Brandmueller, Tom Varney, and Angela Richardson for their generosity in treating me to VIP tours, both virtual and in person, of the *Queen Mary* Engine Room and the *Titanic* exhibit aboard the ship. You have no idea how helpful these were. (Not to mention how much fun!)

Tom Varney, thank you, talented friend, for the gorgeous *Queen Mary* book holder you made exclusively for my trilogy. I love it, and keep it right on my desk.

Tony Strublic, I'm honored that you gave me one of your outstanding maritime drawings of my favorite ship.

Jo Murray, thanks for all the messages, photos, stories of your time aboard the ship, as well as the charming mementos. Your adventures make me grin with delight.

Mark Perry, June Allen, Joe Bertoldo, and Eleni Horgan for being such gracious book trailer guest stars, and to Niko Volonakis and Peter Horgan for film production. I think this book trailer is the best one yet, and I love that you were all part of making it happen.

Tom Guldner, Mark Greene, Jeremy Jorgensen, Bruce Laker, and Andrew J. Thomas for marine safety expertise. Thanks to you, I now know all the ways one can die aboard a ship, and I've crossed 'sailor' off my careers possibilities list.

A special cheer for Joe Bertoldo and Joey Pham, for the remarkably creative and stunning photos of the *Queen Mary*. Particularly memorable is the one for which Joey had to balance a silver tray, a coffee pot, and a vase on his head. And the one for which Joe had to step aboard the *Queen Mary* carrying a woman's high-heeled shoe. (Yes, just the one shoe.) All the photos you've taken for this series are spectacular, but I'm sure you understand why these two in particular have a singular place in my heart. (Oh, and the jellybeans were delicious, and helped fuel me through long nights of writing.)

Speaking of photos: Beat Meienberg, Pyrat Wesly, Robbie Phillips, Michael Crowe, Angela Richardson, Vinny Frittatta. Beautiful photos. Thank you for sharing them with The Secret Spice Café.

Sharon Cohn, Cynthia Faust, and Rebecca Faust of Breathless Wines, who started the Breathless Bubbles and Books Program. We so appreciate your commitment to literature and libraries. Thank you for including this trilogy in your program.

JG Faherty and Becky Spratford of the HWA, the Pulpwood Queens, and The Secret Spice Crew, for your extra support and encouragement. You're wonderful.

My publishing team: Kelly Preston, Jane Hunter, Arnold Knightly, Gordon Warnock, Fuse Literary, along with three very crucial work-in-progress readers, Niko Volonakis, Pete Davis, and Trish Clifford, and HD Media Press's creative and talented graphic artist, Tanya Quinlan. You know it wouldn't have gotten done without you.

"Demons are like obedient dogs; they come when they are called."

— *Remy de Gourmont*

"If you see Rose Mary, tell her I'm coming home to stay
Tell her I'm tired of travelin', I just can't go on this way…"

— *Fats Domino lyrics*

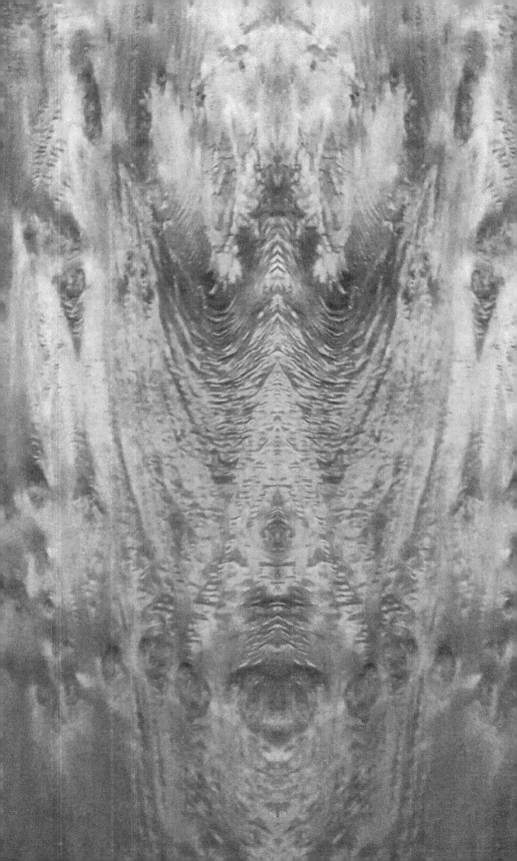

PROLOGUE

The rain was beastly. It blackened the sky. Like a serpent, it sprang from the pavements, coiled around potholes, and slithered along the road's perimeters. But when it hit the car windows, it fell like tears, the tears of the inconsolable, the tears the Queen hid in her heart.

They were almost there. The most arduous part of the journey, the five-hour train ride from Ballater, was over. They were only six miles from Clydebank, thereabouts, and that was a mercy.

She was exhausted already, and apprehensive about speaking in public for the first time. Not to a small gathering, moreover. She'd been told to expect an audience of two hundred thousand at least. That number had her clenching her gloved hand in her lap. Nerves and worry crawled and bumped around inside her in the same way the black Daimler limousine crawled and bumped over the drenched cobblestones and grooved steel tram tracks of Glasgow Road.

Her role was to maintain an air of serenity and confidence, so she kept her jitters to herself. It would be unthinkable to her to voice them aloud, which was just as well, as no one else shared her mood.

Certainly not today. Despite the wet gloom saturating the shoes and clothing of the endless thread of men, women, and children who stood four and five deep on both sides of the streets, their expressions were jubilant as they waved to the Royal motorcade going by. And George, sitting beside her, waved back proudly. As he should do. As he deserved to do.

He'd saved them all.

Granted, some of it was self-serving. The time after the war had been a turning point for their family. Had they ignored the hardships that had plagued the working classes, remained detached from the political unrest, the monarchy might not have survived. That possibility had factored into their actions, undoubtedly. Yet how many would be able to feed their children now, thanks to their King's tireless lobbying on behalf of the Welsh coal miners, the mill hands in Manchester, the shipbuilders in Newcastle, Liverpool, and Glasgow? His persistent, persuasive influence on legislators had compelled them to find a solution, to find the money—more than three and a half million pounds—for the completion of 'Hull No. 534.'

Through the rivulets on the glass, she surveyed the brick tenement buildings smudged black with soot. Although the whole route had been swept of debris in anticipation of their arrival, there was still a grimy feel to the area, a pall hanging in the surrounding atmosphere that had nothing to do with the inclement weather. The only businesses along the road that didn't appear deteriorated were the public houses. There was one on every street, and even this early in the afternoon, they were packed with men. Mary could see them—faces pressed against the façade windows, or huddled outside under the dripping awnings—hoisting their pints in tribute as her procession drove past.

Glasgow lived or died on the dockyards. Its populace had suffered tremendous loss during the Depression, and by 1930, work was stalled on the ship which was to be Britain's pride. Many were reduced to the breadline. And so, her husband did something as King rather unprecedented by previous generations of British Royalty: he stepped in. He'd used all the sway they held with politicians, unions, and bankers to get as many back to work as possible. After much lobbying, and a merger between the two giants, Cunard and White Star, as well as a massive loan, the shipbuilders were back at work, along with carpenters, tile and marble setters, fabric makers, mural artists and other craftsmen. The number employed in the construction, design, and outfitting of such a grand ocean liner totaled in the thousands, all of whom were ecstatic with their King George and Queen Mary, who'd rescued them from destitution.

Edward had taken part too. At least in this, he'd done his duty. In so many other ways, he shirked his responsibilities, and she and George were deeply disappointed in their eldest son.

'David'—as his family called him—preferred to flit about, attending lavish balls and garden parties, carrying on with women, and in general exhibiting behavior unbecoming to a Prince. It had gotten so that he and his father were barely speaking.

And it hurt her. After they'd lost little Johnnie, her other children had become even that much more precious to her. Although maternal love was another emotion she did not find easy to communicate. All she knew was that she didn't want more distance, didn't want this estrangement, not after all they'd endured together.

Now, David had taken up with that woman. That divorcée. An American, no less. Imagine it—imagine him thinking he could choose such a person. Didn't he understand who he was and what was required of him?

Why, she herself had been engaged to George's brother, Albert. Yet only six weeks later, Albert died of influenza. She'd been devastated, of course. Nevertheless, Albert's mother, Queen Victoria, had chosen her—Mary. It was Mary's responsibility—when the time came—to be Queen Consort, and it mattered not which of Victoria's sons ascended to the throne. A year after Albert's death, his younger brother proposed, and Mary accepted. There was no question that she would. George was to be King, and Mary's allegiance was to the crown, first and foremost.

Fortunately, she and George were well-suited. She glanced over at her husband with fondness as he smiled and waved to the multitude.

He was such a good king.

At the outbreak of the Great War, George carried out five visits to the national troops in Flanders, endeavoring to boost morale. During one of these, he was thrown from his horse. His pelvis was fractured, and he never fully recovered his health.

The smoking didn't help. Occasionally, when they were alone in their private quarters, she might sneak a cigarette or two herself. But in the close confines of the car, her nose wrinkled at the strong odor of tobacco. His habit was incessant, and it was killing him. They both knew it. The thought of where that would lead was only one more thing that made her sad.

It pained her to consider that David might not be a good replacement. He was being stubborn—intentionally so—in thumbing his nose at convention. He flaunted Mrs. Simpson, escorting her everywhere, buying her a vulgar amount of clothing and jewels. He was even pressuring them to allow her to attend their Silver Jubilee.

She would never permit that. Never. The very idea made her exhale a long, restless breath.

At the sound, the King turned his head in surprise. "Something amiss, May?"

'May' was the nickname only those closest to her used, and when George said it, it was always said with warmth. His affection for her was genuine, and that assuaged her. At least with him, she could believe she'd done things right. There was no censure coming from him, the kind of condemnation she felt coming from David every time he looked at her.

"Not at all," she hastened to reassure. "I was just—"

Her words were cut off by one of George's coughing fits. He reached for his handkerchief, his body jerking forcefully, and she leaned away to give him room. She didn't dare touch him, not even to pat his back. He hated being coddled. Hence, though it troubled her to do so, she pretended to ignore his ill health, just as he did.

All of it was worrisome—her husband's ailments, her son's defiance, and what might happen to the Empire as a result. There were times, she could admit only to herself, when she grew impatient with it all, when she wished she could just go off somewhere on her own, someplace where there were no obligations to meet, no ceremonies to attend, and no decorum to be mustered.

But this was her life, the life for which she'd been chosen. She was good at it—excellent, in fact. She'd grown accustomed to putting her position as Queen before everything else. It would be impossible to change at this stage. Overall, it wasn't so bad. She glanced at the throng outside again. Indeed, it could be far worse.

Her melancholy did not lessen.

The King's flare-up eased just as they reached their destination. Simultaneously they craned their necks to read the sign hanging over the entranceway: *John Brown and Company, Limited. Engineering and Shipbuilding Works.*

They allowed themselves an exchange of brief, congratulatory smiles. For the time being, she pushed her concerns aside. Today their ship would get a name, a name she hugged to herself.

When their car crossed the gates, she was knocked for six by the view before them. Sprawled for miles were giant derricks and cantilever cranes, and piles of wooden planks that stood taller and wider than ten men. There were enormous excavators and multi-wheeled transporters, dump trucks and concrete mixers, steel molds, air compressors, dredging apparatus, welding and sandblasting equipment, and so much more she couldn't possibly name. She hadn't thought about the meticulous engineering it took to build such colossal ships. The abundance of materials, the immensity of it all, awed her.

The rain pelted on as the driver slowed to a stop. Lining each side of the road, standing at attention, was the Clydebank Branch of the British Legion. A military band set up under a covered dais also stood, their musical instruments at the ready. Several lords, ladies, and other notables waited patiently in the damp to welcome the King and Queen.

The driver came around to open their door, and as soon as Mary stepped out, she was hit by the stench of the shipyard. It reeked even more than George's tobacco. The combination of chemicals used in welding, the anti-fouling paints with which the ship hulls were treated, and the sulfur wafting from the contaminated river made for an unpleasant perfume, to say the least. She wondered what it was like for the men who worked in this environment daily, although not by a glimmer did her discomfort show.

They were greeted straight away by Sir Percy Bates, who was the Chairman of Cunard White Star, and Sir Thomas Bell, the managing Director of John Brown and Company. Also Lady Bates, who curtseyed and presented the Queen with a bouquet of lilies and purple asters.

The flower selections were by no means an accident. Purple was the hue that symbolized royalty, and the asters combined with the deep pink lilies complemented the Queen's outfit to perfection. For this occasion, to set off the King's naval uniform, Mary chose a coat of cobalt blue with a fox collar dyed to match. Her hat was a toque the shade of sapphires, and its velvet brim was anchored with diamonds that looked smart with her pearl-and-diamond earrings. Her ensemble was being admired by the ladies on the platform. She dipped her nose into the bouquet and let them look. The breezy fragrance of the blooms was a welcome respite from the fetid air, and her thanks were more heartfelt than Lady Bates might have thought.

The tendering of the flowers was Their Majesties' prearranged cue to proceed toward the lift which would take them up to the launch platform. As they did so, the band struck up 'Rule Britannia.' When they reached the top, and walked across the enclosed stage to greet the spectators waiting below in the downpour, they were met by thousands and thousands of black umbrellas that stretched far and wide along the shoreline where the great ship stood waiting. They swelled in one great, dark wave when the crowd holding them let out a roaring cheer as their King and Queen came into view. Across the way, hundreds more workmen waved their caps in salute, clapping and whistling as they stood high upon the deck of Hull Number 534.

Everyone was hungry to see the ocean liner that was their salvation be christened and launched when the tide reached full, at precisely ten minutes past three that afternoon. They couldn't wait to learn the name she was to be given, a name that had been kept a closely-guarded secret. And, as it was typically the King who spoke in public or on the radio, they were also looking forward to hearing the voice of their Queen for the first time.

The King would address everyone first. The crowd hushed as he stood before the microphone. Though he read from sheets of paper, his words rang with emotion:

"...Today we come to the happy task of sending on her way the stateliest ship now in being..."

His statement wasn't hyperbole. The ship of which he spoke was one of the largest and most luxurious ever constructed at that point in time, hence the astronomic cost. It boasted two dozen boilers and four sets of turbines, generating one hundred and sixty thousand horsepower. It fueled four propellers that turned at a rate of two hundred revolutions per minute. Its technological innovations and speed were unparalleled for the day. And it would have rusted into oblivion, nothing more than a lost dream to those who had designed her.

Yet, as happy as they were, those there to celebrate that day couldn't know what a legend their sovereign craft was destined to be. Only five weeks earlier, Hitler had named himself Leader of Germany. He would come to despise this particular ship, to do everything he could to see her destroyed. And she would defeat him at every turn.

King George would be gone before that day came. He'd never know by what magnitude his mediation would affect world history, or that his wife—his dear Mary—would live to see the ship he'd rescued help vanquish a tyrant.

The King continued, "During those years when work upon her was suspended, we grieved for what the suspension meant to thousands of our people. Now we rejoice that with the help of my government it has been possible to lift that cloud and complete this ship. It has been the nation's will that she should be completed, and today we can send her forth, no longer a number on the books, but a ship with a name, in the world, alive with beauty, energy, and strength."

He moved aside, and then it was Mary's turn, the moment for which everyone in the Empire had waited, the moment they hoped would usher in a new era of prosperity. She stepped forward and, with a sterling silver filigree scissor designed just for the occasion, severed a cord that broke a bottle of Australian wine across the side of the hull. A photographer from the press was soaked in the process, a mishap that had onlookers grinning.

But all went silent, holding in their collective breaths, as Her Majesty pressed the launching button that would start the liner on its way into the river.

"I am happy," she said into the microphone, "to name this ship the *Queen Mary*—"

The noise from the crowd at the reveal nearly drowned out the rest of the Queen's words—

"I wish success to her and to all who sail in her."

Every eye shifted to the bank. The newly-named *Queen Mary* moved with a sloshing sound, her long hull soared down the slipway, as though she too, had been longing for this day. Bulky lengths of chain, thicker than the laborers' biceps, clanked and scraped as they unfurled, holding her, steadying her, helping to break the momentum of her propulsion into the water. The cheers were thunderous when the great ship freed herself from the confines of the ramp. Her bow hit the river last, raising a wave which inundated everyone on the southern shore, another soaking that brought forth laughter.

The *Queen* was afloat in the Clyde.

And as Mary watched the vessel glide along the water, glistening with raindrops and sea spray, she thought of what her husband had said to describe it, and once more was swamped with sorrow.

It wasn't her habit to dream of things that could never be, nor to make wishes that could never come true. Yet in that singular instant, she knew she would never be as 'alive with beauty, energy, and strength.' Not in the same way her namesake would. She'd never have the adventures her ship would have, never travel across oceans and continents at will, like those who would sail aboard, going somewhere, doing something with their lives. She was bound to her nation until death relieved her of her post. She had made a promise and she would keep it.

Even so, she whispered a prayer right then—too softly for anyone else to hear—that when she left this world, somehow, some way, a small piece of her soul might attach itself forever to the magnificent ocean liner that bore her name.

At the exact time Queen Mary of Teck christened her ship—not one second later or earlier—a child was born more than four thousand miles away, just north of the French Quarter in New Orleans, in a grand colonial country home on Bayou St. John.

Here the time was six hours earlier than it was in Clydebank, just ten past nine in the morning. The weather was warm, the humidity thick enough to slice with a Cajun skinning knife. The scents of the marshland were peppery and ripe, and the water wasn't tainted by shipyard waste. The bayou thrummed with life, slow-moving though it was. The fish and crustaceans swam in languid circles under the surface, making themselves an easy mark for the water snakes and alligators that lay in wait, hidden in the murkiness of the duckweed and hyacinths. The river turtles were a nuisance only to the insects, as they snacked solely on algae, mayflies, beetle larvae and the like. Along the marsh's edge, in the surrounding foliage of cypress and tupelo trees, muskrats, raccoons, nutria, and other marine mammals scuttled and hid, trying to keep themselves from ending up a bigger creature's breakfast, while at the same time searching for a meal of their own.

On the bank of the water, the white-columned manor was built in a style that kept hot summers in mind; the ground floor was enclosed with pastel walls of soft brick. The hipped roof was double-pitched and the *briquette-entre-poteaux* design offered structural support, as well as insulation. The doors were positioned across from one another to keep cool air moving, and extended galleries on both the bottom and top levels of the house kept the sun off the walls and offered outdoor breezeways. An opulent Venetian-style fountain bubbled in the center of the circular drive, birds chirping happily in its dancing spray. Lush gardens boasted sultry-scented magnolias, cerulean-blue irises, camellias as plump and pink as a young woman's lips, and climbing white roses as old as the bayou itself.

The house was fitted with shutters to provide relief from the Louisiana sun, and in the bedroom where the baby had been born, they were shut tight to keep out lizards and prying eyes. But a determined mosquito could always slip in through the slats. That morning, they hovered over the laboring woman's bed and crooned for blood.

They got it. The evidence of a birth gone wrong stained the bed linens red and spattered the elegant Persian carpet. It soaked the towels the midwife had tried to stave it with, covered her apron, smeared across her palms, and made dark crescents under her fingernails. Its tangy, metallic essence infused the air, clashing with the aroma of spiced catfish and eggs the cook had been frying up before the pains started. They came too early and too fast, as though Èrzulie Dantòr had made it happen, had wanted the child to arrive that day. And when the infant girl was brought forth, like so much else in the room, she was marked. But not with the blood of life.

Her mother knew two things: she wouldn't live to see her baby's second day on this earth, and the white man who thought he was the baby's father wouldn't want her.

The young mother's name was Philomène. She was beautiful and she was Creole and she was the mistress of the man who believed her to be carrying his child. After she was gone, there would no one to protect the little one from his wickedness.

The midwife, Celeste, stood at the end of the birthing bed, quaking with grief and nausea as she watched Philomène cradle her whimpering newborn in tremulous arms. Celeste was young too. She'd tried everything she knew, but her experience was limited, and what they'd done had been done in secret and in haste. When it came down to it, the only choice she had was to save the mother or save the baby. It could not be both. Philomène had wanted her child—a child born of true love—to live.

She gulped back tears. "What can I do, Philomène? Please tell me what to do."

Philomène struggled to form words through lips gone dry and chapped. This would be her only chance to speak to her little girl.

"You're wonderful," she told her. Though weak and short of breath, she made a valiant effort to keep her voice soothing, filled with love, just on the infinitesimal chance her daughter might remember it one day. "Don't believe...anybody who tells you different. I love you. And your Daddy...your real Daddy...he loved you too."

She tried to swallow over her parched throat, raised her eyes to the midwife, and Celeste could see acceptance in them through the pain. "Take her to the mambo, and tell her...tell her everything. The mambo will know what to do. Go now, Celeste."

Celeste squeezed her eyes shut. "Philomène. I can't leave you."

"There's nothing you can do for me. You should both be gone. Please. Before he gets back."

Her arms felt too empty the moment Celeste took her daughter from her. Inside, she felt too hollow, too light. She began to shiver as the sensation of warmth pulsing from her womb and onto her thighs grew slower, dimmer. As she felt the pain fading, felt herself floating, one detail she'd forgotten caught.

"Wait." Her words were slurred now, almost inaudible in her final plea. "Rosemary. Tie some around her neck...keep the bad spirits away."

When Philomène went silent, Celeste burst into tears. She beheld the infant in her arms and knew that this child—this little orphan girl who'd been baptized in blood—would need more than an herb to protect her from harm.

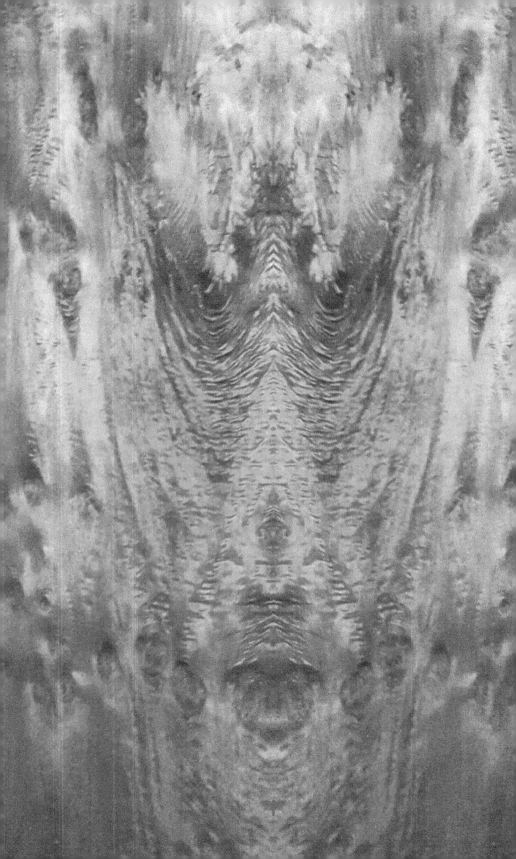

CHAPTER ONE

Saturday, October 31, 2020, twelve hours before the end,
Franklin Avenue Elementary School, Los Angeles

At noon, while she was standing on a hill in the sunny field behind the school where she attended kindergarten, Alana Miceli fell into a trance. It was the first time in her life such a thing had happened, and she had no idea what it was.

The teachers and parent volunteers had gone all out for the fall festival. There was face-painting, apple bobbing, and pumpkin carving. They'd brought in farm animals for the children to pet and feed. There was a haunted house that was more fun than spooky, hay rides, and even a Pinewood Derby. The excited squeals and chatter of the children, the chirping of the birds, the gentle rustle of falling leaves, the scents of popcorn and freshly-mown grass, and every other sensory perception of her surroundings ebbed. All Alana could see in front of her was the big ship.

It wasn't there—it was thirty miles away, floating in the Long Beach Harbor. But in her mind's eye, it was close enough to touch, and it made her feel scared.

She didn't know why. The *Queen Mary* was Mommy's favorite ship. They went there last year when Alana was four, and she loved it. It was as big as the world and so beautiful. It smelled of secrets and stories, and when she walked upon the wooden decks, the soles of her shoes made wonderful sounds. They got to visit the restaurant that used to be Grandma's, the one where Daddy met Mommy. They went into the kitchen, and Grandma's friends, Rohini and Cristiano, were there. Rohini cried when she saw them. Happy tears, she said.

1

"You don't remember me," she told them. "You were just babies when your parents brought you last time. But we remember you, and we're so happy to see you again."

The *Queen* was happy they were there too. Alana caught her murmurs of welcome. When the ship blew her whistle, all who had ears jumped to attention, but when she whispered, only a few took the time to hear.

As Alana stood in the cheerful school setting, she thought she heard the ship calling to her again.

Only this time it sounded different. This time she didn't like it. Halloween was supposed to be scary, but not *too* scary. Besides which, today wasn't just Halloween. It was also her birthday, and they were going to have a Halloween birthday party with presents and balloons. Grandma was coming, and there would be cake. It wasn't a scary day, it was a happy one.

Then why did she feel so scared?

She had the thick, glossy hair of her father, the soft brown eyes of her mother, and more supernatural potential budding inside her tiny being than her parents were capable of, conjointly. They saw her power increase by the day, but they didn't know how far it would go. Not yet, they didn't.

Alana's eyes clouded over and her pupils shrank to pin points. She wasn't moving, but she felt like she was—flying, soaring toward the ship as though she were being pulled through space. It was only when she thought she would crash into its hull that she lurched to a stop and hung, suspended in the air above the water.

She was so close to the *Queen Mary* that she could see the spots where paint was peeling off the metal, and the flecks of orange-brown rust around those big nails she had in her sides. The ship had so many round windows, and Alana thought she might reach one to touch. She pulled back her hand when she saw there was a dark, shiny liquid seeping from the bottom of every porthole as far as she could see. What was it? Her eyes followed, transfixed, as the liquid dribbled down the sides of the ship and plopped into the harbor below.

She sucked in a breath. The harbor was turning red. The ship was bleeding.

"No. Stop it. Stop it, Alana," she said out loud. "Make it go away."

Her breathing was uneven now. She wanted to go home. Though she fought with all her might to send herself back to her body on the hill at her school, she was wrenched aboard the ship and into The Secret Spice Café.

Grandma's restaurant didn't feel the same as she remembered. It wasn't warm and bright. It wasn't scented with melted butter and sugar, with spices and sauces and herbal teas. It was gray and dim, and the sour air made her nose wrinkle.

Through the dimness she searched for a familiar face. Was Grandma's friend here? Maybe she could help her get home.

As soon as Alana wished it, there Rohini was—sitting in the shadows of the dining room, huddled in a chair, her arms wrapped around her knees as she stared at the closed kitchen doors. Behind those doors, Alana could hear men shouting, *Marisol. Marisol!*

Something was in there. In the kitchen with those men. Whatever it was, it made her break out in a cold sweat.

Again, *Marisol!* And again.

"Alana?"

At the sound of her name, she snapped back. Her father was standing in front of her. "You okay, sweetheart? You're shivering. Are you cold?"

Alana mumbled a reply.

Another little girl the mirror image of Alana stood next to him. "What did you say, Alana? You're talking too low again."

Alana's body jolted once more as she threw off the last remnants of her trance. "I said I'm okay, Maria. I'm not cold."

Her father wasn't convinced. "That must have been some daydream. Put your sweatshirt on just in case."

Alana kept quiet as her father took her sweatshirt out of her backpack and helped her tug it on. If she told him, what would he say?

Maria smiled, and grabbed her hand. "Come on. They have goats. We can feed them by ourselves. Daddy said."

At that exuberant news, Alana set aside what she'd seen. Maybe it was just a bad dream. Maybe Mommy's favorite ship was okay and there was no reason to be afraid.

Luca watched as the two sisters ran toward the animal pens, puzzled by Alana's behavior, but not worried.

He should have been worried. It should have been easy for him to recognize that something much more significant than a daydream had occurred for her. She'd turned five years old only that day. Just five, but showing signs for the past year, at least, of having more power than he had.

He had his first experience with divination when he was seven, standing on a bridge with his grandfather. He could never forget what he saw in his mind that day, nor how those horrors played out years later aboard the vintage ocean liner where he'd met his wife. The ship had revealed to him both his greatest love and his darkest tragedy. When it came to the *Queen Mary*, his premonitions should have been especially keen. He should have sensed that the ship was in danger just as he should have sensed his young daughter's turmoil.

But he was oblivious to it all. Given his current circumstances, that was to be expected. His focus was on his life as a father and husband.

He kept watch on Alana and Maria as they neared the pens and a parent volunteer handed them some food pellets. He frowned when she walked away. Weren't they too young to be left on their own to feed animals? Didn't goats bite? Should he join them there, even though he'd promised they could go by themselves?

No sooner did he think that when he spotted the missile from the corner of his eye—an ice cream cone flying at an impossible speed—aimed dead on for a jeering little boy. Whipping around, he just managed to block it from its target with his chest. He stared down at the splatter of chocolate ice cream and rainbow sprinkles on his favorite leather jacket.

"Ha ha—missed me. You stink."

"Shut up. I hate you, Tommy Bertoldo!"

"Niki! Come over here."

After one last scowl at Tommy, Niki turned a guileless face to Luca. "I'm not Niki, Dad. I'm Maria."

"Good try." Luca leveled her a look. "I said, come here."

Niki dredged her sneakers in the dirt as she walked over. "How did you know it was me?"

"You think I can't tell my own kids apart? That's number one. Number two—" he pointed in the direction of the petting zoo—"Maria's over there, with Alana. Nice of you to throw your sister under the bus, by the way. And number three, she doesn't have a rocket for an arm."

He dug through his pockets. Dammit. He forgot to bring tissues, and with Tommy still nearby, making obnoxious faces at his little girl, he couldn't use magicks to clean his jacket. "We don't throw things at people." Especially at that speed, he thought. Just imagine the lawsuit if she'd hit her mark.

"He's always bothering me and saying mean stuff."

Luca shared her opinion that Tommy was a pain in the ass, and his paternal instincts had him wishing he could have let the cone fly. It was a testament to his integrity that he stood firm. "Has he ever hit you? Hurt you with anything besides words?"

"No, but—"

"Then you keep your hands to yourself too." Gently, he tapped her upper arm. "See this here? It's for baseball only. You could have hurt him, honey, and you know it." He held up an index finger. "I catch you throwing anything at anybody again, you're off the team. Understand me?"

Niki kept her head down and nodded. She knew when her father meant business.

Not being allowed to play baseball would be a harsh punishment. She was an athletic wunderkind, practically leaping out of her mother's womb. Two weeks before her first birthday, she climbed from her high chair onto the kitchen counters, opened the cupboards and threw cookies down to her sisters. Currently she was the best pitcher at her school, peanut-sized though she was, usurping the two-years-older Tommy—the reason for the enmity between the two.

With a long-suffering breath, Luca brushed ineffectually at his jacket. The ice cream had seeped into the leather during his lecture, leaving a dark, sticky stain. Now that it had, he doubted his powers could lift it out. Maybe the dry cleaner would have better luck. When he saw Maria and Alana come hurtling over, alarm on their faces, he braced himself for the second crisis of the afternoon.

"Daddy, it was an accident! Honest."

It was Maria who led with the qualification, and that surprised him. She wasn't usually the mischief maker. His sweet-natured Maria had inherited her mother's ability to see spirits and visions. So what calamitous thing could she have done by accident? Summon a poltergeist?

Alana affectionately nudged her sister aside. "It wasn't her fault, Daddy. I did it." Alana's way was to speak softly. With the festival noise, Luca had to lean down close to hear her. "We were by the goats—"

"We felt sorry for them, Dad," Maria interjected. She was too loving to let her sister take the fall alone. "They were so crowded in there. And hungry. No one else besides us was feeding them."

"Uh huh." Luca pinched the bridge of his nose. She didn't have to go on. He knew where this was headed, and he knew who the real culprit was. He addressed Alana. "Did you make the goats disappear, sweetheart?"

"I didn't mean to do it."

Shit, thought Luca. The second time this month. Was this going to be the new thing now?

Alana held out her hands in a helpless gesture as she tried to explain. "I was just petting them. And then I...I started to feel sorry for them, you know, Daddy? Because they were stuck there."

"Stuck?"

"In their cage. I was thinking how much better they would like it if they could be free." She was crying now, tears rolling fast down her little cheeks, as Maria patted her back and Niki edged closer, her face mirroring Maria's sympathy. "The next thing I knew, my brain just went—*whoosh*—and they were gone."

"Aw, Alana, don't cry." Luca hugged her, but he frowned in concern as she clung to him, holding on longer and tighter than the situation called for. She was too distraught, even for missing goats. "I know you didn't mean it, sweetheart. Things like this can happen." But only with his kids, he added to himself. Brushing at the moisture on her face with his thumbs, his asked, "Uh...can you remember where you sent them?"

Alana shrugged, sniffled, and rubbed her sleeve across her nose.

He wished to hell he'd remembered the tissues. He tried another way. "Did the goats stay in California, or do you think you sent them to Grandma and Grandpa's?"

Luca questioned her with loving patience while at the same time his mind was racing. When he was Alana's age he managed to make his pet turtle disappear. But three goats? He had to admit he was impressed, and even proud. Her powers were growing at a prodigious rate. He considered asking her if she could make ice cream stains disappear, but obviously, she still needed practice with control. She might send him to Siberia by accident, and who knew if he'd be able to counteract that? Utilizing his powers in tandem with hers was something they hadn't yet tried. He sure hoped the goats weren't at Cynthia and Raul's. He doubted they'd find them as entertaining as they had the ducks.

Both he and Sarita understood from the start that there was something...extra potent in the daughter who'd been born last of the four. On the *Mary*, when Sarita revealed her birthmark to him, she told him it had appeared when she was twelve. Alana sisters didn't have theirs—if they ever would—but Alana was born with hers, same as Luca was. What that meant he could only speculate.

Mulling that over, a fact blasted into his consciousness as though it were breaking news: 'Born last of the four.'

He had *four* daughters. Missing goats became much less important. "Wait a minute, wait a minute—where's Alexandra?"

"Alex is in the derby, Dad. Remember? You helped her make her car." Niki rolled her eyes. Why was he always forgetting stuff?

"Crap. The derby." He jumped up, checked his watch. "It's going to start any minute, and it's all the way over by the bleachers. Dammit, we have to run. Get your things."

"What about the goats?"

DEMONS, WELL-SEASONED

"We'll figure that out after, Alana. Don't worry about it, honey. Is that your Supergirl sweatshirt by the tree?"

"That one's mine." Maria ran over to get it. "You know, Daddy, you said two bad words."

"Yep. You're right. I'm sorry, sweetheart. Let's go. Alex will feel bad if we're late." He scooped Niki up onto his shoulders, hitched Maria and Alana onto one hip each. "Do we have everything?" When they nodded, he started to run, bouncing the girls along, making all three giggle.

"Think it's funny, huh? Daddy's not strong enough to carry all of you."

"Yes, you are, Dad. You're very strong." With a tender touch, Niki brushed her hand over her father's hair. "Why don't you just pop us over there?"

"Too many people around."

"What's wrong if they see?"

"I thought we talked about this, Niki. We'll discuss it again when we get home."

"Can you make spaghetti for dinner?"

"Again? We've already had it twice this week."

"Come on, Daddy," Maria chimed in. "Please make us spaghetti? You should make it for us, since it's our birthday."

Alana added her vote. "Yes, Dad. Please?"

"We'll see—" he had to pause to draw in air—"what Mommy says."

"Yay," cheered Niki. "Mommy will say yes. She loves it too."

Maria burst into song, and both her sisters groaned. Singing had started as a coping mechanism for her, one encouraged by Luca. She wasn't afraid of the ghosts she saw, but like Sarita, she had visions during the night and sometimes woke up crying. That's when she wanted only her father. No matter where he was or what he was doing,

9

Luca would pop to her bedside and sing to her until she fell back to sleep. She found tunes from the big band era most lulling, and sang her favorites all throughout the day. It irritated her sisters, but Luca was relieved she'd found a way to deal with images she was too young to understand. He grinned as she belted out the lyrics—

"...and I *know* we'll meet again some *sunny* day!"

"You like that song, Maria? Did you know the lady who sang it—her name is Vera Lynn—used to sing it for all the soldiers during World War Two?"

"Was World War Two when you were a little boy?"

"No, Alana," Luca chuckled as Maria switched from singing to humming. "I'm old, but not that old."

Niki rolled her eyes again. "Can't you *please* teach her some new songs, Dad?"

"I like old songs. They remind me of a friend of mine. His name was Elliot. He was a soldier in that war."

Maria stopped humming when something occurred to her. "Hey, Dad, guess what? There were kittens by the goats."

Luca nearly stumbled at that news. "Did...anything happen to the kittens?

"No. But maybe we could get one. Can we?"

"Sure, we can get a kitten. We have to get rid of Mommy first. They make her sneeze."

"*Tch.* Dad, you're so silly. We're not getting rid of Mommy."

"Let's...take a vote on it later. Keep Mommy...or get a kitten."

By now he was panting. As tiny as they were, there were three. And he was running. Damn. The afternoon wasn't nearly over and already he was beat. After he brought the girls home, he still had to pop over to São Paulo to pick up Cynthia. It's a good thing Raul had work, or that would be two trips. At this rate he'd be lucky if he wasn't out for the count by the time their party started.

Alana had a question too.

"What was that, honey? Didn't hear you."

"I said, do you know Marisol?"

Luca spotted the derby setup. Thank God. He didn't think he could hold them much longer. "Marisol? You bet I do. Marisol is my hero."

"She is?" That rattled her. "Why?"

"I'll tell you the story someday. Where did you hear her name? Did Mommy say it?"

"No. Not Mommy."

"Then, who?"

"I don't know who it was, Daddy." The manner in which she said that had Maria eyeing her sharply. Alana was upset about something besides the goats, she could tell. What was it?

Focused on the derby, Luca was still clueless.

They made it to the track just as Alexandra got in position for the first heat. Luca waved and gave her a thumbs up. They spent hours together on that car, and he was looking forward to seeing her compete. After only one run he swore again, under his breath this time, and hurried over to take her out of the race.

"*Dad*, what are you doing?" Alexandra shouted over the music and the school principal's amplified commentary.

Luca moved the girls away from the crowd and bent down to speak with Alexandra quietly. "Your car was going faster than the others. Alex. Way, way faster. Were you cheating?"

"No." She was indignant.

"Hmm. Let me rephrase that. Did you, by any chance, do something to your car?"

She didn't bat an eye. "I modified the specs."

"You souped up your car?" Luca's eyes went wide. "Holy s—" he checked himself. "Yeah. Well, you see, that would be cheating."

Alexandra put her hand on her hip. "How else was I supposed to win? Alana's better than me at everything. Why can't I do something the best, for a change?"

And here was another concern. Alexandra talked in full sentences by the time she was six months old. She was a genius at both science and math. Despite these impressive aptitudes, she'd recently started comparing herself to Alana. The memory of where Santi's envy had led made Luca's insides twist.

But one issue at a time.

He rubbed his palm over his face as he thought of what to say. This was how he spent his days—deliberating over the finer points of his discussions with his daughters—what attitude, what phrasing, what length. Oh, to be a magician in Vegas again. He'd never enjoyed it as much as Santi had, yet how much easier to be eloquent when his dialogue was scripted ahead of time. His quadruplets were a tougher audience than any he'd performed for at Caesar's.

The direct approach was probably best. "You cheated, so you're disqualified." He sliced his hand through the air. "That's it, Alexandra."

"I didn't cheat." She was itching to argue the point.

"Sweetheart." Even though he used the endearment, Luca kept his voice firm. He hoped that would put her on her guard just enough so that she'd listen to him without debate. For once. "We worked on that car together. You know they gave us construction guidelines. You alter the car, you break the rules. You break the rules, that's cheating."

"Sorry to interrupt, Dad. I have a question." When Niki talked she motioned with her hands, as Luca did. "Mommy said that science is one of Alex's talents, like my talent for sports. So if I'm allowed to use my talent to beat Tommy at baseball, why can't Alex use her talent to win the race?"

"Yeah, why not, Dad?" Alexandra stared up at him, her little chin set at a mutinous angle.

"That's…it's not the same thing."

Maria tugged on Luca's sleeve. "Daddy—"

"One minute, Maria. Alex and I are talking."

"But I need to tell you something. It's very, very important."

"Daddy, my tummy hurts."

That announcement from Alana garnered a *tch* sound from Alex. Alana was stealing his interest away from her *again*.

Luca forgot all else. "Your tummy, you said? Just your tummy?" Alana hadn't been herself all afternoon. He'd caught her shivering earlier. If she had a virus, they'd all get it, and there were no words to describe that kind of hell. He felt her forehead. "You don't feel warm. How much ice cream did you have?" He lowered his voice, for delicacy. "Did you go the bathroom before we left the house?"

"It's not that kind of tummy ache." She was mumbling again. "I feel like something's wrong, Daddy."

For the first time Luca noticed how tense she was. "This isn't still about the goats, is it? Because I said I could fix that."

"No. Not that." She looked miserable, but again, she didn't explain.

"Dad." Maria tugged on his shirt a second time. "I *really* need to tell you something. You won't let me tell you."

Alex stamped her foot. "Boy, we never get to finish our conversations, Daddy."

Luca took a steadying breath, mentally counted to ten. "I'm sorry, Alex. I'm sorry, Maria." Man, was he dog tired.

Sarita, he thought to himself. How could you do this to me? She begged him to bring the girls up to the school on his own so she could get things ready for their party. Would he say no to minding his own kids for a few hours when she'd hauled them around by herself for nine months? But it was a bad idea and they both knew it. Letting them loose at an event like this without the second set of ears and eyes was asking for trouble.

He rubbed at his forehead. "All right, Maria, Alex—who wants to go first?"

"You can go first, Alex."

Alex exhaled long and hard. "Ne-*ver* mind. I'm done."

Amused by her dramatics, he asked, "Are you sure, Alex?" When she shrugged, a look of martyrdom on her face, he stifled a smile and turned to Maria. "What did you want to say, Maria?"

"There's a ghost lady over there. She keeps staring at us."

"It's Halloween, honey. Lots of people dressed as ghosts today."

He was tired. He didn't mean to sound dismissive, but his attitude vexed Maria now too. "*No*, Dad. You're not listening to me. She's a real ghost. And she looks like…" she peered at the woman again…"the pictures you have of your mommy."

That got his attention. "What? What did you say, Maria?"

The next minute, Alana slid next to Maria and pointed behind him. "I see her too, Dad."

Alex and Niki scrambled closer. Following their sisters' line of sight, they both started shouting at once.

"Hey, I can see her!"

"Me too. Look, Daddy—she's floating."

It seemed all four could see spirits now, not just Maria.

Luca had gone still. Could it be?

With a twist of his shoulder, he saw that they were right. It was Gina—floating, just as Alex said, about twenty yards away, in the Parent-Teacher Association's pumpkin patch.

Every other thought flew from his mind. As he gaped at her, fatigue evaporated and his heart leapfrogged with joy. His mother was here.

His cherished, deceased mother

He hadn't seen her since she'd appeared on the *Queen Mary* six years before. When his daughters were born, he got a glimpse of her reflection in the window of the hospital nursery. He felt her comforting presence beside him at his father's funeral the following year. But she hadn't manifested herself fully since she and several other spirits aboard the *Mary* had helped to save his life and Sarita's.

To see her again—*see* her—while he was with his daughters, to know they could see her too, made him want to bust out crying.

His elation withered as something else clicked: Her image was pixelated, just as it had been aboard the ship. That meant she wasn't supposed to be here anymore than when she'd appeared to him those years before to warn him of danger. He should have realized immediately this visitation wasn't a social call.

As he was about to go to her, Alana blurted, "Oh, no. She's not smiling. I *knew* something was wrong."

Her words stopped Luca in his tracks. "You knew something was wrong?" he repeated. As he studied her wan, pinched complexion, the brain fog induced by fatherhood began to lift. "Wait a minute. Do you mean...is that why your tummy hurts?"

When she gazed at him helplessly, the dominoes fell. "Alana." Kneeling swiftly, he cupped her face in his hands. "Why did you ask me about Marisol? Did you see something?"

She was still uncertain, her eyes gobbling up her face.

"Don't be afraid to tell me, sweetheart. Is there something Daddy doesn't know?"

It all came out in a rush. "I saw it. In my head. Mommy's ship. Grandma's friend, the lady with the long black hair, she was crying.

And there were men shouting that name. Marisol." She took hold of his sleeve, bunching the material under her small hand. "Daddy, there's a monster there. It looked like a person, but it...it wasn't. And—" she hitched out a whisper—"it wants to hurt the ship. It wants to hurt all of us."

His blood went to ice. "You saw all this today? While we were here?"

When she tipped her head, he hated himself. How could he have missed this? He needed to be more diligent. All at once, the idea that his children had powers wasn't so charming. Right then he understood that they could become damaged by them. As his wife had been by hers. And so much of what they might be capable of was still undetermined.

As smoothly as he could manage, he spoke. "Listen to me, sweetheart. If this happens again—if you see something, whatever it is—you tell me or Mommy right away. Promise?"

To the others he said, "Alex, Maria, Niki—is there anything you need to tell Daddy—anything that scared you?" When they shook their heads, he forced himself to take one calming breath. "Okay." He kissed the top of Alana's head, stood up and pressed his fist against his mouth as he stared grimly in his mother's direction.

What kind of hell were they in for now?

He swiveled back to his daughters and pointed to the ground. "Stay right in this spot. I'm going over to find out why Grandma Gina is here." In a tone that brooked no argument, he reiterated, "Don't move *one* step. Got it?"

At their solemn nods, he left them to walk to his mother. As he drew closer, he saw the fear slashed across her face, and it made his heart pound. Gina tried to push toward him, but it was as though she were being held back by shackles that were imperceptible to him. She struggled to free herself, mouthing words he couldn't hear. He ran toward her, recklessly. Just before he reached her, he slammed into a perdu wall—high, wide, hard as brick, but invisible. His face exploded with pain and he fell to his knees. Gina hammered her palms against the unseen blockade, her voice screaming in his head, *Luciano. Go home. Hurry, hurry!*

Thunder bellowed—the blast so loud and close that Luca wrapped his arms around his head. A jagged streak of light hit the ground, scorching the grass. Smoke rose. When it cleared, his mother was gone.

He clambered to his feet. His face felt wet. When he touched it, to his shock, his hand came away red. Blood was dripping from his nose.

Panicked, he glanced about. A woman turned his way, but she seemed to look right through him. The sun was still out, the day still clear. Parents and children went on with their activities. He saw Niki's baseball coach and several other teachers gathered together. He thought he heard one say something about the empty animal pen. Other than that, everything at the festival was just as it had been. Somehow the noise and flash in the sky had gone unobserved.

The only other witnesses were in hysterics as he raced to them.

"Daddy! Daddy!" A screaming chorus of terror.

"Hold on to me. All of you. Tight." The hell with discretion. He needed to get to Sarita.

His daughters grabbed hold of his ruined jacket and clung. After one more frantic swipe at his bleeding nose, he knelt down and huddled them to him.

A few seconds of crackling, and they were gone.

CHAPTER TWO

*Approximately six months earlier, Memorial Day,
Monday, May 25, 2020, Long Beach*

In the eyes of water, all men are equal.

To a spring, whether he is black or white, he can drink. To a lake, whether he is rich or poor, he can fish. To a sea, whether he is young or old, he can sail. And to an ocean, whether he is good or evil, he can be buried.

She remembered the folklore of her childhood in India, how the wives of fishermen and sailors would throw a precious belonging into the sea—a sacrifice in exchange for their husbands' safe return. Her most valued possession was her wedding ring, but she would never give that up, because the water had already taken her mate. She knew that now.

And yet, every morning, she came down to the spot where they said he'd been lost, and scanned the rippling bay. Every morning for the past seven months since he'd been gone, she walked the shoreline down and back, as he used to do.

Even today she made no exception. Before today, she could still dream that he would be found alive and well, that things would go back to the way they'd been. But Cristiano was never coming back, and today was the day that everything at the restaurant they'd built together officially changed. Their life there was gone forever.

He was gone forever.

Still she'd come down to the shore. To hope.

After one last gaze past the quay, Rohini started back to the *Queen*.

Emilio Guerrero sat behind his new mahogany desk in the office of The Secret Spice Café and steeled himself to keep from scowling as he listened to the impassioned speech Michael McKenna was making on behalf of his daughter.

Perfect. Just damn perfect. Inez and Michael were close family friends, and Emilio was going to get stuck with their brat. There was no way out of it, although the whole time Michael talked, Emilio searched his mind for one.

"I know what you're thinking. She'll never be able to do the job, or if she can, she won't last six months before she quits."

Leaning back in his chair, Emilio raised his brow. "It seems you *do* know what I'm thinking, Mike."

At that blunt retort Michael's shoulders slumped. "Okay, look," he began again, "I admit that her track record hasn't been the best."

Emilio folded his arms across his chest and waited.

"Okay, fine. Her track record is lousy." Michael threw his hands up in acquiescence. "She...there were reasons. Her mother—" he stopped himself, biting back the words. Not even for Marisol would he play that card. It wasn't pity he was looking for. Searching for words, he tried another tack. "I won't say you're wrong, but I will say it's all in the past. She's changed, Em. I swear to you she has. And she'd be perfect for this. I wouldn't suggest it otherwise."

"If she's so changed, Mike, why isn't she in here asking me for the position instead of sending Daddy to do it for her?"

"She didn't send me. I didn't tell her I was going to ask."

That stopped Emilio short. He hadn't expected Michael would give him an out, any more than he'd expected him to come in, his widower's weeds trailing behind him, begging for a job for a girl Emilio knew from family chatter was totally out of control.

It had been a long-held dream of Emilio's to return to Long Beach a successful man, to return to the *Queen Mary*, not as a waiter at one of its restaurants, but as the owner of one. He'd achieved that goal, and when he bought The Secret Spice, he knew old friends would come asking for work. The economy was tanked, and Mexicans were the villains *du jour*. He planned to use his hard-earned wealth to help bring the restaurant back to its former glory, and in doing so, hire as many conscientious, industrious people as possible. Marisol McKenna was not one of them. She was self-centered and spoiled. As far as Emilio was concerned, she'd done nothing but spend her parents' money on whims and frivolity.

There was nothing that irked him more than when children of immigrants squandered what their parents had struggled so hard to achieve. He remembered his own mother rubbing olive oil and granulated sugar on her cracked, chapped hands. When he was a child, Anna Guerrero worked Monday through Friday as a dental receptionist, and cleaned houses on the weekends. His father had a gardening business which kept him busy seven days a week also, but made his hours more flexible. He was the one who fixed his two children's lunches in the mornings, who bundled them into the front seat of his pickup to take them to school, and who helped them with homework each night while his wife cooked. When Emilio asked his mother why she and his father worked so hard, her answer was, "So you and your sister won't have to."

Marisol's mother had subscribed to the same philosophy—work as hard as you can so your children can go to college and earn a better place for themselves in the world than you had. Anna and Inez had known each other for years, and while Emilio greatly appreciated what his parents had done for him, he was convinced Marisol only exploited hers. Even after Inez and Michael were married, Inez insisted she keep her job working aboard the *Mary*, a pursuance that plagued Michael to this day. Emilio had been told by his mother that Michael was convinced it was his wife's long-term exposure to cleaning chemicals that had caused her breast cancer. Doubtful, but guilt compounded by grief was never rational.

Eyeing the disheartened man sitting in front him, Emilio got a flashback of a jubilant Michael and a glowing Inez at their wedding reception, held right there, at the restaurant he now owned. That was the last time Emilio saw Marisol before he left Long Beach for college. She'd been just a few days shy of her fifth birthday. He had an image of her holding a cupcake out of his reach, chocolate smears and defiance on her face when he'd asked her to share it with him.

With these recollections in mind, he found himself relenting. It made a difference that Marisol hadn't used her father as errand boy. He heard himself say, "I'll give her a two-month trial period, Mike. If she proves herself capable within that time, I'll consider hiring her on permanently." He regretted the offer the minute it was out of his mouth, and couldn't help but add the grim prediction, "That is, if she still wants the position after two months."

"She wants it. And I know she'll do well. I know her better than anybody does, and there's more to her than you can imagine." Knowing to quit while he was ahead, Michael stood up, gratitude his eyes. "Thank you, Em. I owe you one."

After he left, Emilio brooded. Like it or not, he had a new pastry chef. And he did not like it.

"Well, you don't look pleased at all." Rohini walked into the office, trying to feel as though she still belonged there. "On the other hand, I just saw Michael leaving, and I haven't seen him grin like that in ages. Something tells me he's convinced you to hire Marisol, and you're not happy about it." She pulled out the chair of her desk and sat, pretending not to notice that the other desks that had been in the room for sixteen years were gone.

Emilio smiled at her with what he hoped was reassurance. He knew how awkward this was for her. "I take it you're not too surprised or troubled by my choice."

"No, I think you made a good one, actually. There's more to her than most people know." Much more, she thought.

"So Michael said, as well. I guess we'll see." He continued to smile, observing her with compassion as she shifted left and right, steeled her eyes away from the empty spaces that only yesterday had been occupied by her husband's desk and Sarita's. "They're in storage," he said, quietly. "I didn't discard them. I can put his back, if you'd rather."

"No. No, there's no need for that," she assured him hastily, too hastily. She forced herself to glance around. "It's so much roomier in here. Besides"—he heard the valiant effort in the words—"This is *your* restaurant now."

"It's your restaurant too," he countered truthfully, but what hung in the air unspoken was that with seventy-five percent ownership, he was the senior partner. She retained only the twenty-five percent she'd always owned, a twenty-five percent for which Emilio had made her a generous offer, an offer she'd turned down.

She couldn't leave. She just couldn't.

Angela had sold her twenty-five percent to Emilio more than a year before when she decided to move to Florida. And with only that twenty-five percent share, he'd chosen to remain a silent partner at first, just as Jane had when she moved back to Italy, and Cynthia had when she turned her portion of the restaurant over to Sarita to manage.

This left Rohini and Cristiano to run the restaurant on their own. But it was a challenge to oversee as well as cook. They realized that

immediately. She'd always wonder if that contributed to what happened. Was it exhaustion? Did he fall and hit his head?

Would she ever know?

With no warning, no time to prepare, she'd found herself trying to
keep The Spice going on her own, while holding on to the fragile hope
that Cristiano wasn't gone for good. Not even now could she say the
words—think the words—the Coast Guard had pronounced to her first.

That Monday, the weather was unusually cold, but he went out for
his walk just the same, and she'd been wondering why he was gone so
long. They had marketing to do. She rang his phone. He didn't answer,
so she went down to the shore to search for him. When she couldn't
find him, she alerted the police, who told her she needed to wait at least
twenty-four hours. The sun went down and he still wasn't back, but by
then, she already knew. She stayed up all night, and on Tuesday, she
kept the restaurant closed. Sarita and Luca came. Luca used his abilities
to explore far and wide, while Sarita made her some herbal tea, and
tried Cristiano's phone at hourly intervals, until Rohini quietly asked
her to please stop. By Wednesday, Jane, Angela, and Cynthia were
there. They waited with her, waited and waited, while there was an
all-out search of the port, of the harbor, of the bay. At last, the restaurant
line shrilled. Jane, standing closest, snatched it up.

She listened to the voice on the other end, then hung up without a
word to the caller. "They're at Reception."

They all went down together, with Jane and Angela flanking her on
one side and Cynthia on her other. Two uniformed guardsman were
standing by the front desk. She could see it on their faces before they
spoke it out loud. And when one of them held out her husband's wet
running shoes—the only things they'd found, the only clue to what had
happened to him—she could only stare at them.

It was Jane who cried first, her silent and decorous tears, reliving her own old tragedy along with this new one, perhaps. Angela looked as though she'd been punched. She'd pressed her hands to her cheeks and said, "Oh, my God, oh, my God," over and over again. But Cynthia did nothing except gaze at Rohini. She understood what this would mean to her better than the other two could.

They stayed aboard the ship for a week, hoping for more news, helping at the restaurant, and it felt good to have them all back again, even as things stood. But when no news was forthcoming, they went back to their lives, to their lovers, and Rohini was left to grieve and wait forever for someone who would never come.

Though she made the attempt, there was no possible way she could manage the work on her own. The staff stayed on for a while in support of her, but as business began to fall off, one by one, they left. Jane told her to come live in Rome, that it would remind her of the beautiful time she and Cristiano had enjoyed there. Cynthia said, without much hope that Rohini would listen, how much she'd love the *padocas* and coffee plantations of São Paulo. And Angela tried to entice her to Florida by sending her a personalized pair of Mickey Mouse ears. When she got them, she laughed until she cried—raw, racking sobs that only stopped when she threw up.

Running shoes and Mickey Mouse ears. That's what she had left, apart from a restaurant that was falling to pieces where it stood, a restaurant that was Cristiano's heart and soul. Until shortly after the six-month mark, when Jane and Cynthia sold their shares to Emilio too.

She knew they meant well, which was why she was trying hard not to see what they'd done as a betrayal. She'd been without Cristiano for only six months and they wanted her to move on—just like that. Six months without laughing with him, without hearing his voice calling out crisp orders in the kitchen, without sleeping beside him in bed, without holding his hand as they walked along the decks of the *Mary*, or as they fed seagulls together along the shoreline. Six months, when they'd been linked at the hip since they met. She'd been alive for more than forty years already before that day, but life had only begun for her the first time he looked at her and smiled.

It was seven months now, and here she had a new business partner, the earnest, lovesick boy she remembered from that first year. He was a grown man now, and he was watching her as though he could read her mind. She hoped he would bear with her, because she just couldn't go. Not yet. Maybe not ever.

Emilio spoke again in that same gentle way. "You know, he was always kind to me. I don't know if he ever told you..." he paused, giving her, perhaps giving himself, a chance to pull it together. As her eyes filled, he found he couldn't finish what he'd meant to say and said something else, which he hoped would help. "You were always kind to me too. I'm glad you're here." He smiled sadly. "I'm sorry he's not, but I'm glad you are."

She couldn't answer at first, then managed to whisper, "Thank you. Thank you so much, Emilio."

When she left the office, he sat there, surprised at himself. He wasn't a hard-nose, but he hadn't gotten where he was by being sentimental. Yet he'd just agreed to work with two women who each came with a lifeboat full of emotional baggage.

He hoped to hell it didn't turn out to be the worse business decision of his life.

CHAPTER THREE

Saturday, October 31, 2020, ten hours before the end,
Miceli residence

At two p.m., while her daughters were with their father at the school fall festival, Sarita was sipping chardonnay with Angela, and reflecting upon her life. There were so many things for which she was thankful. And a few things she wished were different.

Miceli Enterprises was thriving under the sharp eye of Luca's former girlfriend, Desiree. Neither she nor Luca needed to work outside their home. That was a blessing. She couldn't imagine how they'd have managed otherwise. That said, she secretly wished she had a monetary excuse to go back to work. Not fulltime, just a few days a week to clear her head, and give herself time to just...be.

She loved her husband. She loved her daughters. But there was a small, guilt-laden part of her that felt hemmed in by the all-consuming responsibility of bringing up four children with powers that most people believed existed only in comic books. Her family was precious to her, but sometimes she missed being on the *Queen*, missed the orderliness of her work at the restaurant. There, apart from the occasional flying pot and pan, things generally proceeded as expected. Problems that came up were predictable and easily resolved. A missing shipment of foodstuffs or wine, a tardy waitress, she could handle. A dozen ducks disappearing from the neighborhood park—right in front of several neighbors, no less—was another matter.

Luca thought her apprehensions might have to do with her distaste for being the center of attention. True, there was some of that. Most women would be astounded to learn that, if she could, she'd give her breath-stopping good looks to another who pined for them, just so people would stop the gawking. Didn't they realize how rude that was, how unnerving? Even when she and Luca were out alone, people stared. Inevitably, someone would recognize him, then the whispers would start. She'd catch a muttered word about the fire, see people scrolling through their phones for old links to the story, or to Luca and Santi's Wikipedia page.

With quadruplets, there was no chance of not being noticed.

But it was more than the embarrassment of being treated like some A-listers who craved publicity, when she and Luca preferred just the opposite. If one of those staring strangers caught on that her daughters had special gifts, what then? The thought of the possible aftermath for her children was something she fretted about constantly.

Today Luca had given her a reprieve from the worry and madness of her home life. Knowing how tough his day was going to be without her help, she loved him all the more for it. She needed this time to herself, badly. How nice it had been to shampoo and condition her hair without anyone shouting at her from behind the door—"Mommy, I can't find my blue socks that Grandma gave me." "Mom, Alana made my Captain Marvel action figure disappear." "Babe, are we out of Rice Krispies? Should I pop out and get a box?"

Still, even with the blissful quiet, she couldn't relax. Something was making her jumpy and she couldn't pinpoint what.

Angela's company was a happy distraction. She'd phoned ten minutes after Luca left with the girls—"Surprise. I'm in Long Beach for the week. If you already have a cake, put it in the freezer." Now she was standing in Sarita and Luca's state-of-the-art kitchen, assembling a confection that—leave it to Angela—was as unique as the little girls whose birthday it celebrated.

It consisted of four layers, separated by three columns and a plate, respectively, so that each girl got her own tier in a different color and flavor, decorated with its own individual flowers. Angela had kept each layer safe from bumps and bruises by boxing them separately and securing them on the back seat of her rental car. Braving the Los Angeles traffic, she then made the trek from her son and son-in-law's condo in Bixby Hills, to the charming hamlet of Los Feliz where her cousin Luca and his family lived.

"I'm so happy you're here, Angela. This is such a nice treat. You should have told us earlier you were coming. Luca would have come to get you."

"Sweetie, Luca doesn't need to be everyone's private pilot." Angela put together columns and layers. "Before he came along we all managed to get where we had to go."

"Well, battling the 405 takes stamina." She admired Angela's handiwork. "Gosh, that's so pretty. The girls will be thrilled. It's so generous of you to go to all this trouble."

"Oh, anything for those little dolls. Besides, I haven't made a specialty cake in over a year. I miss it. Thank God the oven in that condo is decent. Not that Vincenzo and Douglas would have settled for any less. You know how those two are. I have to say, their tenants were kind of sloppy, though. Place needs a good cleaning. I have to remember to tell the realtor." She looked up to wink at Sarita. "I volunteered to be their go-between. It gave me an excuse to come out here." Surveying her work, she considered it done, put her piping tools aside, and washed the sugar from her fingers. "I'm glad they're selling. They hated being landlords."

"How do they like Florida?"

"They've lived there before. And Douglas loves the new job. It was a great opportunity." She made a face as she carried the finished cake over to the kitchen table and set it down in the center. "I think the real question is whether Harry and I like it."

Sarita set out Wonder Woman napkins and paper plates. Her daughters felt a kinship to female superheroes. "It seems to me it agrees with you. You look great. Younger than ever."

"Aw, sweetie, thank you. But that's not due to Florida. That's due to a good plastic surgeon, one who isn't a felon this time."

Sarita didn't know how to comment on that, so she stuck to the subject at hand. "You've been there...how long? It's not even a year, right? I thought you moved because you wanted to stay close to Vin."

"Yeah, and I think that was a mistake."

Sarita bit her thumbnail. "Don't tell me you two are at odds again?"

"No, that's not it." Angela grabbed her own wineglass from the counter, brought it to the table, and sat. "Thinking back, Harry agreed to it so fast I didn't weigh the pros and cons as much as I should have. Now I'm wondering if maybe he thought I'd go without him if he didn't say yes."

"He loves you, that's for sure."

"I suppose he does." Though it continued to surprise her, even after all this time.

"Yes, silly, he does. Why else would he follow you across the country?"

Angela stuck her tongue in her cheek. "Maybe it was for my tarts. He's always been a big fan."

"Oh, ha ha ha, Angela. Be serious. Are you really regretting it?"

"I think I am." Her tone was rueful. "It's nothing to do with Vincenzo. He and I are fine, thank God." She knocked on the wooden table. "But life there is so different. How many times can you go to Disney? And I miss the weather here. The humidity in Florida makes my hair frizz."

Sarita smiled. "That's the problem—Disney and your hair?"

"No. My not wanting to live in Florida's the problem." She let out a long breath. "And there's Rohini."

Sarita's smile waned. "I know. Does she know you're here?"

"I talked to her Monday and told her I was planning to surprise you. I tried to convince her to come with me, even for just an hour. She hedged—Saturday rush, and blah blah. I guess she's still not ready. When I got in Thursday night, I texted her again, and again this morning before I left the condo. She hasn't gotten back to me."

"We had the same idea. And I couldn't reach her by cell either, so I called the restaurant line. All I got was their recording."

"They must be busy then, if no one picked up. Still, I wish she'd come." Angela spoke the words without hope.

"I wish I could go see her more often. It's so hard with the girls." She didn't want the girls to see she'd been crying on their birthday, but she couldn't help it. She'd been feeling melancholy and restless all morning, and talking about Cristiano always made her sad. "I still miss him so much. It still feels like it's not real."

Angela felt herself welling up too. "I never would have left if I'd known. One month later. One month, Sarita." She smacked her palm to her forehead as if to punish herself for it. "I think she's avoiding us." She paused. "You know, when your mother and Jane sold..." She let the sentence trail off.

"They were trying to help." Sarita defended. "As awful as it is, they did the right thing. It wasn't the money, Angela. You know that. There was no way she could run it by herself. If Emilio hadn't stepped in, she'd have lost the restaurant entirely. And then where would she be?"

"I know." Angela held up a hand to stop her. "I know, Sarita. It's just...I can't help but feel like we abandoned her."

"I get it. I feel that way too." Sarita reached for a Wonder Woman napkin to blot at her eyes. "Gosh. I hate it."

"Yeah, no kidding. At least, if there was some closure."

"I doubt there will be, after all this time."

The profound loss washed over them again.

A stray thought occurred to Sarita, as she sniffled. "You know, when you told me you made the cake, I was sure you went to the Spice to do it."

"I wanted to. Oh, my God—I miss that kitchen. I miss the ship." Angela lifted her shoulders. "But it didn't seem right to barge in."

"Marisol wouldn't mind. How many times did you let her bake with you when it was yours?"

"Maybe. But it's not mine anymore." That fact bothered her more than it should, she knew, and she had nobody to blame for it but herself. "You said it's doing well for them, right?"

"I think so. We've only managed to get there once since they opened, but it was full. And the food was good." She shrugged. "I mean, not Cristiano good, but still pretty good. They should do all right." In an effort to lighten the mood, she added, mischievously, "Rohini and her new business partner. The boy who was nearly strangled by her husband." She blew out a breath. "Whoo. I'll never forget *that* afternoon."

As intended, the memory made Angela smile. "Yep. I'm sure he'll never forget it either. But I have to give the kid credit—your mother fired him, and now he owns the place." She did her best imitation of Cynthia. "Esteban! Get your ass over to table three."

That earned an honest laugh from Sarita. She couldn't help it—the visual was so clear. "He should have had his name legally changed."

Angela chuckled. "Ah, Cynthia, Cynthia," she said, her tone wistful. Thinking about it, she added, "It *is* nice, though. Emilio and Marisol, taking over."

"It is," Sarita agreed. "Since it can't be us, I'm glad it's them. When he and I were kids, we explored the *Mary* from top to bottom. I remember he loved her as much as I do."

"Uh, no, sweetie. Not buying that. He was crazy about *you*. If you were a dentist, he would have told you he loved getting his cavities filled. We all appreciate the ship, but no one could possibly love it as much as you do." Angela poked affectionate fun. "Except maybe the actual Queen they named it for."

"Well, whatever. It's nice he went back. And Marisol. Your protégée." She tipped her glass to Angela. "She's doing great now, by the way. I got a call from her right after Emilio hired her. She was so excited."

"I did too. Ecstatic is more the word." Angela thought back to a time four years earlier. "She went off the rails there for a while, but who could blame her?"

"You're right about that." She shifted in her chair, and caught a whiff of the cake. The scent was scrumptious and familiar. All freshly-baked cakes smelled good, but cakes made by Angela had such distinctive and tempting aromas. Angela said it came from using only the best ingredients, but Sarita knew it was the love she put into them that made the difference. "My mother made me nuts when I was sixteen, but I adored her. If I'd lost her then…" She didn't need to finish.

"Yep. That poor kid. Thank God she had Michael. Although he was just as devastated as she was." Angela pressed her lips together as she thought of it all—so many years of laughter and love, so much change and growth, so much heartbreak and loss. With a motion, she brushed the melancholy aside. "Anyway. Enough about all that. Before my cousin gets back and the bedlam starts, talk to me. How are the girls doing?"

"Well, let's see." Sarita kept her tone light at first. "At least once a week, Alex gets in trouble at school for disagreeing with her teachers. 'Because they're stupid,' she says."

"And they probably are, compared to her."

"Good one. Be sure to tell her that. You're such a good influence, Angela." She went on, "And Niki has broken three neighbors' windows with baseballs, so far."

Angela was enjoying the visuals. "Luca takes care of that, no problem, I bet."

"Maria sings tunes from the Forties all day long, which is bad enough, but sometimes Luca joins in, which is much worse."

"Aw, c'mon. I bet he has a nice voice." With a playful smile, she picked up her glass.

Sarita had no idea why Angela's banter was irritating her. "And the best one lately?" She masked her annoyance with another cautious sip. Alcohol in the afternoon wasn't something she indulged in often, especially since the girls were born. "I got a Facetime from Raul last week. He was laughing so hard he couldn't speak. He turned his phone, and behind him—"

Angela interrupted by nearly snorting out her wine. "I heard about this. Your mother told me. Jane split a gut over it too." She pointed at Sarita. "Ducks, right?"

"Yes." Sarita couldn't believe she was laughing. "That's right, Angela. Ducks."

Angela slapped her thigh with glee. "Don't you wish you could put this stuff on Instagram? It would get so many views."

That was it. Frustrated to a breaking point, she blurted, "Why is this funny? I don't see why everyone thinks this is so funny."

"Oh, my God. It's hilarious. Cynthia said they were just sitting down to eat, and boom—"Angela made a tumbling motion with her arms—"twelve ducks fall from the ceiling and start flapping all over the table." She hooted again, until Sarita's stony expression registered. "What?"

"Nothing. If you all think it's funny, then, fine." She threw her hands in the air. "I mean, I'm losing my mind. My daily life is chaotic, not to mention the possible dangers to my children should anyone learn their secrets, but if I'm the only one who doesn't see this for its entertainment value, then I guess the problem is me."

When she heard how bitter she sounded, she stopped. "Sorry. I didn't mean to be so bitchy." She forced a smile. "Raising my four little sorcerers, or whatever they are, isn't as easy as I expected it to be."

The sarcasm registered for what it was, and Angela tilted her head, studying her. "Correct me if I'm wrong—you two were having sex, right? So what *did* you expect—a toaster?"

"Oh, stop." Sarita was more than just frustrated now. She felt as she often had as a child—unheard and dismissed by everyone close to her, including, on this specific subject, her own husband, who also found his daughters' so-called 'antics' adorable rather than perilous. "That's not what I meant and you know it. We were using birth control. It didn't work. Obviously."

"That doesn't surprise me. Not hard to guess that birth control methods used by ordinary mortals would be next to useless." Still not reading her, Angela smirked. "You know, I knew you were pregnant the minute you threw up my aunt's sauce. Before that you downed it like water. That sauce is probably what got you into this situation in the first place. Luca knew what he was doing there."

But when she caught the real dismay that flickered across Sarita's face, her manner changed in an instant. "Oh, sweetie. I'm sorry. I'm such an idiot. I shouldn't have made light of this. I don't know why I didn't see you were upset."

Perhaps alcohol hadn't been the best idea. There was so much bottled up inside Sarita that it didn't take more than a little sympathy for it all to come rushing out.

"I love my children, Angela. I love them so much. You believe me, don't you?"

"Of course I do, you knucklehead. Anybody can see you love them."

"But I wasn't ready for all this," she continued dolefully, as though Angela hadn't spoken. "I wasn't ready to be a mother of four." She covered her face with her hands as she admitted that. "And for the longest time, I was so worried that if it happened once, it could happen a second time, and I didn't want to be Octomom." She dropped her hands. If she was confessing her truth, she'd have the courage to look Angela in the face while she did it. "That makes me sound hideous, doesn't it?"

"Nope. Not at all." There wasn't a hint of condemnation in the words. "Nothing's out of the realm of possibility for you two. I understand how you felt."

Bolstered by that, she continued. "Luca offered to have a vasectomy. Can you believe that? I wouldn't let him do it. I mean, who knows if it would even be effective on someone like him? And besides, we might want to have another child someday. A little boy, maybe, so we could name him after Luca's father."

Angela's eyes softened. Sarita was in turmoil, but the love she had for Luca was palpable, and it gave Angela pleasure to see it. Luca deserved to be loved. For that matter, so did Sarita.

"And then one night…I think the girls were about eight months old, we…well, we finally got them down to sleep all at the same time. We had the whole evening to ourselves." She blushed bright red.

Angela gave a short laugh at that. She had to. It was kind of adorable. "I think I know where this is going."

"After that night, I didn't get my period."

The laughter died immediately, and she kept her expression neutral. Whatever Sarita was going to tell her next, she would be supportive. "I see."

Sarita shook her head. "No, you don't. I didn't get my period and I haven't gotten it since."

A tiny line formed on Angela's brow. "You're not on some dumb diet, I hope?"

"Me? Gosh, no."

"You went to the gyno?"

"Well, duh. She said everything tested fine. I'm as healthy as can be." Deciding the wine was sharper than she liked, she pushed it aside. "In short, Angela, even though they can't find a reason—"she motioned to her belly with her thumbs—"shop's closed. We don't know why. We don't even know if it's a permanent condition. "

"Huh," was all Angela said.

"It's not that we want another baby right now. It just unsettles me not knowing how my own body works."

"Did you tell Rohini?"

"She did her best, but there's more to this than herbal treatments and relaxation techniques. It's supernatural. There's nothing in any medical book about us—me, Luca, and our girls. We're anomalies. That scares me for my babies." She gulped, finally letting herself cry.

Angela moved to her side and hugged her tight. "Okay. Okay, sweetie, take it easy. Let's talk this through." When Sarita had calmed herself, Angela patted her back, and sat back down, her palms flat on the table. "So. Tell me what's on your mind. Aside from any atypical medical issues that might or might not come up, what else are you worried about?"

"I'm not worried. I'm scared to death. Luca seems to be taking their powers in stride, but I just *can't*. What will happen when people start to notice not just their looks, but that they're different from the rest of the world?" She picked up another napkin and shredded it into strips. "They're personable and inquisitive. They're gifted. They're too daring for their own good. I'm afraid they'll be objects of envy, or ostracized like Marisol was when she was a teenager. They hardly ever listen to me when I try to…to reign them in, to keep them from making spectacles of themselves, and if they're like that at five, what will they be like when they're fifteen?" The thought kept her awake at night. "Alana's the one I'm afraid for most. She already has more power than Luca had at her age." She paused before she admitted to another concern. "Alexandra's showing signs of jealousy."

Angela's reaction to that was quickly masked, but Sarita caught it, and tipped her head in bitter acknowledgement. "That's right—sibling rivalry, round two." With her fingers pressed to her face again, she concluded, "I don't know how to handle it. I don't know how to handle any of this."

When she opened her eyes, Angela was wearing a sad, bitter smile. "Why are you staring at me like that?" she snapped. "It's awful."

"Is it? I apologize again. I'm just thinking how funny life is."

"What do you mean?"

Angela motioned to her. "Look at you. You've become Cynthia."

She cut off Sarita's sound of protest. "I love your mother and you love your mother. I understand her. She had to raise you alone. Stressing over you became a habit. But let's face it—her way of trying to protect you from everything—it made you doubt and dislike yourself. Jane told me that once, and I argued with her. But she was right about it, and about my parents too. Do you know how miserable my mother made me, in her quest to make me happy? Is that the kind of chokehold you want your love to have on your daughters?"

Sarita blanched at the comparison, but she stayed silent. She knew very well how insecure and troubled Angela had been at one time.

"You trying to pretend the girls don't have powers, trying to get them to blend in? That's like me trying to pretend my son was straight when I *knew* he was gay." Angela hated remembering who she was back then. "I made my own baby as itchy in his own skin as I was in mine and ruined my relationship with him in the process."

"Angela—"

"I'm not finished, sweetie. You brought this up, now let me have my say. Please." She reached across the table to clasp the younger woman's hands, wanting so much to help her avoid making the same mistakes she made. "You know what I think? If my family had been more open to our kids being unconventional when Luca and Santi were growing up, maybe Santi wouldn't be locked up in a psych ward now for trying to kill you and his brother."

When Sarita just watched her glumly, Angela pressed home the point. "I'm surprised at you. You had no luck trying to be something you weren't, so why would you think you could make it work for them?"

"I'm just trying to keep them safe."

"Yeah? Well, news flash. You can't."

"What do you mean?" Sarita looked at her as though she'd lost her mind. "That's my job."

"Your job is to love them, to show them how to be the best people they can be. But keep them safe? Ha. Good luck with that," she scoffed. "As long as we're breathing, safety is an illusion." She sat back again. "Jane found that out the hard way, didn't she?"

Sarita bowed her head. "I never thought about it like that. I just want them to be happy."

"What loving mother doesn't wish that?" What she didn't say out loud was that nothing broke a mother's heart more than when that wish wasn't granted.

Instead she told her, "But that's not up to you either. That'll be up to them. The girls are luckier than both you and Luca, if you think about it. They already have adults in their lives who know what they are and who love them just as they are. And they have each other."

She picked up their empty glasses and brought them to the sink. "Here's something else to consider. Maybe I'm crazy, but—" she ticked off the items on her fingers—"the fact that you didn't plan to get pregnant, but did? The fact that you can't get pregnant now? The fact that your daughters were born on Halloween—a holiday Michael and Inez's wedding taught me is a sacred one? You know what I bet? I bet that their conception wasn't the accident you think it was." She wagged a finger at Sarita. "Your daughters were meant to be here. One of these days we'll find out the reason."

The doorbell chimed.

"That'll be trick-or-treaters." Sarita stood up too, dumped the shredded napkins in the trash. "I forgot to put the bowl of candy by the door."

Angela turned back to the sink. "You get that, I'll clean up here."

But there were no pint-sized superheroes, vampires, or princesses waiting for Sarita at her front door. Standing there alone was a young man in his twenties, dressed in a neat pair of jeans, a spotless white t-shirt, and an expensive-looking bomber jacket that matched his sable brown boots. His curly russet hair reached past his shoulders, and diamond posts glinted in both his ears. His eyes were the color of peridots, and his skin was several shades darker than Sarita's. He looked vaguely familiar, but when he spoke, his inflections proclaimed him not from California.

"Ms. Taylor? Ms. Sarita Taylor?"

"Yes, I'm Sarita. How can I help you?"

"My name is Antoine Dupré. I'm here with your grandmother."

"I'm sorry—who?" She couldn't have heard him correctly.

"Your grandmother," he said again, politely. "Mambo Taylor." He motioned to a silver limousine with dark tinted windows that was parked at the curb. "She's waiting in the car."

"The priestess?" Stunned, Sarita stepped out onto the stoop and peered at the limo. "But, we've never met. I mean—she's *here*?"

"Yes, Ms. Sarita. I drove her."

She stared at him. "You drove from New Orleans with an elderly woman? It must've taken you days."

"Yes, ma'am." His good manners never wavered. "She wants to see you. It's very important. May I bring her in?"

From the living room behind her, Sarita heard the sound of popping bubble wrap.

"Sarita!"

"Mommy!"

She whirled and saw Luca standing by the sofa, blood on his nose and a look on his face that did not bode well. He was holding onto the girls, and she could see they'd been crying.

"What happened?' She kept the question casual, for the girls' sake, although her skin went clammy at once.

She knew there was a reason she'd been on edge all day. Her New Orleans visitors temporarily forgotten, she took one step back into the house. "What happened, Luca?"

"Excuse me, Ms. Sarita." Before Luca could answer, from behind her on the stoop, Antoine tapped her on the shoulder with some persistence to get her attention again. "That's why we're here."

The statement made no sense, until she caught the exchange between the two men, a look that terrified her. She glanced back and forth between them, and dropped the pretense of calm. "What's going on?"

Hearing the commotion, Angela came in from the kitchen. She stopped dead when she saw the state Luca and the girls were in.

Antoine Dupré pinned her with his startling eyes. "Ms. Angela, do you know if Ms. Jane is at her home this evening?"

"I…I'm not sure. Why?"

Ignoring Angela's question for the time being, Antoine turned to Luca next. "How long will it take for you to get Ms. Cynthia and Ms. Jane? All of you must go."

"Hold it." Breath jumping now, Sarita looked at Luca. "Go *where*? What's this about?" A stranger was at her door issuing orders and she could see her husband knew why.

"Ms. Sarita, please." This time the urgency behind Antoine's courteous demeanor was unmistakable. He addressed them all. "There's big trouble coming, and we don't have much time. Y'all need to talk with Mambo Taylor."

CHAPTER FOUR

Saturday evening, September 25, 1954,
French Quarter, New Orleans

Her name was Rosemary, and tomorrow she would be twenty years old. That evening was the first in her life she was out on her own. The first time no chaperones guarded her. She knew it was done with love, but lately she felt strangled by it.

If she made it back before midnight, they'd never know she left. At midnight, the mambo would come to her room to offer her a birthday blessing. But for now she'd stolen these few hours of freedom, and she was going to revel in them.

She wore her favorite summer dress—a sleeveless, full-skirted red with white polka dots. The dress had large pockets on the front panel and a light lace petticoat beneath. Her sandals were white, and the polish she'd painted on her toenails matched the red of her dress to perfection. She felt pretty in the outfit, and the cotton material kept her cool.

It was the heat that added to her restlessness. Though it was late September, and the sun had set more than an hour before, the temperature was still in the mid-eighties, and every gas lantern lining the city blocks shimmered white-gold with swarms of mating termites and a haze of humid air.

The weather was in perfect harmony with the sultry tunes of jazz and blues spilling out from the bars, juke joints, and restaurants along Dumaine Street. As she walked, floating from the balcony above her head, its intricate, cast iron railing draped with pots of flowering plants and vines, she heard the wailing, impassioned vocals of the Guitar Slim tune:

"The things that I used to do, Lawd, I won't do no more...I used to sit and hold your hand, baby, crying, begging you not to go..."

The distinctive sights and sounds of the city lightened her mood. It came to her how lucky she was to live in such a place, to possess the spiritual powers that Mambo Zora was teaching her to harness and channel for the greater good. These were very tough times for her people. That was one truth from which Mambo Zora couldn't shelter her. That year, a landmark case had begun to crumble Jim Crow, and the battle for civil rights raged like fire.

Yet, on that evening—the enchanted evening of her bold escape—she focused only on her blessings.

She reached up and brushed her thumb against the star-shaped mole that sat just below her collarbone. A 'divine mark,' Zora had declared it, when it appeared shortly after her thirteenth birthday. That was when her training had begun. Soon she would earn the title of priestess too. Not a high priestess, a *mambo asogwe* like Zora—not yet—but a *mambo sur point*, a junior priestess. If she studied hard and practiced, one day she might achieve the higher distinction.

Luck had not always smiled on her, or so she'd been told over and again. When she was brought to Zora's temple on the day of her birth, they named her Rosemary for the herb in the *gris-gris* they made especially for her. It was her mother's wish that she wear the charm, Celeste the midwife told her, and not a one in the Vodou community would refuse the last request of a dying woman. The *gris-gris* was to protect her from a devil, although what particular devil her mother had been fearful of Celeste had never said. Nonetheless, both she and Priestess Zora felt honor-bound to keep Rosemary safe, and that they'd done for twenty years, to such a point she was beginning to feel like a prisoner in her own home.

She understood the responsibilities that came with being a priestess, that there were those practitioners, those *bokurs* and *caplatas*, who would use the religion to serve the loa with 'both hands.' She knew she must be careful not to allow herself to become ensnared by the temptation of the dark. But she was also in the first blush of womanhood, and she wanted an adventure. She wanted to discover what there was outside of the confines of the temple. She wanted—one day in the not too distant future, she hoped—to fall in love.

A car came up alongside her and slowed to a crawl. It was quite a car at that, a Buick Skylark convertible that reflected silvery blue under the street lights. The top was down, and from her side glance she saw the interior was a gleaming white. She'd never seen the car before, but when she recognized the driver, she stopped and spun to face him.

"Why, Joseph," she grinned. "Look at you, driving such a fancy car. I know you can't afford such luxuries working for Mambo Zora."

Rosemary had known Joseph since they were children, and his mother, Jamilla, had come to the temple to train with the priestess. But the more Jamilla learned from Zora, the more the two women disagreed on how to best serve their community. Zora insisted their magick stay 'clean,' while Jamilla wanted to explore all the sides of Vodou. In the end Jamilla left the temple, but when Joseph was sixteen, he chose to return and work for Zora. Now, three years later, he was one of her most trusted followers, and to Rosemary he was like a brother. At the temple, his duties were wide and varied. Unfortunately one of those duties was to watch out for her, and it was a duty he took seriously.

Like right then.

"Never mind that." Joseph leaned his elbow on the car windowsill, his face stern. "What are you doing out here on your own?"

Stalling, she rocked back on her heels. "You know, you're a year younger than I am. I could ask you the same question. Why are *you* out on your own?"

His expression didn't change. More times than not lately, he was serious and short-tempered, and Rosemary missed his playful teasing. Mambo Zora told her it was because he was growing up and realizing what it meant to be a black man in a white man's world.

"Don't play with me, *cher*. I asked you a question."

She hoped a little wheedling might help. "Oh, come on, Joseph. I just wanted a walk. By myself, for once."

"It's dangerous for you to be out alone. You've been told."

She rolled her eyes. "Yes, I have been told, endlessly. Although nobody's ever bothered to explain what it is I'm supposed to be so afraid of."

The car sat idling as he watched her and said nothing. He put both hands back on the wheel, drummed his fingers, and stared out the front window. Rosemary held her breath as he decided what to do. Finally, he tipped his head to his right. "Get in."

Her face fell. "You're taking me back."

"Nope. We'll...go for a ride."

"We will?" To her trusting ears, that sounded promising. She scrambled around to the passenger side, slid in, and shut the car door. "Where we goin'?"

"You'll see." The Skylark purred as it pulled away from the curb and out onto the street, and he said nothing more as he turned left and right on the streets and avenues, maneuvering carefully over the trolley tracks. It was the perfect weather for a drive with the top down, and since it was the first time she'd ever been in a convertible, she sat back and enjoyed the ride.

"Ever wonder what's it like to be rich, Rosemary?" The question came out of the blue.

"Oh, I suppose. Once in a while. Mambo Zora says we're rich in love and family."

"Does she, now?"

Engrossed in the lovely setting, Rosemary didn't catch the cynicism. "Mmhmm. She does." She ran her palm along the cool smoothness of the seat. "I guess you have a rich friend, and this is his car, then," she teased.

"Something like that."

They were on Lakeshore Drive, and Bayou St. John came into view. "Does your friend live here? He *must* be rich. There's nothing but rich folks down here." She craned her neck to see as much as she could in the dark. "How do y'all know each other?"

It took him a minute to answer. "He's a friend of my mother's."

"Your mother's?" Once again, he surprised her. "Oh."

She didn't see his mouth twist. She was caught by the vision in front of her as they pulled up to a spectacular estate. "Good Lord." She ogled the imposing columns, the vast wrap-around porch, the garden foliage illuminated by strategically placed lighting, the beautiful Venetian fountain. "What a house."

When he switched off the engine, Rosemary could hear the chorus of crickets, the gentle rush of water, the hoot of an owl. She sat, basking in it. The sumptuous car ride, the view of the elegant plantation home, the serene yet mysterious sounds of the bayou, were all so entrancing.

Right up until Joseph spoke again.

"What was it you thought, Rosemary—that I wasn't on speaking terms with my own mother since the mambo threw her out?"

The statement pulled her attention back to him. "What? No. I never thought that." She paused. "But you know Jamilla left because they couldn't agree, right, Joseph? Mambo Zora didn't throw her out."

"Didn't she?" His face contorted, and she was taken aback by the animosity. "My mother *told* me what happened. Zora made her leave."

"Joseph." Her tone was wary. This was a side of her childhood friend she'd never seen. "Jamilla wanted to practice in…a different way than Zora believes. Than I believe."

"So what if she did?" he shot back. "Maybe she wanted more. Maybe some of us want more." He jabbed his finger out toward the mansion in front of them. "This house you're so impressed with? A white man owns it. And another white man owns the next house over, and another the one across the street. And us? Where do we live, Rosemary?" In the dark, his eyes glinted with bitterness and pain. "They don't even want us to go to the same schools."

"There are right ways and wrong ways to get ahead in the world," she said quietly.

"Yeah." She shrunk back when she saw he was sneering at her. "And in the meantime, I wash his fancy car, and do the rest of his dirty work."

A chill went through her. "What do you mean?" she whispered.

He couldn't look her in the face. In fury now, he reached across and flung open her door. "Get out."

"Joseph—"

"I said, get out. Or Lord help me, Rosemary, I will pull you out."

She was sweating with nerves by the time she stepped out of the car. He came around, gripped her elbow and hauled her toward the front door. "Ow. You're hurting me, Joseph. Stop it. Tell me what this is about. Please."

Joseph still wouldn't look at her as he dragged her along. "He just wants to meet you, that's all. He just wants to talk."

"Who?" She dug in her feet, tried to tug away from him, the soggy moistness of the grass beneath her sandals making them slide and slip. "*Who*, Joseph? Tell me!"

Wordlessly, he yanked her up the front steps just as the door swung open, and she felt the blood drain from her face when she saw who was standing behind it. "Jamilla?"

Rosemary had never seen her look so elegant. Jamilla was dressed for an evening out in a white, off-the-shoulder cocktail dress with black overlace, black satin pumps, and black elbow-length gloves. She didn't look at Rosemary. To Joseph she said, "You did good, son."

Joseph also noted his mother's attire. He squinted. "Where you off to?"

"To a supper party. After she leaves." Jamilla kept her face blank.

"What kind of a *supper* party is it that a white man takes a colored woman to?"

"That's my business, and don't sass me." Her tone shut him down at once. "Bring her in."

Joseph had his hand on Rosemary's back, about to push her into the house and get it over with. But, torn between his duty to Zora and his duty to his mother, he wavered. "You gave me your word, Mama. You make sure she's all right."

"Yes, son." Jamilla nodded. "I gave you my word."

As Joseph shunted Rosemary into the house, Jamilla turned to the marble foyer table behind her. On it were writing implements—a gold pen, a metal letter opener with a mother-of-pearl handle, a box of cream stationary with matching envelopes. One envelope had been set aside from the rest. It was filled with cash. Jamilla handed it to Joseph. "He left this for you. What are you doin' for him with all that money?"

Joseph's eyes were bleak as he parroted her words. "That's my business. Maybe we shouldn't ask each other questions we don't want the answers to, Mama."

Rosemary's alarm grew as he stuffed the envelope into his pocket. "Oh, Joseph. It's like I don't know you at all. Do I?"

For the first time, he looked at her. There was disgust on his face, but she wasn't sure if it were for her or for himself. "You said it earlier, Rosemary. I can't afford luxuries working for the mambo." He stepped outside. "Tell him I'll be by at ten-thirty to pick her up."

Rosemary could see Jamilla was gloating, but Joseph couldn't. "That should give them plenty of time for a nice chat, and get her home before she turns into a pumpkin." She closed the door on her son before he was even off the porch. "Right. You come with me."

Rosemary locked her hands together. Her only hope was bravado. "Not until you tell me what's going on."

"Listen, girl." Jamilla leaned in and poked Rosemary in the chest. "You don't want to mess with me."

Though she knew her voice betrayed her fear, Rosemary held her ground. "And what do you think Mambo Zora will say when she hears about this?"

Jamilla's laugh rang with spite. "You won't tell her. She keeps you locked up like a hothouse flower. If you say anything, she'll know you went out tonight on your own, won't she?" Her face went smug at Rosemary's silence. She jerked her head in the direction she wanted her to go. "Get a move on. He's waitin' for you."

When she turned and walked ahead, Rosemary felt she had no choice but to follow. Apart from that, she still didn't believe—couldn't— that Joseph or even Jamilla would let her come to any real harm. But as she passed the foyer table, it was a reflex to snatch up the letter opener and slip it into her skirt pocket.

Jamilla led her past the sweeping staircase and down the expansive hall with its glossy, planked wood flooring, to an ornately-appointed parlor that was large enough for two settees and a baby grand piano. Needlepoint-cushioned footstools of varying heights were scattered about, and a teak card table, inlaid with semi-precious stone, was angled near the fireplace. A mahogany sideboard, polished to a gleam, held a sterling silver tea set, and a Louis XVI-style ormolu clock was set on the mantel. French tapestries and gilded mirrors hung on the walls. Had Rosemary been invited to the house as a guest, she might have marveled at its opulence, although perhaps not if she knew that the wealth of the family who'd lived there for generations had been cultivated by the labor of slaves.

But she wasn't a guest. The man in front of her would tell her what her role was to be.

Like a despot waiting to receive his subjects, he sat in a wingback chair she wouldn't have known was genuine Chippendale. His hands rested on the golden handle of a gentleman's walking cane, an item as showy as the rest of the room. The cane was not an affectation—he'd suffered a mild stroke, and his devout Baptist physician had warned him more were in his future if he didn't change his heretical ways. He'd been a handsome man once. Time and the lifestyle he'd chosen had taken their toll. Though his body was still slender, there was a slackness to it that was hidden by well-tailored clothes. His face was bloated and lined, his complexion pasty from too much Sazerac and too many bennies. But his hair was still thick and it gleamed as silver and polished as the teapot on the sideboard. Like Jamilla, he was in formalwear. His black tuxedo fit him to perfection, enhancing the princely air.

It was his eyes that gave him away for what he was. Once, when Rosemary was gathering herbs from Mambo Zora's garden, she came across a copperhead. Luckily, she knew what it was and steered clear, but she'd never forgotten that snake's stare before it slinked away: Cold, focused, deadly.

That same look was fixed on her now.

"Rosemary." He tipped his head. "Beauregard Clay, at your service. Well, now. You look just like your mama, don't you?"

The glaring question hung in the air, prompting another she didn't dare ask. She knew his answer would change her world.

"I been wantin' to meet you for twenty long years," he drawled on, his soft, raspy voice a whisper of sandpaper across her spine. He lifted one sallow-colored hand off his cane and swept it out toward her, a scornful motion up, then down. "But you. You don't seem very happy to meet me—the man who was supposed to be your daddy."

At those words she froze as if he'd mesmerized her. She had no idea who he was, no idea what he wanted with her. She only knew that everything about him—his voice, his words, the way he was looking at her, gripped her with revulsion.

He waited, continued to watch her in that nerve-tingling way. The silence stretched on, until Jamilla shifted and her petticoats rustled. That one small sound had him jerking his head in her direction, and he frowned in irritation, as though he'd just noticed she was there, like some pesky fly buzzing about. "Sugar, why don't you get Tom to drive you to the party?" he said.

The suggestion displeased her. She wanted to see Rosemary's face when she learned that her mother was a rich man's whore, no better than Jamilla was. Resentment was her motivation. Mambo Zora was training Rosemary for what should have been hers.

She opened her mouth, closed it again in a pout. "You want me to go now? I thought Joseph was takin' you and me together. When he got back."

To Rosemary, the smile he gave Jamilla was equally as chilling as his stare. "Oh now, you're all dressed up. Lookin' so pretty too. Why should you have to wait for me? You go on. I'll be along."

For the first time, Jamilla felt a flicker of unease. Settling a score was one thing, but she never imagined he had anything more in mind than that. She kept her tone light, glanced at the ormolu clock. "It's way past nine, Beau. That old coot is probably asleep for the night by now."

His smile was gone. "Wake him up, sugar. That's what I pay him for."

Rosemary's breath started to hitch, and her knees turned to water. "No, Jamilla. I don't want to be here by myself."

Jamilla's struggle with her conscience was short-lived. He wasn't interested in Rosemary in that way. He couldn't be. He was well past fifty. Philomène was only fifteen when he'd targeted her to be his, but she wouldn't think about that. Nor would she let herself be replaced by Rosemary a second time. To defy him would make him angry, and that would do her no good. Besides, Joseph would be back soon. It would be all right until then.

Her manner changed. Playful and coy with a steel hardness beneath. "Don't be long, Beau. You don't want to leave a woman like me on my own. Somebody else might snatch me up."

Not a trace of humor reflected in his eyes when he chuckled. "Oh, don't I know it." He flicked his fingers, dismissing her. "Run along, now."

"No—" Rosemary made a grab for Jamilla, who shook her off and swept from the room.

And Rosemary was left to face Beauregard Clay in his parlor, in the very house where her mother had died giving birth to her.

On his way back to the Clay mansion, Joseph spotted someone staggering like a drunk along the waterfront road. The figure was still in silhouette, but he knew it was a woman by the shadow of her skirt that billowed and swayed each time she stumbled. As he drove closer, his headlights illuminated her legs. And then she was close enough for him to see a red dress with white polka dots, stained with blood, and her face, soaked with tears.

He slammed on the brake, fishtailed the car to a halt, and bolted out. "Rosemary!"

She collapsed to her knees when she saw him running toward her, and howled like a wounded animal. "You get away from me! You get away!" When he reached for her, on his knees in the dirt, she swung her arm in one great arc with all her fear and fury, to hit him in the face. "You brought me there. You brought me to that monster!"

Icy coldness washed over him. He didn't have to ask. "No. Lord, no." He held his hands to his head. "No. I didn't mean for this to happen."

"What did you *think* would happen? What did you think a man like that would do?" She was still screaming. "He told me you knew who he was—you and Jamilla—you both *knew*."

"Where was she? Where was my mother?"

"He told her to go." She hurled out the condemnation. "He told her to go, and she left me, just like you did."

He didn't try to stop her as she hit him again and again. He stood still for it, stared slack-mouthed at the bruises on her arms, her legs, her split, swollen lip, and felt consumed by shame. "He beat you."

Tears ran down her face in an unbroken stream. "With his cane. He said—" She had to stop to take in gulps of air. She bent forward, pressed her palms against her thighs and rocked forward and back as she moaned out the words she would never forget—"I owe your mama a beatin' for cuckolding me, but she's too dead, so you'll take it for her."

Joseph broke. "Rosemary. I'm sorry, *cher*. I'm so, so sorry." He was crying now too. "Please forgive me. I didn't know. I didn't think. I've been so confused and angry, what with all that's going on. And Mama. She said—"

He couldn't finish. His remorse was genuine, and she finally let him touch her. He put his palm to her cheek so she would look at him. "He'll pay for this." He lay her head against his shoulder. "I promise you."

They both continued to cry as he stroked her hair. Then she started laughing—giddy, helpless laughter between the sobs. "He has paid. I made him pay."

"Ssh, ssh. It's all right. It'll be all right." He rocked her. "What do you mean?"

His shirt was damp where her face was pressed into the fabric. "I stabbed him." The words were muffled against his chest.

His whole body froze. "What?"

"I stabbed him." She said it again, louder this time.

He pulled back and stared at her. "You...you *stabbed* him?"

Knuckling a tear off her face, she nodded.

"Oh, Rosemary," he breathed. He didn't know what he was feeling, whether it was awe or fear. "Is he dead?"

"No, he's not dead." Calmer now, she wiped her hand across her nose, rubbed it on the hem of her dress. "But he's bleedin.' I made him bleed." She looked down at her dress again, and moved her hand over the spot where it was stained. "This is his blood, not mine."

When she lifted her head, Joseph felt the hair on his arms stand up. In her eyes he could see panic, he could see pain, but he could also see power. For the first time he understood why Zora had chosen Rosemary, not Jamilla, to follow in her path.

He pressed his fingers to his eyes to clear them. "How?"

"I couldn't stop him from beatin' me. I didn't see it coming. He just swung his cane at me, hit me in the face, and I fell." She touched her fingers to her cut lip, to the bruise on her cheek. Once I was down, he just kept at me. I...I had my arms over my face..." her voice hitched..."and next I knew, he crawled on top of me." She spoke quietly, but as she talked, every few minutes, her body would spasm with an involuntary shudder. "He told me he was going to give me a baby. That this time, he'd make sure it was his. He said I'd be his mistress, and that I should be grateful for it. The way my mama never was."

She paused to gauge his reaction. She couldn't tell what he was thinking, as he watched her, waiting for the rest. Slowly, she slid the letter opener out of her pocket and held it up so that the car headlights shone on it. "But he never got the chance to touch me like he wanted."

Joseph's mouth went dry when he saw it was caked to the hilt with blood.

"I'm going to jail, Joseph. It's my word against his, and he's a rich, powerful man." She gulped. "A white man." Tears fell again as she whispered fiercely, "But I made him bleed. My life is over, but for the rest of his, he'll remember that I made him bleed."

Without a word, Joseph closed his hand over the letter opener and tucked it into his pocket. He stood up, held out his arm to her. "Let me take you home, *cher*."

She stayed hunched and huddled on the road. "The police. They'll know soon, if they don't already."

"You're not going to jail." He sounded confident and unruffled. Deliberately so. Not by one inkling did he want her to suspect what he had in mind.

But she was wise beyond her years, even wiser now that she'd experienced firsthand the cruelty men were capable of, the ruthless inequities of the world. That wisdom was in the quiet look she gave him.

"Don't you think about going back there. You mustn't ever go there again. Not you, not Jamilla." Her voice shook once more. "You listen to me. That man is nothin' but evil. He's pure evil, Joseph."

His arm was still extended, his palm still open for her to take his hand. "Please, Rosemary. I need to get you back home." When she tried to stand, her legs were still unsteady. He picked her up, cradled her in his arms, and carried her to the car.

By the next morning, he was dead. Mambo Zora sensed it even before Jamilla came shrieking and pounding at her door.

He'd dropped Rosemary home, beat a hasty retreat before Zora, in her distress over Rosemary's condition, could detain him. In the interim, Jamilla had taken a cab back to the Clay mansion when Beauregard didn't turn up at the party. She found him lying where Rosemary had left him, bleeding out his life onto his Aubusson rug. Joseph arrived just as a distraught Jamilla was giving her statement to the police. She was that crazed by fear and resentment that she would have implicated a guiltless young woman. But somehow, she'd raised a decent man who would not let that happen. Joseph walked up to the officers who were taking down his mother's report, showed them the letter opener, and declared that Jamilla was covering for him. The reason he'd stabbed Clay, he told them, was that Clay had cheated him out of some money. Despite Jamilla's denials and pleas, he was handcuffed and taken away. His confession made it easy for the police to avoid an investigation involving a wealthy man from an old, established family.

During the night, Joseph died in his cell. No cause was given, and no inquiry into his death was planned. But when Jamilla saw him, lying dead and cold, his body had more bruises on it than Rosemary's.

Her grief knew no bounds and her rage was displaced. So Zora told her that next day, when the community all came outside at Jamilla's wails to observe the confrontation between the two.

"Don't you lay that child's death at this door, Jamilla. You're the one who lied to him. You're the one who twisted his mind. You're the one who told him to drag my girl to the house of a man you knew has been living off hate for the past twenty years."

Standing on her porch, Zora's face was strained and haggard as she thought of Rosemary's condition. She was so beat-up that Zora was afraid to touch her. She'd called Celeste for help, and together they bathed her, rubbed herbal ointments on her, given her teas and potions to help heal her battered mind and body, until she fell into a fitful sleep.

"Did you *see* what he did to her? Joseph saw. And when that poor boy realized what he caused, he tried to make it right." Her eyes stung and her aging heart ached. Even Philomène's death had not left her as sick and sad as this, and every day the tension in the city, in the country, grew. "Just go. Go on home and grieve for your son. The proper way. Not this way."

Neither women thought to place blame where it actually belonged.

"You always know what's 'proper' don't you, Zora?" Jamilla cried. "You always thought you were better than me."

"No." The mambo felt weary to her bones. "I never looked down on you for your choices. I just didn't want them to be mine."

Jamilla wouldn't let it rest. She screeched, pulled at her own hair, and beat her palms against her chest. "Everything is gone for me. *Everything!*" The shameful truth was that she mourned the loss of a rich benefactor as much as she mourned the loss of her only son. All she could see through her despair was her hatred for Zora and Rosemary.

Clutching the amulet she wore around her neck, she swore an oath on it, right then, for everyone to hear. "I'll make you sorry," she hissed through her tears. "I will not *rest* 'til I make you sorry for what you've done."

As for Beauregard Clay, if only Rosemary had killed him, Joseph's noble sacrifice would have saved so much more than just her life.

CHAPTER FIVE

"Conceited, arrogant asshole."

The mutter wasn't audible *per se*, but the almost too-careful place-ment of butter, eggs, and other perishables Marisol was stacking in one of the new refrigerators told its own story. She wanted to smash them, not put them away.

"Oh, dear." Rohini's smile was sympathetic as she unpacked her own supplies from their latest delivery. "What did he do this time?"

"Nothing." The refrigerator door was shut with a snap. Fueled by frustration, Marisol had no problem hefting a giant-sized sack of flour to line it up next to the bags of sugar and other dry baking goods al-ready stored. "That is, nothing other than be his usual dismissive, con-descending self." She glanced up, and it wasn't just annoyance Rohini saw on her face. There was hurt there as well. "He blew off my mini desserts concept."

"Oh, no. I thought that was a splendid idea." She was just as disap-pointed as Marisol was. "He's making a mistake. People aren't eating such large portions of sweets these days. Besides, suppose someone can't make up their mind which to try, and they'd like a taste of two?"

"Exactly." Marisol flattened the cardboard box they'd just emptied. "I said all that."

"And the sample ones you made looked so delicate and tempting." She felt the need to make Marisol's case, even if only to Marisol.

"I showed him those. I even left some in the office for him. He was unimpressed. And impatient. Just like he always is with me." She set aside the folded box for recycling and reached for another. "Two weeks, and not one word of encouragement. Why hire me if he dislikes me so much?"

Rohini wasn't touching that one. Marisol still didn't suspect Michael's meddling. Wouldn't that go over well when it occurred to her?

"Oh, I don't think he dislikes you." It was the judicious thing to say, although she wasn't at all sure it was true. What she had noticed was that Emilio was aware of Marisol at all times and Marisol appeared to be equally conscious of him. Unless her radar was off, that signified something more than animosity between them.

When they'd emptied all the boxes, Rohini set to making room in the pantry for the additional goods. She retrieved a short step ladder from its customary place, and Cristiano's playful teasing flashed through her mind—*Still can't reach those top shelves? When are you going to grow taller, mi pequeña esposa?*

"Well, if he doesn't dislike me, then maybe he's just a dick." Marisol's blunt indictment cut into Rohini's bittersweet recollection.

"Don't take it like that, darling. He's focused on the re-opening." She climbed up and down the step ladder to place oils, vinegars, and sauces together on one level, assorted varieties of legumes, beans, and rice on the next. "There's a lot to organize in such a short time. That's probably why he seemed distracted." She tried to reassure, though her heart wasn't in it. There was something else on her mind. Something she needed to know, but could not bring herself to ask.

"I guess," murmured Marisol. She didn't pick up on Rohini's canned responses. She was fixated on her own concerns. There was something about the way Emilio looked at her. As though he disapproved of her, for some reason. But how did that make sense? He'd gone out of his way to get her here. Her father told her Emilio had asked if she might be interested in being the new pastry chef.

And she was interested, to say the least. To work at The Secret Spice Café was a dream she'd held since the first time she'd decorated cupcakes with Angela when she was four. The conversation with her father had gone like this:

"Me? He wants *me*? Do you mean it, Dad? Are you sure? He could get anyone—people with tons more experience."

"Well," Michael had said, "maybe he heard good things."

And when she speculated, "Do you think Angela said something to him?" Michael's hedging response had been, "That's always possible, isn't it?"

In that way, without telling a concrete lie, Michael left his daughter with the impression that she was coveted as a team member by the new owner of the restaurant where she'd longed to work for three-quarters of her life.

When she got to the ship on the day Emilio had stipulated, however, pleased to be there and eager to get started, his response to her presence had been tepid, at best. And that was how it was still. Not for the first time did she wonder if she'd said or done something on that first day to put him off, and she'd spent the last two weeks trying to impress him with her enthusiasm and expertise. Which, now that she thought about it, totally sucked. She was starting to feel like a trained seal.

Her musings were disrupted by the scraping sound of the step ladder Rohini was dragging to the cabinet where she kept her herbs and spices.

"Ach. I'm such an idiot. I should have asked if I could hand you stuff."

"That's sweet of you, but it's good exercise."

That was another equivocation sent Marisol's way. The truth was, ever since the fateful day Naag had gasped his last breath on their kitchen floor, Rohini kept an obsessive watch on her herbs and spices.

The cabinet was always locked, and she'd labelled any potentially dangerous medicinals with careful instructions and warnings. Even so, the only person to whom she'd given a key was Cristiano, but not before she'd taught him the possible side effects of each. He'd learned all the Indian names. His pronunciation was excellent too. Such a smart man.

Oh, my love, she thought. Where are you?

Heaven help her, she needed an answer to at least one of her questions. She kept a tight lid on her emotions, and didn't turn to face Marisol when she finally drummed up the nerve to ask. "So. You spoke only about the pastries? There was no mention of...he didn't say anything about a new chef?"

Marisol flushed with shame. Here she was, bitching about stupid Emilio, when the idea of a stranger coming in to replace Cristiano would have to be devastating for Rohini. Inwardly she chastised herself for pestering her about something so minor in comparison, but not by a bat of an eye did she display her pity. She mimicked Rohini's offhand manner, knowing it was what she wanted. "I should have mentioned that he's interviewing one this evening. He invited us—you and me, I mean—to meet her."

At that, Rohini did twist around on the ladder to look at her. "Her?"

Marisol nodded, but kept her eyes on the task of folding boxes. "He's been interviewing female chefs." As much as she hated to admit it, that showed sensitivity on Emilio's part. "He was impressed enough by a phone interview to ask this one to come in and talk. We're supposed to go for Happy Hour in the OB." Sheepishly, she added, "Not that I can drink. Still have six more months to wait for that."

Rohini ignored that last, still reeling from the news that their next chef would be female. "Why not interview her here?"

Marisol lifted a shoulder. "We have drop cloths everywhere. The Observation Bar gives a great first impression." She reached for the last box. "And he said he doesn't want her to assume she's already hired. Wants to keep it formal, so the three of us can get a sense of what she's like."

To herself Rohini could admit that she was weak with relief that there wouldn't be another male in the kitchen, standing in the place where her husband should be. She felt a rush of gratitude that the much-maligned Emilio had been kind enough to think of that. Her mouth curved up. "He said all of that, did he? I thought he was 'unimpressed and impatient'?"

"Well, when I was talking to him about desserts, he was." Even to her own ears, she sounded defensive. "Anyway, it makes sense he'd ask us to join them. We're the ones who'd be working with her."

A simple statement, and yet it hung on Rohini like a hot, heavy blanket. "That's true, isn't it?" She sighed, stepped down off the ladder and closed it back up. There was nothing else to say, nothing that she wanted to say out loud, at least. She was thankful Marisol understood she didn't want a fuss made over this. She wouldn't be able to handle that. As compassionate as Rohini was, she was so intent on remaining stoic, so wrapped up in her own bereavement, she'd forgotten Marisol had dealt with her own loss, a loss that had wrecked her for a time. Of all people, she'd understand the desire for a respite from the raging pain, and the hope that no one jab her where it hurt with well-meaning solicitousness.

When the two women did meet each other's eye, it wasn't because they were both empaths that one knew what the other was thinking. It was perpetual mourning that bonded them.

Marisol broke the connection first, for Rohini's sake. With a sardonic smile and a glimpse of the dimple she'd had since she was a child, she went for the absurd. "'Yippee. I can't wait to meet the person who's taking the job that belongs to my missing husband.' Said no one, ever. Right, Rohini?"

When Rohini managed an answering chuckle, they were both relieved. Ragged around its edges though it was, at least it wasn't a sob.

Please, please, please—she could not be late. Why, oh why, had she felt the need to change clothes? She should have gone to the bar straight from the Spice. This was a business meeting, after all. But then she dropped Nutella on the front of her uniform, and the rest weren't back from the cleaners until morning. No matter how good it smelled, Nutella looked like baby poop, and she did not want to be in a meeting with Emilio Guerrero while wearing baby poop.

It was because she was still trying to impress him, she thought, annoyed with herself. So here she was, sprinting from the parking lot, bypassing the crowded elevators to take the metal stairs, and then across the platform to run up more stairs, carpeted this time. She'd be sweaty when she got there, defeating the whole purpose of dashing home to change.

When she was hired, Rohini had offered her Angela's stateroom. It would be a great perk not to deal with traffic every day. Traffic was why she was jogging up the main staircase from Reception to the Promenade Deck.

But she was reluctant to accept.

First and foremost, though she'd made peace with her paranormal abilities, she didn't think she could deal twenty-four-seven with the sheer number of souls who dwelled aboard the ship. Not that they didn't exist everywhere she went. She was used to seeing them now, even smiled at those she encountered more than once, the same way she might smile at a nameless neighbor who lived down the street, or at a commuter who took the same bus with her every day. But the spirits aboard the *Mary* were more intense somehow, more tethered to the ship, so much so that even those visitors who couldn't see them, sensed them. And as harmless as they were, as heartbreaking as some of their stories were, the thought of stumbling across one in the middle of the night when she got up to go pee was not an appealing prospect.

Apart from that, she wasn't sure she should move out yet. Maybe she was a dork, but she liked living with her father. At least for the time being. It had been four years, but they both still missed Inez fiercely, and took comfort from each other's presence.

When she reached the top step, she checked her phone, and felt like doing a fist pump in the air. Ten to six. She'd made it, with enough time to dash into the restroom to swipe at her armpits, freshen her lipstick, and comb her hair.

The *Queen Mary* Promenade Deck had undergone many modifications since its inception in the 1930s. While still dazzling in 2020, in the 1930s, it had been even more luxurious with its rich teak floorboards and wainscoting, white oak deck chairs, and bronze window frames. In 1940, the ship was converted for war service, and for seven years, her purpose was altered dramatically. Where she'd been a lavish, floating palace to transport the glitterati, she was then stripped of her elegant art, furnishings, and textiles in order to make room for thousands of Allied troops and prisoners of war. During those years, the *Queen* grieved for her lost sumptuousness, but she grieved ever so much more for those young men. The hardships they endured was something she'd never experienced, and it left its mark on her spirit just as much as the graffiti they carved into her wood that chronicled their misery.

After the war, there was a refurbishing that returned her to her former glory. Garden lounges were added to the Promenade near the first-class smoking rooms. Some said she was better than ever. Others said they preferred how she looked before she'd been utilized as a troop ship. All thought of her appearance, but none thought of how she *felt*, of her loss of innocence, of the blood and tears that had seeped into her hull. She would never forget the multitude who'd lost their minds or their lives, even as she gave everything of herself, sailing away from enemies at the highest speeds possible for a ship at the time, in her warrior effort to keep all those she carried safe from harm.

When the *Queen* was forced to retire to Long Beach, the way a senior citizen must relocate to warmer climes so her bones won't creak, she was given another refit. Like a facelift on a dowager, it refreshed her, but she would never again be the ingénue she once was. She had restaurants added, rooms divided up or closed off, never to be seen again. It was no wonder she was rife with mystical activity. For eighty-six years, she'd hosted stars and statesmen, survived storms, war, neglect. It was all still there, cultivated into the very framework of this once most legendary, seafaring ocean liner. She was a microcosm of human history for those who cared to explore her.

As Marisol stepped out of the women's lounge and walked toward the Observation Bar, she wondered if there might be any among the present day visitors who were like her, who could see what she saw right then—the sailors, the soldiers, the men and women of high society dressed in designer cruise wear, the stewards in tuxedos serving them tea. The Long Beach tourists walked right past them, or through them. She thought it humorous that so many were there to hunt for 'scary' ghosts, never realizing that all they had to do was sit quietly and envisage the worlds and times the *Queen* had experienced before most of them were even born.

In the middle of the main shopping area there was the Centerline Boutique, a unique, oval-shaped gift store with ceiling-high windows that curved all around, displaying the books and objets d'art within like Fabergé eggs under a glass dome. A dapper-looking tailor was seated there every day. He'd been waiting patiently for clients since 1936, when the Centerline had been the gentlemen's outfitters, Austin Reed. That tailor stood and made a bow to Marisol every time she walked past, but the pretty young woman who worked in the shop these days never saw him, never knew she had a companion working right there beside her.

There was a time when her ability to see ghosts had made Marisol feel like an aberration. And then a ghoul climbed out of her watery grave, straight up the side of the ship to help her save the life of a friend. She'd thought nothing could be more disharmonious or terrifying than that. Until the day her mother sat her down to tell her she'd been diagnosed with triple negative breast cancer.

Spirits weren't terrifying. Watching the mother you love wither away to nothing, and the father you'd always depended upon fall apart?

That was terrifying.

This was the reason she understood Rohini's reticence in regard to Cristiano's disappearance. The year after Inez's death had been unbearable. If anyone tried to show Marisol overt sympathy, or offer empty condolences, she would just sneer at them. Now, it was better. *She* was better. But there were still times when grief sliced at her, sudden and sharp.

Like the day she was hired. It was the first time in a long time she'd been aboard the *Mary*. She felt fine being there, a little nervous, but mostly excited. She immediately honed in on the new owner's attitude toward her, and wondered what that was about. Her focus was all on her new job. Until the cleaning staff arrived, bringing sounds in with them that flooded her with memories. The waxy smell of her crayons as she colored in one of the staterooms while waiting for her mother. The bubbly excitement of picking out stickers in Michael's shop. And when she was older, the unhappiness of believing she hated her own mother, defying her to sneak into the kitchen of The Spice to bake with Angela.

Then came their turning point, when Marisol helped save Sarita's life.

"You're amazing. You're like Saturn Girl," Inez had praised her. Marisol was shocked her mother knew Saturn Girl was her favorite superhero.

That was when she started to accept herself, to embrace her abilities. Encouraged by her mother, Saturn Girl became her mantra. After that, she and Inez had one wonderful year together, followed by a year of cancer hell, before they were separated forever.

Before she died, Inez said it again, "Remember. You're like Saturn Girl. Saturn Girl always survives."

And Marisol had survived. It was touch-and-go for a while, but what got her through was knowing her mother had believed in her, had believed she was like Saturn Girl.

She was almost past the Centerline when she thought she heard someone whisper her name. She glanced through the glass windows of the boutique to see if the tailor had called to her. But oddly enough, he wasn't there. In his stead was another spirit, a silver-haired gentleman dressed in tails and carrying a cane. It was the first time Marisol had seen him. He tipped his head to her, and she nodded back.

Checking her phone again, she had two minutes before it would be straight up six, and she mentally patted herself on the back that she'd be at the bar in less than one, appearing professional and stylish, not a smudge of baby poo in sight.

She rounded portside, was just nearing the entrance of the bar, when she stopped short to peer at the polished burl panels that lined the hall. The swirls and knots in its highly-figured grain created curious 'faces' in the wood. If one looked carefully, one could see a pug-like nose, a pouting mouth, teardrop-shaped eyes that slanted up under a frowning brow, pointed ears, and even a pair of horns atop the head. These were twists in the wood caused by stress to the tree, fungi or some such. The idea that they were actual faces was too absurd even to a woman with her otherworldly abilities.

Why then, had she been compelled to stop and stare at a panel she'd seen dozens of times? As she kept her eyes on it, it began to morph, its features becoming more pronounced, the brows lowering, the mouth contorting into a snarl.

Marisol. Look.

She'd heard that same voice, that same command, before. In her father's shop, when she was four years old.

She jumped back.

"Watch it!"

A sharp elbow jab to her rib jolted her back to the present.

"Ow!" She swiveled around to confront her assailant, a woman. "What was that for?"

The woman glared back without remorse. "You nearly stepped on my foot."

"I think 'nearly' is the operative word here, don't you?" she retorted, but the woman had already marched on.

Rubbing her side, Marisol sputtered, "Geez. I can't even…"

The whispery voice, the face in the wall were forgotten, as she hurried into the bar and scanned the interior for Emilio. When she spotted him, she saw that the woman he was shaking hands with was the one who'd just tried to give her a rib fracture.

Well. This would be fun, wouldn't it?

Her shoulders were squared as she walked to the table. Under her breath, she said, "Saturn Girl always survives."

CHAPTER SIX
1956, New York City

The Hudson was not the Mississippi, but it made Rosemary feel better to make-believe it was. Two years had passed since she'd seen that river, and she missed it every day. She missed the steamboats churning the water to froth with their paddlewheels. She missed seeing barefoot children dangling their makeshift fishing rods off the docks in the hopes of nabbing a catfish for supper. She missed hearing the longshoremen along the wharf calling out to one another, their familiar Cajun and Creole inflections like a favorite old song.

It wasn't just the river she missed. She was homesick for everything and everyone in New Orleans.

New York City would have been the ultimate adventure for a girl who'd longed for adventure, if only she'd come to live there by choice. After Joseph's death, Mambo Zora knew that Jamilla and her followers, along with any astrals under her supernatural control, would come for them like fire ants raiding a honey bee hive. While Zora could defeat Jamilla's black magick, Rosemary was still a novice at Vodou, so she was sent to practice the art in the house of a powerful *houngan*—a male priest—in Harlem.

In the meanwhile, the South Rosemary longed to see again was slowly becoming the hub of the Civil Rights Movement. A year after she'd arrived in New York, a woman named Rosa Parks did not give up her seat to a white passenger on a bus in Alabama. Blacks united to boycott, and after thirteen months of catastrophic protests in which whites rioted, bombed black churches, as well as the homes of civil rights leaders E.D. Nixon and Martin Luther King, Jr., the Supreme Court struck down laws requiring segregated seating on public buses, at long last. In Rosemary's New Orleans, lunch counter sit-ins were held in Canal Street department stores, and in just four years, six-year-old Ruby Bridges would push her way past protestors to be the first black student at an all-white elementary school in the Ninth Ward.

And yet, the north of the country continued to be a magnet for black southerners who still believed it the way to escape the dire racism of their home cities. By 1956, almost half a million would migrate, the vast majority landing in New York City, with about three hundred thousand living in Harlem. The substantial influx, along with segregation, resulted in a housing shortage which led to toxic crowding. Landlords took advantage of the need for living space and the lack of enforcement of housing and sanitation codes by carving buildings into tiny one-room apartments and raising the rents. Strangers had to share bathrooms and kitchens.

This was how Rosemary had been living for two lonely years. Granted, the priest's apartment—Houngan Toby as he was known—was kept scrupulously clean by his six pupils, and though they were just as crushed for space as everyone else in the 129th Street housing project, they were a close-knit group who were joined in purpose. They kept to themselves for the most part, since Vodou was so maligned and misrepresented in the media and in Hollywood, that even some of their own people were suspicious of it. The houngan was a former student of Zora's, and like her, was a patient teacher who treated his 'children' with kindness and respect. He never let on to any of them, especially not to Rosemary, that he'd written to Zora to inform her that Rosemary had a true gift for the art.

Favored apprentice or not, Rosemary's work didn't stop with her lessons. Bills had to be paid, and they all had to eat, so each of Toby's disciples had a day job. Monday through Friday, Rosemary would walk to the 125th Street Station to take the two bus lines that would get her to the Manhattan Garment District.

New York City first assumed its role as the center of the nation's apparel industry by producing clothing for slaves. Southern plantation owners found it more efficient to buy clothes from New York rather than have their slaves spend time making the clothes themselves. Ninety years after slavery was abolished, it was an irony that Rosemary and others like her labored for low wages in one of these very factories. Just one factory would house hundreds of immigrants—Irish, Italian, Russian Jew—as well as poor minorities, who sewed cut pieces of cloth into ready-made clothes for retail outlets.

After ten hours spent hunched over a commercial sewing machine, and a one-hour commute each way, Rosemary's nights were taken up with studying to be the best Vodou practitioner she could be. What the houngan didn't know was that a big part of the reason she worked so hard to excel was that she wanted to become powerful enough to defy Jamilla. Despite everything that had happened when she was last there, she still wanted to go home.

That desire was about to be replaced by another.

Every weekend she could spare the time, she took the bus to Hell's Kitchen and made her way to the waterfront, by the piers. If money was especially tight, she'd save the fare and walk the five miles down Eighth Avenue and then west to the cruise terminal. At first, she'd been drawn there solely by her yearning to be by the water. But one particularly cloudless, sunlit Saturday, as she was nearing the docks, she heard the boom of a foghorn so loud and deep it pulsated off the river, shook the nearby buildings, and resonated straight through her. She knew whatever ship it was with a whistle that powerful must be huge, but when she saw people hurrying toward Pier 90, she caught their excitement and followed, just in time to see a grand ocean liner propelling toward the terminal, her three red-orange stacks billowing smoke and steam.

When she got to the dock, she didn't think twice about steering her way through the crowd. She knew she was being bold, but she couldn't stop herself. This time it was the vessel that was the siren, drawing the woman to it by its intoxicating, irresistible song. When Rosemary had wriggled her way to the front, she got an unfettered view of the ship, the waves riled up around it, the spray of the water it displaced as it coasted into the slip. Along the ship's side, in gleaming gold, was the name, *Queen Mary*.

Rosemary felt an instant and overwhelming connection. "Oh, my Lord," she breathed. A glimpse of a vision came to her—a regal-looking woman dressed in blue, leaning forward to cut a ribbon with a silver scissor—gone before it was fully formed.

A young man to her immediate left on the platform didn't quite overhear her quiet exclamation, but he took in her rapt expression and grinned down at her. "Impressive, isn't she?" he said in an accent she couldn't place. "That right there is the greatest ship to ever sail the seas."

Rosemary tossed him an answering smile. "It's the most beautiful thing I've ever seen."

She was so wrapped up in the presence of the liner in front of her, she didn't notice the impact her smile had on him. While she goggled at the ship, he stared at her, heard himself say, "Up until this very minute, I'd have agreed with you."

Distracted by the noises of the quayside, the shouts and whistles of the crewmen who pulled on thick ropes to moor the *Queen Mary* in, Rosemary almost didn't register that he'd spoken again. She tore her gaze away from the ship to respond. "I'm sorry. What?"

When he said nothing, she laughed, and to him, it felt like the sun rising over the ocean. "I'm sorry," she said a second time. "I'm being rude. I come down here on the weekends whenever I can, but I've never seen this ship before." Yet somehow she felt she knew it, although she didn't say that out loud.

In all his life he'd never seen a woman who looked like she did. He had the fanciful thought that she must be a naiad who'd lingered there by the harbor just waiting to bewitch him. If that were true, he was thankful for it. When he realized he was still staring, he shook his head to clear it, and held out his hand. "I'm Les Taylor."

She hesitated. She wasn't used to talking to strange men, let alone touching them. But his hand was out, and he had a gentle look about him. The breeze over the water ruffled his short brown hair, and his eyes were a warm, soft blue. She took his hand, then quickly released it. "Rosemary Dupré."

"Dupré? Would that be French?" His curiosity about her was unabashed.

"It's Creole."

When the *Queen Mary* was secured, she delivered one giant blast of her horn. Rosemary gave a little squeal and laughed again. "Oh, my. Up close that surely tests the ear, doesn't it?"

Crew and passengers began to disembark, while photographers waited patiently at the landing for a glimpse of any famous names. Rumors had filtered into their newsrooms that on this particular transatlantic voyage there would be a popular Hollywood actress, and even some British nobility. Then again, aboard the *Queen*, celebrity travelers were commonplace.

Les elected to make a move. "It happens I work on this ship."

Her eyes widened. "Do you? Well, aren't you the lucky one. Why weren't you on board, then?"

"I was here in New York for this one. I'm taking the next one out." He tipped his head toward the *Mary*. "Would you like to go up and walk around? She'll be docked here for a while. I can give you a tour."

"Oh, I don't know." She was tempted. She couldn't believe how tempted she was, considering the last time she'd given into an impulse to go for a walk, it had nearly destroyed her.

He seemed to understand her reluctance, and held his palms up. "I'm harmless, I promise." Letting his hands fall, he stuck them in his pockets, and regarded her with an earnestness she found charming. "I admit I'd like to show off the beautiful girl I met on the dock to my mates, but other than that, my intentions are honorable."

Rosemary chewed on her lip, glanced over to the gangplank where the throng was thinning. She made a decision. "All right. But just for a little while."

Delighted, he took her hand and tucked it into the crook of his elbow. As they walked toward the ship, he did his utmost to put her at ease.

"So. Were you born here in New York, Rosemary Dupré?"

"New Orleans."

"Ah. Never been. Are there lots of Creole people there, then?"

"There are. And you—where are you from?"

"Stalybridge."

"Ah. Never been," she mimicked, and made him grin. "Where is it?"

"Well, it's a little place near Manchester, northern England…"

Over the next six months, every time the *Queen Mary* brought Les into New York, he and Rosemary met. They had one full day together, followed by ten days apart, but it was enough for them to fall in love.

When Les was in town, most of their days and nights were spent aboard the ship, as it held the most welcome for a mixed-race couple. They'd tried walking together in the Manhattan streets, but were given dagger-like stares, condemnation that sometimes bordered on the dangerous. On the *Mary*, Les's crewmates, many of whom had been at sea during the war, were more accepting. When Les proposed, Rosemary did take him into Harlem to meet Houngan Toby, who saw the passion and devotion the couple felt for one another shining around them like a circle of light. Toby gave them his blessing, but like any good mentor, he counseled them on the problems they would face. With their hands clasped together like a sturdy bridge across continents, Rosemary and Les listened to his words and nodded their understanding, but their love felt invincible to them, as young love always does and always should.

They were married by the *Queen Mary* chaplain, though their union would not become legal in New York for two more years. They spent their twenty-four-hour honeymoon aboard the ship. Rosemary felt like a princess bride when Captain Sorell himself came to offer his personal congratulations and, knowing the couple could afford little by way of celebration, invited them to have lunch with him in the first-class dining room, where they dined like royalty on filet, lobster, and crepe suzettes.

After that, Les shipped out again, and Rosemary returned to the tiny apartment in Harlem to practice her craft and wait for his return.

It was the happiest she'd ever been.

She didn't know that word of her wedding had gotten back to Jamilla. Not through Zora, to whom she'd written her joyous news, but through one of Toby's followers and roommates—a spy for Jamilla all the while Rosemary had been in New York. Jamilla seethed when, in the same letter that gave her the news of Rosemary's marriage, she was also told of her increasing skills, and that she'd soon be made a *mambo asogwe*, like Zora.

It was no surprise that Jamilla's powers were growing as well, along with her hatred, her cunning, and her wealth. The cunning was a trait she'd been born with, and the hate she'd had two and a half years to nurture.

As for the wealth, that she appropriated from Beauregard Clay.

Two days after Joseph's funeral, Jamilla visited the hospital where Clay lay recovering from his wounds. The desk nurse looked her up and down, noted the dark skin, the cheap but conservative clothing, the colorful Haitian satchel handbag. "Who are you?" she demanded, with no effort to hide her contempt

Jamilla squared her shoulders with pride. "I am Mr. Beauregard's private nurse," she lied, all the while running her fingers over her amulet until the nurse fell into a trance. "Take me to his room."

Left alone with the sleeping Clay, Jamilla pulled a chair to his bedside, and lay her hands on his temple. "Beauregard Clay," she commanded him softly, "Open to me. What I do now is to punish those who harmed you."

What she told him was only partially true, and for that reason he thrashed, fighting her spell for a minute or two, until he dropped into a deeper sleep.

Once she was certain he was under her control, Jamilla opened the satchel, took out what she needed: a fat black candle, a tiny muslin bag filled with ground cayenne pepper, a darning needle, and a sacred drawing of a cross flanked by two coffins that would help her summon Baron Samedi, the master of the Gede loa, the family of Vodou spirits of the dead.

She lit the candle, placed it on the bedside table. Pulling aside the hospital gown Clay wore, Jamilla placed the drawing on his naked torso, and quietly began to chant. As she murmured the words of the ancient Vodou curse, she punctured the index finger of his limp left hand with the darning needle. Untying the drawstring of the muslin bag, she held his finger over it, pressed down until the blood that had beaded on its tip dripped into the cayenne.

Three drops were all she needed. She shook the bag, the mixture of blood and spice formed a pasty globule within, which Jamilla removed and rubbed over the sleeping man's heart.

The candle flared brighter, its flame rising in one impossibly long, thin column that feathered the ceiling to tinge it with gray. As the dark magick sullied the air, the unconscious man on the bed began to stir. When he woke, the eyes that stared into Jamilla's were no longer Beau's. They were a blazing yellow-gold, the irises dilated and fathomless.

"What do you want from me, Caplata Jamilla?" he asked.

"Revenge, Baron," Jamilla replied. "As is my right."

The next morning, Beauregard's nurses was surprised by how much he appeared to have recovered. He spoke lucidly, his pulse rate was normal, and his blood pressure was down. He even managed to sit up in bed to eat breakfast. And when he finished every morsel, he sent for James Duncan, his lawyer, who, upon his arrival there, was flabbergasted by Beau's request to settle upon Jamilla a sizeable sum of cash and have his home left to her in his will.

"Has that stab wound fevered your mind, Beau?" the lawyer asked.

"I am fine, Jim," Clay assured him. "The woman saved my life. I'd have bled out if it weren't for her, and I want to thank her for it."

"By giving her a boatload of money and willing her your ancestral home?" He was incredulous. This was not the Beauregard Clay he knew.

"Who else am I gonna leave it to?" Beau replied equably. "I have no children, and what relatives I have are pissants, anyhow." He wagged his fork at the lawyer. "You write up that will for me, Jim, you hear me? And be quick about it."

Against his better judgment, Duncan complied with Beauregard's wishes, and brought the revised will and additional documents back to the hospital for him to sign.

A few days later, Beau was well enough to go home, and Jamilla was right by his side to take him there. She fussed over him and cosseted him for two weeks, preparing his favorite foods, giving him foot and back massages, brewing him her special, healing herbal teas.

Despite her ministrations, or perhaps because of them, it wasn't long before Beauregard suffered a major stroke, just as his God-fearing doctor had presaged.

As he lay in his bed, unable to move or speak, Jamilla looked down at him, and thought, Thank you, Baron Samedi. One down, one to go.

She leaned over Clay and whispered in his ear, "For Joseph."

CHAPTER SEVEN

Monday, June 8, 2020, 6:10 p.m.,
Observation Bar, RMS Queen Mary

Elbow jab to the rib aside, Marisol's dislike for their potential new chef was intensifying by the second.

The lowered sun peeked through the wraparound windows of the Observation Bar. Its rays spotlighted the circle of dancing figures of the antique mural on the far wall, lit the wide, sculpted balustrading until it gleamed like polished pewter, and gave the long, flute-shaped torchieres flanking the steps to the seating area a carnelian glow.

The 'OB', as it was commonly known, was not only one of the most beautiful lounges aboard the ship, it was also one of the most historic in existence. Whether one sat indoors or out on the deck, the view of the Pacific was breathtaking.

But the chef—Joy Nettelbeck by name—dismissed her surroundings as easily as she dismissed Barrie, the cocktail waitress who came over to greet them.

Barrie had worked aboard the ship forever, and knew Marisol's parents. She'd even attended Inez's funeral.

"Hey, there." She gave Marisol's shoulder a friendly bump with her elbow. "It's good to see you. You haven't been in to say hello."

"I know, and I feel awful about it," Marisol apologized. She gestured toward Emilio. "We've been working like crazy to get the restaurant reopened. How've you been, Barrie?"

Barrie hadn't even opened her mouth to reply before Joy cut in. "Excuse me," she said, with a stiff, phony smile that set Marisol's teeth on edge, "I hate to be rude, but can I ask that you two save this reunion for after I leave?" She tapped the face of her watch. "I'm afraid I'm on a time-crunch."

Ever the professional, Barrie nodded. "What can I get for you?"

Joy hardly flicked her a glance. "Grey Goose martini, dry as dust. Two olives."

Emilio noted the exchange, but made no comment other than to order for himself. "Chivas on the rocks, Barrie. Thanks," he said, his smile for her sincere.

"I'll just have a club soda, Barrie, with a twist. *Please.*" Marisol emphasized the word, an intimation to Joy, but Barrie merely winked at her. After years at the job, she'd heard and seen it all. Nothing got under her skin. She sailed off to place their order.

"Will Rohini be joining us?" Emilio asked.

"There was a late delivery she wanted to put away." Marisol's nondescript expression gave away more than she thought. Inez would have known immediately that she was lying. "She told me to come ahead."

Emilio expected Rohini wouldn't want to be present for this. He was on to the subterfuge, but without missing a beat, he addressed Joy. "Rohini de la Cueva is the co-owner of The Secret Spice. Her husband was our *cordon bleu.*"

"Yes, I know of Cristiano de la Cueva." She made a moue of sympathy. "A shame. He was a good chef, but most of us in the industry weren't surprised by his mysterious disappearance. He led a troubled life."

Marisol's eyes went to slits. But she steeled herself when Joy turned to her. "And you? What's your role at the restaurant?"

"I'm the pastry chef."

"Really?" Joy drew out the word, her brows raised so high they seemed to fold into her forehead. Her eyes tracked across Marisol's smooth complexion, then down her trim form. "But you look so young." She made it sound like a criminal act.

Marisol smiled thinly. "I guess that's because I am."

"And yet you qualified for such a post in a restaurant of this caliber?"

Her skepticism rang with arrogance, and though Marisol felt her spine go rigid, her smile only grew brighter. "Whose interview is this—yours or mine?"

Emilio stepped in. "Let's get back to the business at hand, shall we?" He didn't give a damn if that sounded high-handed. Two minutes in and already things weren't going the way he'd hoped. That was a problem. Joy Nettelbeck was one of only three applicants who measured up to Cristiano's talent and reputation, in his opinion. Of those three, she was the only female. He wanted to hire her, for Rohini's sake. He knew they'd have to deal with some degree of egotism when it came to a first-rate chef, but this one had no qualms about behaving like an out-and-out ass, on her first interview, no less. And he was just as surprised that Marisol was handling her with such aplomb.

His perception of her had been shifting over the past two weeks, albeit cautiously, as though he were waiting for the other shoe to drop. But he had to admit she'd displayed talent and creativity, boundless enthusiasm for the work, and none of the entitlement for which he'd been braced. There was something about her that made any room seem livelier when she was in it. Apart from that, as much as he had no right whatsoever to think it, it certainly wasn't hard to look at her every day. Her dark eyes, her swingy black hair, her creamy completion—all her features seemed to glow. And that dimple when she smiled—

Whoa. What was he doing? This was forbidden territory. He steered his thoughts back to the issue at hand. If Nettelbeck didn't suit, they were back to square one, unless he were willing to add to Rohini's grief by hiring one of the two men. Either way, they were running out of time. They re-opened in less than a month.

He pulled out some sheets from the folder in front of him, and made an attempt to salvage the meeting. "Since it's now so much a part of the ship, the idea going forward is to pay homage to the original Secret Spice Café, while at the same time adding some new, appealing elements. And we're doing that first by freshening up and reconfiguring the dining room."

Barrie returned with their drinks. Emilio waited until she was gone before he passed copies of the new concept to the women. "My predecessors chose a great designer, but I feel at this point, the look's become dated. Here's the new rendering I received today." Determined to set some boundaries for Joy should they hire her, he asked Marisol first. "What do you think?"

It took all Marisol had to hide her surprise. If she didn't know better, directing the question to her first could mean he was issuing a declaration about her value.

Did he find her valuable, or was it just a show for Joy? He'd have to be pretty thick not to notice the chef's snarky attitude. But on the hope his interest in her opinion was genuine, she studied the drawing in front of her. When she replied, she tried not to come across like she'd just been championed by her nemesis. "It's classy. And…what's the word? Shrewd."

"Shrewd?" Emilio repeated, swirling the ice in his drink. "That's unexpected. How so?"

She wasn't used to him asking her opinion. It was nerve-wracking. After a pause, she motioned to the drawing. "Well, for example, see where the design places the fruits and cakes display? It's the first thing people will see and smell when they walk in. It's enticing. And by having the desserts showcased that way, it's a subliminal message: 'You're out to dinner. Treat yourself.'"

"Naturally the dessert would be your first concern," Joy put in, a smirk playing about her lips.

Emilio couldn't believe his ears. What the hell—why was she baiting Marisol? Was she trying to be funny, or was she just a social ignoramus?

He was impressed when Marisol responded with equanimity once more. "It should be a concern to all of us, if we want to maintain our livelihood. The highest margins are on desserts and wine. It's where restaurants make the bulk of their profits."

"Is that so?" Joy picked up her martini and sipped. "I'm curious as to how you would know that."

Again, Marisol smiled brightly. "Being that I'm so young, right? I've been in and out of the kitchen of The Secret Spice Café since I was four. The previous pastry chef was like an aunt to me. She taught me to bake, and I asked her loads of questions on every aspect of the business," she finished coolly.

"Ah." Joy took another sip of her drink, and said nothing else. She wasn't keen on working with an unknown. It wouldn't enhance her reputation in the culinary world. But she needed the job, having left in a fit of pique from the restaurant where she'd worked previously. And as unimpressive as the girl was in terms of her experience, she wasn't easily flustered. That might be a plus when they worked together.

What Nettelbeck couldn't know was what Marisol had endured at the hands of bullies during her high school years. These days she defended herself. More, she liked herself. Most of the time, anyway. There were always going to be some weak spots in her armor. But everyone had them. How much harm could they do?

Emilio sat back, his jaw tight, as he looked from one woman to the other. There was no getting around it. Like it or not, he'd have to pick one of the two men. He'd talk to Rohini, try to gauge how well she'd handle it. His hopes weren't high on that score. She hadn't even had time to get used to Cris being gone, and they were searching for his replacement. It would be easier on her if they could hire a female chef, but they were asking for trouble if they hired this one. He was just about to terminate the meeting when Joy's phone jingled.

She glanced at the screen. "Oh, I must take this. Excuse me, please."

When she walked out, he took a swig of whiskey. "What do you know? She said 'excuse me,' and 'please.' Might be some human blood running through her veins after all."

His phone buzzed right after Joy's. He read the text, and swore. "Perfect. Just damn perfect."

"Are you okay?" The question was out of her mouth before she could bite it back, and she regretted it at once. It was too personal. This was the first time Emilio was speaking with her as one would with a bona fide colleague. She wasn't sure how long it would last, and she didn't want to mess it up. Then again, between her and Chef Joy, he probably saw her as the lesser of two evils.

"We're screwed." He slid the phone on the table. "One of the candidates for the chef position just got an offer in France. That leaves only Joy and one other. And the other—" he grimaced. "This is funny, in a way. He's Greek. Swarthy. Has an accent. Middle-aged. And his name? 'Christos.'"

"Yikes. Rohini would keel over."

"You're not kidding. We might be stuck with this chick. At least for a while. I can't delay the opening to start a new search."

Joy came back in, looking perturbed. "That was my neighbor. I left her some food for my dog, and somehow, he got sick. I'm afraid I have to go."

"Of course." Emilio tried not to show his relief. He stood up. "Thanks for coming in. We'll...ah...we'll be in touch."

Joy's nod was brisk. "I expect so." Without one glance for Marisol, she dashed off.

On a long, exhaled breath, Emilio sank back into his chair. "Jesus."

Marisol couldn't help it. She chuckled.

His head came up in surprise. "Something's funny about this I missed?"

"Her name is 'Joy.'"

"Yeah. Her parents sure hit the nail on the head with that one."

"Oh, come on. She can't be all bad," Marisol joked. "She loves her dog."

"Does it bode well the dog got sick on food she left for him?"

When she giggled, her dimple flashed. It was the first time she'd laughed in his presence, Emilio realized. He liked the sound of it. "You don't seem very bothered by Chef Joy's less-than-winning personality," he pointed out.

"Honestly, I guess I'm not." She lifted her shoulders. "I mean, if she can cook, what difference does it make?"

"How the staff would deal with her, is my concern. She makes Gordon Ramsey look like Mr. Rogers. "

He was actually discussing work with her. A breakthrough, at last. She did her best to help. "That's just it. Who hasn't seen Gordon in action, even just once? Thanks to him, people expect a chef to be temperamental, don't you think? Not for anything, but Cristiano certainly was." She grinned. "Pretty much everybody who used to work in that kitchen lost their shit at one time or another."

Thinking of his experiences with Cynthia, he grinned back at her. "Boy, do I remember."

Watching his smile bloom, a thought popped into her head, one which she knew was silly even as she thought it: He has such nice teeth. So straight and white. I never noticed that before.

Their accord lasted until Barrie came over to ask if they wanted another round.

"Not for me, thanks." When he turned to Marisol, the Emilio she'd come to know was back. She recognized the sardonic twist to his mouth. It matched his tone. "And you? Another…club soda?"

The pleasure she felt in their friendly exchange died a quick death. She drained the little left in her glass, and nodded to Barrie. "I'll have another, thanks. Oh, and could you bring us some of the pretzel bites with brie fondue, please, when you get a minute? I'm starved."

When the waitress left, Marisol decided to be blunt. "Why do you always look at me like you're mocking me?"

"Do I?" He didn't deny it. "I guess I'm just surprised to see you being so circumspect." He tipped his chin toward her empty glass. "Is that for my benefit?"

She frowned. "What do you mean? I can't drink in public until I'm twenty-one. My birthday's not until November."

"You can't drink 'in public.' I see."

The remark, as well as the contempt in it, baffled her. But for the first time since she started working for him she also got annoyed. He didn't know the particular smile she sent him then was an indication of her rising temper.

She leaned in. "Hey," she said. "Guess what? I have no clue what you're implying. So why not just spit it out?"

"Marisol." Her teeth gnashed at the way he said her name. "My mother and yours were friends for years. I know all about your lifestyle."

Then it came to her. Her 'lifestyle'. His *mother*. Now she knew what his attitude toward her was about. He'd listened to gossip. And believed it, no questions asked. In her lap, her fingers curled into fists so tight, her nails bit into her palms. She wanted to slap him and his mother, both.

"Ohhh. I get it. Okay." Her tone was deceptively sweet and mild. "It must be nice to still have a mom to talk to. You know, my mother insisted I call your mother 'Tia Anna' out of respect, since they were such close friends. She also told me how much your mother loved a juicy story, and that I shouldn't pay attention to her talk. She meant nothing by it. It was just for fun. Isn't that right?"

Emilio's brows drew together. When presented that way, he supposed his mother did love to repeat tales and speculate. But like Inez, he'd never seen the harm in it. It was simply entertainment for her.

Now he wasn't so sure. Every negative thing he'd heard about Marisol had come only from his mother. And when he brought it up to Michael that day in his office, Michael hadn't defended her or expounded upon the subject. Probably, Emilio realized with dawning apprehension, because he hadn't wanted to use his dead wife as a bargaining chip. And in the interim, the Marisol who'd been working with him at The Secret Spice was nothing at all like the Marisol his own mother had put in his head.

She was, as Michael had told him, perfect for the job.

He felt like a jackass.

When Emilio said nothing, Marisol pinned him with her eyes. "So what did Tia Anna tell you, for 'fun'? That I dropped out of school, drank myself sick, spent lots of money, had sex with an endless stream of boys?"

She felt her stomach twist in remembered pain. "Did she maybe leave out the part that I'd just turned sixteen, and for the whole year before that, I watched my mother die, piece by piece? Did Tia Anna mention that I'd go to the hospital after school and, before I got to my mother's room, I could hear her moaning? Or that no matter how much it hurt, she would smile whenever she saw me? And that she died while holding my hand? Did your mother tell you that my father cried himself to sleep for months after she was gone? Or that for a time I wanted to be dead too?"

He saw the tears, saw her effort to hold them back. "I pulled myself back up, though. I got my diploma, and even though Angela had already taught me everything she knew, I went to culinary school, and I did a damn good job there as well." Her voice trembled. "I did it mostly because I knew she could see me. My mother, I mean. For a while, I'd forgotten that. That she's watching, and wherever she is, she'd die all over again if I let myself down."

Emilio wanted to curl up in shame. He'd never in his life felt so petty and small. "Marisol—"

She cut him off. "Why did you hire me if you thought I was such a skank?"

His face went red. "I never said that."

"But you thought it, I bet. So, tell me—what in hell were you doing when you asked me to come work for you?"

He was trapped. He could only stare at her, like a cat caught with his paw in the fish bowl. Michael never told her. She didn't know.

His face screamed his secret, and as he watched her watching him, he saw the split-second it dawned.

She went white. "You *didn't* ask me," she whispered. "You didn't want me at all. It was my father, wasn't it?"

His underarms went damp with sweat. "Listen to me—"

"Oh, I can't believe he'd do this. What was he thinking?" She held her fingers over her mouth and shook her head in mortification. "It all makes sense now—the way you've treated me, the way you've rejected all my ideas. I guess Joy was right. You probably did think I was too young and too inexperienced."

"I never said that either." To his own ears, he sounded defensive and guilty. He hated himself. He'd been so smug, and so, so wrong.

More humiliated than she'd ever been in her life, she stood up, slung her handbag over her shoulder, did her best to stay dignified. "I'll come by in the morning and get my things. I'll be out of your hair by noon." She turned to go.

You moron, he said to himself—say *something*.

"So that's it, huh? You're just going to leave me in the lurch, with no pastry chef? Even after you sat here and *saw* what I have to deal with now, with this Joy person? That's just great, Marisol. Thanks a lot."

He was winging it. He'd made a mess of things, and all he could think to do was to force her into staying by denigrating her pride. It wasn't a good plan by any means, but it was the best he could come up with in a pinch.

"See? This is why I didn't want to hire you," he went on, as his brain tripped and stuttered. "I told your father you wouldn't last. That you'd leave once you got bored or as soon as the job got too tough for you. I was right on the nose, wasn't I?"

She went slack-jawed with shock, as he derided her, belittled her integrity, and the humiliation she felt flipped to such white-hot fury, she quaked with it.

When he saw the wrath on her face, he cringed.

"Okay, pretzel bites and club soda." Barrie came up behind her. "Be careful, cheese is hot—"

Marisol whipped around, reached blindly for the glass Barrie had on her tray, and tossed the contents in Emilio's face. He barely had time to flinch.

"Go fuck yourself, you arrogant bastard. You have the nerve to shame me, when it's *you* who should be ashamed?" She raged at a soaked Emilio, while the entire lounge watched.

One man held up his phone. Emilio caught the movement. "Put it away, dude, or I break it," he warned.

Marisol registered none of it, didn't care. Tears of outrage spilled down her cheeks. "You think I don't have the guts to come back to work? Just watch me, you dick. I'm going to be the best pastry chef ever, and I'll only leave when you fire me. But you better stay the hell out of my way!"

After she stomped off, Emilio pulled at his wet shirt, wiped at his eyes and face.

Yeah, not one of his better spur-of-the-moment ideas.

The unflappable Barrie handed him all the napkins she had on the tray. "I don't suppose you still want these pretzel bites?"

CHAPTER EIGHT

Approximately one month later, Saturday, July 4, 2020

Festooned in red, white and blue from bow to stern, the *Queen Mary* teemed with visitors, all there for the holiday weekend. If any among them saw the incongruity of celebrating American Independence Day aboard a ship that had once been a grand symbol of the British Crown, they were having too much fun to point it out. No matter the occasion, the *Queen* knew how to throw a party.

At dark, there would be a fireworks display hailed as 'the finest in Long Beach,' but while the southern California sun prevailed, there was something exciting happening everywhere on the ship. Outside the Veranda Grill, a swing band dressed in 1940s fashions to commemorate the ship's zenith times, played "In the Mood," and the familiar tune bounced over the bay. Music and laughter also rang in the Royal Salon, where two piano players 'dueled.' For the children, the Sports Deck featured shuffleboard, face-painting, jugglers and gymnasts. There was even an Uncle Sam on stilts, who happily let any child try on his satin top hat.

Hot dogs, ribs, and hamburgers—staple symbols of Americana—scented the air, and could be purchased from open-air stalls. Luscious buffets, featuring everything from shellfish to salads, were being offered in some of the more casual eateries on board. And for those who preferred a five-star dining experience while enjoying the fireworks, there were two superlative choices: Sir Winston's and The Secret Spice Café.

Marisol grabbed a minute to splash some cold water on her face. They were so busy, the kitchen was starting to feel uncomfortably warm. She hadn't thought it was a good plan to re-open on a day when so many other things were going on, but Emilio had made a wise choice. The restaurant was booked solid for the entire weekend. Almost all who came through the doors were impressed with the new décor and tweaks to the menu. Sure, there were those few grumblers who knew the restaurant as it had been in the past, and welcomed no changes, but you couldn't please everyone. All in all, on a business level, she was impressed with Emilio's acumen.

On a personal level, she loathed him still.

True to the promise she'd hurled at him that night in the Observation Bar, she was slaying it as his pastry chef, and carrying out all her other duties equally well. When he spoke to her, butter wouldn't melt in her mouth as she answered. The rest of the time, she ignored him entirely.

That is, she pretended to ignore him. To actually do so wasn't as easy. Right before their hideous confrontation, he'd shown her a different side of himself, and ever since, he just…pulled at her.

Which was idiotic, she knew.

It was idiotic that, up until the night of Joy's interview, she hadn't noticed his smile, but now she had to steel herself against its charm. And when had she become so aware of his body? All of a sudden, she couldn't miss how tight and muscular his bottom looked in his suit trousers, or the way his biceps bulged under his dress shirt when he lifted a heavy box of supplies. His thick hair had a gloss to it like melted dark-chocolate, and his hazel brown eyes were remarkably appealing to someone who claimed to despise him.

Daily, she chastised herself over the unacceptable infatuation she'd developed, and she would have overcome it, if looks were all he had. But there was more to him than that. There was the way he afforded everyone the same attention and respect, whether his head chef, a supplier, or one of the busboys. And he could be so kind. When a newly-hired waitress dropped a dish, Emilio was the first by her side to help pick up the mess. Seeing her reaction, he told her, "Easy, Theresa. It's just a dish. God knows I dropped plenty in my time."

She also thought it was sweet that he treated Rohini as though she were a favorite aunt. On the other hand, Rohini made things so easy for him. Every change Emilio suggested to her was met with, "Oh, that sounds lovely. Good thinking, dear."

She'd only asked two things of him: Could they 'please' keep Shrimp Rohini on the new menu, and would he 'mind terribly' if they also kept the ancient freezer in the scullery until it died on its own?

He'd never deny her that first request. Everyone who'd ever dined at The Secret Spice knew of its delectable shrimp dish the founding chef had named for the wife he adored. Naturally Rohini would want it to remain. But her entreaty on behalf of an old freezer was peculiar, to say the least. The thing was a noisy energy drain. It made no sense whatsoever to keep it, and yet, since it was what Rohini wanted, Emilio let the freezer stay.

If Marisol didn't know better, she'd have thought he was genuinely nice. But she *did* know better. All the more reason she wished the fluttering in her belly whenever he came into her line of vision would cease. This obsession was not good for her, which was why she kept her distance from him, unless her job dictated otherwise.

Little did she know how much her shunning of him stung. Or that he was trying equally as hard to overcome his attraction to her. In his case, he fought his feelings because he thought they were inappropriate. He was thirty-three, and she was four months shy of twenty-one. She was too young for him, and to complicate matters further, she worked for him.

Those were moot points. She hated his guts now, and it was no more than he deserved. The first thing he did after that meeting was phone his mother and give her a piece of his mind. But it was his own fault. He should have known better than to take her words at face value. The McKenna family had been through hell, and all the Guerrero family had done was contribute to it by spreading stories. For a day or so after the incident, he thought about going to Michael to apologize. He decided that might only annoy Marisol further.

So he left it alone, which was probably for the best. He didn't get where he was in life by having no strength of will, but Marisol McKenna, with her remarkable self-possession, honesty, and strength tested it. The pretty face with its dimple that came out of hiding only when coaxed, making it that much more of a treat to see, the enticing laugh, and the trim, lithe figure were, to him, merely gilding on a young woman who, if he were honest, had begun to charm him even before she stood up to two tyrants—himself and Joy—and bested them both. He liked her and—he was surprised to discover—he admired her. But it was wise to steer clear, although he wished he could tell her how sorry he was.

The strain between them wasn't the only lump in the batter that was to become the new Secret Spice. As expected, Joy was obnoxious. When she'd arrived for her first day, both Emilio and Marisol got a pleasant surprise when she was cordial to everyone. She praised the improvements Emilio had made to the kitchen, voice her approval of the equipment chosen and the set-up of the work stations. The hope that they'd misjudged her evaporated when she walked into the scullery, caught sight of Rohini's pet behemoth, and sputtered, "What is this monstrosity?"

Since none of them had a logical answer to offer, the question was left hanging. But as soon as she blurted the words, the freezer motor kicked on with a loud, grinding groan that seemed to protest Joy's disparagement, and she jumped as though it had pulled a gun on her.

Rohini was the spark for the next complaint too. Joy had expected to have full authority over the menu, so it irked her to learn that Shrimp Rohini would remain on offer.

"Is this still to be Chef Cristiano's kitchen, or mine?" she demanded.

Marisol experienced a brief flash of sympathy for Joy when the look Emilio gave her was the same expression of forbearance he'd used on Marisol when she'd first arrived.

"Yours," he said. "But Shrimp Rohini has always been the restaurant's signature dish. It stays."

Joy had no choice but to agree, although Marisol suspected she wouldn't be gracious about implementing it.

And here they were, twenty days later, and Chef Nettelbeck had not endeared herself to her colleagues. The only time they saw her smile was when she called home to check on her dog. A dog she'd given the nauseating name of, 'Puppy Wuppy.'

She'd ask her neighbor to "put Puppy Wuppy's ear to the phone," so she could make cooing noises into it. When she hung up, her displeasure was back, the lines between her eyebrows and at the sides of her mouth furrowed so deep, they looked like endless chasms of gloom.

Their first day open, she'd given no indication of excitement, nor a word of encouragement to her staff. In the three hours since their initial customers had walked through the door, she'd done nothing but scold and bite out commands. To the type of chef Joy was, the kitchen staff wasn't her support team—they were her serfs, and it was plain to see how tense she was making them all. Niko, their easy-going *sous* chef who was about the same age as Marisol, avoided speaking to Joy as much as was practical for someone who had to work in tandem with her. Theresa, the new waitress, jerked visibly whenever Joy shouted her name. And when there was a call for Shrimp Rohini, Joy's already bitter expression went so sour, Marisol was tempted to check the fridge to be sure she hadn't made the milk curdle.

On the other hand, no fault could be found with the woman's culinary skills, and she could handle a busy restaurant. The entire evening she hadn't missed a beat, as servers came in and went out, the double kitchen doors flapping back and forth so fast, it was a wonder they didn't take off and fly.

As for Rohini, she worked by Joy's side, as she had by Cristiano's—with quiet efficiency. Granted, she was quieter than usual. All things considered, that was to be expected. But she kept glancing about the kitchen, tilting her head to one side as though she were listening for something. Marisol worried that the day's events might be overwhelming her. At the first turning of tables, she hurried over to her.

"Are you doing okay? You seem preoccupied." She kept her voice low.

"I'm fine, dear. But..." There was trouble on her face. "Does something about this kitchen seem different to you?"

"Are you serious?" Marisol gave her a wry chuckle. "Everything seems different."

"No, no." She pushed that aside with a dismissive gesture. "Not all *this*. I mean, something different, that only you or I would notice?"

"I don't understand."

Rohini made a small sound of impatience. "Yes, you do. I know you do. Please, dear, this is important. I must know if it's just me. Does anything feel...off?"

When she took in what the question meant, Marisol was on her guard at once. She supposed Rohini must know about her intuitive abilities. They'd played a major role in preventing Angela from taking a neck-breaking tumble down a flight of deck stairs, and Sarita from drowning in her stateroom bathtub. They'd never talked about either incident, which was how Marisol liked it. Now, out of the blue, Rohini was asking her—what, exactly? And she said, 'something that only you or *I* would notice'? Did that mean Rohini was a 'sensitive' too?

"Ladies," Joy snapped out before Marisol could ask, "this is not the time to be chatting. Mrs. de la Cueva, these capons need lemon slices and fresh parsley. See to it, please." She scowled at Marisol. "And I'm sure you have your own work to do."

Marisol gave her a stony look, but went back to her station without a word. The head chef was within her rights to hurry workers along, but she'd spoken to them like they were two bratty kids. She couldn't care less for herself, but for Joy to talk to Rohini that way was not good. It wasn't Marisol's place to point out that Rohini was Joy's boss as much as Emilio was, but she sure hoped Rohini would set her straight. Marisol had taken enough business management along with her culinary courses to know that if Rohini let it slide, an attitude would be established, along with a shift in authority.

The only good thing about Joy's bossy command was that it stopped Marisol from having to discuss something she'd rather not discuss. Although, she was curious about what Rohini might have meant.

If Marisol had asked, she'd have learned that Rohini was unable to put into words what she was feeling. Only that she sensed the energy in the kitchen, on the ship, had undergone a subtle deviation. She couldn't say when this change had begun, but it wasn't to do with Emilio taking over the restaurant, nor with the ache within her since Cristiano's disappearance. This was something else, and her dread of it—whatever it was—was quickening.

Which was why she disregarded Joy's impertinence. In the universal scheme of things, none of it was important— not Joy's dissatisfaction, not Marisol and Emilio feigning a lack of desire for one another, not the new color on the walls in the dining room, nor the fact that she'd put cilantro on the capons by mistake, instead of parsley.

What mattered to her was that while they fretted over the tiny troubles in their lives, the world was diseased by greed, hatred, and fear. Like a festering sore, it became more septic by the day. Most were blind to it, but not Rohini.

If Cristiano were there, he would hug her and laugh away her worries. He would tell her that the world had its ups and downs, and that while they might be experiencing a dark period in its history, things would swing back.

She didn't believe that were so. Not this time. Possibly for the very reason that he wasn't there to quiet her fears. She felt certain, somehow, that in the perpetual struggle of dark against light, the dark was winning. On the news, online, in random snippets of conversation that caught her ear, she heard nothing but mercilessness, and it filled her with grave sadness.

This was why she prayed. In her spiritual wisdom, she felt that while humans partitioned themselves off into groups inflicting harm upon other groups, while they continued to view war—any war—as something to commemorate with parades and flags and fireworks, evil was reveling in its gluttony, consuming all that was worthy and laudable, to burgeon like a plague.

More, she had the most inexplicable, bizarre, and chilling prediction that the first thing evil would come for was this ship.

"Mrs. de la Cueva." Joy's face was puckered with disapproval as she set sprigs of parsley and cilantro in front of Rohini. "Can you tell the difference between these two herbs?"

Rohini smiled. Unintentional though it was, Joy had said something amusing to distract her from dark thoughts. "Why yes, Chef Nettelbeck. I believe I can."

Marisol heard their exchange and gnashed her teeth. *Why* was Rohini putting up with Joy's crap? She was weighing whether or not she should talk to her about it when Theresa approached her.

"Marisol, there's a man in the dining room who wants to see you."

"Did he tell you his name?"

"No, but he said you would know him. He's at table thirteen."

"Table thirteen?" With a glance behind her to be sure Joy wasn't listening, Marisol murmured to the waitress, "We don't have a table thirteen, Theresa. People think they're bad luck. You made a mistake."

"No. He's there. He wants to see you," Theresa repeated, in a dull monotone that struck her as odd.

She studied Theresa's face. Her eyes looked glazed and there was sheen of perspiration on her forehead. Okay, it was hot in the kitchen, but either the girl was coming down with something, or Joy had gotten to her with the bullying. There was no table thirteen. Marisol took off her apron, shook her uniform of flour dust. "Show me where, Theresa."

Theresa moved as though she were sleepwalking, through the kitchen doors, and into the dining room. Her face was devoid of expression as she pointed, "There."

There was a sudden buzzing in Marisol's ears, and the light in the room receded until it was concentrated to one spot and one person—a silver-haired man sitting at a candle-lit table. He was dressed in a black tuxedo. A walking stick with a golden handle was balanced against the side of his chair. A white vellum card that read '13' in bold, black numbers was affixed to a stainless steel holder set on a tablecloth of radiant white. There was a silver candelabra too, that looked for sure like sterling.

As for the man, Marisol had seen him before. Just once, in the Centerline Boutique, when she was on her way to meet Emilio and Joy. The puzzle was, how could Theresa see him too, as he was long-dead?

The man stared at Marisol through strange yellow-gold eyes, and as she watched, his pupils, black as old blood, began to widen and glint like obsidian.

"Marisol," he whispered in a sing-song drawl, "Your time, girl... your time. Oh, your time..."

She blinked. The buzzing stopped, the lights came back, and the apparition was gone. Vaguely, she heard a thud, and several patrons in the restaurant exclaimed. In a daze, she turned her head, looked down. There was Theresa, collapsed on the carpet, blood tricking from her nostril.

Talking with the bartender, Emilio saw her fall, and ran over to kneel beside her. "She's hurt." He was afraid to touch her. "She's hurt."

CHAPTER NINE

1958, somewhere in the Atlantic

The month of March arrived with its customary bag of tricks—tossing New York City one spring-like day here and there, followed by others that were frozen and grim. Three weeks in, it let fly its meanest prank—a nor'easter that dumped over eleven inches of snow.

Les Taylor heard about it while he was at sea, and it worried him. He knew winter in New York was vicious, but it was especially cruel to those in the tenements where landlords were stingy and heat was switched off according to calendar date, no matter what the temperature. That March, the cold crept in through the cracks of run-down buildings, and ice formed crystal crust between window panes in need of repair. Entire families slept on their kitchen floor to be near the stove.

It was no different at Houngan Toby's, where Rosemary stayed while Les was away, and he hated it. One day soon, if they kept saving their pennies, things would change. For the time being, he had to live with the troubling reality that while he was sailing, Rosemary slept on a bedroll in Toby's kitchen with the other students. When he was in port, the *Queen Mary* was their haven. Though the Hudson was bitter cold, and the ship soaked the damp deep into their bones, they slept nestled in each other's arms in his tiny cabin, and kept each other warm.

He couldn't wait to see her again. He checked his watch. Nearly midnight. Wouldn't be long now. They'd dock in less than twenty hours.

Hunching his shoulders, he pulled up the collar of his coat, and looked out at the ocean over the Sports Deck rail. The water was choppy, but the sky was crisp and clear. With any luck, the temperatures would rise, melt some of the untimely snow that had paralyzed New York. He took heart. It wasn't the first time he and Rosemary had navigated bad weather. They'd navigated more than that in the time they'd been together.

He wondered if they always would. He wondered if they would always be this happy, if their love would always overcome society's view of them, and their own essential dissimilarities as well. He'd been in the merchant navy long enough to meet and befriend people from many parts of the world. On the *Mary*, he'd had the thrill of encountering the rich and celebrated. He'd carried Audrey Hepburn's Louis Vuitton luggage, walked the Duke and Duchess of Windsor's pug dogs around the decks, brought Burt Lancaster a packet of Camels. All the exposure to life outside his small-town birthplace had taught him to keep an open mind. Even so, he was still skeptical about spells, curses, and the like. He knew Rosemary's belief was genuine, and he went along, especially now that she was carrying his *bairn*. If it made her happy that he keep her Vodou charm with him wherever he go, he'd do it. He patted his pocket. It was empty. Well, and if he forgot it now and then when he switched trousers, she didn't need to know that, now, did she?

He shivered again, and swore. The temperature felt like it was dropping, not rising. Ah, well. Nothing to be done about it. Spring would eventually come. It was best he go in, anyways, get some sleep. He turned from the rail, and nearly bumped into a passenger. First-class passenger, from the posh way he was dressed.

"Can I hep ye find sumthin' sir?" He always thickened his accent when he spoke to the high-society travelers. They found it quaint. But this bloke didn't answer. He just stood there, giving him the strangest look. Perhaps he'd had one pint too many. "Can I help you, sir?" he said again, clearer this time, in case the fellow had misunderstood.

In the dark of night, the man's eyes began to glow like two small, yellow lanterns lighting up, and Les couldn't seem to turn his gaze away.

The man spoke. "Follow me."

It seemed important, vitally so, that Les do as the passenger asked. He was walking just a few feet behind him when, all at once, the man was a sharp distance away, standing next to the chain locker. He opened the hatch to it, and began to climb down.

"Sir," Les called out. "Ye can't go down there. It's off limits to passengers." Heedless, the man disappeared down the hatch, and Les silently cursed him. A chain hatch was a dangerous place. He hurried over and peered into the hole, but it was too dark to see. Swearing again, Les climbed down after him.

It was only when he got to the bottom of the enclosed space that he realized he was alone. There was no passenger in the locker. There was nothing but damp, and piles of thick, rusty chain.

There was also very little oxygen. It was the rusting metal that sucked it all up, and he knew that very well, as did any sailor who'd been on a ship for more than a day. They were instructed straightaway to stay out of closed spaces unless they were ventilated first.

"Ah, *fuck*." What had he been thinking, trailing after a stranger? It was like he'd been in a stupor. Only a minute in this pit from hell, and he was already feeling it. He had to get back up. Muddled and woozy, he clasped the sides of the ladder, placed his foot on the first rung. Keeping his focus on the night sky through the open hatch above, he made it to the second.

He was on the third rung when someone closed the hatch.

"Hey. Hey!" he shouted, and tumbled off the ladder.

His head spun, and a sharp spike of nausea overwhelmed him. "Help me," he tried again, but his voice was weak and his lungs useless. He started to cry. "Rosemary," he whispered.

Limbs too heavy to hold him, he sank to the floor of his cold, black tomb.

Rosemary knew Les was gone before they came to tell her.

The first omen was the yellow-gold spider she saw scaling its thread when she woke up one morning.

A spider seen in the evening was a sign of hope. A spider seen in the morning was a portent of grief.

"Oh, now, *cher*," Toby said. "It's just a spider."

Then came the storm.

Toby tried to reassure a second time, but she could see his uncertainty. It was a freakish time of year for such severe snowfall.

The night before the *Queen Mary* was due in port, Rosemary dreamed of two full moons rising together in the sky, and a clock that chimed thirteen times. In the early hours of the morning, she pulled back the covers of her bedroll, and sat up. Everyone was still asleep, except for Toby. He was sitting by the kitchen window, gazing out at snow gone slushy-brown with car exhaust and mud.

Softly, she said, "You had a dream, didn't you?"

He didn't turn at first, but when he did, his face was infinitely sad.

She stood next to him by the window. Together they waited for the knock on their door—the three knocks that would herald death.

Under the defense spells of both Mambo Zora and Houngan Toby, Rosemary had felt safe enough to allow herself to marry Les and be happy with him. They'd had over a year of true happiness. In that year, they made plans. Perhaps Les would quit sailing and move to New

Orleans. Rosemary would work with Zora, and Les could have a fishing boat. Or maybe it was best if Rosemary moved to England where their marriage was legal. Les thought Manchester could use a good Vodouist. There'd be less competition there, for sure, he'd teased.

To dream was divine, and Rosemary had begun to believe—to hope—that Jamilla had forgotten them. And so, when she discovered she was pregnant, she felt nothing but joy. Les was over the moon with pride in her, and thrilled at the prospect of becoming a father.

"If it's a boy, shall we name him 'Robert', for my da?" he suggested.

"Yes," she said, happy to agree. "And if it's a girl, we'll name her 'Philomène', for my *manman*."

Barely at the end of her first trimester, her husband was dead. She should have realized how Jamilla's mind worked, that she would patiently wait for her chance to deal Rosemary this far bigger blow.

Not for the first time, Rosemary wondered where Jamilla was getting her information. Her network and reach were growing.

When the three knocks came, Toby took her arm, gripped it. "Maybe it was an accident," he said, offering what little comfort he could. "Maybe it wasn't Jamilla."

The man at their door took off his cap when Rosemary, dry-eyed, but solemn, appeared. His skin was tanned and weather-worn, like Les's. She recognized him from the ship. "Mrs. Taylor," he said. "I'm Ralph Smith."

He spoke the way Les did too.

"Yes. I remember you," she said. "I know why you're here. Is he—" she faltered—"is he on the ship?"

Ralph's expression was pitying. Les had told him about his wife, and Ralph, being older than Les by a ways, knew a bit about Vodou, and believed. It was a relief that she knew, and he didn't have to say it outright. But he would tell her just how it had happened, should she ask, because it was the strangest death he'd ever witnessed at sea.

He shifted from one foot to the other. "Ya, Mrs. Ya. Er—I mean to say, yes. Yes, he's on the ship."

She nodded. "Please come in. I'll get dressed."

When they got to the ship, the Captain came out to meet her. He wasn't the same Captain who'd invited her and Les to dine with him on their wedding day. She searched her mind for his name. "Captain Fasting," she said.

His face was kind as he held out both his hands to clasp hers. "My dear Mrs. Taylor." His inflections were quite different from her husband's and Ralph's. "I can't tell you how sorry I am. How deeply sorry we all are." He released her hands. "Seaman Taylor was an excellent sailor, an asset to our crew, and a fine human being."

Rosemary bowed her head, struggled to get words past her lips. "Thank you, Captain Fasting."

He went on. "I want to assure you that, as his wife, you'll be taken care of." Her head shot up, and he hastened to add, "That may seem indelicate, and I'm sure it means little to you at this time, but you must think of your child." His spoke in a gentle, almost fatherly manner. "The United Kingdom recognizes your marriage." He sounded proud of that. "You'll be awarded a widow's pension, and you shall take it, Mrs. Taylor. You must. It's what your husband would have wished."

She hugged her arms over the small bump of her belly. "Thank you, Captain Fasting," she said again, her voice a hoarse whisper. "May I... may I see my husband now, please?"

"Certainly." The Captain instructed Ralph to escort Rosemary down.

A morgue aboard a ship is especially grim. Holding onto Ralph's arm, Rosemary lost count of the number of flights they descended before they came to a chamber that looked as small, dark, and airless as the one that had killed Les.

From the doorway, she could see his shadowed outline, lying prone on a pallet. "Wait." She looked up at Ralph, a plea in her eyes. "Before I go to him, I have to know. Was it an accident? I don't want to cause any trouble, Mr. Smith. I just need to know."

Ralph's face was creased with sadness. "It's no *mither*, Mrs. I told mi'self I would tell ye. Ye deserve to know. He were a sound bloke, were Les." His dialect was thicker than Les's, but Rosemary got the gist. "It were an accident, but I swear down, I just can't figure it."

He went on to say that Les had gone missing the night before they reached port, and after a thorough search of the ship, the crew suspected he'd fallen overboard. But it was Ralph who found Les's body at the bottom of the closed chain locker. And that was the part that struck everyone as so peculiar.

"He knew better than to go into a confined space without first letting the air in. I'm still scratchin' me head as to what he was doing down there."

Rosemary stayed silent. She could guess who had put the idea into Les' head. She had one more question. "What made you think to check down there, if the hatch was closed?"

When he didn't answer, she got the sense he felt foolish, and she was right. He rubbed his hands over his face. "Well, I suppose ye have a right to know that too, but you'll think me daft."

"I don't think I will, Mr. Smith."

He nodded. No, she wouldn't. "Well, it was like this…"

He admitted to seeing a bloke standing by the chain locker, a bloke who "had something strange about him." She felt the blow to her solar plexus as he described, "silver-hair, black evening coat, and carrying a gentleman's cane."

Beauregard Clay.

He was dead. Bedridden, under Jamilla's care for three years after she'd left New Orleans, and then dead as Judas last year. Zora had written to her about it. His death was one reason she'd started to feel safe.

Clay was dead, so that could only mean Jamilla held him in her thrall. Jamilla was now powerful enough to transport him here, onto the ship.

In her womb, her child stirred, and a fierce protectiveness surged through her. For the first time in the four years since Jamilla and Clay had upended her life, she wasn't afraid—she was enraged. Her sweet, brave Joseph. Her charming, handsome Les. Which one of her loved ones would be next? No matter what Zora or Toby said, it was time for her to take a stand.

First, she would grieve. "Thank you very kindly for telling it to me, Mr. Smith. I appreciate it more than you know. Could I be alone with him? Would that all right?"

"'Course it's all right, Mrs. You take all the time you need."

When he left her, Rosemary moved to where Les lay in final sleep. She caressed his face, his hair, murmured Creole words of love.

"Oh, *bebe*. I'm so sorry," she wept. "I am so, so sorry, *mon kè*. I never should have loved you. But I did. I loved you so. What did she do to you, *amou*? Let me see."

With gentle fingers, she touched his lips, whispered her chant, and his mouth opened just as though he were alive. With a glance at the door to be sure they were alone, she slid a shiny new dime under his tongue, and began to pray.

His body moved, shifting restlessly on the pallet like a man in the throes of a nightmare. She pressed her palm to his heart, and he was still once more. Slipping her fingers into his mouth, she pulled out the coin.

It was black as Hades.

"I knew it," she whispered. "She was going to turn you into one of her astrals, like Clay. But you're free of her now, *amou*. She can't harm you anymore." She slipped the blackened coin into her pocket, and pressed her cheek to his chest. Quaking with sobs, she told him, "I was going to come with you. To England. I'd made up my mind. I was going to tell you when you got back this time that I would live there with you, raise our baby there. I was going to leave it behind, all of it. Not be a priestess, just be your wife." She lifted her head to kiss his forehead, and when her tears dripped onto his face, they looked like they could be his. "We're having a boy. I'll name him after your father, just like we said. He'll be Robert Lester Taylor, and I will love him, as I will always, always love you."

She kissed his lips one last time. "Sleep now, my beloved. We'll see each other again. Good-night."

When she left the morgue, Ralph was waiting. He handed her his handkerchief.

"Thank you. Thank you, Mr. Smith, for your kindness." She pressed it to her eyes, handed the cloth back. "There's just one more thing I would ask of you, please. I'd like to go up to his cabin. There's somethin' there I want you to have."

She stopped when they got to Les's door, and started crying again. They'd made love for the first time in this little room. She remembered how gentle he'd been, how wrapped up in each other they were. How, whenever they would meet, they would still come together with such joy and eagerness. Because of Jamilla, she would never feel his arms around her again.

"I think you should keep this," Ralph said. She gave a short, feeble laugh when she saw he was holding out his handkerchief.

"I'm sorry I'm such a water spout, Mr. Smith. I'll just be a minute. I know where it is." She went straight to the bottom drawer of the wooden chest, rummaged around, found what she was looking for, and handed it to Ralph.

He eyed the small, colorful sack. It felt packed full, of what he didn't know. "What might be this be, then?"

"It's a *gris-gris.* I made Les promise to carry it with him, always. He did promise, but sometimes he'd forget. I don't know if you'll believe me, but if he'd had it with him last night, he'd still be alive." She closed his fingers over the talisman. "I want you to promise that you'll always carry it, for as long as you sail on this ship. If you should lose it, write to me, and I'll make you another. You're not...what was that you said? 'Daft'. You're not daft, sir." She watched him, tried to imagine how he might be taking that information. "Will you promise?"

Ralph studied her tear-stained face. He had a hunch Les's sweet young widow would grieve for him for the rest of her life.

"Yes, Mrs. I promise." He had no reason to doubt her. He'd keep it with him, for sure. "I've got to get back to my duties." He cleared his throat. "The Captain says we're to send ye Les's things, along with the...uh...death record and such others, when they're ready, but why not take a peek around, see if there's something ye'd like to bring home with ye today?"

"Thank you again, Mr. Smith. I'll do that." She smiled—courageously, he thought.

Poor little thing. The cold way the world was, everything about her made her a target. He stuffed the *gris-gris* in his trouser pocket, and hoped the little charms she made would work their magick for her too.

"Right. I'll be off, then." He tipped his cap. "God be with ye, Mrs." And he was gone.

With her heart like a boulder lodged in her chest, she surveyed the cabin. It was so small, Les didn't keep much in it. She trailed her fingers across the neatly made-up cot, picked up one of his shirts and breathed in his scent. He had a photograph of the two of them which she would take with her, and there were some journals and books. She was reading the titles, her back to the door, when the light in the room changed. She looked up. And promptly dropped the book she'd been holding.

Standing before her was a woman. She was wearing a long, cream-colored gown embroidered with roses, thistles, and shamrocks, all glimmering with gold thread. A blue sash was swept across her left shoulder. There was a circlet around her head with eight high arches that sparkled with so many diamonds it dazzled the eyes. More diamonds, as well as pearls, glittered at her ears, around her neck, wrists, and fingers.

Rosemary was stupefied. She'd had visitations from spirits before, but this was unprecedented. Why would this particular herald come to *her*?

The vision spoke. "My dear Rosemary."

It was a reflex for Rosemary to slap her hands to her mouth. It was that astounding to hear Her Majesty, the Queen Mary, call her 'my dear'.

The Queen continued, "You will need to be strong. You will need to put duty first, as I did, and to make decisions that are for the greater good, even if those decisions break your heart." Her own grief, her own life regrets, swirled in her eyes as she continued, "You were born to be a queen, as I was, and you will suffer for it. That I can assure you." Her face softened, almost imperceptibly. "I wish you luck. Now, go home. There is a traitor in your midst. You must find him."

Her image receded, and disappeared.

It would be decades before Rosemary fully understood their connection, but for now, all she could do was stand riveted, her head swimming with what the Queen had said. She was a twenty-four-year-old Creole girl, working in a factory, about to become a single mother. What kind of an impact could she possibly have on 'the greater good'?

With her arms filled with mementos—all she had left of her brief time as a man's wife—she left the ship.

She would be aboard the *Queen* again, but not for more than sixty years.

In New Orleans, Jamilla sat on the wide veranda of her white-columned manor and watched the water in her fountain waltz up and down. The sun shot through the droplets, making them sparkle like diamonds. The rich, sweet scents of flowers floated around her, and the trill of birds, the whirr of insects flitting through her garden and the nearby bayou, tickled her ears.

The only minor irritation was the fly that kept circling, no matter how many times she swished it away. It was one of the big, blood-hungry, greenhead horse flies that buzzed around the marsh. When they bit, it burned like the devil. They were a nuisance. Dozens of them had been in Clay's room when he died.

Of course, they'd been attracted by the filth she'd left him lying in for days at a time. Toward the end, she'd made no pretense of concern, fed him only enough so that when he passed, there'd be no untoward inquiries by the police. She bathed him less frequently than that, only when there was a pending visit from his business manager. No one else came, not a one of his society friends, once they knew he couldn't speak or move. She had free reign, and she exulted in it.

The first time she left him unwashed after he shat himself, he managed to croak out one word, "Why?"

She chuckled bitterly to herself when she thought of that.

'Why.'

He didn't even know. He was so unmindful to her lot—hers and everyone else's like her—that he didn't know *why* she would exalt in seeing him laid so low. Every minute of every day in this time and place where she'd been set down on this earth, she felt invisible at best, scared mindless at worst. But most days, it was a never-ending onslaught of frustrations that made her want to throw herself into the Mississippi and drown.

This very house she now owned would not be standing here were it not for the subjugation of her people. And apart from a proclamation that decreed otherwise, they were still slaves. Every time she had to give up her seat on the bus, every time she drank from a fountain marked, 'Colored', or was denied entry where Beauregard Clay and his ilk were free to traverse, she seethed. Then she'd go home to that hellhole side of town, where even the air they breathed seemed as if it were being doled out to them in stingy increments, just enough for bare survival, by the rich and white who could take in great lungfuls whenever they wished.

The only thing she had plenty of was desperation.

And he'd asked her 'why'.

So, she told him. She leaned in to him, covering her nose to hold back the stink, and whispered in his ear, "I wanted you to smell to yourself how you smelled to me, every time you put your hands on me because it was your right. You'd have taken me, you'd have taken any other women like me, whether we wanted you or otherwise. I hate you for that. I hate you for all the unmerited privilege you were granted, when it was denied to me. But I used you, best I could, even when it was all I could do not to shudder in disgust at the feel of you. Now you know how I felt."

When she saw his eyes go wide with shock, that made it worse. That he didn't know, that he'd never entertained one thought of what life was like for her and her people, was worse than if he'd known of their misery and enjoyed it. At least then it would mean he saw them as human.

The fly looped around once more, and she flapped her arm in the air yet again, dismissing it with the same disregard Clay had dismissed his wrongdoings.

Clay was dead—so to speak—and under her control, and the only ones who mourned his passing were those whose liquor he'd supplied. None of her people would condemn her for what she'd done to him. It was irrefutably just, and as satisfying as the lush sights, smells and sounds spread before her. She basked in it all, the satisfaction of the oppressor who'd once been the oppressed.

Her plans for Rosemary Dupré would be harder for folks to endorse.

Like Rosemary, she knew without being told that Les had succumbed to her curse. She knew Rosemary was aboard the *Queen* right then, sniveling over her dead husband's body. Rosemary, who'd been born into the same life-suffocating circumstances, but had refused to be suffocated.

There were those she knew who accepted the world as it was. She would never understand it. When she saw those women, sitting on their sagging, tiny wooden porches in the summertime, laughing, telling jokes, stealing a minute or two of escape from an otherwise dreary life, it made her want to scream at them. How could they be happy?

But Rosemary did more than make her want to scream. Rosemary made her fume. Where those other women found contentment in things as they were, and she—Jamilla—had been made broken and hard, Rosemary was different yet. She was happy *and* she fought back. She fought back against Beauregard, she fought back against the world, believing she could shape it into what she wanted it to be. Never with her powers. She would only ever use those to heal, to counsel, to spread bounty and love.

Miss High-and-Mighty.

This was the true motivation behind Jamilla's vendetta. She was jealous of Rosemary's capability to rise up in the face of adversity. Since the injustices of society had not daunted Rosemary's resolve, Jamilla was determined to do so herself. She couldn't be like Rosemary, but she could crush out Rosemary's fight, trample every seed of goodness and hope Rosemary would ever hope to sow.

She searched inside herself for any vestige of remorse or pity for what she'd done to Lester, for what she planned to do to Rosemary in future, and was gratified to feel none. Rosemary made her feel lesser simply by her existence, and she would not tolerate that.

Just then, the fly found purchase on her arm. She waved her hand over it. It didn't scare, and before she could slap at it, its scissor-like mouth cut into her skin, a bite that drew blood. With a yowl of pain, she slammed her palm down on it, smashed it dead, and flicked at the carcass with her fingers.

It didn't budge. Swearing, she reached down, plucked a leaf from a nearby magnolia bush, and wiped it across her bleeding arm.

The fly still did not move, not by a millimeter. She held her arm up to get a closer look, and saw the carcass wasn't on her arm, but in it. Somehow, when she killed it, it was absorbed into the top layers of her skin—like a tattoo—in the shape of a squashed greenhead fly. Repulsed, she stared at it.

A second fly landed on her other arm.

CHAPTER TEN

Saturday afternoon, October 17, 2020,
The Secret Spice Café, RMS Queen Mary

"Please, dear, there's no need to make a fuss. It's not important."

"It's not? Then why are you hiding back here, crying?"

"Nonsense. I was cutting onions."

"Honestly, Rohini, you're a terrible liar. There's not a cut onion within twenty feet of us." She pointed to the prep table. "That's shrimp. And the only reason it's making you cry is because that bitch changed Cristiano's recipe."

Marisol's whispers were vehement. She and Rohini were alone in the back scullery, and she didn't want anyone in the kitchen to over-hear. Especially not Joy Nettelbeck.

"I'm just being silly. It's not a big deal."

"It is so. She changed a signature dish without permission. Why are you letting her get away with this? She's been walking all over you for the past three and a half months. It's *your* restaurant, dammit."

"It's not my restaurant." Her voice wobbled.

"The hell it isn't. You still own just as much as you ever did. One partner or three, it's the same."

When Rohini said nothing, did nothing but dab at her eyes with her apron, Marisol huffed in frustration. "I don't understand why—*Ow.*" She breathed through clenched teeth. "Dammit."

In an instant, Rohini set aside her own woes. "What's wrong?"

"Just a headache. Nothing to worry about." She sank into the near-est chair, pressed her fingers to her forehead.

"You've gone white as a sheet." With a feather-light touch, Rohini placed her palm against Marisol's forehead. It felt cool. "Any sensitivity to light?"

"It's not a migraine, if that's what you're thinking. I don't get migraines. I don't get headaches at all, usually. At least, I didn't until recently."

"You've had a headache like this before?" Rohini's brow creased with concern. "When did they start?"

Marisol shrugged, the movement making her cross-eyed with pain. "I'm not sure. I guess...maybe right around when we opened. I didn't pay much attention the first couple of times, because it goes away so fast." She stopped, waited. "There. See? It's gone."

"Seriously? Only seconds ago, you looked about to faint, and now it's gone, just like that?"

"Totally." With a relieved laugh, she stood up, took a steadying breath. "Whew. I should get back to work."

Her attitude alarmed Rohini. "Dear, wait a moment. Severe headaches that come and go so quickly should be discussed with a doctor, don't you suppose?"

She bit Rohini's head off before she could stop herself. "I said, I'm fine. Maybe instead of worrying about me, you should worry about yourself." With that, she stalked off, leaving Rohini staring after her in surprise. She regretted her outburst by the time she was back at her station. How could she have been so snotty to her, and right after she'd been crying?

She wasn't wrong either. Marisol knew she should get the headaches checked out, although she was pretty sure they were stress-related, since she always felt so irritable right before and after they came on. Why lie to herself? She'd been irritable for three solid months. There was just so much to deal with. Too much.

Theresa was still in the hospital. In all this time, her condition hadn't improved, and Marisol couldn't help but feel she was somehow to blame. Right before the paramedics lifted her onto the stretcher, she'd looked at her, her gaze feverish.

"You saw him too, didn't you?" she whispered.

And Marisol whispered back, "Saw who?"

"You saw him. I know you did." Theresa reached for her sleeve then, held on as though she'd never let go. "Marisol. Tell me you did."

And when Marisol had stared at her helplessly, Theresa grew even more agitated. "No. You saw him. Tell me you saw him…"

She was still whimpering those words as they carried her from the restaurant. She was out again by the time they got her to the hospital, and hadn't regained consciousness since.

Marisol felt sick at the thought that if she'd just agreed, that short time awake wouldn't have been so distressing for Theresa. But she still had no clue what the girl meant.

"She didn't mean anything," Emilio tried to reassure her the day after it happened. "She had a hemorrhage. People say all kinds of things that make no sense when their brain is bleeding."

"But she asked me to go into the dining room with her," Marisol had reported, guilt jabbing at her. "She said there was someone who wanted to see me."

"And was there?"

"I didn't see anyone. And as soon as we walked out there, she fainted."

Every time Marisol thought back to that day, her head ached. It ached each time she and Rohini went to see Theresa, lying so still in that hospital bed, attached to all that horrible apparatus. At least there was still hope. The doctors said she was young and strong, and she was fighting. They all clung to those words.

Emilio stopped by the hospital too, at least once a week. From Theresa's mother, who sat by Theresa's bedside day and night, Marisol learned that he'd also arranged to pay all expenses not picked up by the family's insurance.

And here was another thing stressing her out. It was getting harder and harder to convince herself she hated Emilio. Because the fact was, she so definitely didn't. She couldn't reconcile the man she worked with every day with the one she'd encountered those first two weeks after she was hired, the one who'd acted like such a jerk that night in the Observation Bar.

She wasn't sure which was real, and she wondered—what would this version of Emilio Guerrero do if he knew how Joy was treating Rohini? If he knew that Chef 'Nettlebitch'—as she was called behind her back by everyone—had this morning decided to switch out Cristiano's Shrimp Rohini recipe with one of her own?

She supposed he'd find out about it as soon as one of their regular patrons complained, which they would, for sure. The only thing the two appetizers had in common was their main ingredient. Nettlebitch was so egotistical, so arrogant, she couldn't stand to honor another chef's memory, so she'd done a 'bait and switch.' She'd promised to keep Shrimp Rohini on the menu, and she had—in name only.

It was infuriating.

Her timer dinged, and she switched on the oven light, peered in to check the tart shells.

She loved the new ovens. The pastry was cooking so evenly—gold in color, but not too brown, which was perfect, as she had to cook them again once the shells were filled. She set the tray down to cool, lowered the oven temperature a notch, and prepared the chocolate filling.

As she heated milk and cream, added chopped chocolate and sugar, blended beaten eggs carefully into the saucepan, along with her own secret spice—a dusting of cinnamon—she considered telling Emilio about Joy's perfidy.

No. Bad idea. After their altercation, she'd sworn she wouldn't do a damn thing that could give him an excuse to fire her. She was an employee, that's all.

The chocolate mixture smelled heavenly as she filled the tarts, the whiff of cinnamon giving it that extra punch. She reset the timer. Another fifteen minutes, and the chocolate would be set, the surface rich and glossy.

Rohini was the one who should talk to him. Why wasn't she stepping up to inform her business partner about their signature dish? Did he even know that their best *sous* chef, Niko, was ready to quit because he was so sick of Joy's crap?

As these thoughts ran through her head, from across the busy kitchen, she heard the chef say, "Where *is* that woman?" She knew who Nettlebitch was referring to, and she wanted to kick herself knowing she'd made Rohini feel worse by sniping at her.

Were headaches any surprise with all that was going on?

"Marisol," Joy called out, in her usual imperious way. "Where did Mrs. de la Cueva get to?"

That did it. Marisol could feel the heaviness in her temples as she turned to give Joy a cool-eyed look. "*Mrs. de la Cueva* doesn't answer to me," she emphasized, letting Joy know she was aware of her contemptuous use of Rohini's surname. "Nor to you. Am I right?"

After she threw down that gauntlet, part of her hoped Joy would respond in kind. When Joy backed off, as most bullies do when challenged, Niko gave Marisol a wink, and everyone went on with their work.

But Marisol was still fuming. How satisfying it would be to leap across the cook station and rake her fingers down Joy's face, hear her scream with pain, and watch her bleed.

No sooner did the brutish urge manifest than she was revolted by it. Where had *that* come from? It wasn't like her at all. Her head started to ache again, a dull throb this time.

The timer she reset went off. Still focused on Joy and Rohini, as well as what might be wrong with her damn head, she slapped on an over mitt, absently pulled out the tray without checking it first. The smell of mud hit her nose. She glanced down, and every other thought dissolved.

The tart shells were no longer filled with chocolate. In its place was dark, damp soil mixed with small stones and clumps of hair. No, not stones. They were *teeth*. Teeth, and what appeared to be fragments of bone.

Graveyard dirt, used in black majick.

With a strangled sound, she dropped the tray. Warm pastries fell to the floor and broke apart.

Niko rushed over. "Did you burn yourself?"

At the sound of his voice, Marisol jolted. She looked down at her feet. There was nothing on the floor but the tray and her beautifully baked tarts, ruined.

"No." She stared at the mess, her hand clenched at her sides to stop herself from trembling. "No, I'm fine."

It was just her damn luck that Emilio would choose right then to push open the doors, making the incident even more unnerving. He almost tripped over them while she and Niko swabbed up pastry and chocolate.

"Whoa. Sorry." He gave an apologetic chuckle. "Oops—what's going on here? Everybody okay?"

Joy put on a smile for him, but it was laced with spite. "Marisol has butterfingers today. Niko, leave that be. I need your help more than she does."

Emilio might have taken Joy's comments in stride, but he intercepted the venomous look shot at her by Marisol. And perhaps that was a lucky thing. He skimmed the room. The waitstaff avoided even a glance at Joy as they went in and out, preparing the tables for that night's service. The teenage boy loading the dishwasher looked positively morose. Marisol's spine was stiff enough to snap in two as she dumped pastry crumbs into the bin. Niko kept his shoulder turned slightly away from Joy, even as they now stood together at the cook station. And Rohini was nowhere in sight.

Inwardly, he sighed. The delectable scent of baking chocolate had lured him to the galley. He'd stopped by only to snag a freshly-baked tart, and had walked in on an episode of *Kitchen Nightmares*.

Hoping it wasn't too late to do damage control, he tipped his index finger at Marisol. "Could you spare a minute? Something came in from one of our baking suppliers," he lied. "I wanted to get your input." He motioned with his thumb. "In the office?"

The last thing Marisol had the stomach for was a restrained interaction with Emilio. Still shaken by her bizarre vision and her violent internal reaction to Joy, she was at the edge of her self-control. Her emotions were everywhere. She distrusted him, while at the same time she admired him. She knew she should stay away from him, while at the same time she wanted to jump his bones.

She had no choice but to follow him into the office.

Emilio got right down to business as soon as they were alone. Leaning a hip against his desk, he crossed his arms. "All right, what's going on in that kitchen?"

He'd caught her off guard. She schooled her expression. "What do you mean?"

The prevarication annoyed him. "Come on, Marisol. Don't bullshit me. I saw the look you gave Joy. Spit it out."

Holding onto her temper by a thread, she took a deep breath in and a deep breath out. "First of all, I'd appreciate it if you would *not* speak to me that way. I don't care if you are my boss—I don't take it from Joy, I won't take it from you. Second of all, it's not my place to discuss any… situations there may or may not be in the kitchen. That's for you and Rohini. If you think you can goad me into saying something inappropriate so you'll have grounds to fire me, it won't work."

For some reason he was amused by her rebuke. "Goad you into saying something inappropriate? That's funny. I already *did* goad you into saying something inappropriate—you called me a dick and told me to go fuck myself. If I didn't fire you then, what makes you think I want to fire you now?"

That threw her. "Wh…what?"

Watching her, he saw genuine surprise, and he was amazed by his continued cluelessness when it came to her. He thought she knew by now how much he'd come to value her work, while all this time, she still believed he didn't want her here. She should only know how wrong she was.

"Hey, you know what?" He held up his palms. "Let's just clear this up right now, okay? I have no intention of firing you. I think you're an excellent colleague and a fantastic pastry chef. In fact, if I had to choose, I'd say you're even better than Angela." He paused to let her process that. "But if you tell her I said that, I'll deny it." He needed to make the joke, because this next part would be harder for him. "I owe you an apology. I made some assumptions about you I shouldn't have made." Keeping his eyes on her face, he shrugged. "I don't have an excuse."

Marisol was floored. But true to form, she had a comeback. "Why did you wait almost four months to tell me this?"

"Because I—" he bit back what he was about to say. He'd almost blurted out the truth—because he wanted her, and it was better that she dislike him, better that she avoid him. But it was wrong to have her thinking she was in danger of losing her job. "Because I'm an idiot."

"No, you're not an idiot. You were just mean."

He bit back a grin. She wasn't going to make it easy for him. Good for her. "Yes," he agreed, as contritely as he could manage. "I was mean. Will you forgive me?"

She gazed back at him. It wasn't fair. It wasn't fair that he was so cute. And now with this apology, he was damn near perfect. "Fine. I forgive you."

"Great." He beamed at her. "That's great."

"I still don't want to be your stoolpigeon," she added the caveat.

"Marisol, please." He put his palms together, held them in front of him as though he were about to pray. "I'm begging. Everybody in that kitchen looks like they want to slit their wrists. And when I ask my business partner for reports, she says, 'Everything's just fine, dear.'" He made his voice a falsetto, mimicked Rohini so well, Marisol had to laugh.

He'd definitely lifted her mood. She was silent as she wrestled with her scruples, then decided to come clean.

As he listened, all the warmth drained from his eyes. "She made Rohini cry?"

To Marisol, it was just one more point in his favor that Rohini's emotional state was his priority, rather than Joy's duplicitous over-throw of the restaurant's classic dish.

This was not the way he remembered The Secret Spice. The ener-gy in the kitchen had not been the same since Nettelbeck stepped in.

While it was true that at one time or another, Cristiano had reprimanded every staff member who worked with him, including his own wife, he'd made it clear to all, be they a dishwasher or an assistant chef, that he valued them, considered each one of them a vital part of what was to him, something miraculous, something big—the creation and presentation of beautiful food. He saw what he did through more than his ego—he saw it as art, as life. Whether they agreed with that premise, they understood he was motivated by love. They felt needed by him, and he'd treated them like family.

Someone like Joy could never appreciate that. She had plenty of talent, but not one ounce of empathy.

Emilio would never forget the compassion with which Cristiano had handled him when he was seventeen and so crazy in love with Sarita. She was his first love, and it was genuine on his part. He'd gotten over her years before, had even fallen a time or two since, but he remembered how much that first heart blow had hurt, and it was Cristiano who was there to help him through it. He could still hear Cris's words: *I know what you're feeling is real, amigo.*

When he accepted that he and Sarita weren't to be, he left the ship, but not before asking Cris to look after her as a father would. He'd held no grudge against Sarita because she couldn't love him back. At that time, she was still his beloved, and he wanted her to be happy.

And Cris had said, *I will, of course.*

It was his turn now to look after Cris's beloved.

Without another word, he pushed away from his desk and stalked toward the kitchen.

Just as she had earlier, Marisol followed him, but this time not only was she glad to do so, she scurried to keep up. She wouldn't be human if she didn't want to see Joy Nettelbeck get her comeuppance.

She imagined the chef wouldn't be so trying to work with after Emilio reprimanded her.

But that wasn't what he had in mind at all. His jaw tightened as he heard the chef's mouth going even before he got to the galley, yelling at his employees, talking to them in a way she'd never dream of talking to her dog. He pushed through the double doors like Wyatt Earp walking into a saloon. One glance at him and everyone froze.

He fixed his eyes on Joy. "Get out."

Her eyebrows winged up. "I beg your pardon?"

"I said, get out." His voice was quiet, but lethal. "Pack your things and go."

"How dare—"

"Save it." He cut her off. "You don't have time. If you're not out in five minutes, I'll have Security throw you out." He ignored her stuttering outrage, and focused on Rohini. Her eyes were still red. It incensed him, but he kept his voice calm. "Are you all right, dear?" he asked, and Marisol melted. He'd called her 'dear', just as she called them.

"Yes." Rohini was bemused by Emilio's gallantry. She'd always assumed he would have preferred her gone. She was pleased to discover that wasn't the case. "I'm fine."

"Good, because you'll have to take over as head chef. Can you handle it?"

"I can, yes." She'd done so when Cristiano went missing. It wasn't the cooking she hadn't been able to handle, it was the running of all aspects of the restaurant on her own that had tripped her up.

Emilio knew she could do it, but he also knew he was dropping her in at the deep end, so he planned to give her backup. To Niko, he said, "You'll work with Rohini. We'll talk about a raise on Monday."

Niko gave him a thumbs-up and a beaming smile. No Wicked Witch of the West, and an unexpected promotion. He couldn't wait to text home with the great news. "Happy to help."

"Thanks." Emilio surveyed the surprised faces all around him. "I'm sorry things have been so rough. You can expect them to improve now. Let's all get back to work. We have reservations starting in one hour." He nodded at them, then spotted the platter of shrimp and eyed it with distaste. "Has that already been seasoned for her recipe?"

Rohini kept her eyes down. "It has."

"Do something with it, but don't serve it."

"We'll need to prep more, then," Niko told him. "It'll be a crunch to get it done before we open."

"I can do it." Marisol volunteered.

Emilio blew out a breath as it hit him how much extra work he'd just dumped on his crew. "Are you sure? Don't you have that tray of tarts to replace?"

"Those were for tomorrow. We're all set with desserts for tonight. I don't mind staying late to bake." Emilio's reward for being the white knight was the brilliant smile she gave him as she hastened to the scullery to start on the shrimp.

"You're ridiculous to put a dead chef ahead of *me*." Joy took her parting shot as she stomped toward the door. "You'll never get someone of my caliber to work here again."

Emilio gave her his patented look of bored irritation. "For the sake of us all, I hope that's true." With one turn of his back he dismissed her, and went into the dining room to prepare for the evening.

Nearing midnight, he was still in the office tallying receipts. Working short-handed on a Saturday night had been a stretch, but the whole staff pitched in however they could, giddy, he noted, that they'd seen the last of Joy Nettelbeck. The woman needed a damn good therapist.

He rubbed the back of his neck. He hoped the afternoon's events had convinced Rohini that she could trust him. If she'd felt comfortable enough to talk to him, the situation with Joy would have been rectified before it got out of hand. It just wasn't in her nature to be that forthright, he supposed.

He chuckled to himself as he tried to picture Rohini cursing him out and throwing club soda on him. Marisol didn't struggle with bashfulness, that was for damn sure. And thank God for it. When a party of twelve regulars walked in, all ordering Shrimp Rohini, they dodged a bullet there, because of her. After so many years, locals and tourists came aboard the *Queen Mary* solely to sample it. The Secret Spice Café without Cristiano's Shrimp Rohini would be like Chelsea's without clam chowder, or Sir Winston's without Beef Wellington. It said a lot about Marisol that she didn't relish ratting on Joy, but did so for the benefit of the restaurant. How thankful he was that she'd stuck it out with him, had forgiven him for his stupidity.

His thoughts went back to Rohini. He believed she could handle being head chef, especially with Niko's help. He was a fast learner and talented in his own right. But it meant they needed another cook right away. They'd all be running their asses off to pick up the slack until one could be found.

As he was putting the receipts and cash in the safe, he heard a soft knock. His mood lifted when he saw Marisol standing at the door.

"Hi." She smiled. "I saw the light was on in here."

"Wow, you're still here too." And a sight for sore eyes. "I knew you'd have a late night."

"Oh, I finished baking a while ago." She was carrying a covered dish, and she set it down by the coffee cabinet. "I stayed to chat with

Rohini after everyone else left. She just went up to bed. It was a…a big day for her."

"Ha. 'A big day'. That's one way to put it." He tipped his chin toward the dish. "What have you got there?"

Her eyes danced. "It's Joy's shrimp. It was a shame to waste it, so Niko grilled it with rice, and we all took some for home."

Emilio laughed, appreciating the twist. "Hey, her cooking wasn't the problem."

"No, it wasn't. I'm bringing it to my father. He'll enjoy it, without any of the bad juju attached."

"There's a good point. If I try to eat any, it'll probably poison me."

This time when she smiled, her dimple peeked out. He loved that—loved that it had to be cajoled. It felt like a victory when he said something that brought it forth.

And he absolutely shouldn't be thinking about her dimple, he admonished himself.

He didn't know whether to offer her a seat, or come up with a polite way to end their conversation. It was late, he was tired, and that meant his resistance was low. They were alone, standing close enough together that he could smell her perfume—something both woodsy and citrusy that melded in an intoxicating way with the scents of baked sugar and cinnamon she always seem to carry with her.

Marisol felt just as drawn to him right then as he did to her. She could see the long day was catching up on him. He'd loosened his tie. His shirt was slightly rumpled and rolled up at the sleeves. It was the first time she'd seen him with a shadow of dark stubble on his face. It brought out the amber lights in his eyes. All evening, she couldn't get them out of her mind—how they'd sparked with fury when he'd told Joy to leave, how they'd gone soft when he asked Rohini if she were all right.

Dammit. He was so hot. She knew she was wading into treacherous waters, knew she should grab her dish of shrimp, say goodnight, and go, but she couldn't bring herself to leave, couldn't take her eyes off him. "He'll be glad you didn't let her change the recipe."

"Who will?" He hadn't looked away from her either. He couldn't even remember what they'd been discussing only a minute ago. He had to send her on her way. Fast.

"My father. He has a special fondness for Shrimp Rohini." She brushed back her hair, and with some satisfaction, saw him follow the movement. "He told me Cynthia believed it had some mysterious properties that brought him and my mother together."

"I didn't know that." When she shifted closer, he almost retreated back a step, and then felt foolish. To distract himself, he starting talking, could hear the jitters in his voice, a man who suddenly found he was standing at the edge of a cliff. "I guess that's why they served it at their wedding. Seemed an unusual choice, what with all of Cris's Mexican dishes."

"Oh!" She laughed with the sudden memory. "That's right—you were there. I'd forgotten." She lifted her finger, pointed at him. "You banged into me."

"Pretty sure it was the other way around, but okay."

"You wanted to steal my cupcake." Her voice caressed the words.

"I—"

"You *said*," she cut him off, and the way she looked at him then, he could feel his body respond. "Can I have a taste?" Now she was close enough to touch him, to run her hands up the front of his shirt.

His hands circled her wrists at once. Desire was brewing in him like a storm. He wanted to stop her, but he could feel her pulse throbbing, just as his was. "You were four, Marisol." He said it to remind her of their age difference, to remind himself.

Her dark eyes were filled with promise, with longing. "I'm not four now." She stood up on her toes, and kissed him.

It was a kiss that nearly sent him to his knees—the sweetest, hottest kiss. He couldn't help but surrender to it, releasing her wrists, cupping his hands to the back of her neck, her head, sinking into her. Though he felt delirious with need, his hands were gentle as he moved them along the sides of her face, touched her, held her, as he'd longed to do ever since she stood up to him in the bar.

At his fervent response, she went limp, only to surge up again, madly, plunging her fingers into his hair, pressing him closer, drawing him in, to feast.

And then with a suddenness that was stupefying, she pulled away.

"What am I doing?" she whispered. "Oh, my God." She stared at him. "I'm *sorry*. I practically tackled you. I'm so embarrassed. I don't know what came over me."

Panting as though he'd just run a race, he gazed back at her in wonder, unable to speak. She looked mortified. Why was she sorry? What did it mean? He was so lightheaded, he didn't know what to think or say.

"I'm sorry," she said a second time, as she backed toward the door. "I feel like an idiot. I should go. I have to go." She turned and fled before he could call her back.

He had no idea how long after she left he was still staring at the empty doorway.

Marisol dashed out into the parking lot, berating herself. He was her *boss*. He'd just started to respect her, had even apologized, but had she responded to that like a career-minded professional would? No, she responded by throwing herself at him—*on* him, like some horny, insecure kid—the minute he'd been nice to her. How was she going to face him tomorrow? She'd sexually harassed a co-worker, is what she'd done. And she had no idea how to fix it, if it could even be fixed. She'd have to google it.

On the other hand, he hadn't exactly been fighting her off. Her body still felt flushed.

Oh, that kiss. It was epic.

"Who'd have guessed," she murmured.

She kept walking as she pulled her parking ticket out of her hand-bag, then stopped short. Damn. She'd left the dish in the office, and she'd already texted her father to tell him she was bringing him a treat. A glance at her phone revealed it was just past midnight. He'd be asleep by the time she got home.

She was the only one in the lot this late, was almost to her car, when it hit her that she was hearing a strange noise—a noise she'd been too preoccupied to register—like dozens of cellos being tuned. The sound bounced off the harbor. She stopped to listen, turned back to face the ship, and saw every spirit of the *Queen Mary* lining up along the top deck, their energy thrumming. There were so many gathering in one spot, the temperature around the ship dropped rapidly, creating a veil of fog.

Familiar with them all, she identified each one. At the front of the line was the nanny who'd help her rescue Sarita, staring down at her with no look of recognition or welcome.

"What are they doing?" Marisol whispered to herself.

As she edged closer to the ship, the wind picked up, and the spirit hums escalated. She was about ten feet away when they pointed to her, their faces contorting with wild terror, their mouths opening wide to release wails so loud Marisol clapped her hands over her ears. En masse, they fled from the ship, diving into the water with a speed so tremendous they blurred, blended into the fog, until she could make out nothing but trails of steam, hear nothing but their ringing cries.

"Wait!" She tried to shout over the din. "Please, what's happening?"

Marisol. That same voice beckoned—the voice in her father's shop, the voice by the burl wood panels. *Marisol. Marisol.*

Another blinding headache hit her, the agony of it so intense this time, she felt sick, nearly blacked out. Mustering every bit of strength, she staggered to her car.

Hours later, Rohini was debating whether to stay in bed letting her mind race, or get up and make tea. The clock on her nightstand read four a.m. Sleep had eluded her again.

She used to love to pull open the curtains, lean out the open porthole with her first cup, and watch the seagulls dip and fly over the water. The ocean no longer held the same enchantment for her. She dressed in the dark, and went down to the restaurant. These days, she rarely got the chance to be in there by herself.

In the shadowed dining room, she stood motionless, listening for the sighs only she could hear, the murmurs she'd heard since she that first day, when she walked in, carrying her sacks of spices and herbs, along with her wishes and worries.

There were no sighs, no murmurs beckoning to her that morning.

She moved into the kitchen, waited for the hanging pots and utensils to twirl and swing in mystical greeting as they always did when she was alone.

The pots and utensils were still.

"Your Majesty?" she said, a thread of hope in her voice, but when her question was met with silence—a silence of nothingness—she sank to the floor.

The spirit in the kitchen was gone. She didn't know why, she didn't know when, but she couldn't bear it. Not when everything else was gone too.

"Cristiano...Cristiano..." Like a prayer, she repeated his name.

Her senses were off. Loss was all that was tangible.

What she should have felt was fear.

CHAPTER ELEVEN

Friday afternoon, October 17, 1958, somewhere between Savannah and Charleston, South Carolina

Robert Lester Taylor came red-faced kicking and squalling into the world, as though he knew what his life would be like and wanted no part of it.

When Celeste cleaned him up and handed him to his mother, she felt she'd come full circle. She'd brought hundreds of children into the world but had never been blessed with one of her own. She was fifteen years old when she'd wrestled Rosemary into being, shrouded by dark secrets and looming death. Twenty-five years later, here she was again, delivering Rosemary's son under that same cloud. She ached for both mothers, both babies. She'd known the infant Rosemary would lose her mother on the very day she was born, and so little Bobby would lose his mother too. Unlike Philomène, Rosemary was healthy and strong, yet she still would be handing her newborn to Celeste for safe-keeping, just as Philomène had done.

And she—Celeste—would finally have a child to care for, a child the world would be led to believe was hers.

Rosemary turned the fussing child to her breast and, with ancient instinct, pushed her nipple between the tiny, bow-shaped lips. Her baby boy mewled, flayed his tiny fists about a bit more before he settled in. When she felt those first tiny tugs and suckles, the beauty and wonder of it made her smile, even as tears fell.

Seeing that, Celeste pleaded, "Stay, Rosemary. Just for a while. Just until he's weaned."

"I leave tonight, or risk his life. You know that." Her voice was soft now that the child was relaxed and content at her breast, but Celeste could hear the determination in her words. She knew Rosemary spoke the truth, so she said nothing more.

When Celeste turned to tidy the room, Rosemary swiped at her cheeks. She cried when she lost Joseph, cried when she lost Les. It hadn't done her any good then and wouldn't do her any good now.

She gazed out the window. Lowcountry was beautiful, the weather perfect this time of year. Where the summers were humid enough to rival New Orleans, an autumn in Lowcountry begot warm days, but offered nights that were as soothing and cool as a spearmint leaf in a julep.

The first time she saw the sun rise over the Savannah, its glow spread out across the water like the golden wings of a seraphim. The river teemed with so many kinds of fish, hugged more wildlife and plant life to the bosom of its shores than a rainforest. True, its distinctive smell of puff mud—that mix of clay minerals and decaying sea organisms—had taken some getting used to. But it was so much better than living in a Harlem tenement. It would be a wondrous place for her boy to grow up.

Apart from that, Vodou tradition permeated the area. Like the gardenia flowers that infused the very air, Vodou was imported, but had blossomed and spread until it was now so integral, the region would be unrecognizable without it.

And this is where her Bobby would live. In this sweet little house in the midst of the Vodou village. A house that would soon be protected and blessed by Toby and the other spiritual leaders. Her son would never see her, nevermore be held by her. He wouldn't be raised by her, but he would learn her traditions, her beliefs, her values. He would discover his ancestry here, and by way of that, would come to know her.

It was all she could hope for, all she could have of him. Or else Jamilla would steal it all.

The community had taken Rosemary under their wing, protecting her from the *caplata*'s long reach for the six months leading up to her son's birth. They would disguise Bobby's parentage so that he could never be used as a weapon against her. In exchange, she would fight the scourge that Jamilla and her ilk had become.

It was a simple plan devised the day after Les was killed, the day she'd had a visitation from a great queen of the past, a queen who had warned her she would need to put duty first. Rosemary went home and told Toby what she'd learned: they were harboring one of Jamilla's spies. With the use of fire powder and a white hex breaker candle, the traitor was revealed. Toby had wanted to expose and destroy him, but Rosemary had the better plan to use him, to feed him only the information they wanted Jamilla to have.

Now, here she was, gathering the strength and courage to give up her and Les's beautiful son to Celeste.

"You have the bank information in a safe place?" she asked her.

The midwife's shoulders stiffened with pride at the question. "Rosemary, I said, I don't want—you don't have to—"

"Yes, I do. Please, Celeste, don't make this harder than it already is. I've told you and told you, it's Les's money. He would want his son to have it. A child needs so much. And someday, he'll be wanting to go to school. Promise me you'll take it."

Celeste was still reluctant. Rosemary reminded her, "If you don't, I'll know." She could feel herself starting to well up again. "*Please* tell me you will. I have to know you'll both have what you need. I can't stand it otherwise. Please, Celeste."

The agony on Rosemary's face banished Celeste's objections where words couldn't. "All right. I promise." She bobbed her head, pressed her hand to her heart. "I promise, Rosemary."

The baby shifted and detached from his mother's nipple. He was sound asleep, his brow innocent and untroubled, his cupid mouth pursed, droplets of her milk still clinging to his bottom lip. This was the image of him Rosemary would take with her.

"You're wonderful," she told him, and the tears Celeste had fought so valiantly burst forth as she heard Rosemary repeat, almost verbatim, her own mother's words to her. "Don't believe anybody who tells you different. I love you. And your Daddy…he loved you too."

From outside they heard murmurs, shuffling, the stirring of tcha-tcha rattles and drums.

"They're starting." Rosemary placed her lips on Bobby's brow. "Good bye, *bebe mwen*. Good bye, my angel." It took everything she had to hand him up to the weeping Celeste. "Toby will want to leave as soon as they finish."

As she washed and dressed in the other room, put together her things, she heard the beating drums, the stamping and chanting of the protection spell floating around the cottage:

"Au nom Monsieur Danbala-Wedo-Toka-Mirwaze, Da, Sa Lavatya…"

So began the rest of her life.

CHAPTER TWELVE

Sunday morning, October 18, 2020, RMS Queen Mary

Seven days a week, Michael McKenna stepped into his Queen Mary Memorabilia and Postcard Shop one hour before opening. He used that hour to make sure his establishment was in pristine condition for his customers. This was a ritual he'd begun right before he started dating Inez, and he continued to observe it though it was no longer a necessary one. With Inez gone and Marisol grown, he spent more of his waking hours dusting where no dust existed, simply as a way to pass the time. It didn't stop him from thinking about Inez, but it helped him get by.

The truth was, he missed her with a physical ache still, and nearing the age of fifty, he assumed he'd miss her to that extent for the rest of his life. It was the reason he'd taken to having tea with Rohini weekly. Though he preferred a dark beer or good strong coffee, he drank herbal tea with her as a way to comfort and commiserate. Her loss was much more recent than his, and he knew how engulfing that loss could be. That they were both lonely was their one commonality.

He was thankful he had his daughter. Not only had his interest in Inez inspired him to turn his finances around, she'd made him into a husband when he was sure he'd always be a bachelor, and into a father when he thought the closest he'd ever come was to be a doting uncle to his sister's children. Marisol was his daughter in every way but one, and he was glad—selfishly so, he readily admitted—that her biological male parent showed no interest in being part of her life, had willingly signed adoption papers after Michael and Inez married. Michael would never burden Marisol with the knowledge, but the truth was, she was the one source of joy he had left.

Though he knew the time would come when she would leave, he was pleased she still lived at home. He was fine with that, but why shouldn't he enjoy her presence while it lasted, just as he enjoyed the fact that she was now working aboard the ship? It wasn't like they lived in each other's pockets. They were on different schedules, rarely saw one another more than the one evening a week when he would go to the Spice for dinner, same as he'd done for years. He'd have a fine meal, feel like a V.I.P. when he got a visit to his table from their fantastic pastry chef. He looked forward to it, just as he'd come to look forward to chamomile tea with a grieving friend.

He had his daughter, his family and friends. And he had his shop.

Overall, it wasn't such a bad life. And if sometimes, in the midst of sleep, he forgot where he was in that life, reached to the other side of the bed for the cute, chatty girl with the big dark eyes, felt that cold pit in his stomach when he remembered she wasn't there, it was nobody's business but his own.

That morning, with still half an hour to go before he flipped the sign, he heard a tapping on the glass, and his brow raised in surprise when he saw Emilio peering through the window, a covered plate balanced on one hand.

With a smile, he unlocked the door. "Can't say I expected you at nine-thirty on a Sunday."

"I come bearing gifts." Emilio handed him the plate. "Marisol forgot it last night."

"Oh, man. Thanks." Michael tipped his head toward the back of the shop. "Lucky thing I've got a fridge. And a coffee maker. Was just going to make a cup. Got time?"

"Sure." Did he ever. He was hoping to wangle an invitation. He needed to talk, badly. He followed Michael into his office.

"Marisol was just getting up as I was leaving. She said you fired your chef." He put away the plate, got out the coffee.

"Did she?" Emilio grabbed one of the two chairs in the small space. "She tell you what happened?"

Maybe he shouldn't have mentioned that Marisol had broached the subject. He sometimes forgot that Emilio was her boss. "Uh, she's pretty groggy when she wakes up. Just said you all worked shorthanded last night because the chef was dismissed. I heard her come in pretty late."

"Yeah. We all ended up staying longer than we usually do." He'd soon have to add that in his case, it was partly because he'd been all over Mike's daughter.

So, how to begin?

He cleared his throat. "Listen, that's what I wanted to talk to you about." To his own ears, he sounded nervous, unsure. "Marisol. I wanted to talk about Marisol."

"Oh, crap." Michael's shoulders slumped. "You want to fire her."

"No. Hell, no. She's great. She's a great pastry chef. A great co-worker. Just like you said."

Michael noted the repeated emphasis on the word, 'great.' "Well, that's—ha ha—*great* news. She was mad as hell at me for interfering on that score. So what's the problem?"

Emilio took a deep breath. "She kissed me."

"Holy shit." Michael paused in the midst of spooning coffee to gawk at him. "She came on to you?"

"*No.* I mean, yes. But...no." Michael's perplexed frown confirmed to Emilio that he was making a mess of things, just as he knew he would. He squared his shoulders, looked Michael straight in the eye. "What I mean to say is...I kissed her back, Mike."

There. It was out. Emilio braced himself for a punch. If Michael threw one, he'd take it.

The only sound in the room was the perking of coffee as Michael stared at him. "And you're telling me this, why?"

"Come on, Mike. You know why. I took advantage of your daughter. You asked me to hire her in good faith, and I took advantage of her." Saying it out loud, he was ashamed of himself.

"I don't see how. *She* kissed you first, isn't that what you said?"

"Yes, but I shouldn't have encouraged it. I shouldn't be as attracted to her as I am."

"Why the hell not? What's wrong with Marisol?"

"Nothing!" Emilio threw his hands in the air. "That's the problem. She's smart and brave and talented. She has integrity. She stands up for herself and others. And she's your daughter, Mike. Your young daughter," he finished lamely.

"Oh." Michael drew out the word. "I get it. You like her. And you think she's too young for you."

"Don't you?"

"Hee, hee, hoo." Michael's laugh was uniquely his own. He poured coffee, handed a cup to Emilio.

"What's funny?"

"You are. You and your dramatic Latin tendencies. Hoo, boy, this brings me back. It's like the conversations I used to have with Cynthia."

That stung. And the casual attitude was confusing. "You're serious? You're saying you wouldn't object if she and I were a couple? I'm thirty-three. You know that, right?" He hung his head, embarrassed. "She's twenty, for godssake."

"She's old enough to vote. To join the military. In less than a month, she'll be old enough to drink. And you know what? I pretty much think she's old enough to date who she wants without asking her dad's permission." His grin had an edge to it. "You're not Humbert and she's not Lolita. But even if I thought you were too old for her—which I don't—or didn't think you were a decent guy—which I do—my opinion wouldn't stop my daughter from doing what she wanted. And it shouldn't. The year is twenty-twenty, Em."

Emilio took a gulp of coffee, nearly burned his tongue. "I'm not dramatic." When Michael arched a brow, he insisted, "I'm not. I just don't want to be that guy. You know what I mean?"

"Yeah, I do." He chuckle was dry. "I do know what you mean, because *I* was that guy. When I was your age, I dated a lot of girls in their early twenties. They were the only ones who put up with my immaturity, and the fact that I was broke as fuck." Emilio's head shot up at Michael's candor. "It was only when I met Inez that I started getting my shit together. You're not immature. You're certainly not broke. But if you were either of those things, I know my daughter, and she wouldn't find those qualities appealing. You're judging her by the average twenty-year old, but you wouldn't be so drawn to her if she *were* the average twenty-year-old, would you?"

Emilio couldn't argue with that, so he sipped mutely. After a while, he said, "What if she changes her mind? You know—" he gestured with his cup as he tried to illuminate his concern—"being that she's young, she might decide in six months or so she doesn't want me."

The unguarded comment had Michael studying him. "Well, hell. That sounds like more than just an attraction, Em. Are you in love with her?"

"No." He answered the question as frankly as it had been asked. "No, I haven't let myself fall in love with her." He paused. "But if we start something up, I could see it happening pretty quick."

Michael scratched his ear, debated what to say, how much to say. "Look. I'm sure you already know that more than I want my next breath, I want Marisol to be happy. She had a year after her mother died that she...well, you know about that. I figure she was entitled. And I knew common sense would eventually prevail. Marisol is...how can I describe her, so you'd understand?"

He thought back to when he first met her. She was three, and what a sweet, obedient child she'd been. Even at that age, she sensed her mother was relying on her to help get them through, as Inez scrimped and scrounged to keep a roof over their heads. He thought about her rebellious years. His wife had never fully understood, but he'd always believed those years were owed to Marisol as a recompense for what amounted to her having to mature far more quickly than her peers. It was as though she knew that once he was in the picture to help Inez, she could relax and just be a kid. Lastly, he thought about her abilities, what she'd accomplished with them, what they'd cost her before she fully accepted them.

"Marisol is an old soul," he said, at length. "But that doesn't guarantee she won't change her mind, just as there isn't one that you won't." He shrugged. "There are no guarantees, Em. You know that. Look at me—my wife was so young when she got sick." His expression was bleak but resigned, and he knew it. "I don't mean to be a downer. I'm just saying, live your life. If you and Marisol make each other happy, go for it. And if she ends it or you do, just don't be dicks about it. I like eating at your restaurant. I'd hate to be barred from it."

At that, Emilio snorted out a laugh. "Always thinking about your stomach, aren't you?"

"Hell, yeah. Who else will if I don't?"

A tremendous weight lifted from Emilio's shoulders. He looked at Michael with gratitude. "Thanks for trusting me, Mike. And thanks for the advice." To change the mood, he added, "It was pretty good, coming from somebody who used to be immature and broke as fuck."

"Yeah, it was pretty good, wasn't it? Sometimes I surprise myself."

Emilio was in a much lighter mood as he made his way to the Spice. It probably was antiquated of him, but he felt better about pursuing this thing with Marisol—whatever it was, or would turn out to be— now that he'd spoken to Michael. He was pretty sure she wouldn't be happy to hear he'd talked to her father, but he'd cross that bridge...

Just as he reached the main hall, he saw a cluster of maintenance and security near the Centerline Boutique. Avi, the manager of Chelsea's, and Danny, one of the tour guides, were there too. All who'd gathered shared the same grim-faced look.

"Some kind of a sick prank," Danny was saying. "We gotta get it cleaned. And find out if anybody on this deck saw anything."

"Right, but we have to cordon it all off, first thing," one of the security men told him.

"Can't we just go ahead with cleanup?" Avi quietly protested. "I'd rather not—"

"I get you, man, but that's not the priority. Nobody without clearance in or out 'til the cops come, get photos, whatever." He turned to Danny. You'll need to close the tour office too. Suspend any scheduled walks."

Danny nodded, reluctantly. "Okay. Shit. I got a big group this afternoon. How long we talking?"

"Shouldn't take us more than a few hours."

"Fingers crossed," Avi put in.

Emilio walked over. "What's going on, guys?"

They turned. "Oh, hey, Em. It's a mess." Danny jabbed his thumb toward the Observation Bar, lowered his voice. "You know the burl wood outside the bar? Some asshole poured blood down the wall."

"Blood?" Emilio took a step back. "Real blood?"

"Yup. We don't know what kind yet—animal or human—but it's real, dude, and it's all over the wall. The somabitch placed it so it looked like it was leaking out of the—" Danny tapped his lids—"parts of the wood that look like eyes holes."

"Christ."

"We're thinking, most likely kids, on the ghost tour late last night, got drunk, stayed late, and so on. At least, we sure as hell hope that's what happened," Avi said. He didn't think so. Not at all.

"Most likely, yeah," Danny reiterated.

"Uh huh." Emilio couldn't help but notice that neither seemed convinced of that scenario. "Where would they get blood?"

"Who knows?" Danny thrust his neck in response. "I just hope it's some poor fucking cat."

"A cat?" Emilio was horrified. "What the hell, Danny—why?"

"He didn't mean he *wants* it to be a cat, Em. He meant…" There was a sheen of sweat on Avi's skin. "Because of the amount."

The implication was now clear. "You guys mean—?"

"Yeah." Danny's face went rigid. "If it's human blood, we're looking at a homicide."

Before long, the ship was crawling with police, forensics experts, and cadaver dogs. Emilio and all other restaurant and shop owners contacted their staff to let them know not to come in to work. Room and restaurant reservations were cancelled for the day. Only those tourists who'd stayed over Saturday night were told to remain until they were questioned, after which time they were escorted off the ship. A wedding scheduled for that evening with a reception in the Veranda Grill was also cancelled, the bride in hysterics, the groom and the parents berating detectives and managerial staff.

Little sympathy was spared for them, as the blood had indeed tested human, and the *Queen Mary* was officially deemed the site of a murder. Somewhere on the huge ship the police expected to find a body, a body tapped of blood. Emilio, Rohini, and others who lived aboard were asked to stay in their staterooms while the ship was searched.

All non-essential persons had been dispersed for nearly an hour when the dogs went wild. Their yipping was incessant, they strained against their leashes, scrambled over one another, pushed and pulled toward the exit and the boardwalk that would take them down to the engine room. Growling and sniffing, they clambered across steel platforms, their nails clicking against metal stairs, nearly falling over themselves in their rush to get down there. But after searching in and around giant pipes, electrical equipment, thrusters, every square inch of space and machinery, nothing was found in the *Queen Mary* engine room.

At five-thirty in the afternoon, still no corpse was discovered anywhere aboard, and with the sun due to set in less than an hour, a Coast Guard cutter docked nearby, while several divers searched the waters in the harbor and beyond. The local news got wind of the mystery, and their vans, cameras, and lights, their questions and live reports were a nuisance to those who were trying to work while there was still some daylight to catch.

Around seven p.m., The Secret Spice was deemed free of dead bodies by the police. After it was sanitized by the cleaning crew of dog hair and other muck from the search, Emilio and Rohini were permitted to return to it.

This was welcome news. They were famished. Neither kept much food in their staterooms, and they'd been confined to them all day. Emilio set a table for two, lit candles, and uncorked wine to breathe. Rohini prepared a chicken dish with a zesty paste of onion, garlic, gingerroot, cinnamon, cardamom seeds, cloves, peppercorns, bay leaves, and red pepper. The scent was mouthwatering, and she served the chicken with a particularly fragrant white rice that came from her region of India.

Nothing would stop them from having a good meal. With all they'd experienced when it came to the *Queen Mary*, they'd learned that fearful attitudes helped stir up an energy upon which negative forces would thrive. They remained upbeat because it was the wisest thing to do.

"A pity we don't have naan bread. From time to time, I get a hankering for food from home," she said as she served.

"It smells delicious, Rohini."

"Thank you. Did you know that no Indian uses commercial curry powder? To me the word `curry` is as degrading to India`s great cuisine as the term `chop suey` is to China`s."

"That doesn't surprise me. My mother laughs when Americans talk about 'authentic' Mexican food."

"I blame the British. They tried to standardize a blend of spices, but they oversimplified, and hence destroyed Indian cuisine."

Emilio poured wine, as Rohini sat. "I thought a light Pinot Noir would go well."

She took a sip. "Perfect," she pronounced. She placed her napkin in her lap, and smiled at him. "Gruesome mysteries aside, this is pleasant. I do believe it's the first time you and I have dinner together on our own."

Emilio smiled back. "I do believe you're right. And while we eat, I have some good news to share. It seems Marisol and I have settled our differences."

"Oh, that's lovely, dear. I can't wait to hear about it."

CHAPTER 13

Twenty-four hours later, the source of the blood was still undetermined. Law enforcement reluctantly gave the go-ahead for regular activities to resume for those who lived and worked aboard the ship.

For Emilio, this meant paperwork and lots of it. For Rohini, it was her usual Monday trip to the farmer's market. She would be accompanied for the first time by her new assistant, a pleased-with-himself Niko. Marisol often went with her on the weekly shopping trip, but she begged off, having other plans for the morning. She had other plans for Emilio's morning too, as he was about to discover.

She made her way to his stateroom, *tch*-ed in disgust at the rapacious reporters, the packs of pseudo-ghost hunters who were milling about, mentally rubbing their hands together at the opportunity to sensationalize an incident she was sure would turn out to be nothing more than a macabre prank.

He'd just stepped out of the shower, and was toweling off when she knocked.

"Emilio. I know you're in there."

Crap. He recognized the voice and the tone. She'd heard about his visit with Michael, and she wasn't pleased. Not that he'd expected any different. Hoping to stall, he spoke through the door. "Marisol, I'm not dressed."

"I don't care. I need to speak with you. Open up."

In silence, he stared at the closed door.

Now, Emilio."

When he unlocked it, there she stood, glaring, her foot tapping, her left hand fisted at her hip, still in her street clothes. She was angry enough to have marched straight up to his room, no detours to the restaurant to change.

He braced himself. "Go ahead. Let it out. I can see you're ready to bite my head off."

Oh, she wanted to bite him, all right. He looked delicious standing there with just a towel wrapped around his waist, those buff abs, that muscular chest on display, his dark hair damp and curling, the smell of soap on his skin.

Could her timing have been more perfect?

She stepped in, shut the door behind her. "You went to see my father yesterday."

As though she'd pointed a gun at him, he held his palms up. "Guilty."

Now she fisted both hands at her waist. "And you told him you wanted to have a relationship with me."

"That is correct, yes."

They gazed at each other, the air between them throbbing.

At last, she said, "Next time, you idiot, tell *me*." With that, she leapt at him, and he caught her just as she wrapped her legs around his waist.

"Well, look at this," he said with a happy grin, as his hands circled her bottom and he bounced her in his arms. "I seem to have caught a beautiful pastry chef."

She didn't realize she was mimicking Michael's famous arched brow. "What are you going to do about it?"

"I'm sure I'll come up with something," he murmured. As he walked them to his bed, she reached down to yank his towel away.

Some while later, they lay back against the pillows. Marisol breathed a deep sigh. "Whew. Thank God that's over with."

"Uh…That's not what I was hoping to hear."

When she realized how it sounded, she giggled, nudged him with her foot. "I didn't mean it like that, silly."

"Well, feel free to elaborate. I'm all ears."

With a contented smile, she turned on her side, reached over to play with the hair on his chest. "I meant, I've wanted to do this with you for a long time. I'm glad we finally got to it. It was starting to affect my concentration at work."

He burst out laughing. "Anything to improve employee productivity." With his eyes closed, he savored her touch. "So, how long?"

"How long…what?"

"How long is a long time?"

"Well, certainly not from the beginning, when you were acting like an arrogant jackass." Her hand stilled as she thought about it. "I think it was when Theresa's mother told me you visit the hospital every week."

He smirked lazily. "I was an arrogant jackass, wasn't I?" He continued before she could answer. "Know when I first wanted you? It was when you threw your drink at me in the bar."

"Well, what did you expect? You said—"

In one swift move, he shifted over her to silence her with a kiss. "I know what I said. We both agree I behaved abominably. I only said what I said to galvanize you into staying."

"Galvanize me?" She looked up at him quizzically. "Why didn't you just *ask* me to stay?"

"I don't know."

When she saw he meant that, she continued to study him, thinking back on their misunderstandings. "You know what?" She reached up, traced the outline of his lips. "I think we have a communication problem."

"We might." As much as he didn't want to agree, she had a point. They liked each other, they were drawn to each other, but they didn't know each other.

"From now on, let's just be honest, okay? I hate bullshit, Emilio. I…" she dropped her hand. "I've been through a lot. And it's made me see that life is too unpredictable to play games."

He frowned down at her. Michael had said something along the same lines. "Is it the loss of your mother, or is there more?"

"My mother's death did hit me hard. But there's more. A lot more." She paused. "I'm not sure what you'll think if I tell you. But if I don't tell you, then it's not being honest, which is what I just said I want us to be."

"Try me." When she still wavered, he added, "Whatever it is, it stays between us. I promise."

"Okay. I'll tell you." She took a deep breath. "I can see ghosts."

"Ghosts? Did you say ghosts?" His eyes went comically wide.

"Very funny. I take it this is not a big surprise?"

"If that's all there is to your secret, no. Believe it or not, I've seen a few myself. You'd have to be obtuse not to around here." When she visibly relaxed at his words, he went on. "As a matter of fact, you're not the first girl I've dated who had the ability."

"Huh. I didn't think there were that many of us. The only other girl I know who has it is Sarita Taylor. You must remember her, right? You worked for her mother."

He never suspected there was a quicksand pit in the center of his mattress, but he was about to get sucked down into it. "Oh, that's right. Of course you know Sarita. What was I thinking?"

"Wait a minute." She slid out from under him at once, sat up when he rolled aside at her sudden move. "You *dated* Sarita?"

He noted her body language. The silence stretched until it was taut enough to snap. "Why do I get the feeling I'm about to be relegated to 'jackass' status again," he said, trapped.

"Did you or didn't you?"

"I...uh...it...it was a long time ago."

"You mean, when you worked here?"

"Yes. She was sixteen. I was seventeen. And you—need I remind you once again—were four."

She squinted at him. "Why do you keep bringing that up? Why is that such a fixation with you?"

"Because you're asking me about something that happened long before you and I could have ever possibly been a...a thing."

"Oh, I see. So you slept together."

"Whoa, *whoa*—hold it right there, okay? That's off limits territory. I don't want to know about your past relationships, nor do I care to discuss mine. It's one thing being honest, it's another thing comparing...comparing." He was starting to sweat, couldn't believe they were arguing. Again.

"Fine." She lifted a shoulder. "You're right."

"I'm right? Now I'm right?"

"Yeah, you're right. We shouldn't discuss it." She waited a beat. "Besides, I already know you slept with her. You wouldn't be getting so defensive about it otherwise."

"*Jee-zus*, Marisol." He nearly said something scathing, but caught the vulnerability in her expression in time to bite his tongue. That's when it occurred to him that, just as he fretted he might be too old for her, maybe she had her own anxieties about their budding relationship.

He was right. As much work as Marisol had done on herself, as much as she'd learned to present a confident front, she still wrestled with stints of self-doubt that had become entrenched during her adolescence, the time in her life when her powers made her feel like a changeling in her own family, and a misfit among her peers. And in those years, the one person who understood her, the one person she'd looked up to, was Sarita. To learn that her mentor and her new lover had once been an item was disconcerting. And she didn't want to tell him that, because it made her feel pathetic.

Watching the emotions play across her face, Emilio's eye softened, and he made a decision. He sat up too, smoothed his hands over her bare shoulders, kissed her forehead. "Sarita and I did not sleep together. Okay?"

She believed him. And as foolish as it was, she felt relieved.

"We haven't seen each other in years. You know that, right?" he went on.

"She was here after we reopened," she reminded him.

"That's right, she was. With her husband." He pressed home that point. "They seem to be very happy together. And they have four children, Marisol. Four little girls."

"I know."

"Our relationship—such as it was—was a lifetime ago. We were kids, cariña."

The endearment mollified her. "I know," she said again, and smiled softly. I'm being silly."

"All right, then." He smiled in a way he hoped reassured her. "So, can we stop talking about Sarita now? It would be nice if we could make love one more time before I have to get downstairs and hit those books. I don't know about you, but I have a lot of work to do today."

She nodded, feigned nonchalance. "So I guess you don't want to hear about how I saved her life." She couldn't help it—she had to get that in, just so he would know that while Sarita might be a force of nature, so was she, dammit.

His eyebrows shot up. "You saved her life?"

"Uh huh. And actually, Angela's too, pretty much."

"No kidding? Wow. That's impressive. Is this to do with the seeing-ghosts thing?"

"It is. Did you want to hear about it?"

"I'd love to hear as much about you as you want to tell."

"Hmm." She mulled it over. "If we're on a time crunch, I think I'd rather make love again now, and tell you the stories over dinner."

When she pushed him back down to the sheets, his lips curved. "An excellent plan."

They had twelve happy days and nights, during which time Marisol's headaches seemed to disappear. This led her to conclude they had indeed been stress-related, or possibly even related to her unfulfilled desire for Emilio, a desire he was now satisfying with frequency and gusto.

She liked him so very much. Truth be told, she could see herself loving him, although it was imprudent to envisage that so soon. Besides which, for the first time since she was hired, she was enjoying work unreservedly. She wanted to bask in that without worry over the possible complications down the road of a love affair with her boss. As he'd pointed out more than once, she was young, but she'd never *felt* young, never allowed herself to be carefree. With a job she loved and a satisfying personal relationship, she gave herself that gift, at last.

The kitchen's ambience was vastly improved now that Joy was no longer there to drain the vitality from it. Rohini had watched her husband cook for so many years, she could replicate his style, but she surprised everyone by daring to add her own flair. And there was a new special on offer—Emilio insisted they add the chicken and rice dish she'd made for him the night they'd eaten alone. He also insisted upon the name. Thus 'Chicken Rohini' was born. As for Niko, he and Rohini worked flawlessly together. He was learning so rapidly, Marisol was sure he'd be in charge of his own restaurant in no time. He also had a great sense of humor, cracking jokes over everything, whether it was an oddly-shaped vegetable or a finicky patron who kept sending back his food. It was part of the waitstaff's job to be warm and pleasant to customers, but thanks to Niko's sense of fun and Rohini's kind manner, their smiles and bright moods were now authentic.

Michael picked up on the improved work environment on his weekly visit to the restaurant. His daughter looked happy and relaxed, and that pleased him no end. He knew Emilio was at the root of her happiness, and though his heart gave a little pang at the additional evidence that his baby girl was a grown woman, he patted himself on the back, not only because he'd been instrumental in getting her in as pastry chef, but because he'd made the right call in reassuring Emilio.

Em was a good guy, Michael knew with certainty. Even Rohini was less forlorn when they next had tea. She'd gone so far as indulging in some gossip—a pastime that was unusual for her—by giving him a detailed and, he noticed, gratified account of Joy's ouster from the kitchen. And while he knew she wasn't happy, would likely mourn Cristiano forever, he could see he might have underestimated her strength. If she could go on and make a life for herself, maybe it was possible for him to do so too. After all, when people lost a limb, they didn't stop living. They adjusted. Didn't they?

PATRICIA V. DAVIS

All in all, things were looking up for those who were connected to
The Secret Spice Café. They never dreamed that blood on the walls of
their treasured ship had anything to do with them, or with a woman
they'd never met, a woman who'd dedicated her life to protecting them
from a vast and unimaginable threat. As the hours ticked down, she
and those with her began to contemplate the horrifying possibility that
her valiant efforts might have been in vain.

As for the ghosts, Marisol had confided in Emilio that she had the
ability to see them, but for some reason, she didn't notice they were
gone. Their flight from the ship, an exodus she'd witnessed, was wiped
from her memory, as was the memory of the man with the cane who'd
been drinking Sazerac in their restaurant at a table that didn't exist,
when Theresa collapsed.

Since that night in the parking lot, whenever Marisol walked
through the main shopping area, she was oblivious to the absence of
the 1930s tailor in the Centerline Boutique, the forever-young soldiers
who stood along the promenade smoking their C-rations cigarettes, the
socialites in their pompadour hairstyles and long, tiered cocktail dress-
es, and all the other unearthly inhabitants who were part and parcel of
the *Queen*. Unlike Rohini, she hadn't picked up on the lack of the spirit
presence in the kitchen either. The ghosts were gone, and it was peculiar, to say the least, that their lack was not noted by someone whose
life had been so marked by their presence.

But they weren't all gone. One or two remained. In the initial hours
of the morning of the thirteenth day after Marisol and Emilio had come
together as lovers, with none of the other spirits around to stop them,
those remaining few had their chance.

The prior evening, Marisol and Emilio had stolen away from the
Spice early for a romantic dinner on their own. They didn't go far, only
to another restaurant aboard the *Queen*, Chelsea's.

158

Avi, the manager who knew them both, gave them one of the best tables in the house, with a grand view of the water.

"Do you think they'll notice we lit out?"

"Yeah, I do, *cariña*, considering I dragged you out of the kitchen. But they can handle things for a few hours without us."

"Well, if you're sure, then I'm going to enjoy this little outing." She purred with pleasure, surveyed their surroundings. "Look at that view. Did you notice the moon? It's almost full."

"It'll be full tomorrow. And it's a blue moon."

"I've never known what that is, other than in the literary sense."

"The thirteenth full moon in one calendar year. Doesn't happen often." Emilio smiled with mischief. "I ordered it up just for us."

"A blue moon on Halloween." She fluttered her eyelashes playfully. "How...well, I can't say it's romantic, so I'll just say, how unique." Opening her menu, she perused it with satisfaction. "I'm so glad we're eating here."

"Oh, yeah?" It pleased him that she was pleased.

"Yes. Their clam chowder is incredible."

"Let's get two bowls, then."

Avi came over with a bottle of wine. "This is on the house, y'all."

They chorused their appreciation and thanks, and if there was a sharpness in Avi's eye as he studied Marisol, neither she nor Emilio caught it. They delighted in their stolen hours together. Marisol had her bowl of clam chowder, and when she dipped her spoon into Emilio's bowl too, he was happy to indulge her.

Later, in his bed, he indulged her again, and she him, when he whispered to her how much he'd love for her to stay overnight.

"What about my father?"

"You could text him." In the dim light, Emilio's eyes gleamed wickedly as he nipped her bare shoulder. "Not sure if there's enough room in here for him, though."

"Oh, you're so funny."

She texted Michael: *Daddy, staying aboard the ship. Love you. Sleep tight. Don't let the bed bugs bite.*

Avi used his phone too, after Marisol and Emilio left Chelsea's. "Antoine? *Kisa ki pase?* How far out are you, bro?" He listened. "Make it fast. It's already started, and I won't be able to call you again. No, she's not. Not yet, poor girl. The kitchen? It's going to be tough on my own. *Kisa?* Cristiano's wife? I'll try, but she hardly knows me."

Rohini had been tip-toeing down to the restaurant every night after everyone was asleep. At last, she'd put aside her own heartache to listen to the quiet, to analyze, to finally understand that something was very wrong.

Why had the presence in the kitchen left?

At three-fifteen that morning, she was alone in the restaurant again, when a sound of rushing wind came from the scullery. She raced toward it, slid to a stop by the freezer, elated to see its door wide open, blowing cold air out into the room, in the same way it had welcomed her on her first day.

She stood in front of it. "Your Majesty?" Two eager words.

As the stillness dragged on, and the icy air enveloped her, pricking like needles along her spine, she understood.

She was staring at the face of Naag's crypt. The freezer was where he'd first lay before he was condemned forever to the bottom of the sea. This time, the freezer door hadn't opened in greeting.

It had opened to let something escape.

Her muscles went stiff, immobilized with terror. She knew this day would come. She could sense something—someone—behind her. She knew who it was.

But when she turned, it was only Marisol, standing several feet away, watching her.

Her body went limp with relief. "Oh, good heavens, dear, you scared me half to death. What are you doing down here at this hour? Couldn't you sleep either?"

"Did you think you'd get away with it forever?"

"I...What?"

Marisol stepped forward until she loomed over Rohini. "I *said*, did you think you'd get away with it forever?"

When her face twisted, Rohini saw it—Naag's face under Marisol's. Naag, as he'd been in death, dripping in his own malice and bile.

Before Rohini could scream, she was shoved, viciously, into the freezer, the door slammed and locked from the outside.

CHAPTER FOURTEEN

Saturday, October 31, 2020, 3:00 p.m.,
nine hours before the end

When Mambo Taylor stepped through his doorway, Luca was struck speechless. He was seeing his wife, fifty years down the road. At eighty-six, Rosemary wore the vestiges of her youthful beauty with the same grace and nonchalance she wore her tignon, her traditional clothing, and her sacred cowrie-shell jewelry.

The second thing that flummoxed him was to see her pull Sarita in for a fierce hug the minute she laid eyes on her.

"Sarita! *Bèl pitit fi*—my beautiful granddaughter—at last. Oh, how I've dreamed of this." She rocked her back and forth, back and forth.

Flustered by the unexpected display of emotion from a woman she'd never met, Sarita stiffened. But then she thought of a gift sent to her when she was child—the *gris-gris* that had kept dark dreams at bay—and she felt her body ease into the embrace, as the love, the words, came to her. "*Granmè*. I've wanted to meet you for so long."

"Let me look at you." With an ear-to-ear grin, Rosemary pulled back, pressed her palms to Sarita's cheeks. "A beauty," she declared. "Just as I was told." Still beaming, she said to Antoine, "Avi was right, wasn't he?"

"He was, Priestess, yes. Ms. Sarita is very beautiful."

Avi? Sarita knew only one Avi, from the *Queen Mary*. They couldn't mean him, could they?

Rosemary saw Sarita's uncertainty, and gave her a reassuring pat. "In good time, *cher*. We'll tell you all. But for now—" she smiled at the quadruplets, who were still clinging to their father—"I want to meet my great-granddaughters too."

"Let's see." With the four little girls gazing at her wide-eyed, their tears forgotten, she pointed to each one in turn. "You're Maria. You'll have to sing for me, later, I hope." Maria was transfixed by Rosemary's spiritual dress, so much so, she didn't take note that she'd been recognized at first look by a stranger. "You have a scarf around your hair," she said shyly. "It looks pretty."

"Thank you so much. I'm glad you like it." Rosemary smiled warmly at Maria, and ignoring the astonished reaction of Luca, Sarita, and Angela, she went on to the next little girl. "And this here's Niki." She touched Niki's knee. "Scraped it playing baseball, did you?" When Niki nodded sheepishly, Rosemary grinned. "Thought so. I got somethin' to put on that, in my bag." She turned to Alana, softly brushed at the tears drying on her face. "And Alana. It's all right, sweet pea. No need to fret. We'll fix it." Spotting Alana's birthmark, she studied it, her expression pensive. "We'll fix it all."

Alana took a minute to scrutinize her great-grandmother before she whispered, "You look like Mommy."

Luca was amused when Rosemary tittered, obviously pleased by the comparison. "A few more wrinkles than your mama, I think."

When she got to Alexandra, she bit back a smile at the suspicion on the child's face. "And why, may I ask, are you givin' me such a sassy look, Miss Alexandra?"

"How come you can tell us apart?" Alex demanded.

Antoine had to hide his laugh behind a cough. The mambo wasn't used to being spoken to in such a direct way, in particular by a child.

"I know who you are because we're related."

"Then, how come we've never seen you before?" Alex pointed to Antoine. "And why did that man call you 'Priestess?'"

"Full of questions, aren't you? Good ones too." She nodded her approval. "They'll be answered, as I told your mama. In time."

It was Luca's turn next. "Luciano."

"Priestess Rosemary. It's nice to meet you." His tone was polite but guarded. He still didn't know what his mother's warning was about, and now—out of the blue—Sarita's grandmother, who'd never been part of her life, was suddenly in their home.

He had a right to be wary, and Rosemary knew that. "Your nose. May I?" She placed her hand on his forehead, and the bleeding stopped. When she touched him, he could feel her hand shake, and it revealed the anxiety under her valiant mask. "You're going to hate it when you find out why I'm here," she murmured to him. "I pray you don't end up hating me along with it."

Before he could respond, she pivoted to face Angela. "Well, now," she said, as cheerily as she could manage, "I hear you make great cakes."

"That's what they tell me, Priestess." Angela said nothing else. She had the same questions they all had.

"I would surely love to taste some." With a gallant smile, she addressed them all. "This is supposed to be a party, right?"

By six p.m., despite the wild excitement of the day, as well as sugar overload from too much birthday cake, the quadruplets were sound asleep.

It was Rosemary who made sure of it. They needed to be rested for what was to come, although she hadn't discussed any of that with the others as yet. They were waiting for Luca to get back from Rome with Jane. Cynthia had arrived as scheduled a few hours prior, apprised of the day's events by Luca when he picked her up. The adults made a big happy show of cake and candles, presents and games for the children, but they were dreading what was to come. They knew whatever

Rosemary had to tell them was big and scary, and Cynthia, in particular, was growing restless with the wait.

"Can you at least give us a hint, *Mamman* Taylor?" She prowled across the living room rug, as the others sat, trying to contain their nerves.

"I don't want to tell it twice, *cher*. They'll be here soon."

"What's taking them so long? He usually pops in and out before you can blink."

"It's two in the morning there, Cynthia," Angela reminded her. "They'll be asleep. I hope to God my brother doesn't think it's a prowler. He's liable to hit the poor kid with a bat." She jiggled her foot, ran her hands up and down her arms, every movement a statement. "I wish we could have called to let her know. It's bad enough we weren't able to get in touch with Ro, and now I can't try her again. She has no idea any of this is going on."

Rosemary exchanged a sideways glance with Antoine, but said nothing.

"We have no idea what's going on either, do we?"

"We can't take the chance, Ms. Cynthia. We don't know if our phones are being monitored," Antoine explained again, patiently.

"By whom?" She threw up her hands. "Who are we talking about?"

"Mae, this isn't helping." Sarita felt like she'd eaten lead. The whole afternoon, as she entertained guests, took photos, smiled and sang 'Happy Birthday' to her daughters, she held the image of how they'd looked when they came back from the school. There'd been no time alone with Luca to discuss it, and as the day stretched into evening, her apprehension grew. "Sit down. Please. You're making me dizzy."

"I need a drink."

"There's still some wine left."

"A real drink, Sarita."

Her loud, drawn out sigh was meant to both ease the tension and shut her mother up. "I'm sorry. I forgot to pick it up. I don't drink anything stronger than wine, so I don't keep it in the house. My husband's in recovery, remember?"

When the crackling noise that signified Luca's return came from the kitchen, Rosemary was the first to say, "They're back." It no longer surprised anyone that she recognized a sound they would have assumed she'd never heard. She and Antoine stood at the same time. She took his hands, clasped them. "You know what to do. When you're done, take the back roads home, and be careful. Bondye beni ou—God bless you."

"Thank you, Priestess." He leaned down to kiss her cheek, then said to them all, "I hope we'll meet again, under better circumstances next time."

"What's he—?" Cynthia bit back the question when both Sarita and Angela gave her baleful stares.

As Antoine strode out, Jane trudged in with Luca trailing behind, carrying her overnight case. "There better be a bloody good reason for snatching me out of a sound sleep," were her first words.

"Well, look what the cat dragged in." Even with whatever it was they were soon to face looming over them, Cynthia was happy to see her. She and Jane kept in touch with holiday cards and social media, but they hadn't been in the same room together in far too long. Distance and differing lifestyles had been their excuse for not properly tending to a friendship that had developed slowly but grown rock solid by the time they went their separate ways. And that was a shame, she thought, as she beamed at her old friend.

"Too right," Jane harrumphed, just as pleased to see Cynthia. "Like something the cat dragged in is precisely how I feel at this ungodly hour." She glanced down at Cynthia's low-heeled pumps, and teased.

"Oh my. Look at you, wearing a sensible pair of shoes. What brought this about—Vegas showgirls get tired of you nicking their footwear?"

Cynthia's lip turned up. "Old age and gravity brought it about." She looked Jane up and down, knowing she expected her to return the shot. "Apparently they've affected you as well."

Jane grinned in appreciation. "Indeed, they have. Not to mention I've just had my hair scared white." She scowled at Luca. "I haven't seen Antoni jump around in bed like that for ages."

"I was on a time crunch. I'm sorry. I tried my best," Luca apologized again.

"I'm sure you did, cousin. In your own cack-handed way." She blew a kiss to both Sarita and Angela where they were sitting, then frowned. "Where's Rohini?"

"We couldn't get her this morning, and now we're not allowed to call." Angela gestured to Rosemary to indicate who had given the order.

"Oh, I beg your pardon." Jane turned to the priestess. "Where are my manners? I should have introduced myself straightaway. How do you do? I'm Jane."

"Trust me, Mambo Taylor knows who you are," Angela assured her, when Rosemary simply gave her a small smile.

"Well, that certainly makes things less awkward, doesn't it?" Unfazed by meeting a Vodou priestess for the first time in her life, and behaving as if there were no urgency to their gathering, she unzipped her overnight case. "After breaking into my bedroom, Luca told me to bring along this." She pulled out a bottle of single malt and set it down on the coffee table.

"See? That's a son-in-law." Cynthia said.

"Why does he get the credit? It's a good job I had it on hand." Jane scanned the area for a spare seat.

"What—like you just 'happened' to have it in the house?" Angela tipped her chin toward the bottle. "I'll bet you a hundred bucks right now you have at least two more stashed where that came from."

Jane tipped her nose in the air. "And what if I do?"

Sarita was amused by their familiar banter. "You're all in cahoots, encouraging my mother's proclivities."

Luca shrugged as he pulled over chairs for Jane and himself. "What do you want from me? She's been jonesing for a drink since she got here. It would be rude not to oblige." But he made the joke half-heart-edly. He wanted to get on with this. The sooner they knew what they were facing, the sooner they could deal with it.

Rosemary shared his sentiments. "Be nice if y'all stop talking about it and start pouring it. Pretending we're sitting here for a social isn't going to turn it into one." There was a beat of silence after she made that assertion, and then she patted Sarita's knee. "Go on, sweet pea. Get some glasses. I could use a drink for this, myself."

When they were all settled in, Rosemary clasped her scotch like a lifeline, but her face was perfectly composed, belying the turmoil whirling through her. "I'll start by giving you, Cynthia, my apology. I know you hated my Bobby all your life for leaving you and your baby girl." When Cynthia opened her mouth to protest, Rosemary cut her off. "Please. This is so hard for me. It's a tale sixty years in the making, one I hoped I'd never have to tell. I gave up everything for that hope, but I failed in it. I failed all of you. And I'm here, where I've always wanted to be—with my family—and it's both the happiest moment and the most terrible one."

"*Granmè*." As always, Sarita's first reaction was compassion. She reached for Rosemary's hand. "Why do you say that?"

"I say it, because your Daddy didn't leave you." With a look of en-treaty at Cynthia, she said, "I know he was failing you both, but he didn't leave you. He was killed."

"Killed?" Cynthia's face went blank with shock. "When? Why didn't you tell me?"

"Because you would have been in danger if I'd done that. Because the same thing that took Bobby took his father. And unless you help me stop it, it's the same thing that wants to claim you—every one of you."

Luca looked at the stupefied faces around him. The women were buying her story wholesale. Their faith in her was too immediate, and that didn't sit well with him. He'd learned, in the most terrible way possible, that people weren't always trustworthy just because they were family. "What do you mean, 'help you stop it'? What is it that needs to be stopped, and how, specifically, do you need our help?"

Sarita gave him a sharp look. He was regarding her grandmother as skeptically as Alexandra had earlier in the day. She nearly asked him why, then bit back the question. Rosemary tugged at her heartstrings, but she trusted that Luca had his reasons.

"A long time ago, there was another priestess who sought revenge on me for a tragedy in her life. The death of her son."

It was hard to tell them about Beauregard Clay, Jamilla, and Joseph. When she got through it, she closed her eyes so she wouldn't have to see their pity.

"He tried to...to..." Angela couldn't get the words out. "And she blamed you? I don't get it."

"I don't either," Sarita jumped in. "You were *dragged* into that repul-sive man's house. It makes no sense that she'd lay the fault for what happened to her son on you, *Granmè*."

"Doesn't it?" Rosemary opened her eyes, gave Sarita a short, bitter smile. "Who else could she blame? Her lover? Herself? How was she to have lived with that?"

Still reeling from the revelation that Bobby Taylor hadn't abandoned her and his baby daughter, sickened by the injustice of what Rosemary had endured, Cynthia spoke without thinking. "Nobody thought to go after the people who actually killed him?"

"You mean, the police? Accuse them of causing the death of a black man in their custody—a black man who'd confessed to stabbing a rich, white man." Rosemary did her best to keep the mockery out of her voice. "Bless your heart, Cynthia."

Cynthia winced. "That was stupid of me. I should learn to keep my mouth shut."

"That's not likely to happen after all these years, so never you mind." Jane reached over and patted Cynthia's knee. "We've gotten used to it." As she intended, her flip remark smoothed over any awkwardness, and she ventured to ask Rosemary, "We can assume that's why she killed Sarita's father. She killed your son because she blamed you for the death of hers."

Rosemary thought back to the day she'd seen her son for the first time since he'd been born, walking toward her, his pregnant wife with him. It was that one and only visit to her that had caused his eventual death. "Yes, ma'am. That's why she killed my Bobby. But first she killed my husband." As one, the women recoiled when she added, "Fact is, I was pregnant with Bobby when I got the news. Lester was on his ship when it happened."

Luca was the only one whose first reaction wasn't empathy. God help him, he already sensed where this was going. "Was he on the *Queen Mary*?"

Rosemary knew he'd put it together quickly. She could only hope he'd hear her out, let her get through it all before he turned her down, as she was sure he would. "Yes." Looking at the others, not at him, she went on. "Bobby's father was an English seaman. He and I met when the *Queen Mary* pulled into port in New York. We had a long distance romance, and we were married aboard." She smiled as she recounted one of her few happy memories.

Cynthia shook her head in wonder, looked at Sarita. "I didn't know any of this."

"You didn't know, because Bobby didn't know. Just like he didn't know who stabbed him and dumped him in the desert for the coyotes." Rosemary held onto her dispassionate tone, but her eyes belied the emotion she felt. "Most likely, he thought it was just somebody he owed money to who caught up with him." Steeped in regret, she leaned forward. "Cynthia, *cher*, I don't know if he would've grown up a better man if I'd been able to raise him. I know the folks who did bring him up were good folks who did their best. But I will always wonder…"

She let her voice trail off on the thought, finished off the contents in her glass, and a sympathetic Angela refilled it to the brim.

"With Les, they told me it was an accident on the ship. But I knew it was Jamilla who set an astral after him."

"What's an astral, *Granmè*?"

"In this case, it's a spirit that's under the control of a practitioner who wants to use it to do harm." Luca answered Sarita before Rosemary could.

"I don't do that," Rosemary said adamantly. "I don't use my power to hurt. Vodou is used for good purpose by most. The idea that it's wicked is a wrong-headed idea, a lie put out to discredit us, to frighten folks away from the glory of it. Jamilla was an exception. She fed off the dark side until it ate her alive. I have devotees—*hunsi*—like

Antoine. They've gone through the rite of fire, they're qualified to assist with ritual activities, and they abide by my orders. They've been helping me in the fight against the foulness she created. But they do only good, not harm."

She watched them as they watched her, knowing that these moments were the most important of her life. If she couldn't convince then of her sincerity, of the danger, they were all finished. "Jamilla and I chose different paths, and after Les, I saw she wasn't going to stop. So I gave up my baby, my little Bobby. I hid him from her as best I could. I thought, if Bobby's safe from Jamilla's eyes, I could use my own powers to hinder her. She was growing so strong, you see. I was told in a vision it was my job, my lot in this world, to thwart her. I gave up my whole family, my whole life, in trying to defeat this."

"This? You mean, this one woman?" Luca's eyes narrowed.

"She's no longer a woman." Rosemary tried to think how to explain. "She's altered. By the enormity of her deeds, she's been absorbed into something much bigger, much darker, and much more dangerous. Whatever you want to call what she is now, must be stopped."

They all sat, silently absorbing it. The only sounds to be heard were the shouts and laughter of the Halloween revelers outside that filtered through the windows as they went door to door. Antoine had cast a circle around the perimeter of the property to hide its occupants from those intent on harm. The spell wouldn't last indefinitely, but while it did, it concealed the house from everyone, friend and foe alike.

Rosemary continued, "That's why I stayed so far away. I thought...I hoped and prayed, that if she believed I had no interest, she'd leave y'all alone. And she did." She added, "Until now."

"It's on the ship, isn't it? Whatever this thing is."

"On the *Queen*?" Sarita stared at her husband. "Why would you say that? Did you have some kind of vision?"

"I didn't. Alana did." Luca bit off the words.

"Alana? What did she see?" Sarita's heart lurched. The fears she had for her daughters were coming true.

"I'll tell you. But I need to ask your grandmother something else first. Is Avi one of your *hunsi*, Priestess?" Luca already knew the answer. The pieces were falling into place for him, Alana's premonition running through his head:

Daddy, there's a monster...it wants to hurt the ship. It wants to hurt all of us...

"Yes, he is." She looked at Sarita. "He wanted to help you. When Santi hurt you."

"Avi knew about that?" Sarita's jaw fell. "But he's the one who brought me the drugged coffee. If he knew it was drugged—"

"He didn't know, sweet pea. Not until later. But even if he had done, I told him we couldn't interfere. That chapter in your lives, it wasn't for us. Certain things have to play out as they're meant. It was for the spirits onboard, for you and Luca to handle. And Marisol."

Her eyes shifted over to the others, then latched back onto Luca. "That experience changed the whole direction of that young woman's life. Knowing she saved Sarita made her stronger. And Lord, she will need that strength now."

"What do you mean, *Mamman*?" Cynthia cut in. "What's happened to Marisol?"

"Oh, my God." Angela's whole body jerked. "She's on the ship. With Ro."

As it all sank in, Jane breathed, "But why? Why the ship? Why Marisol?"

Rosemary shifted her attention to Jane. "I can't answer that first question. It's another long tale, and we don't have the time. But as for Marisol..." She thought of what the girl was experiencing as they spoke. "Marisol's abilities were what drew the monster to her. She's grown much stronger over the past few years, but buried underneath, there's still a lack of confidence. That self-doubt leaves a rip in the *ti bon ange*—a part of the soul where the devil can sneak in." She focused back on Luca. "She saved your wife's life. Now you have to help save hers. All of you."

Daddy, there's a monster…Daddy, who's Marisol?

Luca sprang up out of his chair. "No. Hell, no. Don't even think it, Priestess. It's out of the question."

"Luca! Why would you speak to my grandmother like that?"

Rosemary and Luca ignored all as they faced off. "I can't do it without them, Luciano."

His face was hard and cold. "They're five years old. You're talking about my children."

"They are strong, powerful beings. More powerful than any of us. And they will die tonight, if we don't stop this now." Rosemary pushed herself up too. "They either come with us, or we all die here, together."

"I saw Alana's face today. She was scared out of her mind." Luca was shouting now. He didn't care.

"And she'll keep on bein' scared until we get this done, but at least she'll be alive," Rosemary shot back, while the others watched them, thunderstruck.

"Stop it, both of you, and talk to us." Sarita was trembling, but she spoke up for the other three as well as herself. "*Granmè*. Please."

"It's grown bigger than Jamilla, Sarita, much, much bigger than her petty revenge. Whatever she started, whatever she did to gain the dark power she harnessed, it's become something grotesque." Even with her best efforts to stay calm, there was a hitch in her voice as she looked from face to face. "Don't say you don't feel it. The bad energy. It's everywhere—evil breedin' more evil. If we don't stop it—all of us, together—*tonight*—the night of the thirteenth moon of the year—it wins. It'll take the ship first. Then it will take the rest."

"You're asking me—us—to use our daughters. You're out of your goddamn mind."

"Get a hold of yourself, Luca. What's gotten into you?" Angela sounded mortified. "You weren't raised to behave like this."

Luca reverted back to childhood when she scolded him. "*Cugina* Angela, do you understand what she's asking? She wants us to bring our little girls to face some kind of demon." He turned to face Rosemary again, shaking with fear, furious with her for causing it, but trying hard not to say anything more that would shame his family. "Do I have that right, Priestess?"

"Yes. That creature has taken over Marisol. She will die in less than four hours if we don't try to stop it."

She paused to let that sink in. "Are you going to let that happen, Luciano? Those four little girls of yours—my great-grand-babies—wouldn't even be in this world if it weren't for Marisol. And your wife—my only grandchild—would be in the ground, like my Bobby and my Les."

"No. No. This can't be." He pulled at his hair with both hands. "It's crazy. You're crazy."

"I am *not* crazy, and I think I've had just about enough of your sass. What did you think, boy—that you were given those powers of yours so you could pop over to Italy to eat ice cream with your wife when you had a mind to? You have a *responsibility* to your magickal heritage. Do you know what my life has been like while you've been enjoying yours?"

"Oh, I've had it easy, have I, according to you?" He laughed bitterly, choking back tears. His pain had started to ease, just a little, with his father's death, knowing he was finally at peace. But Santi, whom he visited regularly, showed few signs of improvement. "You're kidding me, right? The only happiness I've ever had is with my wife and daughters, and you want me to put them in danger."

"No, honey, I don't." Rosemary was so drained she could barely stand. "I want you to help me save them." Her body quaked visibly. "You don't have a choice. None of us do. It's this or death. For more than sixty years now, I have fought this, done all I can to keep you safe. I'm wore out. I can't do it anymore. Not alone. I need all of you. Thirteen souls, on the thirteenth moon, if we have any chance at all to beat this thing."

"Luca." Sarita came up next to him, and placed her hand on his back. "She's telling the truth."

"No." Like a child in a nightmare, he had his eyes squeezed shut, afraid to open them.

"I can feel it." Her voice shook. "Can't you?"

He broke down. "Oh, God. Oh, my God, Sarita. They're *babies*. They're our babies." He pulled her in, sobbing. "They're *my* babies. I *can't*. I can't lose them. I can't lose any of you."

Angela and Cynthia edged closer to the young couple, Cynthia with her arm around her daughter, and Angela's around Luca. While they held onto one another, and Jane pressed her hands against her mouth in a gesture of helplessness, the priestess stood, straight and still, bearing it all, as she had for decades. She let them cry out their grief, their anger, their frustration, knowing full well that once they had, they would be prepared to do the necessary.

Still, she had to tell them, one more time, because she loved them, "I am sorry. I am so sorry to bring this to your door."

"How can we help, Priestess—Cynthia, Angela, and I?" Jane wanted to know. "I don't mean to say we don't want to. I'm sure I speak for all three of us when I say we do. But, in what way?"

"You ladies have more power than you know."

"Us?" Angela gawked at Rosemary, then at the other two. "*We* have power?"

"Yes, Ma'am. There's all kinds of power. Regular folks don't see the ghosts that are all around us. Not because they can't, because they won't. They're too darn scared to see anything but what somebody else tells them to see. But Angela, Jane, Cynthia—y'all forced yourselves to see—took a good, hard look at your mistakes, your weaknesses, and changed for the better because of it. You helped each other change for the better. You are the wiser and the tougher because you looked your own demons in the eye. I expect you can look this one in the eye just as well."

"Sure." Angela hadn't bitten her nails in years. But now she chewed on her thumb cuticle until it bled. "Easy peasy."

"Easy or otherwise, we'll help however we can." Jane looked back and forth between the other two, as resolute as she'd been when she convinced them to get rid of Naag's body. "Am I right?"

"Yep. I'm not saying I'm not scared to death, but I'm not leaving Ro or Marisol to face whatever this is on their own."

"You know I'm in. If my daughter and granddaughters go, I go." Cynthia's brow creased. "*Mamman* Taylor, you said, 'thirteen'. With the girls—" she risked a glance at Luca, who still looked shattered—"we're only ten."

"You're right." Exhausted, Rosemary finally sat. "I should have said, thirteen, if the others are still alive."

CHAPTER FIFTEEN

Saturday, October 31, 2020,
nineteen hours before the end

In her initial panic, she banged on the door and shouted. When she realized no one would hear, she tried to remain calm, searching around the door frame for a hidden interior handle or a way to break the seal. But the old freezer was not up to code. And to think they'd kept it only because she insisted.

There was nothing within but an empty cardboard box, which she had the presence of mind to flatten and fold, making a cushion between her thin clothing and the metal floor. She knew that to preserve her air supply, she should try to remain still, but wouldn't the lack of movement only lower her body temperature that much faster? Her expertise in herbalism didn't much help when it came to hyperthermia. How long did she have until she was in serious trouble? The morning crew wouldn't be in until six. It was unlikely she could last much longer without serious harm.

Only one hour later, her hands and feet were already aching. She knew this was due to the surface capillaries constricting. Her muscles had tightened. In reaction, she couldn't stop shivering. At less than ninety-five pounds there was little fat to insulate her, and the cold was quickly penetrating her core. Soon her nerves would be too frozen to signal any pain.

Why hadn't she let them unplug it, at least? Had she, on some level, known this was where she must die someday, in penance for Naag?

By five a.m., she wasn't afraid anymore. She was too numb to be afraid. Her brain was so sluggish, she couldn't even remember how she'd gotten trapped in the first place. She knew how it worked. She'd fall asleep, effortlessly, and wouldn't that be a nice change for someone who'd tossed and turned fitfully for months? All in all, this was one of the easier ways to leave this world.

And why not? What was left for her? Her husband was gone, her friends had moved away. As the heat leached out of her, she thought about that. Why was she still here? She was no different than the spirits on the ship who stubbornly clung to this realm, longing for something that no longer existed. She was already a ghost, in all ways but one.

Leaning her head on the frozen side panel, she gave up the fight, and let her eyes drift close.

In the dark, from far away, it seemed, someone called her name.

"Can you hear me?"

Behind her lids, she sensed light. Someone grasped her shoulders, shook her gently.

"Rohini. Can you hear me?"

That voice. She knew it. She tried to open her eyes, but they felt so heavy.

"Rohini." Now came light taps on her cheek. Whoever it was, would not let her sleep. "Move. Stand up. *Por favor, amada mía.*"

Dimly, she remembered the words.

Her eyes fluttered, opened. The enclosed space seemed warmer, brighter. And then—

"Cristiano?" she whispered.

In disbelief, she felt his touch, the heat of him, as he ran his hands up and down her arms. He frowned "*Dios.* You're freezing."

"Cristiano?" she said again, as she struggled to sit up. "Oh, God. Are you truly here?"

"I'm here." He smiled at her, and his eyes misted. "I'm here, *sangre de mi corazón*. I've missed you."

"Oh, Cristiano, I've missed you too." She launched herself at him, joy flooding through her at the feel of his arms around her. "I've missed you so." She couldn't cry. Her tear ducts were blocked from the cold. "I thought you were dead."

"I am dead. I would never have left you otherwise. I told you that once. Did you not believe me?"

Her own fingers had a nebulous quality to them, as she touched his face, his lips. "Then, how? How can you be here—like this? I can feel you."

"We're trying to save your life. You have to get out of here. You have to call for help."

"No, no." She didn't think to ask who he meant by 'we', and didn't care. He was *here*. She tightened her hold, as if by will alone she could hold him forever. "Talk to me," she murmured against his shoulder. His strong, solid shoulder. "Please. Oh, my darling, I've been going mad."

"I'm sorry. I couldn't prevent it."

"What happened to you?"

"I had a heart attack." He said it as though he was surprised she didn't know. "I knew it would happen one day."

"We searched and searched." Trembling in his arms, she told him, "I never stopped looking for you."

"I know. I saw you. You couldn't find me because the tide took me." He chuckled. "The last thing I did here was feed the fish. Appropriate, don't you think?"

She stared at him. "You can joke about it?"

"Everybody dies," he reminded her. "My only regret was leaving you." He kissed her forehead, jiggled her lightly once more. "Stand up, *menina*. Move."

"*No.*" She gripped him tighter. "No." Though her voice sounded vague to her own ears, she clung to him like a burr. "I want to come with you. I want to be with you."

"It's not your time. Not for a long while yet. You have important things to do. Your friends need you. Marisol needs you."

"Marisol?" She couldn't remember. Her shivering was so severe now, she couldn't form the words. "I'm so tired of being alone."

"Oh, come on now." He made a sound of mock impatience. "This is not the brave woman I married."

"I'm not brave." Her words slurred as she slumped against his chest, swam in and out of consciousness.

He rocked her and caressed her, transferring as much warmth to her as he could. "Yes, you are, yes, you are." Laying his cheek on the top of her head, he rubbed against her hair, and grinned as he thought of something that was sure to rouse her. "You're the girl who seduced me."

"I...what?"

"You seduced me. We knew each other only one week, and you took my virtue."

She lifted her head to gaze at him as she tried to think, to remember. "That's not what happened. You kissed me first."

"No, no, no." He laughed at her indignant expression. "You gave me the signal. Admit it, *chica*. You wanted me. And you were brave enough to take what you wanted. Thank God." He was wearing the warm, beguiling smile she'd yearned to see again, and it was then that she noticed how wonderful he looked—how vital and young.

She had so many questions. What was it like where he was? Was his family with him? But her body was shutting down, quaking so much she thought her bones would snap. If she were going to save herself, she needed to do it soon. "You're saying you want me to be brave."

His smile faded, and he gave her a look of longing. "You must live your life as if I were still with you. Because I am, *mi alma*. Always."

If only she could cry. If only she had the tears. "Kiss me. Please, oh *please*, kiss me. Just once, before you go."

It all came flooding back when his lips touched hers—everything they'd shared—every conversation, every meal they'd created side by side, every walk by the sea, every squabble, every time they'd joined their bodies in passion. It was all still real, still cherished within her. The memories infused her with heat, with strength.

He was right. She *was* brave. She'd been brave enough to leave India on her own, brave enough to outwit a madman for ten years, to endure being shunned by her family, to use every penny she had in the world to open a restaurant with three strangers. That's what he'd loved about her. That she, like he, had persevered.

She'd been a fool. A fool to wallow in sorrow. She should have known he would want her to live—fully live.

When he released her, he brought his mouth to her ear and whispered, "Make me proud. I'll be waiting for you, I promise. But for now, *wake up*."

She jolted and her eyes flew open. The freezer was dark and cold, and once again, she was alone. But she could hear sounds coming from the scullery. Someone was there.

"Help me." Her cry was faint, but summoning all her remaining strength, she willed herself to use the cardboard she sat upon to slide across the metal base of the freezer, and reach the door. She pounded on it. "Help. *Help*."

It was wrenched open, and Avi went wide-eyed to see the woman he'd been told to recruit tumble from the freezer. She grabbed for his trouser leg just as he reached down to swing her up into his arms.

"I've got you. I've got you. You're safe."

"Marisol." If he hadn't already known, he wouldn't have understood. Her lips were stiff and blue, and she felt like ice in his arms.

"I know. We'll fix it. First we need to get you warm."

Unsure, she peered at him, trying to place him. Then she remembered. "Clam…clam chowder?"

"Yes, ma'am," he said, shifting her from right arm to left, as he shook off his suit jacket one hand at a time, to wrap it around her.

At eight a.m., three hours or so after Avi brought Rohini back to her stateroom, bundled her with blankets, brewed her one of her herbal teas, and cautioned her to drink in small, slow sips, Michael McKenna woke up, abruptly alert, with a sense of urgency he couldn't fathom.

It was the smell, a smell he recognized with dread: Acetone, bad eggs, and bitter almonds. Every day, for weeks before Inez succumbed to the disease that ravaged her, he would leave her hospital room carrying those odors with him. No matter how long he stood under a hot shower, what soap or shampoo he used, the acid-sour smell of terminal sickness that clung to his skin and hair would never wash away. That morning, the smell filled his bedroom, and before he even adjusted his eyes to the early sunlight filtering through the blinds, he knew what he would see.

He sat up. Inez was standing at the foot of their bed, looking just as pallid and skeletal as she had two hours before she died. After years of working aboard the ship, hearing tales of hauntings, he understood that if she appeared to him as she'd looked in death, if that ominous odor was still with her, she was not at peace.

What did it say about him that he was still so happy to see her?

She stared at him, her eyes welling, as she struggled to speak.

"What is it?" he said, his tone gentle, coaxing, while his heart slammed against his chest. "Tell me, love. What do you need? What can I do?"

When she tried again, the sound was savage with terror, words that eviscerated him:

"*Michael. My baby. Help my baby.*"

He didn't think. He leapt from his bed, threw on clothes, shoes, grabbed keys, and was out the door without a backward glance at the apparition of his wife.

As a panicked Michael was speeding toward the *Queen Mary*, Emilio stirred, stretched out his arm to reach for Marisol. To his disappointment, her side of the bed was empty. There went his plan for early morning lovemaking. He should have guessed she'd take advantage of her overnight stay aboard to get an earlier start on her day. He'd sure as hell misjudged her work ethic, hadn't he? And so much else about her besides. Never was he so glad to be wrong.

Pressing the pillow she'd slept on to his face, he breathed in. Did he detect the scent of cinnamon and sugar he'd come to associate with her, or was that wishful thinking?

When he realized what he was doing, he chuckled to himself, and thought, Dude, you're like a lovesick puppy.

After basking in the feel of her in his arms as he fell asleep the night before, he wondered if he might be able to persuade her to make the arrangement more permanent. Not marriage. Not yet. Ever mindful of her relative youth in relation to him, he thought he might present the idea of her living on the ship as one of convenience. He'd be more than willing to share his stateroom, but if she preferred, he could offer her one of her own. The suites the women had used were still leased to

The Spice. He'd toyed with the idea of subletting them back to the ship managers for hotel guests, but for the time being they sat empty. Which seemed wasteful, is what he could tell her.

That would be a good way to approach it, he thought, as he got out of bed and headed for the bath. A casual offer of accommodations, in the name of expediency. A perk of her employment, a gesture from him and Rohini, for a job well done.

And she'd see right through that. He grinned, trying to guess what smart-alecky retort she'd make in response.

By nine a.m., he was showered, shaved, and dressed, anxious to get downstairs to see her, when there was a soft knock. It was more than a little surprising to see Rohini standing at his door with Avi, whom he and Marisol had just seen the prior evening at Chelsea's.

"Uh oh, is this a coup? Are you stealing my partner and taking over The Spice?" he joked, pleased he'd come up with the off-the-cuff quip. His mood was so lighthearted, he didn't notice at first that Avi had his arm around Rohini. He was sure they didn't know each other very well. When it clicked that there was trouble, his smile faded.

"Can we come in?" Avi said.

They'd just entered, he'd just shut the door, when there came another knock, a forceful one this time. "Open up, Em."

When Michael stepped in, Emilio was paralyzed by the crazed fear on his face. "Where's Marisol? Where's my daughter?"

"What do you mean? Isn't she downstairs?"

"Your place is locked up," Michael panted. "I've been running all over this ship. Where is she?"

"It's locked because I locked it." Avi told them. He reached into his pocket and handed Rohini back her keys. "More than that, there's a spell on it. Marisol's in there, and she's safe, for now. But before you go tearing downstairs again, there are some things you both need to know."

CHAPTER SIXTEEN

Saturday, October 31, 2020,
fourteen hours before the end

For Avi, the adage about the messenger had genuine substance. Even if they were successful in their mission, forever after, whenever Michael McKenna saw him on the ship he'd be reminded of this, and he, Avi, would always be associated with his ineffable suffering.

They were in the sitting area of the suite, Emilio and Michael on the couch, Rohini in a chair across, and Avi leaning with his back against the wall facing them. Not by one centimeter had Michael moved. His eyes stayed locked on Avi, and his skin went gray. Emilio grabbed hold of Michael when he slumped forward, slapped him on the back until he breathed in, red washing over his face.

As for Emilio, all the life punched out of him. His forbearance was for Michael's benefit. Only he knew what a thin veneer it was, that it might easily crack. He'd lived the last decade of his life taking charge, but now he felt what he hadn't felt since he was a child. He wanted to cry in his mother's lap.

He kept his 'man mask' in place, and said the expected and inane. "You're sure? There's no mistake?"

"I'm afraid not, dear. She locked me in early this morning. I'd have died if Avi hadn't found me." Rohini shuddered again as she remembered the distortion of Marisol's features, how they'd warped into Naag's. She couldn't look at Michael, not while she was saying this. "It isn't her. It's not Marisol."

"So what do we do? What's the plan?" Emilio sounded more belligerent than he meant to, and forced himself to reign it in.

"The spell I used should hold until the priestess gets here to perform the ritual." Avi paused, decided it was best to be blunt. "The operative word being 'should.' I'm pretty good at this, but I'm not up there with Mambo Taylor. As the hours wear on, for the amount of time we need it to work, it might be like trying to use a squirrel trap to hold a wolverine."

He checked his watch. "It's ten fifteen. She'll be here with the others in just under eleven hours. Until then, your job is to stay with it"—he gave Michael a swift side glance and amended—"with Marisol. Talk to her, keep reminding her of who you are, who she is. She's still in there, but she's being...restrained." What he didn't say was how life-threatening to her that struggle for control was.

"Where?" Emilio wanted to know, since Michael still hadn't spoken.

"In the back room behind your kitchen."

"The scullery, where the freezer is?" Rohini asked, to be sure.

"Yes, ma'am. I expected it to go down there this morning, and I managed to charm the perimeter. That's why I came across you, Ms. Rohini. It went in later, after you and I left. She—the entity, I mean—will try to trick and confuse you. Don't let it. Don't give it any information. It wants to break the bonds of the confinement, but it can't. Unless you do it."

Emilio frowned. "What do you mean?"

"It's restricted to that room," he clarified. You can go in and out of there, but if you go in and pull it with you past the boundary of the room, it escapes." Seeing the impact those words had, he tried to reassure them without being overly confident. "I can guarantee it can't get out for now. But it's very powerful, and it'll raise hell while we're holding it. That's also a guarantee. Unfortunately."

"For the love of God, stop saying, 'it.' You're talking about my daughter." Michael's voice was scarcely above a whisper when he finally spoke, but saying the words out loud crushed him. "My daughter." Rohini went to him, and he was flanked by her and Emilio as he wept.

Avi closed his eyes briefly. What could he say? "Mike, I swear to you, we'll do everything possible to get her back."

"Why eleven hours? Why do we have to wait that long?" Michael choked out.

"The moon has to be up. The priestess has to start the ritual at a certain point before midnight." Rohini didn't know much about Vodou, but she'd done some reading years before, when she'd learned that Sarita's grandmother was a practitioner. That brought something to mind. "You know Sarita will be with her," she told him. "Isn't that right, Avi?"

"Yes, ma'am. So I'm told."

With a nod of approval at the young man, she turned back to Michael, her hand on his arm. "See there? Marisol loves Sarita. That should help."

Emilio wasn't so sure. Not of anything, other than he was glad he hadn't had breakfast, because he was sure he would sick it all up. He wanted to run downstairs, grab Marisol and get the hell away. Michael was in pain, but so was he. It was time to ask the hard questions. "What are the chances of us beating this? Tell the truth."

Avi thought about hedging, but to what end? "I'm not sure. But I know if we don't, we're all pretty much done for."

It crystalized then. "Theresa. Our waitress." Emilio pointed to him. "You heard..."

His voice trailed off when he saw the look on Avi's face. That's when he knew. Whether they won the day or lost it, Marisol might already be dead.

When that hit him like a gut punch, he willed himself to stay put, to not jump up and break everything in sight. He turned his face, kept his hands balled in his lap, and prayed he could hold it together, as one image after another came to him. Her eyes—those lovely, intelligent eyes—sparked with excitement as she pitched him her mini pasties, lit with dry humor as she challenged Joy, burning with righteous fury as she tossed her drink, and glowing like candlelight as they tumbled together in his bed.

Marisol McKenna, smothered, extinguished—just like that. He didn't look at Michael. He'd fall apart if he did.

It was with macabre timeliness that static came over the ship's broadcast system just then, and a cheery female voice intoned, "Good morning, *Queen Mary* visitors and hotel guests, and a happy Halloween to you all! It's come to our attention that our house lines are down and guests are having trouble with cell reception. We should have those issues cleared up shortly. In the meantime, enjoy the ship's festivities, and be sure to visit our onboard restaurants for some spooky and delicious lunch and dinner specials." The speaker clicked off.

"It's started," Avi said. "We won't be able to get calls in or out. You'd better get down to the Spice. My guess is they'll be evacuating the ship soon. I have to leave you. Things are about to get ugly. There are some on board who'd never leave the ship willingly if she's in trouble. I need to work some more spells."

"Thank you, Avi." Rohini smiled softly. "Thank you for everything. And do be careful."

When he was gone, their guide through the madness, they were left with nothing but their horror.

The screams began as they were leaving the stateroom.

A group of revelers had rented a suite down the hall for the weekend to attend the ship's popular Dark Harbor celebration held annually during Halloween week. They'd spent the night getting drunk and gleefully being chased by actors in ghoulish makeup and campy costumes. But those vaudevillian scares were nothing compared to the fright the early riser among them got when he took the opportunity to get dibs on the shower while his friends were sleeping off hangovers. He twisted the vintage knobs in the tub. Brownish-red water gurgled from the spigot. He thought the pipes were corroded. The scent was not foul, but strong, like iron. It looked too viscous to be water. He held his hand under the flow.

His was the first voice that called out in terror.

More screams belted through the decks that housed hotel guests, as others turned their taps. Some were already immersed in showering when the water above their heads began to gush red. Covered in blood, they ran crazed into the halls.

Squeezing past the multitude of Carries, Michael, Emilio, and Rohini stayed close together as they scrambled down the steps that led to the restaurant. They were nearing the entrance when a burst of noise—indescribable, but ear-splitting as a sonic boom—ripped through the ship. For the first time in over fifty years, the *Queen Mary* bucked and swayed as though she were back on the high seas battling a hurricane. Whether of its own volition, or due to an overzealous crew member, the *Mary*'s horn blew—seven short blasts that indicated a ship in distress, creating more hysteria for those who knew what the signal meant.

The broadcast system snapped back on, and the three stopped to listen, straining to hear over the background pandemonium of shouts, pounding feet, and suitcases slamming against walls.

"Visitors and guests of the hotel *Queen Mary*, please do not panic. We're experiencing a small electrical problem—very small—that is *absolutely* not dangerous. We're working on it. In the interim, as a precaution only, we're asking everyone to exit the ship via the gangway by the main lobby." Though the spokeswoman now had to shout over the swell of noise in her vicinity as guests pushed their way toward Reception, she deserved a medal for remaining so calm. "Please do not take the elevators. If you can't walk down the steps, someone will be along to assist you. Hotel guests, we ask that you leave everything behind that is not *absolutely* essential when you vacate your room."

She paused. Someone could be heard whispering nervously to her. "Oh." She spoke into the mike again. "Uh, yes. There…there's a rumor circulating aboard that blood is coming from some of the stateroom taps. This is *absolutely* false. It's some kind of a…Halloween hoax. But if you feel you've been affected by this negative misinformation—if you imagine you saw a liquid substance coming from your taps that is *absolutely* not blood, please come see me, Kellyanne, at Reception, and I'll give you a voucher for another local hotel, where you can get cleaned up. Thank you."

Once the three entered The Secret Spice dining room, they locked up again, in case any officials came by and tried to force them to leave. When they reached the kitchen doors, Rohini and Michael almost collided with Emilio as he stopped short.

"Wait." Pressing his fist to his forehead, he breathed deep, fought to gather himself. "Wait." He turned to Rohini, and her heart broke to look at him. For the first time she saw how much his control was costing him. "What do I say to her? I don't know what to say."

"Speak your truth." She touched his cheek, gave him a fond smile "Remember what Avi said. She's still there."

But when they reached the back room—

"Guys, what the hell?" In exasperation, Marisol raised her arms out sideways. "Where *were* you?"

—she seemed her same self. Emilio was startled. Even Rohini faltered.

Behind her, ingredients were laid out on one of the stainless steel tables. She'd been mixing dough, as always. "I tried calling both your phones," she went on. "The lines are all down, and...oh, hi, Dad. What are you doing here? Any clue what's going on outside? I heard the announcement."

As for Michael, all he needed was one look at her. "Sweetheart, I brought something for you. It's in the dining room." With his jaw clenched, he tipped his head indicating she should follow. It was a test. A test he already knew was futile.

She swiveled to face the table, and with her back to them, continued kneading dough. "I can't stop now. This won't rise the way it should. Just tell me what it is."

"It's a surprise," he said, never looking away from her.

"Well, just bring it in here." She glanced over her shoulder at him with a quick smile, went back to her work, her hands steady and sure.

"Marisol." With a hand held out to stay the others, he stepped into the scullery, could feel the invisible barrier that Avi's spell had created between that room and the kitchen—a pronounced, tingling sensation that traveled across his shoulders, down his spine, to the tips of his toes. It was unpleasant but nothing more, and that was because it hadn't been put there for him.

"Marisol," he said again. "Look at me." His touch gentle on her shoulders, he turned her to him, and gazed down, straight into her eyes.

"Dad. Geez." She made a *tch* sound. "What is it? Kinda busy here."

Every gesture, every intonation was so exact, he wanted to fall to his knees and weep. But he didn't. His daughter could not afford his succumbing to that self-indulgence. "I know you're in there, Marisol. I love you, sweetheart. I *love* you with everything I have, and I won't leave you. I will die before I leave you—do you hear me? No matter how long this takes, or how hard it is, Daddy is here. Fight it, baby. Fight."

Her mouth hung open as she stared at him. "Have you lost your mind? What is *wrong* with you?" She looked over at Emilio and Rohini, who were still standing on the other side of the barrier, watching in helpless confusion. "Guys, what's going on?"

"You think I don't know my own daughter?" Michael said, mildly. He let go of her shoulders. "Rot in hell, you fucking piece of shit."

"Dad!" A look of shock on her face, she stepped back, and stared at Michael, saw his devastation, the defeated face of a father ready to give his life. And she couldn't help herself. She started to laugh. It was a thick, guttural laugh, emitted with triumphant relish, as though it had been waiting to be released for half a century. And it wasn't Marisol's. But when she smiled, Emilio's heart splintered to see that dimple he adored. "Why, sugar," she said to Michael, all at once speaking in a southern drawl, "is that any way to talk to your little girl?"

Michael went cold, submerged in it, like a man thrown into an icy lake, weighted down with rock, to sink into the endless murk. Not even when Inez's monitor had stopped beeping, not even the drawn-out, monotone, techno-cry of the flatline to follow, had dug this depth of terror into his soul. He needed to leave the room at once, before she saw, before she knew the victory she'd scored. He turned away from the thing that had taken over his child's body, and strode out.

Rohini hooked her arm in his. No matter how much anguish she or Emilio were feeling, she knew it couldn't compare. "Let's get you something to drink."

"I don't want tea," he bit out.

"Tea wasn't what I was suggesting," she said, and pulled him into the dining room, straight to the bar.

That left Emilio alone with the entity. He stared at her intently, looking for any hint, any trace of the girl he'd held in his arms throughout the night. He could see none. "You son of a bitch. What did you do to her?"

"Who can say?" Gaily, she shrugged. "Maybe she's down in the hull with the other lost, hopeless prisoners. Remember them, Emilio?"

The hair on his arms rose at the reference, but he schooled his expression. "What do you want from us? Why are you here?"

She laughed again. "You wanted me here. All y'all did."

"Huh. I don't recall any of us summoning a demon."

"Oh, don't you, now? You know how evil grows, sugar? It's like toxic mold. By the time you see one tiny dark spot, there's a whole bunch more, hidden, where that came from. You ignore it, it just gets bigger and uglier, now doesn't it? But nobody likes to clean it up. It's messy. So y'all pretend it's not there, y'all make excuses for it. Now it's choking you to death, and that's just fine by me."

Emilio had no response to that. But he had to know. "Why take Marisol? She's a good person."

"*Was* a good person," she corrected him. "Past tense. She was vulnerable enough to let me in, but strong enough to withstand me. I needed that resiliency." Her sympathy seemed so sincere, especially presented on Marisol's face. "But I am sorry for your loss."

"Yeah, I bet you are." He needed to leave. He needed five minutes alone, before he could face this again. He pivoted, started to walk away, when she called out, in Marisol's voice.

"Emilio, wait. Don't go."

How were they supposed to endure eleven hours of this? He clenched his eyes shut. "Stop it."

"I can't. Look at me, please, look at me. It's really me. I don't know how much time I have."

He remained still. With his back turned, she couldn't see the uncertainty and pain on his face as he deliberated.

No. Avi said it would try to trick them. Even when she called to him again, he kept going.

He made it to the kitchen doors, was about to push them open, when something made him peer out through the diamond-shaped windows.

In the dining room, Michael and Rohini sat side by side at one of the tables that overlooked the harbor. Daylight, dingy though it was, shone in on them, and Emilio could see Michael crying, his head in his hands, a shot glass of amber liquid in front of him. Rohini was leaning toward him, patting his shoulder, murmuring what he was sure were words of comfort, if any such words could exist for Michael McKenna. As different as night to day, he knew they'd become true friends, connected by tragedy, bonded by the shared loss of the one great love they would each have in this lifetime.

Was Marisol his one great love, he wondered? He'd certainly felt headed in that direction. Only a few hours earlier, he'd been thinking about asking her to move in with him, and now he was to believe she was gone, stolen from them all.

But, had she been? Or was she still here? Avi said she was, the creature told them she was not. It appeared that Michael, as her father, hoped she might be here, sensed she might be here, but also believed she might not.

Schrödinger's cat.

So what did he, Emilio, as her lover, believe? Until he knew for certain, did he deserve a seat at that table with Rohini and Michael? How could he mourn Marisol if he wasn't sure she was gone?

Decision made, he went back to face her, and when he looked in on her this time, his doubts grew. She was sitting on the high top table, a forlorn look on her face. Her legs hung off the side, and she swung them back and forth while she played with the flour she'd poured in a bowl, running it through her fingers.

It was *her*. It had to be her.

"Marisol?"

She looked at him, slid down from the table.

As he passed through the barrier, he felt discomfort, like a minor jolt of electricity. When he reached her, she circled her arms around his waist and buried her face in his chest.

"Something's got me, Emilio. Something terrible."

"I know, baby. I know." He tipped her face up to his. "We're working on it. We're going to get you free."

"Can you? How? Tell me, Emilio."

"We—" He stopped. He'd almost told her about the priestess, but thought better of it. "I can't tell you. You have to hold on. Just for a little while."

"I don't know if I can. It's so strong, whatever it is. And it overpowers me, no matter how much I try to fight it."

"How long have you been fighting with this?"

"I'm not sure." Her brow puckered as she thought back. "Weeks now, maybe."

The color drained from his face. "Weeks?" God help him—did that mean it wasn't her when they came together? That possibility was appalling.

"I'm not sure," she said again. "It all blurred." She dug her fingers into his arms. "I feel it happening again."

"No. No, Marisol, don't let it take you." He hung on to her, like a drowning man snatches at passing driftwood. Willing her to remain, he put everything he felt for her into his kiss.

The kiss *felt* like Marisol, like it had the first time and the last. He pushed his misgivings aside, relieved and nearly convinced they could beat this. Until he noticed that, as they were locked together, she was slowly backing him toward the barrier. If he passed through it with her in his arms, she would break loose. His opened his eyes. Hers were already staring at him with something much darker than determination.

He locked his legs. When she saw she could no longer propel him backward toward her freedom, she clamped onto his lower lip and bit down hard. He struggled, unwilling to shove her off, to hurt her physically, as long as she—*it*—was wearing Marisol's body. She broke through skin, and he tasted his own blood. He pushed back just as she released him.

"You sucker." Her laugh, wild with derision and fury, was changed again, and the creature spoke in another voice, one of many it had stolen from its victims. This one belonged to a real estate mogul from New York who'd made his millions as a slum lord. "Ha. Got ya. I grabbed onto ya good. Oh, man, it's true. There's one born every minute. Whadja think—love would conquer all? This isn't *Harry Potter*. She's dead. Get it? Dead. You'll never see your precious lover again."

Emilio drew the back of his hand across his bleeding mouth. "You're a liar. Marisol is coming back to me. She's coming back to all of us. You won't win."

This time when he walked away, he kept walking, his eyes stinging, his lip throbbing, his lungs like ice in his chest. He'd join Michael in that drink. Maybe two. They'd get through this, but damned if they had to do it stone cold sober.

"Ya won't be able to keep me in here forever!" With a roar, it picked up the bowl of dough and chucked it at the doorway. The bowl reached the barrier threshold, sprung back as though someone had smacked it with a bat, and crashed to the scullery floor.

By five that evening, just when Rosemary was stepping into Luca and Sarita's home, and Sarita was face-to-face with her grandmother for the first time in her life, circumstances aboard the *Queen Mary* were precisely as Alana had seen them in her mind while at her school's fall festival earlier that day.

The fiend, in its efforts to break free, was mauling the ship. Blood, both human and animal, slid all along the decks and seeped out of portholes into the waterway below. Directly above the ship, and no-where else in Long Beach but above the ship, wind blew and thunder peeled. All communications were cut off to and from the vessel. When the last remaining carloads of guests and employees had peeled out of the parking lot, thinking of nothing save their own immediate preser-vation, the *Mary* became abandoned.

Strangely, there was no press covering this phenomenon. Whereas the previous sighting of blood, along with the possible homicide aboard, had been covered as a scintillating whodunit and rehashed ad nauseam, this—the irrefutable presence of evil—was treated as though it did not exist.

The *Queen* had not been rendered invisible. She was right there in the port—a bastion of pride as definable and majestic as she had been for more than five decades. The dark clouds, the lightning and thunder that hovered above her, were evident to anyone who drove past or who might be strolling along the waterfront. The dripping blood, if not immediately recognizable as itself, was nonetheless obvious—a red fluid trickling into the harbor, impossible to miss. And yet, flagrant though it was, the malevolence remained unremarked upon by the media and general public, as though by ignoring something so sinister, it could be made trivial and therefore inconsequential.

Everyone familiar with the *Queen Mary*, who knew her history, who knew her to be one of modern man's noblest achievements in terms of inventiveness, art, engineering, determination and courage in the face of dire circumstances—in summary, a testament to the best the human race had to offer—should have been appalled that she was under siege by a menace that had settled in, for no other reason than its own narcissistic pleasure, to systematically pillage one of the greatest monuments of civilization.

But they were not. Somehow, it went unnoticed, save for those few who were, just as Alana had told her father, fighting a monster who wanted to hurt them all.

And that monster had trespassed onto a noble ship via the tiny fractures in the spirit of a valiant, loving young woman named Marisol.

CHAPTER SEVENTEEN

Saturday, October 31, 2020,
three hours before the end

At nine p.m., Luca walked across the *Queen Mary* parking lot with his wife and daughters. Even though the night was cool, sweat beaded on his forehead. To say he was terrified would do no justice to the enormity of what he felt.

What did Cepheus feel when the gods demanded he sacrifice his daughter Andromeda to a sea monster? Could it have been merely 'terror'?

His four little girls cried over baby goats locked in a pen. They loved piggyback rides, and sometimes needed him to sing them to sleep. Because of a fluke in their genealogy, he was compelled to offer them up to a beast who wanted to destroy mankind.

What his brother had devised to torture him had been terrifying. Seeing his mother's murder had been terrifying. But this. There was no word for this.

Holding Alexandra's and Alana's hand as Sarita held Niki's and Maria's, he thought of how often his wife had said she felt her powers were more a curse than a gift. He'd always tried to dissuade her from that mindset, but today he understood it to be true. He had more money than anyone could possibly need in one lifetime, but it hadn't bought him the one thing he'd longed for. He'd felt bereft of family all his life, until Sarita and their daughters. And now he had to gamble with them against the unspeakable.

He knew the how of the priestess's plan, could even say he understood the why. What he didn't know was whether or not he'd be able to go through with it.

Niki's voice broke into his thoughts. "Mom, did we bring any juice boxes?"

"Grandma has them. You can have one as soon as we get to Cousin Angela's car."

"How come we drove?" Alexandra wanted to know.

Before Sarita could respond, Maria put forth her theory. "Because Daddy's getting old. He's tired. And Grandma and Cousin Jane are getting a little bit fat. They're hard to carry now, right, Dad?"

"Maria, it's not nice to comment about people's weight. And Daddy's not getting too old." The gentle reprimand was automatic.

Her focus was more on Luca just then. She was as scared sick as he was, but knew she mustn't let him see it. In this instance, she had to be the stronger. He was barely hanging on. She could hear the cries in his head, like the death-moan of a bear caught in a steel trap. And she had no comfort to offer. She was parched of everything but fear. Even the saliva in her mouth had gone dry.

"So, why did we drive?"

Alex persisted in her interrogation, and Sarita thought carefully before she responded. "It's a good idea to have our cars here. In case we need them."

In case your father doesn't make it out alive, we needed another way to escape, if escape is possible. She kept that harsh reality to herself.

"What about your grandma, the priestess lady?" Niki piped up with her own question. "I know you told us, but I forgot."

"Daddy's going home to get her after we all meet at the car," Alex answered in Sarita's stead. "Because she's going to do the magick," Maria added. "Right, Mom?"

"She'll perform the ritual, yes. And we're all going to help," Sarita explained once more.

Under the circumstances, she'd done her best to outline things to the girls. They were told that what they were doing was necessary, but dangerous. Being so young, danger was an intangible concept, so to them, there was a sense of adventure in the outing—they got to stay up late, they got to go to the big ship, and best of all, they got to be with the people they loved most. But it was possible the adults had overplayed their composure. The quadruplets had no idea how helpless their parents felt. As a result, they weren't frightened at all.

Except for Alana. She stayed as silent as her father, kept her hand tightly in his as she gazed up at the ship, and wondered if she were the only one who'd noticed the dark liquid dribbling down its sides.

There were few lights glowing on the *Queen's* decks. In all her years in Long Beach, she had never been cloaked in such bleakness. Dark clouds clung to the sky above the ship as though they'd been pinned there, and from them lightning struck with eerie regularity, illuminating her hull in stark, jagged intervals. Yet high in the atmosphere, the moon shone full and bright, making it easy for the family to spot Angela's car as it pulled in.

The three women stepped out as soon as they were parked.

"They're here. Oh, good—I'm so thirsty. Grandma, can I have some juice, please?" Niki called out.

"Yes, you may, *menina*." The girls ran to her as Cynthia reached into the backseat and pulled open a cooler.

"Unlock the boot, and help me get the rest," Jane told Angela. "Sarita can help Cynthia carry the cool box. It's too heavy for her to manage on her own."

Juice wasn't all they'd brought along. When they saw that Sarita and Luca were hard-pressed to put one foot in front of the other after the priestess's revelations, Cynthia, Angela, and Jane took over the outlying details. Determining what they should bring was one. Not knowing how long they'd be, or if the *Mary* had lost her electricity as well as her phone service, they brought plenty of food and beverages.

But what else might one need to wage war against evil? Rosemary assured them she had everything in hand, including ritual clothing for them all. But when she was out of earshot, Jane insisted they err on the side of caution, and after much debate, they also brought along the following: a first aid kit, in case the one at the restaurant wasn't enough, four pocket flashlights and extra batteries, three plastic lighters, three rolls of duct tape, several dozen feet of paracord, bug repellant, six space blankets, an air horn, six containers of pepper spray designed to look like lipstick tubes and, solely at Angela's behest, a jumbo-sized bottle of milk of magnesia. They were prepared to fend off everything from a case of dysentery to a posse of muggers.

Tucked into Cynthia's handbag was her trusty old Derringer, which she'd squirreled out of hiding from a shoebox at the top of Sarita's wardrobe. But like Sarita, she never let on to her granddaughters how scared she was. While she handed out 100-percent, organic apple juice, she behaved as though they were having a tailgate party.

While Cynthia did that, Sarita took the opportunity to pull Luca aside. "How are you doing?" she whispered, and realized even before her husband gave her a frustrated glare how absurd the question was.

"The sooner we get this done, the better I'll be." He hated himself for sniping at her, but he was in torment. "Let's just get on with it."

When she bent her head, nodded in absolute understanding, he only felt worse. "*Granmè* said forty-five minutes after we're all onboard. I won't be able to call you, and I don't trust the telepathy, so let's set the timers on our phones. They should be exact."

He gave her a look of desolation. "This is insane. What kind of people do this to their children?"

"Desperate people. People who know they have no other option." She touched his face. "We have this one shot—one chance to be free of this thing—or certain death, Luca. You know it as well as I do."

"Why can't I come onboard with you now, and then go get her?"

"It senses majickal beings. The fewer at once, the better. *Granmè* said she wants us to try to take it by surprise."

"*Granmè* said, *Granmè* said," he mimicked bitterly. "I'm sick of hearing that old lady's name."

"It's not her fault, Luca."

"How do we know that, Sarita? We only have her word she didn't do something sixty years ago to have a curse brought down on the whole family." They'd been whispering, but the more agitated he became, the louder his 'whispers' got. "It's like the goddamn house of Atreus."

"Ssh." She shushed him, glanced over to where the others waited. "Please. Keep your voice down. And don't swear. If they hear us arguing, they'll get scared. I can't go through with this if they're scared. I *can't*."

That brought him back from the brink. She had as much to lose as he, and for the sake of their children, she was doing a much better job of holding it together. "I'm sorry." He pulled her to him, held her tight, kissed the top of her head. "I'm sorry."

When he let go, he had himself under control. "All right. Let's set the timers."

As Cynthia kept the girls distracted while their parents talked and embraced, Jane and Angela stood together on the sidelines, watching the couple. They couldn't hear what was being said, but Luca and Sarita's body language spoke volumes.

"Look at those poor kids." Angela murmured to Jane. "Did you ever think when we decided to do this—open the restaurant, I mean—that we'd be shoving dead bodies into our freezer, or holding an exorcism in the storage room?"

Jane thought about it. "I can't say it's wholly unexpected."

Angela gaped at her in disbelief. "You can't?"

"Well, no." She raised her shoulders. "I mean, Rohini and Cynthia might be our good friends now. But after all, we *did* meet them online."

Leave it to Jane to make her smile at a time like this. But their smiles were erased when the crackling commenced and Luca dematerialized.

Cynthia watched as Sarita fought to get her game face back on, then turned to address her daughters. "Okay," she said brightly, "time to go."

"Can we bring our juice?" Niki wanted to know.

Michael, Emilio, and Rohini had been grappling with the entity for nearly eleven hours.

Rohini proposed they work in shifts. On their first break each, they took turns driving to Michael's to shower and change. While he was home, Michael picked up a bunch of photos to bring back.

The three sat together, directly in front of the doorway between the kitchen and the backroom, past Avi's barrier, but within earshot and view of the creature. There they discussed Marisol, loudly, as though they were trying to get through to a coma patient, in the hope that while they talked about her, they were also talking *to* her. For Emilio, the photos Michael shared were both enchanting and heartbreaking: Marisol at age four, with her collection of sticker books and her favorite Mary-Kate and Ashley dolls. There was one of her at age eight, wearing a Saturn Girl Halloween costume. Of her high school graduation, arm-in-arm with her best friend Lizzie. Of her and Angela holding up Marisol's first successful attempt at Raspberry Chocolate Truffle Tarts.

And another of her and Inez sitting under their tree that last Christmas before Inez died.

The creature ignored them, other than to scoop up spoonfuls of wet, sticky dough to flick toward them. The dough bounced off the barrier and ricocheted back to end up splattered about the room, clinging to walls, table surfaces, appliances, even the ceiling. When there was no dough left to throw, it opened cupboards. Giant jars of olives, marinated artichoke hearts, sun-dried tomatoes—whatever was stored there was smashed—an antipasto of vegetables, olive oil, and broken glass across the floor. And the whole time this destruction was wreaked, thunder boomed, and the *Queen* shifted and groaned like a sick old woman whose death was near.

But it was excellent forethought on Avi's part to confine the creature to the back room. Being a restaurant manager, he knew the purpose of a scullery was mostly for storage. Knives and heavy cookware that could have been used as weapons were kept in the main kitchen. The creature was limited to petty vandalism. Nonetheless, the mess on the floor only made the thought of food that much more sickening. The three had gone without breakfast or lunch. But about six hours into their ordeal, Rohini scrambled some eggs, insisting they all had to eat like it or not, to keep up their stamina.

Which brought up another point—what about Marisol? Her mind had been taken over, but was her body being drained or sustained by the entity? It was when these speculations occurred that Rohini began to scrutinize the creature for any signs of thirst or hunger, in the hope that should any become apparent, it might mean that Marisol was still alive. And if she were, surely her body needed fuel too, to be at its best when the time came to fight.

With that in mind, Rohini filled a fourth plate of eggs, and the men watched warily as she went inside the circle to place it on the table, along with a glass of water.

For her trouble, it took two seconds to have the eggs and water dumped on her. When she did nothing but glare, the creature chuckled derisively and went back to speaking in the voice it had usurped from Jamilla.

"Tougher than you look, aren't you, sugar? I thought for sure you'd die in that freezer this morning. It won't matter one bit, because you're still going to die. *All* y'all are going to die. Your species is doomed," it prodded, as Rohini shook egg out of her hair. "I have already ushered so many of your politicians and so-called holy men into the blackest pits. You obey them like my astrals obey me. At least my astrals have no will of their own, but you—y'all choose to be zombies. That's what made this all so easy."

"Oh, blah, blah, *blah*." Rohini retorted as she left the circle. "Is this your great plan—to badger us to death with childish pranks and trite lectures?"

She brushed off the rest of the mess, annoyed with herself for losing her temper. Her experiment had failed. They still didn't know if Marisol might be hungry or thirsty. How long could she last without food or water?

"Let's take a breather, together," Emilio suggested. "Just ten minutes."

They needed it. What they were doing was like running a marathon across hot coals. After a while, they became accustomed to the brutal workout, knowing that to give up, to stop short, would set them ablaze and reduce them to ash.

They carried their plates into the dining room. While they were eating, Emilio got the idea to set Marisol's phone down outside the barrier, and open her playlist. They considered it a point for their side when Cardi B's "I Like It" played, and the creature shrieked, "If you had an oven in here, I'd stick my head in it."

It seemed implausible that Avi's spell continued to hold. If the creature could summon lightning and thunder, if it could make blood leak from pipes and walls, they had the prickling sense it was just toying with them while it bided its time. Yet, the barricade held, although for how long was anyone's guess. The creature tested it hourly, and each time, she seemed to withstand it for a longer period.

Day passed into night. At five minutes past nine, Rohini left the restaurant to go down by Reception and wait for the others. She descended the steps just as they walked in.

Sarita, Angela, Jane, and Cynthia did not register her presence at first. They'd stopped dead at the entranceway to stare at the damage their *Queen Mary* had sustained in only one day. Light fixtures were shattered, the vintage, rare wood paneling was splintered and stained, the brass rails tarnished and spotted. On the wall panel above Reception, it looked as though someone had taken a hammer to the sterling silver Thomas Mercer clocks that had once displayed the current time in six major cities throughout the world. The glass faces were smashed, the inner workings of springs, gears, and wires eviscerated and scattered across the black marble counter. Behind the desk, the replica medallion with the relief profile of Mary of Teck was split crossways, bits of plaster dusting the carpet below. And the carpet itself, with its whimsical fish design, was torn to shreds.

Observing the tableau from the steps, Rohini's eyes watered. She'd had hours to absorb the destruction, but seeing it through them, she was overcome by it again.

Angela was the first to spot her. "Ro! Oh, thank God." She dropped the bags of supplies, ran to her, hugged and rocked. "We were worried sick. We kept calling."

"I'm sure. The phones are useless." Rohini held on to her old friend just as firmly. "It's so good to see you." She looked past Angela's shoulder. "It's so good to see all of you." Releasing Angela, she bent to address the girls, who had four matching sets of eyes locked on her. "Hello, my darlings. How are you?" She noticed Alana's fretful expression. "Oh, my gracious, such a sad face. What's the matter, dear? Do I look a fright?" She touched the long braid going down her back, which she'd tied hastily hours earlier, and picked out a speck of scrambled egg she'd missed. "It's been a rather long day. I'm afraid I'm not at my best."

"Are you crying?" Alana whispered.

Rohini studied her with a keen eye, and summed her up, just as she'd summed up her mother when they'd first met. "Some. But I'm much better now that you're all here."

"Are we going to the restaurant?" Maria asked her.

"We will, shortly. I have some things to discuss with the grown-ups first."

"Alana says there's a monster on this ship." Alex stated directly. "Is she telling the truth?"

Rohini decided they needed straightforward answers. She stood up. "I'm afraid she is."

The silence from the children after that declaration was broken by Niki slurping the last drops of juice through her straw. "Oops. Sorry." She giggled. "Where's the trash?" She looked around for a bin, seemingly oblivious to the wreckage around her. Until she spotted the liquid dripping down the walls. "Ew," she said. "What's that?"

It was familiar yet sinister. Angela's eyes fixed on it, then shot back to Rohini. "Oh, my God. Is that…?"

Rohini closed her eyes briefly, and nodded. "It's also coming out of the taps."

"Holy shit," Cynthia muttered.

Sarita swayed where she stood. "How can this be real?"

"It's not exactly real." Rohini said, cautiously. Children were always less frightened by the truth than they were when they sensed the adults they depended on were lying. But she wasn't sure what Sarita wanted her to say or not say in front of her daughters.

"The monster did it. It will only go back the way it was if the monster goes away. It's a very bad monster, and we have to make it go away." That Alana's voice rang out clear and sharp was equally as extraordinary as her commentary.

Sarita fought past the obstruction in her throat. "Thank you for telling us, Alana." If nothing else proved her grandmother right, it was those words, spoken with such self-possession by her little girl. Unconsciously, she reached for Cynthia's hand. When she was a teen, she hadn't realized her mother modeled what strength in a woman meant. It was her turn to show that strength to her daughters. "I guess we better get started, then."

Fighting her own emotions, Cynthia clasped Sarita's hand in return. "How much time do we have?"

Sarita checked her phone. "They'll be here in thirty minutes."

"Right. Let's go change in Rohini's stateroom." Jane took charge. "I don't know the condition ours are in." She eyed the dripping blood with distaste. "I assume there's no water?" Being Jane, the question was posed as though someone had simply forgotten to pay the bill. "Mambo Taylor said we must wash our hair before we put on our tignons."

"We've been using the five-gallon bottles in the restaurant. I'll tell Emilio to bring some up." Rohini paused. "After we're ready, perhaps it's best if we wait in my room until the priestess and Luca arrive. We should all face what's in the Spice together."

The children ran up ahead as they climbed the steps to the suite.

"You wouldn't happen to have a blow dryer, would you, Ro?"

"I'm sorry, Angela. I don't."

"Darn it. I should've thought to bring one. I'm going to frizz up like a Brillo pad."

"Are you joking?" Jane said, irritably. "You're worried about your hair at a time like this?"

"You don't have Italian hair, Jane. You don't know what it's like. I'll be lucky if I can stuff it all under that scarf she wants us to wear."

"You could have brought two blow dryers what with the size of that bottle of magnesium hydroxide you insisted we bring. Why in heaven's name would you think we'd all need a stool softener?"

"Milk of magnesia has a lot of uses, Jane. I just thought—"

They almost tumbled backward when Sarita braked on the step above. Much to her mother's surprise and amusement, she whirled around to the two bickering women. "*Stop* it. I don't need this right now." The defilement of the ship she loved had only added to her terror, and she was hurt that Jane and Angela were indulging in their usual pecking at one another as if nothing out of the ordinary were happening. She couldn't know this was their coping mechanism, but she had no tolerance for it, not just then. "You two can play your stupid little game later. Or, I swear, laxative or not, I'm going to lose my shit right here, in front of my kids."

Neither said another word until they reached Rohini's.

Sarita answered Emilio's knock when it came. One look at him and her heart rolled over in pity. He seemed to have aged ten years since they saw him only four months earlier. It brought back to the forefront of her mind that she and Luca weren't the only ones who had everything on the line in this fight.

"Emilio. Come in." She glanced down at the water jugs he'd set outside the door. "Those must be heavy. Let me get one."

"I got them, thanks." They weighed forty pounds each, but he lifted one in each hand easily, hauled them in, and set them down by the bath.

"Everyone's in the bedroom, getting ready. I'll tell them you're here."

"Wait, just one sec. I wanted to ask you something, privately. It's about Marisol."

"Um. Sure."

She sat down on the couch, and he took a chair, tapped his fingers against his knees, as he thought about how to start. "Look. We never talked about this, you and I, when we were kids. But Marisol told me...she said you and she have a special connection." He kept his head down, didn't look at her, while he waited for what her reaction might be.

"Yes. Yes, we do." She no longer felt self-conscious discussing her powers with people she trusted, but for the life of her, she was so preoccupied, she didn't get where he was going with this.

Until he lifted his face to hers, and she saw the plea in his eyes. Just as pretty and long-lashed as they were when he was a teenager, they were now red-rimmed with exhaustion and terrible grief. "Can you tell if she's still in there? Because I can't tell. I can't, Sarita."

He let the tears he'd been fighting for hours fall. Years back, she'd have been the last person he'd want to see him cry, but now, it mattered not one whit what she might think.

"Oh, Emilio." Her eyes brimmed too, and she kneeled next to his chair. "I wish I could tell you yes, but the truth is, I don't know. I have no idea what we're up against. I'm following directions, same as you. But listen—" she reached for his hand—"we *all* love her. That's one of the reasons we're here. We want her back as much as you do."

He couldn't speak. But he nodded, pressed his palms against his eyes, tried to pull it in, to get himself under control.

When he was calmer, she said, "She's very brave. She saved my life. Did she tell you?"

"Yeah, she did." The words sounded rusty. "I know she's brave. I know if anybody can get through this, it'll be her."

But he looked so lost. And with that in mind, she hugged him, and he hugged her back. They held on, two old friends who'd once shared so much, and would now be on the same side of an apocalypse.

"Hey. Who are *you?*"

Emilio looked up from Sarita's shoulder to see the cutest little girl he'd ever seen, giving him the dirtiest look he'd ever gotten.

Sarita did the introductions. "Alexandra, this is Emilio. He brought up some water for us."

Emilio tipped his head warily in greeting while Alexandra continued to glare. "Why was he hugging you, Mom?"

"Emilio and I are friends." Sarita was the picture of composure. "Friends are allowed to hug."

Alexandra was not convinced. Her eyes narrowed at Emilio. "We already have a daddy at our house."

"Uh...that's...good to know." He patted his trouser pocket as Sarita stifled a laugh. "Where's my pen? I better write that down."

With one last stony stare at him, Alexandra turned, went back into the bedroom, and slammed the door.

Sarita couldn't help it. Even under the circumstances, she had to smile. "I'm sorry. She's our spitfire." And she was thankful, because Emilio smiled a bit too.

"Alexandra, huh?" he said, his tone droll. "Not Cynthia Junior?"

A short while later, there was no more laughter. Emilio was back in the restaurant with Michael. The women and girls were gathered in Rohini's sitting area, washed and ready.

Angela and Jane sat side by side on the couch, their hands clasped. Cynthia and Sarita were to Jane's left. Sarita with her head on her mother's shoulder, as Cynthia absently stroked her hair. Maria, Alexandra, and Niki sat crossed-legged on the floor in front of their mother and grandmother, but Alana had chosen to nestle into Rohini's lap, in the chair across. The quadruplets were quieter than usual. They'd had a long, restful nap, courtesy of their great-grandmother's spell, but even so, it was way past their usual bedtime.

The women were silent. As one might expect, they were reflecting back on so much, most especially on that fateful day they'd first stepped aboard the *Mary*, years before. How much that one daring decision had altered them all, in the most intrinsic ways.

The *Queen* had saved them. Now, they must save her.

Softly, Jane cleared her throat. "I'm not one for speeches," she began.

Cynthia grunted. "That's not the way we remember it."

"Oh, be quiet, Cynthia." When Angela snorted out a laugh, Jane elbowed her in the side. "You hush up too." She started over. "What I wanted to say, in case—" she darted a glance at the little ones—"well, in case I haven't made it plain, is that…I love you all." She paused. When she spoke again, her voice sounded hoarse. "I just wanted to be sure you knew."

None of them were surprised by the depth of her feelings, but they knew what it took for her to say it out loud.

Cynthia blinked rapidly. She would not face the devil with her mascara smeared.

"Of course we know, sweetie." Angela patted Jane's knee.

"We love you too," added Rohini.

There was nothing left to say. In continued silence, they waited for Luca and the priestess. Angela gnawed on a cuticle. Jane squared her shoulders. Cynthia held onto her daughter. Sarita prayed to herself.

And Rohini thought of Cristiano's words to her, 'Make me proud.'

When Rosemary boarded the ship, what dripped down the walls slowed, as though a healing hand had been pressed upon a wound. The entity lurking in The Secret Spice sniffed the air like a dog in heat. And the particles within it that had once been a woman named Jamilla sensed her presence, and wished she could tell Rosemary to run.

Contrition after six and a half decades came too late to help either of them. What Jamilla had lost was much greater than this longed-for victory.

The worst thing that had happened to her was not the thing she'd railed against the whole of her life. No, it was that she'd been given power. Had she not had it, she'd have continued on in anger and re-sentment, victimizing others even more unfortunate than she, holding up her circumstances to justify her mean spirit. Eventually, she'd have passed from this universe a dried-up shell of discontent, with no one to mourn her loss and plenty to give thanks she was gone. That would have been the end of her existence.

But she'd had power. Power in her hands had no chance of being used for anything but destruction. For the kind of woman Jamilla had been, it was inevitable that her feelings of envy and bitterness would one day become so uncontrollable, they would devour her.

It wasn't the first bite that did her in, nor the second, nor the third. But each time she perpetrated an abominable misuse of the gifts she'd been given, flies flayed her skin like tiny razors. Yet she didn't stop, couldn't seem to stop. With each enactment, her power burgeoned, and the headiness of it was impossible to resist. She hid herself away in the mansion she'd so coveted, as the fly stains crisscrossing her body proliferated, until not an inch of skin was left unmarked by mottled green and gray. She oozed from raw bites, while the scabbing of a thousand others itched relentlessly.

When the entity came for her, she went willingly. Anything to end the agony. She didn't know her agony had just begun.

So many Jamillas had been taken in this way—Jamillas of every race, sex, and creed. It was a triumph to pull them in, for they hadn't started out as evil. The indisputably wicked—pedophiles, News Corp. executives, physicians who took bribes from Coca-Cola—were easy pickings who knew what they were doing going in, and figured the pay-to-play was worth it. They were merely appetizers, while the ones like Jamila were much sweeter an attainment, both main course and dessert, challenge and reward. Wronged in some way, those like her rationalized their means to an end, but when that end came, they'd caused as much harm in the procurement of it as those who'd had intent to injure from the start.

It was interesting to the creature to observe how, over time, those fly bites, painful as they were, didn't even make a body flinch. Over the centuries, it saw that certain human beings would accept flies under their skin in the same way they reasoned away the deterioration of their compassion and decency—as a necessary compromise of conscience. Until they had no conscience left, and were enshrouded by a pestilence whose sole reason for stealing blood was to breed upon itself.

This was the entity using Marisol as host. It was not an impish being that threw eggs and smashed olives. It was a pandemic that collected souls, and the more it gathered, the stronger it became.

But Marisol was blameless. Seized, just as the *Queen Mary* had been seized, by a parasite sapping them of their will and energy, using them as bait to lure the best humanity had to offer—Rosemary Dupré Taylor.

Like the ocean liner she was now aboard, Rosemary had weathered much, survived all, and remained indomitable. This was the reason the demon craved both. If one were swallowed, so would the other be. They would be its gourmet meal, its *haute cuisine*.

Tonight, Rosemary would die, and the *Queen* would splinter into the sea. Their reign was over.

CHAPTER EIGHTEEN

Saturday, October 31, 2020,
two hours and fifteen minutes before the end

The odor pushed up her nostrils. It left a fetid taste in her mouth, burned past her throat into her lungs. When she and Luca materialized onto the ship in the hallway outside the women's staterooms, she didn't have to ask him if he could smell it, she could tell he couldn't, and neither would any of the others.

It was the tang a bad spirit gave off to keep good Vodou away, which was why it only affected her. Over the long decades she'd been a priestess, she'd eventually pinpointed the melded scents of caramelized sugar, dead frogs, and Clive Christian cologne. The combination produced a stench unlike any other. This time it was so pervasive it took all she had not to gag.

She pulled a white handkerchief and a tiny bottle of geranium oil out of her skirt pocket, sprinkled a few drops onto the cloth, and waved it in the air. The smell dropped back to barely tolerable for her, and she held the cloth over her nose, breathing through it until her airways cleared.

The deafening sounds of suffering she could do nothing about. The blaring wails being played for her as a soundtrack were human, even if they didn't sound it, certainly not the first time she'd heard them. The voices of broken souls had a different quality, especially with the entity broadcasting them from deep within its core. The creature took the remains into itself and amplified their screams, as though boasting, celebrating their acquisition. If the redolence of depravity wasn't unpleasantly familiar enough, the keening and laments officially welcomed her back to an old battleground.

They were its war cry, its campaign music. It was an attempt to demoralize her. And it worked.

Year after year, the number of lost multiplied. Each time she was subjected to their utter hopelessness, their entreaties for compassion, the part of her that wanted to scream back at them that they'd triggered their own ruin, dragged down multitudes with them, grew more caustic and querulous with her restraint.

As with the odor, the others were spared these voices. But if Marisol were still alive, those fiery cries were in her head, and being unprepared for them, they might do more than just drive her mad.

Rosemary still held on to Luca's sleeve. Hesitantly, he covered her hand with his. For the first time he was cognizant that what was taking place went beyond him and his family. The bloodstains and other fresh wounds to the *Mary* were his first wake up call, sights he knew must have demolished his wife. And though his senses weren't as tuned to the sounds and smells Rosemary was experiencing, he *was* a sorcerer. He could feel the malevolence. It perched on his shoulders like a vulture.

She spoke first. "Lord, have mercy. This is the worst I've ever borne. Give me strength, Lord, give me the strength."

At first, Luca thought she was talking to him, but when he looked down at her, her eyes were closed. She was praying:

"Oh dear Lord, please let me stay
Don't let the devil take me today
Give strength to this worn old body of mine
Restore the ship, restore mankind."

It came to him then that Rosemary was here to sacrifice herself. While he was taking that in, she let go of his sleeve.

"Let's get this done, boy."

They walked down the hall and knocked on Rohini's door.

The women were dressed in the ceremonial white clothing—ankle-length, flowing skirts and matching blouses made of cotton, the color a symbol of modesty and purity. They had wrapped tignons around their hair after it was washed, a cleansing that was a vital part of the ritual. They were now circled around the priestess on the deck outside the restaurant. Luca stayed off to one side, holding onto his daughters as though he'd never let them go. For now, he and the girls were only observers.

Rosemary carried her *ason*—the sacred gourd rattle that denoted her rank as high priestess, the title she'd worked so hard to earn under Toby and Zora's guidance many years before. In her satchel she carried herbs, oils, candles, rum, and other essentials she would need for the cleansing.

They'd not yet gone inside The Secret Spice. Emilio and Michael were still left to stand watch over Marisol, a task that was becoming more challenging as the minutes ticked by. The creature kept testing the perimeter, which was starting to give off sparks. As the hour grew closer to midnight, Avi's boundary was giving way.

This was why the priestess's first duty was to create a *veve*—a sacred drawing made with a powdery mixture of cornmeal and wood ash. It would help keep the creature contained, but its primary function was to act as a 'beacon' for the *loa*—a spirit who would assist in this most arduous of rituals. Within the circle of women, Rosemary began to fashion the drawing upon the wooden deck. When the loa descended from the heavens, it would walk through the drawing, scattering it to make its presence known.

The barrage to her senses, the sounds and smells that only she was subjected to, were an interminable strain on her constitution. She was concerned about the tremor that manifested itself these days when she was stressed or tired, but her movements stayed steady and sure as she knelt to pour the powder substance, first into a crossroads that called on Papa Legba to open the gates between the realms, and then into shapes—stars, triangles, two snakes touching heads, two flags—the representation of Danbala, the spirit whose assistance was most vital to their cause.

"I call upon Danbala, the Sky Father," she began, in a strong, clear voice, "the Creator of all Life on Earth, the creator of all Earth's waters—"

The blood that had slowed upon her arrival began to flow once again, and Luca herded the girls away from the walls. There came a low humming sound, and Rosemary recognized it at once as the beating of flies' wings. This did not bode well for their success. Abandoning the drawing, she stood up so quickly, her knees popped like bubblegum.

"Keep your arms covered and your hands in your pockets," she ordered. "Everybody stay in the circle. You too, Luca. And the girls."

Reaching into the satchel again, she pulled out another bottle of oil, rosemary this time—the most powerful oil one could use to repel bad spirits—and pressed a drop onto each of their foreheads. Around their periphery, the flies came in little black clouds, but the oil kept everyone safe from bites and deterred the flies from entering the circle. They zoomed round and round, looking for a way to breach Rosemary's majick. When none could be found, the more tyrannical among them gathered in the air near the humans, menacing them with their presence like tiny, buzzing henchmen, while the less ambitious gave up, settling themselves onto the fissured walls and splintered wood of the ship to feast upon the dripping blood.

Jane, in particular, detested flies. They put her so on edge, she was sure everyone could hear her nerves jangling. "Priestess, we brought insect repellant. Shall I get it?"

As soon as the words were out of her mouth, she wished she could take them back. Her face went pink at the look Rosemary gave her.

"Insect repellent? Well, darnation, why didn't I think of that, Ms. Jane?" She swept her hand over the drawing. "Would have saved me a whole lot of trouble here."

"I...er...I beg your pardon. It was a silly suggestion."

Rosemary dismissed her with a glance around the circle. "I'm goin' to ask you all to please not interrupt. I need to concentrate."

What she did not tell them was that this evil was the most potent she'd ever faced and their likelihood of conquering it was slim. At eighty-six, her store of energy was limited. She felt drained already, and she'd barely begun her task. The toughest part was yet to come.

But there was one among their assembly who could sense the priestess was wilting. And it was not Rohini the empath, nor Sarita the seer, nor Luca the sorcerer. It was someone else, someone they might not have anticipated.

Rosemary went back to the *veve*, continued her chant to the spirit Danbala, raising her voice over the escalating drone of insects. She managed to finish the drawing and the prayer, but moisture beaded on her forehead, and her hand shook like a violinist playing Bach. The rest of them were too focused on the increasing number of horse flies to pay her any heed. She'd been upstaged.

Sarita's heart skipped when Alana twisted out from under her father's hold, walked to the center of the deck, and with her back to them all, held up her hands, palms out.

Silence descended, sudden and absolute. The flies had vanished.

With a smile of triumph, Alana whirled to face them. "I did it! And I remember where I put them this time. I know where they are." They were so caught off guard they could only stare at her.

"*Menina,* you did a good thing," Cynthia managed, with a slight edge of panic in her voice. "And I will not get angry, I promise. But tell me the truth—did you send them to Grandpa Raul?"

"Uh uh." Alana shook her head, proudly. "I sent then back to where they were. Before."

"Where, sweetheart?" Though her mind was blown by her child's power, Sarita asked the question in the same way she'd ask where Alana put her pencil box. "Where did they go?"

Every one of the adults felt their hair stand on end at her answer. "Back inside the monster."

She was so pleased with herself. She even remembered where the goats from school had gone, and was about to give her father that happy news, when she got a good look at him, and her face fell. "Oh, Daddy. I'm sorry. Are you mad at me?"

"No." In two strides, he was next to her, knelt to fold his arms around her. "No, sweetheart. Why would you think that?"

She pulled back to study him. "You're not mad. You're scared," she determined. "Aren't you, Dad? You're scared something bad is going to happen to me."

"I'm *not* scared. And nothing bad is going to happen to you." Even as he denied it, he could see she knew he was lying.

"It might," she whispered. "That's why you have to let me help." She placed her tiny hand against his cheek. "I know you don't want me to. But I have to. Great-grandma needs us. She...she's tired, Daddy."

"Alana." Luca couldn't believe his baby was trying to comfort him, a grown man. Her father. It wasn't right. It shouldn't be. But he knew what he was seeing on her face as she spoke. Her eyes on his were not the eyes of a child. They were the eyes of a wise woman.

They were Rosemary's eyes.

That staggered him. He had no way to protect her, no way to shield her from her calling. How could he go on living if she were harmed, if he failed her? He'd shouldered so much loss, but this would break him. He knew it. And he couldn't stop it.

He didn't know he was crying, on his knees, crying, until Maria, Alex, and Niki huddled around him too, murmuring to him.

"Daddy, don't cry." Maria put her arm around his shoulder.

"Yeah, Dad." Niki imitated her baseball coach, gave him a light punch on the arm. "We got this. We can do this."

"Dad, if anything happens to Alana, you still have three of us. We all look the same."

Despite the pathos of the moment, that observation from Alex made him spit out a short laugh. It was a must they start chipping away at her sibling rivalry. "Three is good, Alex. But you're all different. I want all my girls." He look across to Sarita. "All five of my beautiful girls."

Watching them, Rosemary was overcome. A father's pure love was a miracle she'd longed to experience. Her mind flashed back to Les, placing his palm tenderly against the slight rounding of her stomach. One brief moment in so many long years.

"Luciano. It's all right, *cher*," she said, gently, impulsively. "The girls don't have to be here. I can do it without them."

"No, you can't." Sarita spoke up. "Alana's right. You're reeling on your feet, *Granmè*. This thing is strong, isn't it? Too strong. I can't feel it as well as you can, but I can feel it." She turned to Luca before Rosemary could reply. "I'm sorry. I know this is hard. They're mine just as much as they're yours, and I'm as terrified for them as you are. Maybe even more so." She glanced at Angela, gave her a soft smile of gratitude for what she'd told her earlier that day.

"Sarita—" Luca tried to interject.

"No. No more. Look around you, Luca. *Look* at what's happening here. This is our reality right now. And our daughter just sent hundreds of flies back to Hell or whatever it is, without even breaking a sweat. My girls and I are helping my grandmother. That's it." She exhaled and looked at Rosemary. "Tell us what you need us to do."

Rosemary didn't answer right away. She had a question for Luca first. "Can you handle it if I give you, Maria, Alex, and Niki a job, or are you going to keep cryin'?"

"He can handle it," Maria piped up, still with her arm around her father. "Don't worry. He's just having a bad night."

Niki rushed to Luca's defense too. "Yeah, we all get them at our house."

"He doesn't usually cry." Alex thought back. "Not this much, anyway."

"Mom says he's more dramatic than Grandma Cynthia," added Alana softly.

"Is that so?" Cynthia raised a brow at Sarita.

Sarita blushed and shrugged her shoulders at her mother.

Rosemary bit back a smile. She took one brief moment for herself, to be thankful. No matter what the outcome tonight, she'd experienced her family. This family, these children. They had certainly been worth the wait.

"All right, then, young ladies. If you're tellin' me your Daddy can handle things, then he can. Now, you three, come on over here."

From her stash of supplies, she took three blue candles and two small bottles of oil, handed one candle each to Alex, Niki, and Maria, and held out the bottles of oil to Luca.

"This vial here with the brown cap, is nutmeg oil. This one's ver-vain. Do not get them mixed up. Brown cap, nutmeg, blue cap, vervain, you hear me?"

Luca walked over, his mumble sullen. Regrettably, his resistance to the plan was now coming across as petulance.

"What was that?"

"I said I hear you. Geez." He took the vials, stuffed them in his pockets.

Rosemary cocked a brow. "All right, then. I need you to go down to the engine room—" she stopped, glanced over at Niki—"don't play with that wick, sweet pea. If that comes out, we don't have another, and we need all three"—and back to Luca—"go to the propeller box, and pour that vervain into the water."

"Why does he have to do that?" Alexandra was already enthralled.

"To make Juno's Tears." Before Alexandra could ask, Rosemary stopped her. "I'll explain it to you tomorrow, sweet pea, I promise. Right now, just pay attention. We're in a hurry, and this is important work you're doin'." She looked up at Luca again. "That's the first order of business. The next thing is to set those candles down, light them, and sprinkle that nutmeg oil around them." She knew Alexandra couldn't help but ask, so she told her, "That'll help bring the good ghosts back."

Luca frowned. "Ghosts?"

"The *Queen Mary* spirits, dear," Rohini chimed in. "They've been gone for weeks now. I'm sure they were driven away."

"That's right. And if we can bring them back, that'll help us turn this thing around." Rosemary patted her pockets. "Where did I put those matches?"

"I won't need them, Priestess."

"We brought a lighter, Luca. Take it." Angela tossed him a plastic lighter, but Niki stepped in front of him and caught it with ease. "Here."

She delved into the box of supplies they'd brought, stuck a flashlight in Alex's back pocket, and looped the coiled paracord across Maria's shoulder like a handbag.

"Why do we have to carry all this stuff, *cugina*?"

"Just in case. Don't rely on the majick, sweetie. With the way things are going, you never know."

"I think you're all set." Rosemary gave the three girls a smile of reassurance, as everyone circled around them to say goodbye.

"How come Alana gets to stay here with you?"

It was Alex who asked the question, of course, and the tone of it was unmistakable. Before Sarita or Luca could respond, Rosemary frowned at her. "Excuse me? Did I hear what I just heard? It sounds to me like my great-granddaughter is questioning my judgement on who should do what and go where."

Alexandra's eyes went wide. She wasn't accustomed to old-school child rearing. But being the girl she was, her recovery was quick. "I just want to know why *she* always gets to do stuff I don't get to do."

"Well, now." Rosemary folded her arms over her chest, looked Alexandra up and down. "What kind of ugliness is this? Is there somethin' wrong with you that I don't see? Because where I come from, only a person with nothing to offer is jealous of another person."

"There's nothing wrong with me. I'm not jealous." Alex's chin jutted out so far she looked like a prize fighter.

Rosemary cocked her head. "You sure? Because it sounds to me like you are. And of your own flesh and blood, no less. That must mean you don't think much of yourself. And if you don't think much of yourself, that must mean there's not much to you."

"Now, hold on." Cynthia didn't like this, and was about to say so.

To her surprise, she was forestalled by her daughter and son-in-law. Luca put his finger to his lips and gave a quick shake of his head. Sarita wasn't nearly as kind, giving her a jab in the side that actually hurt.

The timing wasn't the best, but the opportunity had presented itself, and Rosemary, even with all she had on her mind, had addressed it, as Sarita and Luca knew they should have done before this. Alex *was* jealous of Alana, and if they'd had their doubts, she'd just proven it. Luca wished someone had spoken to Santi the way the priestess was speaking to Alex.

Rosemary went on. "Is that right, Ms. Alex? Is there not much to you? Because I thought there was. When I look at you, I see Alex. When I look at Alana, I see Alana. Why would you want to be her? Why on God's green earth would you want to be *anybody* else but yourself?"

"I want to be myself."

"That's right, you do. Because there's not another you in this whole wide world." Rosemary leaned down so they were eye level. She pointed behind her to where Alana stood. "Your sister is about to go into that kitchen and face a demon. You are about to go downstairs, into the heart of this big ship, and help your Daddy find some ghosts. They're different jobs because you're different people. But I tell you this—they are dangerous jobs, and one or the other of you might not come back from them. Is this how you want to leave things—with harsh words between you and your sister that you might never get the chance to say you're sorry for?"

Alex didn't know how it happened, but suddenly she felt wrong. And when she thought back to some of the things she'd said and done to Alana, for no other reason than because Alana was Alana, she felt mean and small. She hung her head. "No."

"No? No...what?"

She bit her bottom lip. She would not cry in front of everyone. "No. I don't want to leave with harsh words."

"Then you stop this nonsense. Today you have a woman's job, not a child's. So, you get your woman on, and you go help your Daddy." Rosemary straightened. Her work was done here, and not a moment too soon. They were just nearing the time when the cleansing should start in earnest. "Go on, now."

Sarita stepped up to embrace her three girls, gave kisses all around, with an extra hug for Alexandra after her inquisition. "Love you, all of you. Listen to Daddy. Promise?" When they murmured their promises, and went to say goodbye to their grandmother, to Jane, Rohini, and Angela, Sarita tilted her face up to Luca. "We'll get through this," she whispered. "I love you. More than ever. And for always."

He pulled her to him, heedless of their audience, and gave her a kiss that even after six years together made her toes curl.

"Blech." Niki was disgusted. "I hate when they do that. Why do they have to do that?" she asked Jane, who just happened to be standing next to her.

"I can't imagine why," Jane replied, using her hand to fan herself. "It certainly does look dreadful."

Luca knelt to Alana again, cupped her face in his hands, a gesture of his that always comforted her. "You know no matter where I am, I can hear you if you call to me in your mind, right?"

She nodded.

"Mommy's with you. I know you're both going to do your best in there. I know you're both so brave and so strong. But listen to me—" he kept his voice steady—"it's okay to be scared, and if you feel *too* scared, and you need me to come, I will, Alana. I promise. Okay?"

Her smile looked a little sad. "Okay, Dad."

Alex watched them. For the first time, she wasn't envious of the attention Alana was getting. She was thinking about the monster her sister kept talking about, the one she'd seen in her vision at the fair. The priestess said it was a demon. She wondered what it was like to see demons in your head, real ones that wouldn't go away, no matter how much you wished they would. While she—Alex—had been having fun playing with her classmates, going on rides, and hoping to win the derby, Alana had been trapped by her own dark thoughts.

When her father stood up, Alex went with impulse. She stepped forward and flung her arms around her sister. Over her shoulder, Alana blinked in surprise, and grinned.

"You can do it. I know you can," Alex whispered in her ear.

She released her, ran to Luca, and amid crackles and sparks, she and the other three ghost hunters disappeared.

Alana looked up at Sarita. "Poor Daddy. I feel so sorry for him tonight."

CHAPTER NINETEEN
Saturday, October 31, 2020,
one hour and fifty-five minutes before the end

The moon blazed white and round and high by the time Rosemary ushered Alana and the five women into the restaurant. In her head, the cacophony of the damned was all the more invasive this much closer to their target, but she felt stronger than she had earlier, and she knew some of the positive force she was drawing came from their belief in her. They might not know her well enough yet to love her, but they had faith in her. She'd even earned Luca's trust, as much as he feared what they were about to do. His was especially hard-won. She did not blame him for it, and was determined not to let him down.

Standing on the dining room side of the double kitchen doors, she turned to her companions. "Hear me now. Every hardship and heart-break that's come before, they were only practice for this. I pray you're ready for it. That skunk in there, it can be whatever you're afraid of. It knows every pain from your past. No matter what it says or does—and it will provoke you, I promise you—pay it no mind. Don't talk to it." She wagged a finger. "I see how much y'all like to talk, so I'm tellin' you. Speak only when absolutely necessary." She looked at Sarita. "You and Alana stay here in the dining room for now. You'll be needed later."

Sarita gnawed on her lip. "How will I know when?"

Her grandmother tipped her head toward Alana. "She'll know, sweet pea." To the others, she said, "Let's go."

As soon as they pushed through the doors, the four former business partners felt the change in the kitchen. There was the hiss of something that bred a depthless cold in the womb. Unconsciously, they all hugged their arms over their abdomens.

Emilio and Michael looked up when they entered. They'd also been apprised by Avi there was to be minimum chatter, and they were to follow the priestess's instructions to the letter. Michael couldn't stop his eyes from filling when he saw Angela, his daughter's favorite person when she was a little girl. Angela smiled at him, and silently pressed his hand. They all noted how defeated he looked. Emilio had not fared much better. However, nothing compared to the toll taken on Marisol, after being fed upon for more than twenty hours.

Rohini was prepared for it. Naturally, Rosemary knew what to expect. But when Angela, Jane, and Cynthia peeked into that back room, what they saw hit their eyes like hot vinegar.

She was as gaunt and yellow as someone with liver disease. Her eyes were no longer dark and shiny, but coated with a rheumy film, and so shot through with blood, the whites looked solid red. She hadn't eaten or had anything to drink since her meal at Chelsea's with Emilio the night before, and she sat slumped and lifeless in one of the metal kitchen chairs.

Angela took one look at her and burst into tears. She couldn't stop herself.

Its host might be in frightful shape, but the creature was feeling right as rain. It looked at them and smirked. "Well, now. Look who's here. Scary, Baby, Ginger, Posh, and Sporty."

"Hold hands. Stay by me. Don't move from my side."

How did he let himself get talked into this? He must have been out of his mind. To be forced to bring his children down here was his own twisted version of the Harrowing of Hell. They were in the cavernous engine room only five minutes, and already he was so rattled by the changes to it, his shirt was soaked with sweat.

Pumps, turbines, tanks, ventilation shafts, condensers, motors, steering gears—every piece of historic equipment that had always looked preserved and cared for—was orange with rust. Cobwebs, some speckled with the carcasses of greenhead flies, hung from the starting platform controls and gauges. For the first time ever on the ship, he heard scuttles and squeaks, and prayed that the rodents would be frightened enough by his movements and voice to stay hidden. The overhead lights were dim, as though the wattage were being siphoned for something else, something that sapped the vitality of the ship, and left her engine room—her very essence—sluggish, illuminated with a queasy-green tinge. And the air—

"Ew. Dad, it smells awful."

"Yeah. It didn't smell like this when Mommy brought us down here."

"Maria, did you fart?"

"Shut up, Niki. Dad, tell her to be quiet. It happened one time—"

"Okay, everybody *stop*." He bent to his daughters, and the look on his face made them snap to attention.

He didn't look like their father right then. That was more frightening to them than what was happening around them. But it occurred to him that they were too innocent to grasp how much peril they were in, and the only way to keep them safe was to scare the crap out of them himself.

"You're going to do *exactly* what I tell you to do, *when* I tell you to do it. You're going to be quiet, so I can concentrate, get this done, and get us out of here. Because if you don't, I'm going to give you the first spanking of your lives, and believe me when I tell you it'll be one you'll never forget. Are we clear on this? Don't say a word, just nod if you get it."

They nodded. He'd never seen their eyes go so round. They were terrified. Not of the fucking demon that was attempting to destroy the human race. Of him.

He felt like a piece of shit.

But he might as well get some mileage out of it. He pointed to Niki. "And you. We all remember the day Maria...had a very upset tummy."

He doubted he'd ever forget.

"It wasn't her fault she ate something bad. It happens to the best of us, and I don't want to hear you tease her about that again. You understand me?"

Niki's head bobbed up and down with such vigor he thought it would snap off her neck.

"Good." He gave them one last warning look for good measure, still feeling like a heel about it, but better safe than sorry. "Now, let's move it."

They were walking aft, starboard side of Shaft Alley. The passageways were narrow, lined by steel railings on either side. The partitions and archways were also thick steel, and there were giant rivets everywhere, along with steps and platforms shooting off every which way. In his current state of mind it all looked too similar. He thought the propeller box was this way, but wasn't sure.

"Where the hell is it?" he mumbled to himself. How could he not remember? He'd been down here countless times with Sarita.

His three little girls remained painfully quiet, the only sounds coming from them the knocking of their sneakers on the metal flooring. Niki kept her eyes down, trying not to cry. Alex knew exactly where to go, and stole glances at her father, wondering if she dare tell him.

And while Luca, Niki, and Alex were preoccupied by these thoughts, Maria caught a glimpse of a man up ahead. A gray-haired man, standing in a doorway marked with the number '13'. He was wearing a tuxedo and twirling a cane. When he saw she'd spotted him, he smiled.

A terrible smile that slid through her insides.

She gasped, and he disappeared.

"What's wrong?" Luca asked, still sounding gruff.

"N...nothing."

He knew better. "Maria, tell me what you saw."

"I—"

Every light snapped off. There was nothing but solid black. Luca swore, and the girls squealed. They heard a loud blow, and felt a tremendous force of air rush by.

And then silence.

"Dad?"

"Daddy?"

"Why isn't he answering?"

Alex was afraid to release her grip on her sister's hand for fear she'd never find it again. She bent down and poked around cautiously in the dark.

"He...he's not here."

With a practiced nonchalance, Rosemary studied Marisol, trying to gauge how far gone she was. She turned her back on the creature with not one word, and emptied her satchel on the kitchen side of the barrier. Her eyes flicked to where Angela sat at her old pastry station, rocking back and forth, her arms folded to her chest. Jane kept a hand on Angela's shoulder, taking deep, steadying breaths herself.

"Angela, *cher*, that's not helping us," the priestess said quietly. But her heart went out to her. Evil, the first time one faced it, was a wallop to the psyche. Which was why most people spent the whole of their lives pretending it didn't exist.

"I'm sorry," Angela whispered. "Just give me a minute." She dabbed under her eyes.

Marisol. The little girl who'd been so excited the first time she let her decorate cupcakes, the defiant adolescent who would sneak into her kitchen to learn how to bake, the teenager who'd cried in her lap when her mother died.

"Oh, Rose-*maaary...*" the creature sing-songed, "you're not gonna get rid of me." It pushed Marisol's weakened body into standing, moved as close to the barrier edge as it could get, and heckled Rosemary as she worked.

"Beauregard sends his best wishes. You remember him, don't you, honey? You left him to die. You'll be paying your dues for that soon. Yes, ma'am. Just you wait."

Emilio clenched his jaw. Rohini pressed her lips together. Michael glanced over to where Angela sat with Jane.

Rosemary kept unpacking.

"Bobby's here. Your baby boy." When it added, "I bet he'd *love* to say hello to his wife and little girl," all eyes flew to Cynthia, who crossed herself, and the creature laughed in the throaty laugh that wasn't Marisol's. "Joseph and Lester are here too," it went on. "They all hate you for comin' into their lives, Rosemary. You were their ruination. They're here with me because of you."

True to her word, Rosemary continued on silently, while the voices of the suffering raged in her head, and the demon's taunts snapped at her like teeth. She held onto the thought that the majickal barrier had resealed, more secure than ever, once she'd fashioned the *veve* and completed her chant to Danbala.

The creature's hatred for her was so ferocious, they could all feel it, coming at her in waves of heat. Old and feeble though she was, she was still a powerful force, a powerful foe. No matter what the outcome of the night's battle, the entity knew she must die.

Luckily, it had an ace up its sleeve.

The group focused their attention as Rosemary used Rohini's work station to line up vials of sacred oils, candles of different scents and colors. She lay down sprigs of rosemary and mint, put eucalyptus leaves and cinnamon sticks in a small bowl. They knew they'd all have a part to play. To Emilio, she murmured, "I can assume your bar here stocks white rum? Bring us a bottle, please, *cher*."

He left on that task, and Rosemary set down the last items—two blindfolds, and a sea sponge.

Cynthia crossed herself again, and slid her eyes in Michael's direction, so heartsick for him, she could taste her pity. She sure hoped some of that rum was for him.

Alana and Sarita were sitting on bar stools, at Alana's request. She liked that she could swing her chair side to side, and she was doing just that when the kitchen doors swung open and Emilio came out.

"Hello."

That one word was stated with such trepidation that Sarita chuckled. "This isn't Alexandra, Emilio. This is Alana."

"Well, hi, there." He beamed at her, hoping to make a better impression on this sister. "Nice to meet you." When she gave him a cheerful grin in return, he was relieved. To Sarita he said, "The priestess asked me to get some rum."

Apprised of the ritual particulars, Sarita nodded. "We're just waiting for—" she tilted her head toward the kitchen—"our turn to join you."

"Yeah, I know." He was so tired, it was an effort just to bend behind the bar, pull out an unopened bottle, and stand back up again. "There's paper and some pencils in the office. No crayons, but maybe she'd like to draw in the meanwhile."

"Oh, that's a good idea. Thank you, Emilio." She gave him a smile of encouragement.

Bottle in hand, he left them to go back to the kitchen, and Sarita turned to Alana.

"Would you like to draw?" When she nodded, Sarita winked at her, and slid off her chair. "I'll be back in a sec. Stay right here, okay?"

While Alana waited for her mother, she folded her arms on the bar and rested her head. It was so late, later than she'd ever stayed up before, she knew. Even though she'd taken a long nap, she was starting to get sleepy.

The phantasm that presented itself as Beauregard Clay peered in at her from the glass doors at the restaurant entrance.

They'd left her by herself. After knocking out the sorcerer, this would be much easier.

No sooner had he thought it, then her mother reappeared.

Not so easy, then.

He watched them together, the mother smiling, scribbling something on a sheet of paper that made the girl giggle. And he hatched what he thought would be a better plan.

Sarita felt a prickling between her shoulder blades. She swiveled around to scrutinize their surroundings. Her gaze darted to the entrance doors.

There was something…

"What are you looking at, Mommy?"

"I'm not sure." She walked to the doors, unlocked them and peeked out, left to right. When she spotted what had given her the twinge of unease, she smiled, closed the door, and went back to Alana.

"Nothing to worry about. It was just a cat."

"A cat?" Alana was charmed. "On the *Queen Mary*?"

"Uh huh. A pretty white cat. With all that's going on, I'm not surprised one managed to sneak on board."

Alexandra was trying to 'keep her woman on', as the priestess had said, and pretend she wasn't scared. She *had* to. Her two sisters were a mess. Niki was bawling her eyes out, and Maria kept sucking air into her lungs and forgetting to exhale.

"Maria, you have to stop breathing like that, or you'll hyperventilate."

"What does that mean?"

"I don't have time to explain it. Just breathe like a normal person."

"Where...*where* is he?"

"He's here. Somewhere." She swallowed hard. He had to be. "We'll find him." But she couldn't think how. It was like being buried alive. They were standing side by side. She could hear her sisters talk, breathe, fidget, but she couldn't see them, not even an outline, a shadow of them. They were so blinded by dark, they hadn't moved from the spot where their father had disappeared.

"He was mad at us. At me, especially. Maybe he popped away because he was mad."

"That's the stupidest thing I've ever heard you say. He's been mad at you...at us...lots of times, Niki. He wouldn't pop away and leave us here just because he was mad. He'd never leave us, no matter what." Alex was as sure of that as she was her own name.

She was trying to think, to plan. "Wait—I forgot." She tugged at something in her back pocket that didn't want to come out. She elbowed Maria accidentally, as it finally came unstuck.

"Ow."

"Sorry."

A clicking sound brought a small beam of a light. It was better than total darkness, but still not much help.

"Where'd you get that?"

"Cousin Angela, remember? And she gave you a lighter."

"*Oh.* That's right." Niki fumbled around in her pockets too.

"We can light the candles with it."

"I dropped my candle when the lights went out."

"Me too."

Now that Alex thought about it, she'd dropped hers as well. "They have to be right around here." She waved the flashlight. The beam reflected off the railing and along the narrow walkway. "Oh. I think I saw one." She moved the light back again, and screamed blue murder.

"What is it?"

"What is it?"

Maria and Niki were jumping up and down like they were on the trampoline in their backyard.

"I'm sorry. I wasn't prepared for it. It's okay."

"What did you see, Alex?"

"Mmm. Never mind."

"What *was* it? Tell us what it was," Niki demanded.

Alex didn't understand why she wanted to know. It was obvious she wasn't going to like the answer. "Um, well…it was something with a tail. It ran away when I screamed."

"Ew, ew, *ew.* I bet it was a rat." Next to her, Alex could feel Maria tremble.

"Oh, that's so gross. I wish we could get out of here." Niki was crying again.

Alex aimed the flashlight right in her face. "If you want to leave without Daddy, go ahead. I'm not going. Not until I find him."

"I don't want to leave without Daddy either," Maria spoke up. "I want to find him too."

Niki covered her eyes. "I didn't say I wanted to leave without Daddy. I didn't *say* that."

"Then stop crying for five minutes, and let me think." Alex wanted so badly to sit. Her thoughts—the ones that made sense, anyway—came to her more easily when she could sit still. But she didn't, in case there was another rat. And while she was trying to figure out a strategy, Maria started humming. "Maria could you stop that? I'm trying to think here."

"No. I can't." Her voice quavered. "It makes me feel better."

"Let her hum, Alex. You know how she gets."

"Okay, *fine*. That'll just make it harder for me to figure a way out of this, but go ahead, Maria."

To her surprise, her sister's humming didn't distract her. In fact, it was such a familiar sound, she found herself being calmed by it. Even so, she bit her thumbnail, a habit she'd picked up from her mother. "First of all, I'm not sure we should light any candles down here anyway. Or use the lighter."

"Why not?" Niki had been about to see if she could flick it on. She'd never even held a lighter before. She wasn't allowed to play with them. This seemed the ideal opportunity to get away with doing something she wasn't supposed to do.

"Because even though you were kidding about the farts, they contain hydrogen sulfide gas, and it does smell like sulfur down here. Which means there could be methane too."

"We'll meet *again*...don't know *where*...don't know *when*...but I know we'll meet again some *sunny* day..."

In the dark, Alex sighed loudly and raised her eyes to the heavens. Maria was singing now, not just humming.

Niki paid no heed to the singing, nor to Alexandra's irritation with it. "What's 'methane'? How come I can't use the lighter?"

"Um...well, long story short, it means there might be a gas leak. And if we use fire, we could cause an explosion."

"...keep smiling *through*...just like you always *do*...'til the blue skies drive the dark clouds far away..."

"So what should we do?" Niki frowned. Was the room getting brighter?

"...they'll be happy to *know*...that as you saw me go...I was singing...this *song*...we'll meet *again*..."

"I don't know yet." Alex glanced around. "How come I can see now?" She could, faintly, as though they'd lit the candles after all.

"You can too? I thought my eyes were getting used to the dark."

"Maybe..."

But Alex didn't think that was it, and she wasn't only puzzled, she was getting scared all over again. From her position, she tried to remember where she'd last seen one of the overhead lights.

"Alex?"

"One sec, Niki." The closest light should be to her left, about ten degrees or so. She shifted her gaze. It was there. She could see it now, but it still wasn't lit. The electricity was still out, so what was causing the iridescence?

"Alex," Niki said again, her voice sounding odd. "Look."

Alex turned to see her staring at something behind Maria, who was singing her heart out, her sweet, young voice resonating, bouncing off the machinery. Following Niki's line of vision, Alex gave a soft cry of alarm.

Spirits hovered around Maria, each one radiating a soft, cool light. Alex's apprehension faded when she noticed they didn't look the least bit menacing. In fact, they were smiling. They seemed focused solely on Maria, and as she sang on, more and more were gathering around her, until the room blazed bright.

"You know what I bet?" Alex said, awestruck. "I bet these are the ghosts the priestess sent us to find."

They were. Thin, hollowed-eyed young men in tatty military uniforms the children didn't recognize were from a war fought long before their grandparents were born, a coifed, elegant woman in a floaty white gown, a short, bespectacled man in a double-breasted suit, a dark-haired, meaty sailor—the children hadn't met them, but their mother certainly had, and Marisol knew them too. Dozens who'd fled after evil had infiltrated were now there with them in the engine room of the ship they loved, listening to a little girl sing.

"It's Maria's song, Alex. They love it." Niki was amazed. "It's the same song she was singing at the festival."

It was a song the spirits might have danced to when they lived, a song that reminded them of their sweethearts, of a war that took away their loved ones, or brought them home. Or perhaps it was a song that reminded them of why they were still here, what they were still searching for. It was a song linked to so many who'd once sailed the *Queen Mary*, and with it, they'd been called back to her.

"I'll never again tell her not to sing," Alex declared. She stood still, listening to the melody, to her sister's perfectly pitched soprano, and decided they were both wonderful. "Maria, keep singing. Niki and I are going to find Daddy."

Maria's song came to a halt. "No. Please, Alex, don't leave me here by myself. That scary man might come back."

Alex felt her stomach jump. "What scary man?"

"He was there." she pointed. "By that door. Just for a second, right before the lights went off."

Niki and Alex looked at each other, and back at Maria. They'd had the same thought. Alex held out her hand. "Come on, Maria. We'd better go look for Daddy."

"I know where he is, girls."

They jumped, whirled around at the quiet voice behind them. A pleasant-looking young man dressed in crewman's clothes was standing by Door 13. He had short brown hair, and his eyes were a warm, soft blue.

"I can take you to your da."

Niki leaned toward Maria, and whispered, "Is he the man you saw?"

"No," she whispered back. "He doesn't look scary at all."

The young man smiled. He understood their reluctance, and held his palms up. "I'm harmless, I promise." To the girls, the way he said the words was new. Clipped, with a different sound to the vowels. It made him seem all the more like a stranger, and they hung back. But what he said next convinced them to trust him. "Your da is in trouble. He needs help. Come."

They hurried after him, past the door, down the tight passageway and up not one, but two old escalators that weren't working, that looked as though they hadn't worked in decades. By his fluid movements, they could tell he was a spirit, although he was solid-looking, unlike the ethereal others Maria had brought back with her song.

When they reached the top, he swerved left, and the girls followed him into a smaller room that housed hydraulics, pumps, valves, and navigation instruments.

"Where are we?"

"This is the Rudder Control Room," Alex told them.

"How do you remember all this stuff, Alex?"

"I don't know, but this is the way to the propeller box."

She remembered, all right, and didn't understand how her sisters could have forgotten. The propeller was ginormous—twenty feet wide and weighing thirty-five tons. When the *Queen Mary* still sailed, she had four of them.

A tiny line creased her forehead. The propeller box was where they'd been headed when the electricity went out. Their father wouldn't have gone on without them, would he?

They could hear the reverberating drip and rush of water coming from the sealed off box where the one propeller still bolted to its shaft was lit by submerged blue lights. When they entered the area, they slammed to a stop, their minds emptied of everything but terror.

Luca was knocked cold, hanging suspended over the pool, caught on something below the railing that encircled the box. His head flopped to one side, his body slumped lifelessly, out of their reach, and his legs dangled up to his knees in frigid water. There was a long gash on the side of his face and up into his hairline that stood out in stark red. The ripples of blue light against his skin bleached it of color. Next to the gigantic propeller, he looked tiny and helpless.

To his three little girls, the scene was not only petrifying, but surreal. To them, Luca was the tallest, the bravest, the handsomest, the strongest. He seemed indestructible—their very own superhero, who had *real* superpowers. Now they saw this was not the objective truth. He was as vulnerable as any other human. That realization, discovered in such a way, was nothing short of traumatic.

This time, Alex couldn't stop herself from crying. She didn't even think to try.

"Hang on, now, hang on. E's not dead," the crewman assured them. "But we have to hurry. He's got little time left."

Things were not going any better several decks up.

The five women had managed to get Marisol onto one of the stainless tables and unclothed, but weakened though she was, she was younger by decades, and didn't make it easy for them. She sunk her teeth into Rosemary's wrist, and gave Cynthia a black eye as soon as they put their hands on her. Though they all did their best not to hurt her, the creature inside her struggled against them, and her skin was mottled with bruises. The sounds that came out of her were feral, but when that didn't work, it used Marisol's voice to plead.

"Daddy, help me! Emilio, *please*. How can you let them do this to me?"

When she started to sob, Emilio lost it, completely. He'd been holding it together for the sake of others—endless, agonizing hours of watching something depraved take over the mind, body, and soul of his darling Marisol. She'd been imprisoned in a small room all day with no food, no water. And he'd helped. She'd suffered so many indignities already. She, who so loved The Secret Spice, had to endure it when whatever was within her used her own hands to vandalize it, to fling dough and smash glass. She was fastidious in her cleanliness, yet twice her father had gone past the barrier to clean a mess on the floor when her body had succumbed to human needs. How must she feel, trapped inside a body that was no longer hers to command, that was defiling everything she was, everything she stood for?

He'd already promised himself that when this was over, every appliance, every chair and table, everything down to the last teaspoon, would be replaced, so she'd never have to lay eyes on any of it again. If he could, he'd have burned the restaurant to the ground.

And now this. To be held down and stripped, on the stainless steel table in the room where she stored her sacks of flour and sugar, where she and Rohini had whispered secrets, laughed together, and prepared foods. How could he *know* if they were right in this? He'd been given no choice but to accept their conclusion, but what if they were wrong? The news ran stories all the time about victims killed by zealots who believed them to be possessed.

Her cries for help were his undoing. It was that simple. The veneer finally fractured. He burst through the barrier, and it took Michael, Angela, Jane, and Rohini every ounce of muscle they had to stop him from flinging himself at the two who were left holding her down, Rosemary and Cynthia.

"That's enough. Let go of her. Leave her alone!"

Rosemary kept her hands steady on Marisol, never glancing behind her once. "Get that boy out of here. If we stop now, she's lost to us. Cynthia, turn your head back over here, please, *cher*."

But Cynthia couldn't tear her eyes away from Emilio. He was a madman—kicking and twisting against the arms and legs that were locked around him, holding him back from Marisol.

"You bitch," he shouted at Cynthia, as his friends hauled him out. "You've always been a bitch."

"You're right." Cynthia held back tears. "I have." Her heart broke for him. He was just one of those who was unlucky in love.

"Cynthia Taylor!" Rosemary snapped. "Pay him no mind, and help me here. She's flopping around like a fish."

Cynthia spun back around, clamped her hands on both sides of Marisol's waist, and got a solid kick to the shin for her trouble. It didn't hurt as much as seeing Emilio fall apart.

"He didn't mean it." Rosemary broke her own code for a brief moment in order to comfort her daughter-in-law.

"Yes, he did. He owed me that one."

"Did he? Well, all right, then. Now you're even."

The comment helped Cynthia get her focus back where it should be. Together, they pulled the last shreds of Marisol's clothing to the floor, and pushed them into a pile. "We'll get one of the others to burn these."

"They all dragged Emilio into the dining room."

Jane and Angela came running back just then, and Cynthia didn't have to ask. The looks on their faces were answer enough. They snapped to attention when Rosemary cried out. In one swift move, the creature had managed to sit back up, and wrench her arm behind her back.

Jane's first instinct was to pinch the hand that had a hold on Rosemary.

"No, don't try to hurt it. It won't feel the pain. Only Marisol will." She grimaced as the creature jerked her arm again. "Pull it off me! Hurry up. We're goin' to start running behind if we don't hop to it."

It took all three of them to wrestle the creature away from Rosemary and get it back down on the table.

It fixed them with its bloodshot gaze. "You're all murderers." It grinned when it saw the indictment hit a nerve. "Tell her. Tell her what you hid in that freezer over there."

"Ignore it. I told you." Rosemary was out of breath. She held the creature's hands. "Let's get this blindfold on."

The creature bucked and squirmed as Angela pressed down on its shoulders and Jane held its ankles. While it could still see, it leered at Cynthia. "Your father's with me, Cintia Bianka di Azevedo. I burned out his tongue and ate his black heart raw." Cynthia's hands shook as she secured the blindfold, but she didn't respond.

It had more success with its torment of Jane, who was hit all at once by the scents of silt and sea water. "Can you smell that?" she said, already sensing what was to come.

"I don't smell a thing," Rosemary lied. They should only get a whiff of what had been making her want to heave up Jonah since she got there. "But whatever you think it is, it's not real." The reminder came seconds too late, and wouldn't have helped. As she'd told them, the creature knew every button to push.

"Mama!" the thing on the table called out. "I can't breathe."

Jane screamed and released her hold. The demon scissored its legs until Cynthia managed to grab hold of them again.

"Mama. Help me!"

Short, whimpering cries came from Jane with every breath.

"That's does it." Angela let go of Marisol, shouldered her way past the priestess and Cynthia. "Jane, sweetie, take a break."

Jane couldn't answer. She stood frozen, staring at the creature.

"Jane," Angela said again. "Go in the kitchen. *Now.*" Gently, she turned Jane's shoulders about face and pushed her past the barrier.

Rosemary and Cynthia were left alone scuffling with the creature, trying to keep her hands away from her blindfold and her body on the table.

But not for long. From behind them came the sound of duct tape being ripped from the roll. Angela stomped back over to Marisol, pressed the tape over her mouth, and swore at the creature. "Shut up, *cagna schifosa.*" She tore off more tape, and with Cynthia's help, secured the ankles.

Rosemary winced. "Ms. Angela, try to keep in mind your Marisol is still in there. I don't take such harsh measures during a cleansing."

"Yeah, well, I'll apologize to her when this is over." She yanked the creature's hands together, and bound them with tape too. "And I hope you forgive me for stealing your thunder. But I'm Sicilian. *This* is how we clean demons."

In the dining room, Sarita jumped out of her chair when she heard Emilio's bellows. He swore, she heard an answering voice, and her mouth dropped open.

Was he swearing at her *mother*?

She grabbed Alana's hand to bustle her out of the restaurant. They'd gone two steps when the kitchen doors crashed open, and he burst into the dining room, with Michael, Angela, Jane, and Rohini trying to hold onto him, calm him, slow him down. It was like watching barrelmen steer a bull at a rodeo.

Rohini locked eyes on her, sprinted over to them faster than Sarita had ever seen her move, scooped an arm around Alana, and scurried her away. "Come along with me, darling. This is grown-up business."

They disappeared into the office only seconds before Emilio shook himself loose, picked up a dining room chair and heaved it. Everyone jumped when it hit a wall, knocking down one of the paintings. He reached for a second chair. Michael grabbed him by the shoulder, spun him around, and slapped him across the face with such force, they both tottered. Angela and Jane fled back into the kitchen.

"Get a grip on yourself."

Emilio charged at him, then checked, remembering he was Marisol's father. "How can you let them do this to her?"

"It's *not* her. Don't you get it yet?"

"How do you know that? What if they're wrong?"

They were shouting, loud enough to pound down walls.

"Because I *know* her!" Michael slapped his palm to his own chest. "You've been with her only months, but I've known her all her life. You think I'd let them touch her if I didn't know?" His face contorted with fury, but he could no longer shout. His next words whispered past a throat gripped by pain. "This is her only chance." He jabbed his finger toward the kitchen. "That thing in there is not Marisol. I want my daughter back. Whatever it takes. If you can't handle it, then just stay the hell out of the way."

Lurching on his feet, Emilio stared at Michael. "You're right." His voice was quieter now too, but the reality was unbearable. The girl he loved was in agony, and he was useless to her. "You're right. I can't handle it." A muscle ticked in his cheek. "I need...I need five minutes."

"Then take it." Michael's tone tempered. He'd been thinking only of her suffering, of nothing and no one else. "Take a walk around the deck. Come back when your head's clear."

Like a vodou zombie, Emilio moved past Sarita, without seeing her, without saying a word, and exited the Spice.

For the first time, Michael looked Sarita's way. His eyes were raw as they surveyed her trembling form, her pallor, her cheeks wet with tears. "Don't let your little girl go in there," he told her. "No matter what the priestess says."

He turned away, back once more to fight a fiend that had his daughter's face.

Hugging herself, Sarita sank back down into her chair. She needed to give herself time to stop shaking before she retrieved Alana. Thank God she was with Rohini. But even with the office door closed, there was no way she hadn't heard the men. She must be terrified.

Eyes closed, Sarita took slow, deep breaths, and prayed for answers, prayed she was doing the right thing.

While she did, the white cat slipped in through the door Emilio had left ajar, and settled itself into a corner.

Jane was pacing behind the kitchen doors when Michael went back in. He saw she'd been crying, and his world collapsed. "She's dead."

"No." She clutched his arm. "No, she's not. I'm *so* sorry I frightened you."

"I see." He was still out of breath as he studied her, looked in the direction of the scullery, where it seemed much quieter than it had been only a short while ago. Neither of them had been present to see Angela take matters into her own hands on that score. "Emilio wasn't the only one. It got you worked up too?"

"She…it…spoke to me in Gabriella's voice." She felt strangled by the words.

It took him a minute to remember the name on Tony Miceli's fishing yacht. "Your daughter."

"It's been so long, you see."

She bowed her head, and when her breath came out on a sob, he reached out, thought better of it, and pulled back. The shape she was in, it might crumble her to be touched.

But nothing would stop Jane from speaking of it. She had to. Her baby's voice. That hideous being had stolen it, even if just for a moment. "Her birthday's coming up. I was looking at Marisol, and I was thinking about her. About Gabriella, I mean. It must have plucked the thought right out of my head."

That her own child had come to mind while she was tending to his was something he appreciated more than he could express. The other comment she made registered. "You were thinking about Marisol's birthday?"

"No, Gabriella's. I don't know why I was, at that particular moment. But it's in just a few days. November third. She'd have been twenty-five."

He smiled, and to Jane, there was a quality to it that told her he was a man who did not believe in happenstance. "That's Marisol's birthday."

"Is it?" Jane stared at him.

"That's why I asked. I wondered how you knew it was coming up."

They stood there, bowled over by the twist of fate.

He thought back to the early days of his marriage, to his novel role as husband and father. "You know, Angela baked her a cake every year from the time she was five. Never missed a year. We told her she didn't have to, but she said—" he stopped, realized this might not be a story he should share with her.

"Go on," Jane prompted. "What did she say?"

"She said we had to let her bake them, because she never got the chance to bake one for her niece." He'd been so wrapped up in his newfound happiness back then, it hadn't left room for much else. "I'm ashamed to say if she mentioned the dates were the same, I guess I forgot."

"No need for that." She waved a hand in dismissal of his apology. "I was here for Marisol's fifth birthday, now that we're thinking back. It was that first year we opened the Spice. I'm sorry to say, I forgot about that too."

"Yeah. It was two days after Inez and I got married."

It came to Jane that she and he had crossed paths many times, but each time, they'd exchanged nothing more than a few pleasantries. She'd known his wife, she certainly remembered that Marisol had saved Angela's life. She and Antoni had even danced at his wedding. But they'd never had a real conversation. Not until this. In her mind, their daughters were now forever connected. And by more than a birthday.

She felt herself getting weepy again, and she shut it down, taking on a resolve that bolstered him as much as it did her. "Well, then. We shall have to celebrate this year, all the more."

"We'll do that." He wished he could believe it. "I should get back in there."

"No. That's why I was out here. I was waiting for you." She bent to pick up a plastic trash bag filled with clothing. "These are Marisol's. The priestess says they must be burned. She wants you to do it. The parking lot would be a good place for it. There's not a soul here but us tonight." An odd look crossed her face as she held it out to him.

"Why me?"

Jane acknowledged defeat. She was no good at deception. Likely she'd gotten stuck with this job for just the same reason Michael was being assigned his—the priestess didn't need any more emotional outbursts. "All right. I'll tell you the truth. She believes it's best you're not present for this part of things. And, frankly, I agree."

"Is that so? And why is that?"

Now he'd argue. Who could blame him? "Because this part is going to be ghastly," she burst out.

Though he paled at the reminder, he told her, "I know. The priestess explained it. All the more reason I should be in there. Marisol should know I'm with her."

"And if you can't handle it, as Emilio couldn't, as I couldn't? Do you think it will help her to see you fall to pieces? Apart from which, assuming she's aware, which we most certainly hope she is, this part of the process must be mortifying for her. It can't be helped, but she doesn't need her lover and her father looking on. For pity's sake, it's bad enough having a man watch you give birth." There was empathy in her eyes, but determination too. "Please, Michael. You and Emilio both should stay away for now."

It made sense. But… "She'll be so afraid."

"She has Angela with her and Rohini and Cynthia. They love her too. She'll be comfortable with them, as comfortable as she can be, all things considered." She held the bag of clothing out to him again. "Take it."

He didn't want to say it aloud. "What if she dies while I'm not here?"

"If she dies, we're all done for shortly thereafter," Jane said, brusquely. "The priestess explained that to you as well, I suppose?"

There was something about the woman that brooked no argument. But if he didn't think she was right, she'd never have convinced him to walk away. He'd go find Emilio. God willing, they'd be coming back together in a short while. He took the bag.

Rohini came through just as he was about to leave. Her glance went from the bag to Jane and then to Michael. She held his gaze. "You're doing the right thing."

"I hope so." With that terse reply, he left.

The five women were now alone with Marisol.

"*Manman* Taylor, will Sarita be coming in with Alana?" Cynthia had been fretting about that since Sarita had agreed to it. Michael wasn't alone in his opinion that the little girl should be barred from participating. All were having second thoughts on that. It was true Alana had powers which would be a great help, and this was a life-or-death fight, but she was still a child, with a child's sensibilities. She and her sisters cried when they watched *The Lion King*, even though they'd seen it dozens of times.

"All in good time, *cher*." Rosemary was more focused on the spiritual bathing of Marisol.

There were two parts to the bath. First came the 'bad bath', which removed the evil spirit. This was most taxing to both practitioner and subject, and in this particular case, it would be excruciating. The spirit that had trapped Marisol in its grip was formidable, and had no intention of being cooperative. If they survived it, they would move on to the second part, the 'good bath' which would bring positive elements back.

Don't think about the good bath before you get through this, Rosemary chided herself. You know better. Don't be arrogant. Danbala wouldn't like that.

She took several cleansing breaths. "Hold her down the way I told you." she said.

Jane and Cynthia took one arm each, Rohini and Angela the legs. The creature went limp and still, as though it were shoring itself for what was to come. Rohini felt heat rush to her face. This was too hideously familiar. They all had the same thought at once, it seemed, as their eyes slid a guilty glance toward the freezer.

Rosemary sensed their distraction. "Focus," she scolded. "I need you. This will be foul."

She placed a casserole pot filled with heated rum and her mixture of herbs on the table, and tested a few drops against her own skin, the way a parent might test the temperature of a baby's milk. "For this, her blindfold stays on, but she must be ungagged and unbound."

"Marvelous news," muttered Jane. They wrenched at the tape around Marisol's ankles and wrists. Once untied, the creature kicked, bucked, and made such sounds behind the gag, Rohini was thankful Michael had listened to Jane, and was down in the parking lot burning clothing.

When Angela pulled the tape off her mouth, the creature spat at her, the spittle hitting her chest.

"Ew. It's a dead fly. It spit a dead fly at me." Angela grabbed paper towels.

That went without comment from the others when Rosemary sponged the first pass of hot rum over Marisol, and the creature's ear-splitting squalls filled the room. Ice shimmied over their skin.

Rohini pressed her palms to her ears. "I can't bear it."

"Don't do that," Rosemary snapped. "I need your hands on her."

"Oh, my God. This is terrible," Angela cried. But she held onto Marisol's leg and didn't let go.

Another pass of hot rum, and Marisol screeched and sobbed as though she were being scalded.

Even Cynthia spoke out. "*Manman* Taylor, are you sure it's not too hot?"

When Rosemary huffed out a breath, they piped down at once, sure she was about to tell them off for questioning her. But when she huffed out another breath, and another, they realized she wasn't exasperated with them, she was gasping for air. With jerky movements, she dropped the sponge on the table, clutched at her chest, and sank to her knees.

"*Manman* Taylor!" Cynthia started to go to her.

"Leave me be," she rasped. "We can't stop."

"But—"

"Dammit, girl. What part of the word *demon* don't you understand? I said we *can't* stop. Somebody grab that sponge. Hurry. Keep on washing her 'til all the liquid is gone out of that pot."

Jane snatched it up. "Cynthia, take her other arm." Though Jane's hands were shaking, she went to work. But there were no piteous screams this time when the rum hit its skin. This time it laughed, and the laughter was raucous, hyena-wild, and giddy with triumph, a sound that paralyzed them.

"I told you. I told you I'd kill you, Rosemary Dupré Taylor."

A sheen of sweat sprung up on Rosemary's skin. She reached up and grasped the edge of the table, trying to pull herself up off her knees.

The others held onto Marisol, went on with the bath, but they couldn't help but be preoccupied by Rosemary's battle to stay conscious. It was right then that they fully absorbed the enormity of the evil staked out in their restaurant, being held down and soaked with white rum. They'd faced so many fiends. Up until then, they'd seen the creature as just one more, and the steps of the cleansing as just another kind of recipe. But this was different.

Angela voiced it first. "Maybe we better call in Sarita and Alana."

"*No*. I forbid it, do you hear me?" Rosemary rasped, while shadows pulled in at the edges of her vision. "You leave them out of this. They're right where I want them to be." She was too weak to stand, but her eyes blazed at them.

"Let's just do what she says." Rohini nearly got hit in the face with a foot, and she grabbed for Marisol's ankle again. "We're stressing her all the more by arguing."

"Finally." Rosemary leaned her head back against the table leg and closed her eyes. "Somebody says somethin' that makes sense."

Sarita was having grave misgivings. The terrible noises in the back room were audible from the dining room, and there was nothing she could think up that might put a positive spin on them.

She wasn't sure she should try. Wasn't it better for Alana to know what they were facing? She was so out of her depth here. This evening, it had been made clear how extraordinary her five-year-old's powers were. The situation they were all in had been outlined to them accurately, she believed. If she'd had any doubts, all she needed was one look at the condition of the ship. If they survived the night, there would still be emotional damage to her children, and she hoped like hell she and Luca were up to mitigating it.

Yet, as she observed her daughter sitting across from her at the table they'd switched over to from the bar, it struck her that Alana didn't appear to be all that frightened. She stayed focused on drawing, lifting her head from the paper in front of her only occasionally at a sound coming from the kitchen. Sarita wondered if Alana might be blocking what she was hearing out of her mind, as a defense mechanism.

The cat was still hiding in the corner. It was perfectly still. Like Sarita, its focus was on the child, and on the scullery, but its reasons were explicitly different. On some level, Sarita sensed its presence. She didn't feel right in her skin, but with all that was going on, why would she?

Then she saw what Alana was drawing.

The child had switched from her depictions of their house, their family, Grandpa Raul and the ducks, to a variety of symbols that looked remarkably similar to the *veve* the priestess had made.

"Alana, what's that?"

"I'm making the *veve* for Agwe. He's the loa in charge of the sea and all the ships. He protects them." She turned the paper around as Sarita leaned in to get a better look. "These are the symbols he likes, see? Fish, boats, and other kinds of things from the water."

At that detailed response, alarm bells pealed so loudly in Sarita's head, they drowned out everything else. No one had given Alana any lessons on the art of Vodou. Each time Sarita learned something new about her children, she was thrown. Sooner or later, they were bound to catch on to that, bound to catch on to the irrationality of *her* being in charge of *them*.

But for now, her secret was safe.

"Well, that's...they're pretty." She smiled. Tranquilly, she hoped. "And how did you learn about him?"

Alana shrugged. "I'm not sure. But he's there, in my mind, with all the rest."

During this exchange, the white cat left the corner to slink silently along the far wall, edging its way closer and closer to the kitchen doors.

Sarita didn't notice. She was focused on Alana. "The rest? The rest of what?"

"The loa. I know Erzulie, and Papa Legba, and a whole bunch more."

"Gosh. I didn't know that, Alana." But her eyes were being opened. "So, you've drawn these before today?"

"Uh huh. I can draw lots." She yawned. She was really tired now. She wanted to go home. "Mom? Remember when Daddy and me, and Maria, and Alex, and Niki went to the festival today?"

"Sure I do."

"When were there, you know what? Daddy told us cats make you sneeze."

The change of subject was baffling, but it was all part and parcel of the same. Nothing Alana said or did should surprise her. "Did he?" The creepiest laughter ever came from the kitchen, and it singed her nerve endings. "Well, he's right. They do make me sneeze. I'm allergic to them, which is too bad, since I like cats."

"Are they any special kinds that don't make you sneeze?"

"Huh." A crease formed on Sarita's forehead as she got that sensation at her shoulder blades again. "I don't think so. Why? Were you hoping we could get one?"

Alana was looking at her intently. Her gaze shifted, and something made her eyes go big and bright. Sarita heard a sound coming from behind her, a soft, vibrating growl, and she whipped around.

The white cat was staring at Alana through yellow-gold eyes. As Alana stared back, the cat began to glower and spit.

Sarita stood up, her breath coming in short, fast bursts. She backed slowly toward Alana.

The spitting turned to a crooning cry, and the cat arched its back. It looked enormous. Then bigger still.

"Don't look at it," Sarita whispered. "Don't look at it, Alana." But Alana kept her gaze locked on the cat, and the cat was just as fixed on her.

It bunched, ready to attack.

With a yelp, Sarita lunged for her little girl. The cat sprang, its leap impossibly high. Mouth open, claws extended, it soared toward Alana.

Alana held up her hands, and the cat stopped, suspended midair, soundless, motionless, eyes wide, shocked, and almost human.

She turned to Sarita. "Mommy," she said, with her usual softness, "this is not a real cat. You didn't sneeze. Can I make it go away?"

Sarita couldn't breathe. She got two words past her lips. "Yes, please."

The fake cat didn't disappear the way the flies had. Sarita watched as it was thrust upward to the ceiling. For an infinitesimal blip of time it looked not like a cat, but like a shrunken, white-haired man. Whatever it was, it shot back down like a bullet. A deep black hole appeared in the carpet and the floor, and the next thing Sarita knew, the cat was sucked down into it. When the hole slammed shut like a steel door on a prison, the entire restaurant shook.

In the kitchen, the women felt the floor under their feet quake, and the creature on the table in front of them began to jerk and jolt.

From her spot on the floor, Rosemary saw the demon's juddering movements, and praised Danbala. She knew what would happen next. "Duck your heads, and hold onto her tight," she warned.

Marisol's mouth stretched wide open, and flies belched out by the dozens. But no sooner had she expelled them than they dropped to the floor, dead or dying.

They were all disgusted. Jane was practically hysterical. "I hate flies. I hate them."

Angela groaned. "How can anybody ever prepare food in this room again?"

But Rosemary smiled, and it held a pinch of wickedness of her own. She'd done it. Alana had done it. Her great-granddaughter was stupendous. Rosemary knew she would be. They'd have another *mambo asogwe* in the family one day.

She could feel her strength flowing back, and she sent up another prayer of gratitude. Her breathing was still laborious, but the women were astonished to see her pull herself to a standing position, and get straight back to work. When she saw the casserole pot was emptied of rum, she placed her hands on Marisol's head. The demon knew her touch, and bayed like a wounded wolf.

If it astonished them to see her up and functional when minutes before she'd been near death, it was even more astonishing to hear her speak directly to the creature. Not only speak to it, have an actual conversation.

"It's time for you to leave. You lost your lieutenant to a five-year-old girl. You played your trump card, and you lost."

"You're gloating. You're glad he's gone. You're even glad for what Jamilla did to him. Admit it. You're not so pure."

"I am gloating. He deserved everything he got. And I never said I was so pure. You're the one who says that."

Marisol was whimpering. "It was so close."

"That it was. Go on, now. Go away."

The demon turned its head toward her to spit out one last fly, but there were none. "You bitch. You should have died right there on the floor."

"Oh, don't you fret about that. I will die. I promise. But not today."

She took the blindfold off Marisol, and for the first time since the cleansing began, the tautness in the young woman's body released. Her eyes closed, and she went still.

Rosemary placed her hand over Marisol's heart. "Beating," she pronounced. She fired out orders. "We're not done yet. Not even close. We need to get some water into her, slowly. Wrap her in that white robe. When we get back from the engine room, we'll need to scrub this room from top to bottom. You were right about that, Ms. Angela. For now," she motioned to Rohini's chef station, "let's light those crescent candles over there, and place them all around this room. That'll keep the space clear of bad spirits until we get back and can cleanse it properly. Once we're done here, we can take her down to the propeller box to bath her again, and the sooner that's done, the better. Luca should have things ready for us there by now. Let's get to it, ladies." She grabbed a bottle of sesame oil. "I'll be back shortly to pick up those flies. They need special treatment. Don't anybody touch 'em." As if they would. "I want to let Sarita know Alana's job is done, and done well."

Cynthia spoke up. "You had no intention of bringing her in here, did you?"

"Of course not," Rosemary scoffed. "I'm no fool." She pointed to the freezer. "Like that. Don't you think I don't know what y'all got up to with that. Tomorrow morning, first thing, get rid of it."

She walked out, their boggled eyes following her.

"Oh, my God." Angela had never uttered the phrase with more reverence. "She's amazing."

Sarita was standing next to Alana, both of them gawking at the spot where the phantasm had been suctioned out of existence, when Emilio and Michael came rushing back into the restaurant.

"We felt this whole place shake. What happened?" Even as he asked, Emilio dreaded the answer.

"It was Alana." Sarita had a dazed look. "She killed a cat."

"She...?" He was sure he'd misheard. "I'm sorry, what?"

"That was no cat." Rosemary came in, her bottle of sesame oil in hand. She beamed at Alana. "You did very well, sweet pea. I'm proud of you. Where'd it go?"

Alana pointed. Rosemary walked over, uncapped the bottle, and drizzled oil in the shape of a cross over the spot. She straightened up, looked at Emilio. "That'll stain."

"Oh." Emilio wasn't sure what to contribute.

"But even so, I'd leave it be."

Michael locked eyes with Rosemary. "Priestess?"

"We're not out of the swamp yet, sir, but it looks like we're getting there."

He clasped his hands together, wanting to kneel at her feet. "Thank you. *Thank* you, Priestess."

He and Emilio exchanged face-splitting grins, and Sarita collapsed into the nearest chair with relief.

"Don't get ahead of yourselves. Like I said, we got a ways to go yet. As soon as they have her dressed, you boys can both go back in and talk to her. She's unconscious still, but she'll hear you, and it'll do her good. Then we'll carry her down into that engine room for the good bath."

"Why not complete the cleansing here, *Granmè*?"

"Ordinarily, that's how we'd do it, but this whole ship's been poisoned. If we finish down there in the water Luciano's consecrated for us…" she stopped, looked around. "Where he'd get to?"

"They haven't come back up yet."

Rosemary stared at Sarita, her face wiped clean of emotion. That was not the response she'd hoped to hear.

He should have been dead, drowned at the bottom of the propeller box. That's what 'the scary man' Maria saw had anticipated. The phantasm Beauregard Clay had pitched his unconscious victim over the railing, then disappeared to go after Alana next, fully expecting the body of Luciano Miceli to be found resting atop the thousands of good luck coins thrown into the box over the years.

It didn't happen. The *Queen* had other ideas. Like Rosemary, she'd been weakened hour by hour under the onslaught of atrocities. But they were two tough old birds who'd dealt with atrocities all their long lives, and neither would succumb without a fight. The *Queen* used what strength she had left to pull one of the perpendicular rods away from her rail, bend that rod forward, and hook Luca under his shirt tail as he fell.

The rod wouldn't hold indefinitely. Under Luca's weight, it was beginning to tilt. Very soon it would snap free of the rail altogether, and both it and Luca would topple into the water. He needed to regain consciousness. Failing that, he needed to be rescued without delay, and the only living creatures nearby were three five-year-old girls.

"Alex, please don't cry," Niki pleaded, even as she cried too. "You have the best brain. If you're crying, you won't be able to think of anything to do."

"I *can't* think of anything to do. We can't reach him from here."

She lay down on the floor, scooted as close above the spot where Luca hung below, stretched her head and shoulders as far out under the bottom rung of the railing as she could without tumbling off the platform. "Wake up, Daddy. Wake up!" she shouted down to him. When he didn't stir, it brought on a fresh spate of tears.

Her little face twisted with misery, Niki looked up at the spirit who'd brought them to their father. "Can you help us? Can you fly down there and bring him up?"

Before he could explain the physics of spectral anatomy, Maria did. "He can't. He's energy, Niki. If he tries to touch Daddy, Daddy will freeze."

Alex stood back up, scrubbed at her eyes. "How do you know that?"

"Mommy told me. Up until today, she and I were the only ones in the family who could see spirits." She rubbed her temple. "Maybe we should try to run back up and get one of the grown-ups."

"There's no time. That pole won't hold," the crewman told her. Then he noticed what she had looped around her neck. "Is that paracord?"

"The rope!" Niki exclaimed. "The rope Cousin Angela gave us." She grabbed for it, tugged it over Maria's head.

"Ow. That hurt, Niki."

"Sorry." But she was on a tear. She'd just had a great idea, and was proud of it. "We can loop it on the rail and around my waist, and then I can swing down next to Daddy."

"Are you crazy? You'll fall."

The lack of confidence was insulting. "I will *not*. I know how to make knots, Alex. And I know how to climb ropes. *And* I got a medal in swimming." She threw back her shoulders. "I'm the best person for the job, and you know it." The crewman hid his grin at that, but Alex and Maria still looked doubtful. Niki was determined. "Please. Please let me do this. Alana's helping, and you did something to help, and Maria did something. I want to help too."

"You have to make a bowline knot," the crewman told her.

She gave him the side eye. "I know that." And before any of them could protest any further, she shook out the rope, and looped it around the rail.

"Test that railing, little girl. Make sure it's still sturdy. The old gal's taken some hits today. There's rust everywhere." He was trying his best to be a help in his limited capacity.

Niki didn't appreciate that as much as she should have. She wished he'd stop calling them 'little girls.' Did he think they were babies? She grumbled, "I was going to test it."

But he was right. Together the sisters pushed on the rail above where Luca dangled, to be sure it hadn't been damaged by the on-slaught to the ship. When they confirmed it would hold, Niki made her bowline knot around it, then stopped. "Alex, how many feet do I need?"

Alex peered down into the box, pursed her lips. "Mmm. I think about seven."

The crewman smiled. "Clever, aren't you?" he complimented, and Alex preened, just a little. She'd been pretty much in charge this whole time, and it felt good. The priestess was right. Only a person who didn't think much of herself was jealous of someone else.

Niki let out the sufficient amount of rope. She looped the rest around her neck and secured it around her waist with another bowline knot. She grinned at her sisters and gave them a thumbs up. Had her father not been in danger, this daredevil act would be pure fun.

By now, all the spirits had gathered around. If they'd had breath to hold, they would have been holding it, as they watched the young girl wriggle under the railing and lower herself down, letting out rope little by little, pushing herself away from the side of the pit and back, inch by inch, foot by foot.

She looked up, her smile wide. "I did it. I'm right next to him." Then her brow lowered. "What do I do now? How do I wake him up?"

"Swing into him," Maria suggested.

"If she does that, he might fall," Alex cautioned.

The decision was made for them when the rod gave way, and Luca catapulted into the water. He missed being slammed into the propeller by mere inches.

The spirits gasped collectively, but terror dug its claws so deep into the sisters, they couldn't make a sound. Niki didn't think. She loosened the rope from around her waist and plunged in.

Alex and Maria held on to each other as they watched their father slowly sink and their sister push herself back to the surface. When Niki came up, she was already shivering. The water was cold, the coldest she'd ever been in.

"Behind you, Niki." Alex shouted. "Daddy's right behind you."

Maria jumped up and down. "His shirt is stuck on that thingee. Get him, Niki, get him. He's under the water. He can't breathe!"

Niki twisted and dived after Luca.

Luca had been knocked on the head with enough force to keep him out for a good long while. But factoring in that he'd been hanging over the water for some time now, rather than drown him, the water was brisk enough to help bring him around.

...He was submerged in the tank, trying to free himself from the locks and chains, an illusion they'd done numerous times. He would rarely let Santi do it, of course, since Santi would have to use real skill, not sorcery.

But something was wrong. His majicks weren't working. He struggled against the restraints, seconds away from mortal danger, from losing consciousness for good this time.

The tank door opened, spilling gallons of water onto the stage, along with him, soaked and choking. His brother loomed above him, the one who'd saved him.

Santi kneeled down, shook his head. "The hell was that, bro?"

Still gasping, Luca looked out. The seats were empty. It was only a rehearsal for the show. He coughed and coughed, spitting up water. "I don't know. Something happened. I lost control. Thank you, bro."

Santino smirked, gently helped him up. "You want to thank me? Let me do it tomorrow. I won't screw it up." They laughed, he and his brother, together…

Except, Santi wasn't there. Luca's eyes opened. The water was back in front of him, all around him, submerging him. This time, there was blood in it. It wasn't there before, with Santi. Where was it coming from?

There was someone else in the water. A figure shining in front of him. Was it Gina? Had she come to rescue him again, or to greet him now that he was dead?

No. It wasn't his mother. It was his daughter.

Clarity hit him, and with it came instant fear for the daughters he'd left alone, a fear that ground his heart to mincemeat. With panicked movements, he untangled himself from the rod, and propelled upward. Something tugged on his shirt tail. He turned his head, and to his absolute disbelief, his daughter *was* under the surface with him. When she grinned and waved, he thought he was still hallucinating. But when he snatched her hand, she felt real, alive, safe. He scooped his arm around her and with two powerful kicks, he brought them to the surface.

With her first breath, she told him. "I did it, Daddy. I saved you."

"You saved me?" He was drawing as much air into lungs as he could get.

"Yes." She linked her arms around his neck, and beamed at him. He looked up at the platform, where, to his immeasurable relief, Maria and Alex were cheering and waving down at them. And all around them were the spirits of the *Queen Mary*.

"My God." In genuine wonder, he stared. "You did it. You really did it." He lifted Niki high above his head. "My hero!" She squealed with glee. To her sisters, he blew kisses. "My three amazing girls."

Niki's lips were turning blue. "Let's climb out now, Dad, okay? It's cold." He was still disoriented and short of breath, so she pointed to the ladder at the far end. She knew he couldn't teleport out of water.

Above them, Maria turned to the crewman. "You helped us. You helped save our Dad. Thank you so much." She blew him a kiss, and said shyly, "I wish it could be a real kiss."

His smile was warm. "Well, thank you very much. But I didn't do a thing. It was all you. You three brave lasses." With pride in his voice, he added, "You're as brave as your great-grandma."

"The priestess?" Alex scrunched up her nose. "You know her?"

"I do indeed. She's my wife."

They were speechless. And perplexed. The man in front of them looked much too young.

Alex put it together first. "I guess you died a long time ago."

Maria caught the look that crossed his face. Was it sadness? She couldn't be sure.

"I wonder if you might give her a message for me?"

They nodded.

"Tell her I found Bobby. And that we love her." He touched his hand to his forehead in a quick salute, and disappeared.

Niki and Luca reached the ladder. "Wait, Dad. Remember, we have to put the oil in the water."

He felt around his back pockets, pulled out the two vials, and frowned at them. "Which one—?"

"The blue one, Dad." Niki rolled her eyes. She knew he'd forget.

While the others were in the kitchen keeping watch over Marisol, it was Rosemary, Alana, and Sarita who looked out the glass doors at the entrance of The Secret Spice, waiting for Luca and the girls to return. Rosemary held Alana's hand, and Sarita had her arm around Rosemary. The priestess was about to send out the troops, when once again, the *Queen Mary* trembled.

This time she trembled with joy. She knew her metamorphosis would soon begin. Rosemary breathed a long sigh of relief. "They're coming."

No sooner had she said it, then they could hear the sound of Luca's arrival, a sound that was so natural to them.

Alana grinned up at her great-grandmother. "I love bubble-wrap. Don't you?"

Rosemary laughed. "I do." She lay the back of her hand against Sarita's cheek. Her granddaughter's cheek. What a blessing it was to be able to show her that small gesture of affection. "Do you prefer the girls stay here with you, or do you want them to be with us when we bring Marisol back?"

"I want to go," Alana said, before Sarita could reply. She turned hopeful eyes to Sarita. "Please, Mom. Can we go?"

Sarita glanced up at the clock on the wall. Twenty-two minutes before midnight. Just that morning, she would have responded with a definitive no. Just that morning, she'd been laying her soul bare to

Angela about her fears for her daughters. She'd been worried they were 'too daring' for their own good. She had wanted them to fit in, had been afraid of what would happen when people started to notice not just their looks, but how different from the rest of the world they were.

How wrongheaded she'd been. But it wasn't the first time, and it certainly wouldn't be the last. Now, she couldn't wait to see what her daughters would do next. Her daughters. Hers and Luca's. If the world wasn't ready for them, that was too damn bad for the world.

She lay her hand on her daughter's cheek, just as the priestess had done to her. "Yes, Alana. Yes, sweet pea," she said, imitating Rosemary. "We can go."

The rest of the quad squad came barreling in, along with Luca, who was wearing a sheepish smile and a gash from ear to forehead. "Sorry we took so long. We—" he touched his wound—"had a few mishaps, but we got the job done."

Niki chimed in. "I rescued Daddy, Maria brought the ghosts back all by herself, and Alex—" she stopped. How to explain what Alex had done, that the whole campaign would have been impossible without her?

Alex cut in. "I scared a rat." She looked bashfully at the priestess, who winked at her.

Watching them, listening to them, Sarita was filled with gratitude that they were returned to her, and more love than she would have dreamed possible. Tomorrow was early enough for them to discuss the particulars of their adventures. Tonight, they had twenty-two minutes to save a friend. A friend without whom none of them would exist.

Sarita Taylor Miceli, she told herself, this is not the life you envisioned. And aren't you damn lucky about that.

She wore the white robe, and a fresh blindfold. Emilio held her hand. Like her father, he would not let her go.

Michael wanted to be the one to carry her down to the engine room. Luca had offered to teleport her, but the priestess was taking no chances by adding outside majicks into the mix. Marisol was still unconscious, and although that was a sign her body had been cleared of intrusion, not until the good bath was complete would she be wholly free of the demon's grip. Unfamiliar with the physics of teleporting, Rosemary thought it best to stick to tried-and-true methods when it came to banishing bad spirits, even at the risk of being labeled a Luddite.

Cynthia, Sarita, and the quadruplets were holding bowls of white primrose petals, Rohini held the fresh herbs, Jane, Luca, and Angela the candles and anointing oils. It almost looked like a wedding procession, with a Sleeping Beauty for a bride, but it was a renewal, a restoration of balance, light, integrity, and godliness.

They entered the engine room, and already Luca noticed a difference. The space was repairing itself. The cobwebs and rodents were gone, departed as soon as the spirits returned, and they could see the rust dissolving even as they walked up to the propeller box.

When they got to the platform, Michael stopped, turned to the priestess, who anointed Marisol with oil: rosemary on her forehead, orange oil on the insides of her wrists, both to attract good. She rubbed vinegar oil on her ankles to keep the bad spirits from ever returning.

"Ms. Jane, Ms. Angela, light the candles, please, and set them on the platform floor."

While they did that, Rohini stepped forward. Thanks to Niki's reminder to Luca, the water had been sanctified with vervain, but now the rest of the ingredients integral to the good bath could be added. Standing on her toes, Rohini leaned as far over the railing as her petite stature would allow to scatter herbs across the surface—parsley, mint, marjoram, and once again, rosemary. When the priestess followed that by sprinkling a few drops of mecca oil—an oil to cleanse dwellings of the presence of evil—the pool began to bubble and foam.

To the flower bearers, she said, "After Marisol is in the tank, throw your flower petals in a few at a time."

She nodded to Emilio, who, fully clothed with the exception of his shoes, climbed down into the tank.

The water was freezing. He tread in place by the bottom rung of the ladder. Michael and Luca lifted Marisol under her arms, lowered her down into the box as far as they could, and waited for the priestess's signal to drop her down. The tank was deep, the water surface, as Alex had calculated, seven feet below the platform. The unconscious Marisol would get a shock to her system once she fell, but Emilio was there to retrieve her as soon as she hit the water.

In one fluid motion, Rosemary shook her sacred rattle and raised her arms above her head. The room was hushed, save for the sounds of dripping water. She could sense the spirits, though they did not show themselves. She closed her eyes, and began the prayer:

"*Adje, kite m montre chante Bondje*
gwo lwa m yo reklame mwen
(Oh, heavens, let me teach God's songs
The loa have claimed me)
Let me call upon the pure, the loved, and the righteous
To wash away the unclean, the wicked, and the soulless."

She tipped her head toward Michael and Luca, who released Marisol. Emilio caught her before her head hit the water. As she lay in his arms like a beautiful mermaid, he tilted back her head and cupped more water over her forehead and through her hair. He did that three times, and each time he did, she stirred a little more.

But the wonders had only begun. When the women threw their petals into the water, destruction, vermin, blood—every stain, every disfigurement was being erased, deck by deck by deck. Right before their eyes the engine room began to transform, layer by layer, as though pages were being flipped in reverse, taking them backwards in time to the golden days of the *Queen Mary* when she was, as a king had once said, 'the stateliest ship in being.'

And as the clock struck midnight on the night of the thirteenth moon, Emilio removed Marisol's blindfold. Her eyes fluttered open, and they were her eyes again. Dark, luminous, clear. They looked straight into his.

With infinite gratitude and love, he smiled down at her.

"Hello, beautiful," he said.

CHAPTER TWENTY

Sunday, November 1, 2020, 5:00 p.m., Long Beach

A syrupy, faux-pine scent of disinfectant. A taste in her mouth like school glue. A repetitive click, click, click she knew was the sound of an IV pump. A blurry, pale blue wall. The feel of someone's hand in hers. One sense at a time, Marisol woke up.

Her head lolled to the left, and Emilio came into focus. She gave him a weak smile and said the first words she'd said of her own volition in over twenty-four hours. "I have to pee."

A look crossed his face, and she knew what he was thinking. "Don't worry, Beelzebub is gone." Still in a haze, she shifted, and the hand with the IV line attached jerked. "What's in this?"

"The nurse said it was to hydrate you."

"No wonder I have to pee." She smacked her lips together. "And yet, it's not helping the dryness in my mouth."

Still holding her hand, he shifted from his chair to the edge of her bed. "You've been sleeping for almost fourteen hours."

"Have I? How do you know?" When he said nothing, she slowly shook her head. "You were here, weren't you? Amazing. Most men would have gone screaming in the opposite direction."

His eyes darkened. "You say that like you remember what happened. Do you?"

"I think so." It was like being strangled slowly. "A few hours after we fell asleep, I woke up, and I wasn't alone anymore. Just like that, I couldn't speak. And it felt...you know how, sometimes, when you're just waking up, and you want to move, but you can't?"

Leaning across, he brushed back her hair. "You mean, sleep paralysis?"

"Yes. That. I wanted to call out, to snap free of it, but I couldn't." Of all the terrors she'd experienced, the terror of not being in control of her own body was carved into her, would remain so until her last breath. "And, oh, God—there were thousands of voices in my head. The things they were saying, the pleas…" She couldn't finish. Didn't have to. He'd been there.

He said nothing, just kept stroking her hair. Knowing she'd want to talk about it—*must* talk about it—was why he'd forced himself not to sleep. He wanted to be right here, ready to help her when she woke up. He was determined to stay awake for as long as she needed to talk.

Through her lethargy, a thought focused. "My dad."

"He's all right," he hastened to reassure. "He's fine. At the ship, in my room, out for the count. The priestess gave him something to sleep. He…he was in pretty bad shape." He paused, and she felt his hand tremble against her forehead. "We thought we'd lost you."

"No. I was there. It wanted me to die. I know it did." She remembered the debilitating fatigue, the effort not to succumb to it. "But I had to hang on. If for no other reason than for my father. I heard him. Everything he said. Everything you said." She tightened her grip on his hand. "It was what kept me sane, knowing you were both with me. That you were all there for me."

"Marisol." Undone, he kissed her forehead, lay his cheek against hers. "I'm with you for as long as you want me." But he didn't know what to do for her, didn't know how she'd be, going forward. Whatever was ahead for her, he would face it with her. "Just tell me what you need, and you'll have it. Anything, and it's yours. I swear it to you."

It startled her to realize he was near tears. And where his chest was pressed against her side, she could feel his heart beating way too fast. She pushed at his shoulders to get a good look at him, and her brow knit when she took in the gritty eyes, the pallor and day-old stubble.

Discreetly, she sniffed the air. He needed a shower too, though it would be churlish to mention it. Then again, maybe it was her. Either way, it was clear he hadn't slept or bathed since—call it what it was—her exorcism. He was dead on his feet. They needed to remedy that right away.

"What do I need?" she countered softly. "I need a bathroom. I need to shower, brush my teeth and gargle for at least an hour." She could still taste dead flies. "After that, I might even want something to eat. How about you?"

He stared at her. "That's it? You're not...I mean...aren't you...?" His sleep-deprived brain was having trouble processing her mindset.

"Traumatized?" she finished for him. "Of course. It's not something I'm going to forget, that's for sure. But I'm here. I won. *We* won. For the rest of our lives, we can say we stood up to the most powerful evil in existence." She kept her eyes fixed on his bleary ones, shook his shoulders for emphasis. "We beat that fucker, Emilio. All of us, together. We did it."

The rapid rebound confused him, even troubled him. He thought for sure when she woke up she'd still be in turmoil. He studied her face, those lovely eyes that had only yesterday been bloodshot and glazed. "But, Marisol—"

"No, just listen. Will you listen?" She wanted so much to tell him, to make him understand. "You didn't know me while I was growing up. I hated myself. I wanted to be like everybody else, and if I couldn't make that happen, I wanted to be invisible, Emilio. I had only one friend. I felt like a freak, and spent most of my time reading comic books." It took a leap of faith for her to tell him, "I wanted to be Saturn Girl." She was embarrassed by the admission, but all he did was give her a commiserative smile.

"We all had a favorite superhero, *cariña*. At least, I know I did." A memory came back of himself at age eight, standing in front of the full-length mirror in his parents' bedroom in his Spider-Man costume, and dreaming.

"I guess so. But because I felt so…I don't know. Weird, I suppose is the word, I never spoke up when I was bullied in school. It's true. I know it's hard for *you* to imagine," she quantified, when he gave her a look of skepticism. "But after this…" Her throat tightened. "You were there. You heard it. Apart from it being so terrifying, it was so smug and arrogant. It was sure it was going to win, but I didn't let it. I faced the worst there is, and it couldn't defeat me. For the first time in my life, I feel like I really *am* a superhero, Emilio."

"You are." Reassured to some extent that she wasn't in shock, he smiled wearily. "You are Saturn Girl. And Saturn Girl always survives." When she gave him the most poignant look, he frowned. "What? What did I say?"

"My mother used to say that to me," she whispered, as one tear fell. "It's silly, but I still repeat it to myself sometimes."

"It isn't silly at all." Moved by her confession, her trust in him, he stroked the tear track with his finger, leaned in.

With a screech, she shoved him away. "Don't *kiss* me. I'm gross." She wriggled, tried to sit up. "I want to get out of bed."

"Just one more thing. I need to know something. Please."

"You better make it fast." If she didn't get to the toilet soon…

This was going to be tough to ask, even tougher to hear her answer. But he had to know. "When we made love…it was you, right?"

"Oh, Emilio." At her warm smile, relief washed over him. "Of course it was me." Her eyes went soft when she saw how much that mattered. "I'll be happy to prove it as soon as we feel up to it." With that, she verbalized the question, the anxiety she'd had since the second she woke up. "*Will* I be feeling up to it? What I mean is…did they find anything?"

He got the subtext of what she was asking, and was so thankful he could ease her mind on that score. "They ran all kinds of tests, and came up with a diagnosis of exhaustion. Apart from that, you're healthy. There was no permanent damage, Marisol."

No permanent damage. She closed her eyes on the sound of those words, three words that meant everything. "Wow. I guess I was lucky, wasn't I?"

He stared at her, saw she was perfectly serious, and his mouth quirked up. "Yeah. You were lucky."

She was still groggy enough for that to go over her head. "What did you tell them when you brought me in, by the way? I don't think our health plan covers demonic possession."

"I told them you fainted at work, which is true."

"Does that mean I don't have to stay?"

"We can leave whenever you're ready."

That was the best news she'd had in a while. "Great. Then would you please help me up? And let's get a nurse to take out this damn IV."

Carefully, he raised her to a sitting position, moved the drip line over so she could stand. "You know, while you were asleep, I was thinking." Wheeling the drip, he held on to her as she made her way to the bathroom door. He hoped the timing was right to mention it. "I was thinking, maybe we could…you know, sell the Spice and start fresh."

She frowned. "You mean, just give it up?"

"No. I mean open our own place. Another restaurant, or maybe a specialty pastry shop. You and me, as partners." He cleared his throat. "Business partners." He said nothing about his long range plans. Now was definitely not the time to declare himself.

"Hmm. It's an intriguing idea." She didn't need to ask him why he'd come up with it. If she were honest, she didn't relish going back, all things considered. "What about Rohini?"

The smile he gave her was sly. "I have a bead on someone who might be interested. I think they'd hit it off."

"Well, it's definitely something to talk about." She pulled the IV stand in with her, and smirked before she shut the door. "We can call it Beelzebub's."

Emilio went back over to the bed and sat down. He didn't know anybody could feel as tired as he did without being dead. His legs shook from it, and his stomach, empty of everything but too much caffeine, roiled. But for the first time since the nightmare had started, he had hope.

Yesterday afternoon at this same time, she was in the throes of the unspeakable. And now, she'd made a joke about it. If nothing else convinced him she would recover, it was that she could be flip. She'd deal with the aftermath in the same way she'd dealt with the demon, he thought with pride.

She hadn't dismissed his suggestion out of hand that they get a place together. It was a good sign she might be looking in the same direction he was, toward their future. When she was feeling better, he would suggest they take a few days to go somewhere—anywhere. Just to breathe. Just to be a couple. If he had his dates right, her birthday was in two days. He chuckled to himself. She would be twenty-one. Finally. How glad he was she was here for it. He'd make it a celebration she'd never forget.

He thought about texting the others, but they might still be sleeping. It would better if they could see her for themselves anyway. He pressed the call button for the nurse, then shook his head as he thought of it again.

"Beelzebub's," he muttered. "Yeah. That's just not funny."

It was late in the afternoon before Angela took the stairs to the upper deck. When she saw what was waiting for her there—in the precise spot where she'd had her life-changing encounter with a soldier named Lee—she smiled a misty-eyed smile.

New wooden lounge chairs. *Four* of them.

"Thank you," she whispered to the air. "Thank you."

She chose the one on the far left, sat back, and looked at the sky. At this time of the fall day, it was resplendent with color. Angela gazed at the dappled layers of orange, purple, and yellow, and thought of them as shades of spice—cayenne, sumac, saffron.

"I thought I'd find you up here." Jane's steps slowed when she registered the chairs. "Where did these come from?"

"I guess they showed up after the…shall we call it, 'the makeover'."

"The number could be a coincidence, I suppose."

"It could." Angela smiled, and patted the chair next to hers. "But I'd say these are special gifts."

"From whom I can't begin to contemplate, but gifts and horses." Jane sat next to Angela, stretched out her legs, and leaned back with a satisfied sigh. "I've just finished walking the entire ship, and I must say, I'm very pleased."

"She looks gorgeous, doesn't she? Like brand new."

"Mmhmm. Even the decking looks as though it were just hammered down today."

"Yep. Not a drop of fiend blood anywhere."

"Please." Jane grimaced. "Don't remind me."

"Are you likely to forget?" Cynthia caught their commentary as she came up. With a shudder, she chose the chair next to Jane's. "It was worse than the keggers I attended in college."

Angela gaped at her. "What college did *you* go to?"

"Don't ask." Jane reached over and poked Angela's thigh. "Just be thankful you were lucky enough to have me for a roommate."

"Oh, I am, I am." Angela's mouth twitched. "You were very refined." To Cynthia she said, "Where's everybody else?"

"I don't know about the others, but I'm right here," Rohini piped up. She climbed the rest of the stairs. "I called Emilio. Marisol is doing very well, and they're on their way back."

"Oh, thank God."

"Marvelous news."

"It is. I was going to mention we have a waitress in the same hospital who was also affected. She woke up this morning for the first time in months, and they wanted to pop in to see her before they headed back." Rohini settled into the last empty lounger. She was smiling, but then remembered something else. "Oh. Emilio wanted to know if anyone brought anything for heartburn. I offered him peppermint tea, but that didn't appeal."

Angela looked smug. "Did you hear that, Jane?"

"Yes, Angela, I'm sitting right here. If it pleases you to hear me say it, from henceforth, I shall carry a bottle of magnesium hydroxide wherever I go."

Still overawed by it all, Cynthia touched her eye, the eye Marisol had blackened. The priestess put something on it to ease the swelling, but it was still sore. An image flashed in her mind of Marisol as a little girl, seeing and hearing things no child should have to. And she thought of her own grandchildren, Alana especially. What heroes they all were. What a road they had ahead of them.

How thankful she was that *Manman* Taylor would now be in their lives. The woman had remained steadfast throughout the entire experience. Cynthia had never seen such courage. Rosemary could teach the girls how to handle their powers, to be like her. Not just the quadruplets either. Sarita could benefit from spending time with her too. In fact, they all could. Life was miraculous, but it could also be vile. And when it was, better to face it with the audacity Rosemary had faced it with all her long life.

Rohini said, "I saw Michael as I was coming up. He was going home to change after he heard that Marisol was leaving the hospital. He said…" She had to stop, then start again. "He said he wanted to stop by Inez's grave."

On cue, Angela's eyes went damp. "That doesn't surprise me."

"Nor me. He'll be back to see Marisol, of course. And to eat with us." With a small smile Rohini added, "I promised him shrimp."

"Ah. Naturally," Jane said. "I'll look forward to that, myself."

"The poor guy needs a good meal after what he went through."

"At the very least." Cynthia decided to kick off her shoes. "Luca and Sarita were taking the girls to the aquarium. Sarita thought it might be best to get them away from the ship for a few hours. Although I think she did that more for Luca's benefit than for the children's."

"Wise of her. Even apart from that whack on the head, he suffered far more than the girls did. But he knew what was at risk. What he'd been forced to risk," Jane mused.

"*Manman* Taylor slept in quite late, as you can imagine," Cynthia continued. "Last I saw, she and Avi were in the dining room with their heads together discussing—" she waved her hand around—"whatever it is Vodouists discuss after forestalling Armageddon."

"I wondered about that. They did a great job of keeping people away while we dealt with everything, but now what? How do they get everyone to come back?"

"I don't know that either, Angela," Cynthia said dryly. "Maybe they use WhatsApp."

But she was about to discover that Angela wasn't as provincial as she'd once been. With a mild expression, Angela told them, "Did you know that in the Vodou tradition, the spirits of the ancestors are celebrated today?"

Struck, Cynthia turned her head and stared.

"Yep. November first. It's called 'Fet Gede'—the 'Feast of the Ancestors. The ancestral dead are honored. The Vodou faithful regard them as walking with us all through our lives."

Jane managed to keep the astonishment out of her voice. "No. I most certainly did not know that, Angela."

"Interesting, isn't it? And the way they celebrate, it's like the Vodou equivalent of Mardi Gras, the Mexican Day of the Dead, and Halloween, all in one. I think that's more than a coincidence, don't you?"

"Sounds like it must be a great party," Cynthia commented, astonished by the changes in Angela.

But Rohini smiled knowingly. Had she been asked to choose, she wouldn't be able to say who had been most transformed by their years and experiences—herself or Angela.

"Oh." Jane sat up. "I can't believe this nearly slipped my mind again. Today is their wedding anniversary."

"You're right, it is. No wonder he went to her grave. He's taking her flowers, I bet." Angela paused. "And I'm sure he wants to tell her what her other anniversary present is."

"What other anniversary present?" Cynthia was not at her sharpest after what they'd been through.

The look on Jane's face said it all. "Her daughter is her gift, Cynthia. We brought her daughter back."

They went quiet as it ran through their minds. That same date, November first, sixteen years earlier. Michael and Inez's wedding reception, right there aboard the *Queen Mary*, in their restaurant, The Secret Spice Café.

It was on the very deck where they now sat that Jane and Antoni, from their fishing yacht docked in the harbor below, saw two spirits encircled by light. The sight of her little girl smiling and waving, the burst of fireworks over the ship when she and Jackie disappeared, the warm, secure feel of Antoni's hand in hers. An indelible memory. A gift of bittersweet joy.

Angela was thinking of the moment Vincenzo and Douglas showed up in time for the reception. The emotions on her son's face—surprise, forgiveness, love.

Rohini could hear the music, recalled how flustered she'd been when Cristiano pulled her up to do a tango. She told him she didn't know how, but he just grinned and twirled her into the steps. And to her wonder, she discovered she could dance.

As for Cynthia, that day was the day she let Sarita grow up, the day she allowed herself to be captivated by a very sexy man, a man she still loved with a passion she'd assumed would have abated by now. On Michael and Inez's wedding day, she and Sarita went from being defined exclusively as mother and daughter to friends, as well as women, by and for themselves.

"Maybe we should all go," murmured Angela.

Rohini looked at her. "To Inez's grave? I was thinking that myself."

"We should," Cynthia decided. "Tomorrow, for sure. Today, I just want to sit. Right here."

"Absolutely," Jane agreed. "I for one, am happy to have the *Queen* to ourselves. We needed the time to recoup. And people will come back, Angela, referring to your earlier comment. No worries there. They'll carry on as though nothing happened."

"For them, nothing *did* happen." Cynthia stifled a yawn. None of them had gotten much sleep. Despite sufficient hours abed after it was over, the images and sounds were impossible to escape. She imagined it was the same for the others. "And believe me, any who might have recognized the danger signs but had no stomach to do anything about it, will never thank us for dealing with it in their stead."

Abruptly, she changed the subject. "God, I've missed this view." When Jane and Angela murmured in assent, she added, "I've missed this ship, the restaurant. All of it."

"Truer words." Angela heaved an enormous sigh, and gave her own confession. "I'm kicking myself that I sold my share." She sent a glance toward Rohini that was heavy with regret. "I don't want to live in Florida. I don't want to play golf every week. And I hate Early Bird dinners. Why did I do this to Harry? Why did I do this to myself? I'm not ready to be retired."

"Then don't be. I think we're at a point in our lives where we should be able to do whatever the hell we want, whoever likes it or doesn't." Cynthia paused before she dropped the bombshell. "Which is why I offered to buy Emilio out."

"You did?" They all had the same thought at once, a thought Cynthia could read as clearly as if they'd written it in black marker across their foreheads.

"Yes, I did. And no, Raul and I are not having problems." She shrugged. "At least, I hope not. I don't know how he's going to feel about this. But I guess I'll find out."

It was Angela who put forth the question. "If you're not having problems, why would you...?" she trailed off.

"I'm bored, that's why. Raul loves what he does. The different cities, the anticipation of landing a new deal—it's all exciting to him. And he does quite a lot of good with the money he makes."

"Travel, a private jet, homes all over the world. It certainly does sound boring." Jane was having a hard time disguising her sarcasm.

"I'm not being pretentious." Cynthia defended herself. "It's lots of fun. Sometimes. But I'm not the one sitting in those boardrooms making those deals. I'm the one having lunch with the wives of his colleagues, or getting my nails done." She made a face. "I've been doing it for more than six years. For godssakes, don't tell me you wouldn't be bored."

With a little smirk, Angela shifted in her chair. "I'm thinking, Cynthia. I'm thinking."

"The lifestyle is exactly what I put behind me when I left my birth family. And apart from the lean years when I could barely manage to feed Sarita, and wished I had some of that money I was so careless with growing up, I never once missed it." She stopped, thought about what she'd learned only one day earlier about Bobby Taylor's disappearance from their lives, and felt saddened by it. All those years of anger at him...

"How do you propose to have both a marriage with a man who travels for business, and a restaurant here in Long Beach?" Jane wanted to know.

Cynthia shrugged again. "I'm not sure yet."

"I just thought of something," Angela swung her legs around the side of her chair to lean toward them. "I have this book—"

She was forestalled by a chorus of groans.

"Please tell me you're not still reading Dr. Phil," begged Jane.

"Yes, please do," agreed Cynthia. "He's a hack, Angela. Not much better than a televangelist."

"Excuse me, I happen to like Dr. Phil. But this is not one of his. This book was written by two women. It's called *The New I Do*, and it's excellent. They write about different kinds of marriages and partnerships, how people aren't tying themselves together at the knees anymore after they commit to one other."

"Tying themselves together at the knees. Doesn't that paint a picture?" Jane was showing interest. "My father couldn't even watch an hour of telly in peace before my mother dragged him off somewhere. He was lucky he died before she did. If she'd gone first, she'd have insisted he go along with her, I bet."

"They were happy for over fifty years, and you know it. Everybody's different. And we're getting off the subject." Angela turned back to Cynthia. "I encourage you to read it. It's got great tips. You'd be surprised how many couples spend time apart yet manage to have successful and happy relationships."

"It's a clever title," Cynthia admitted. "Who wrote it?"

"I can't remember their names off the top of my head. But I saw them on *Ellen*. She squinted as she tried to remember details. "I think they're California authors."

Cynthia rolled her eyes. "God help us. Was this a book you found on Gwyneth Paltrow's reading list?"

"I'd be interested in reading it."

Angela's head snapped toward Jane. "Are you serious?"

"I am, actually." When Angela eyed her in silence, Jane hastened to reassure her. "There's not a thing wrong with my marriage either. I love your brother, as you very well know. And I quite like the life we have. But..." She raised her shoulders. "Antoni goes off on long fishing trips with clients. I don't always feel like going along. And if we're getting the band back together, I wouldn't want to be left out."

"But, Jane, I don't get it. You didn't even stay the whole first year we opened."

"Well, she had to leave, Angela, didn't she? She and Antoni had just reconciled." Cynthia would have said more, but she stopped herself. Perhaps this was a family matter.

"You're right." Angela pointed to Cynthia. "Not only that, you hadn't even grieved together," she said to Jane, with compassion. "You needed time with him for that."

"That's precisely it." Jane nodded. "But it's been fifteen years. And that first year here I…" She couldn't finish, not knowing quite how to explain.

"You weren't yourself." Cynthia helped her again. "You were unhappy, and now you'd like to try this as a happier person than you were at that time, wouldn't you?"

"I would." She looked down at her feet. "And…I don't know." She smiled over at Rohini. "Perhaps it's foolish to think that if we'd all been here together, none of this might have happened."

"You know, there should be a way for you two to figure out a schedule and do it part time." Angela was mulling it over. "It wouldn't be hard, not with Luca to help. He can pop in here, pop one of you back wherever you need to be. He wouldn't mind, I bet."

"Maybe Sarita would want to fill in sometimes, when we're not here." The idea bloomed in Cynthia's head, and it thrilled her. She would get to see her daughter and granddaughters more often if she were back in Long Beach.

Remembering their conversation shortly before the girls' birthday party, Angela thought Sarita might enjoy being at the Spice now and again. Even so, friendship compelled her to rein Cynthia in. "Yeah, maybe she would. But I say this with love, Cynthia, as one mother to another. What with her having magick quadruplets to handle, if you start being Helicopter Mommy again, she'll be the next one spitting flies out of her mouth, before we can say 'Father Merrin'."

Jane barked out a laugh at the ghoulish quip, but Cynthia hastily crossed herself. "*Santa Maria*! Don't say that. Don't even think it. What's wrong with you? That's not funny."

"Have we got any of that duct tape left?" Jane said, as Angela chuckled. "We should keep it on hand."

Cynthia was scandalized. "How can you joke about this? It could have been Sarita in that back room just as easily, and you know it."

"True, but I wasn't speaking about Sarita when I mentioned duct tape. If we're going to be working together again, I propose we put a piece of it over your mouth every morning. That should make the transition back easier for everyone, including Sarita. "

That got a laugh out of Cynthia too, and they were still laughing when they realized that Rohini hadn't joined in. In fact, through this whole exchange she'd remained silent. Ominously so.

"I wasn't aware that Emilio wanted to sell," she finally said.

"I think he does. After all, he's in love with Marisol," Cynthia pointed out. "It makes sense he wouldn't want to be here after what happened to her."

"Of course it does. And of course Marisol would want to go with him."

For the first time since they'd hatched this new plan, the possibility entered their minds that it might not be welcomed by Rohini. She'd had to adjust to losing Cristiano, and then again to new partners. Maybe the vicissitudes were too much to cope with.

"Look, Ro, I regretted moving almost as soon as I did it. I can't think why Harry didn't try to talk me out of it, when it's pretty clear he'd rather be here too. You can ask Sarita. I was telling her how I felt yesterday morning, before any of this demon stuff got started." Angela twisted her hands together in a nervous gesture. She would have thought Rohini would be jumping for joy to have them back. Apparently not.

With a nod, Rohini stood up and walked over to the railing.

"So, what do you think? Do you like it, or not?" Cynthia asked her bluntly.

She looked out at the harbor. Did she like it? She *loved* it. Although, she wasn't going to be a pushover about it. Cristiano's words to her when she was in that freezer came back to her again. He'd made her see she could be bold when there was something she wanted badly enough. It was high time she stopped concealing that quality. There hadn't been anyone in her life for decades who would chastise her for it.

Still facing the water, she responded to Cynthia's question. "I might. I do have a few conditions, if I'm to stay on with you." She knew that caught them by surprise, but when she turned to face them, their expressions were bland.

"All right." Cynthia was up for the challenge. "What are they?"

"To start, I remain head chef with Niko as my second. I quite like being in charge of the kitchen, and I'm doing very well. You can ask Emilio and even Marisol to verify that, if you wish, but those are my terms. I won't go back to being second in command."

Jane glanced at the other two, saw they were about to acquiesce, so she countered quickly with a caveat. "Are you open to additional training, cookery lessons, should the need arise?"

"I am. In fact, I'd quite enjoy studying with another chef to hone my craft."

Cynthia bit back a smile of pride and affection. "Oh, would you?"

"Yes. As long as the expenses are paid by the restaurant."

"That seems fair," Angela said. "Don't you think, Jane? Cynthia?"

When they agreed, Rohini told them, "There's more."

Cynthia grinned. "Keep going, then. You're batting a thousand, so far."

Rohini gave Angela an apologetic look. "I'm afraid you're not going to like this one."

"Me?" Angela stiffened in defense and pointed to herself. "You're talking to me?"

"I'm afraid so. I think we should keep Marisol's Raspberry Chocolate Tart recipe on the menu. Quite frankly, I prefer hers to yours."

"Thanks a lot, Ro. I like that." Angela pretended to be indignant, when secretly, her heart was singing. Rohini was working her way through her grief. She was better. And if Angela were honest with herself, so was Marisol's tart recipe.

Jane laughed. "Well, it's good that you like it, because it appears that's the way it's going to be. Although we probably need to discuss it with Marisol."

"The Spice is entitled to retain it, I believe. I'm sure we won't have a problem with Marisol over it either way. I think she'd love the idea of her mentor using one of her recipes." Cynthia arched a brow at Rohini. "Any other demands?"

"One more." She took a deep breath. "I want us to take one week off together. As soon as possible. I want us to go to Disneyland."

Jane stopped laughing. "I'm sorry, did you say Disneyland?"

"I did. I've never been, and I realized recently I'd quite like to see it. Angela has already given me my own set of the mouse's ears."

"Yeah, I did. But geez, Ro, does it have to be Disney? Can't we go someplace else?"

"Suck it up, both of you." Cynthia wanted to throw back head and guffaw. She was loving this new Rohini. "I agree to your terms, Rohini. In fact, I think we should all go. The girls would love it. We can even take *Manman* Taylor, if she's up for it."

"Okay, look—I'll deal with one more trip to Disney, if we get to go to Universal too. They have the *Ghostbusters* ride."

"Oh, you can't be serious." Jane looked like she was chewing moldy bread. The indignity of American theme parks.

"Why not?" In her inimitable way, Cynthia spelled it out. "We just rid the world of a soul-sucking monster. Why the fuck shouldn't we go on rides?"

Jane grumbled a bit more for form, but relented. "Fine, we'll go. But if anyone falls to their death before we can reopen the restaurant, it'll be on your heads." She gave Cynthia a dire look. "And you had better bring sensible shoes. I'll not carry you on my back if you get a blister."

Cynthia pointed to her bare feet. "Did you get a look at these bunions? I haven't worn stilettos in years."

"She's telling the truth." Angela kept a straight face. "She made a pyre in her backyard and burned every pair after Bowie died."

"Well, then." Rohini interjected, beaming at them all, "It appears to be settled. I think we should have champagne to celebrate."

Angela suggested, "We'll get Emilio to open one of the best bottles."

"Yes, let's, while he's still footing the bill." Cynthia was thinking that she couldn't wait to break the news to Sarita, when she heard young voices floating up to them.

"I think that's grandma up there!"

She sprang up, went over to the rail opposite Rohini, and looked down into the parking lot. "Oh, perfect. Sarita and Luca are back with the girls." She waved down at them, and smiled. "*Manman* Taylor is with them. I thought she was still in conference with Avi."

Angela stood next to Cynthia and peeked over the rail. "Aw. How sweet. Luca has his arm around her." She waved down too, then raised her brow at Cynthia. "I guess they're friends now. God bless her for having the energy to go to the aquarium after the night she had."

"Yes." Cynthia blew a kiss to her granddaughters. "I expect she feels she has a lot of time to make up for."

Rohini's phone beeped. She read the text and laughed out loud. "Marisol says she wants scrambled eggs."

"Lovely that she's texting." Still comfortably ensconced in her lounge chair, Jane gave Rohini a puzzled look. "But why is that funny?"

"I'll tell you the story while we're fixing dinner." Rohini could feel Cristiano watching from above, and knew he was pleased. "We must invite Avi to dine with us. He was a great help."

"Quite right. Now, let's see…" Jane calculated, ever the one to organize, "how many of us does that make, in total? We'll have to push some tables together…"

They stayed out on the deck, planning, reminiscing, laughing. And as the sun dipped into the sea to glaze the surface with a sheen of copper, its last rays glowed against the *Queen*'s newly-restored hull and smokestacks, and sparkled off the golden letters of her name.

It filled her with pride. The women had saved her, and once again, she was beautiful.

Soon the air would be fragrant with their cooking. The pots and utensils hanging in the kitchen of The Secret Spice would be dancing once again. Rohini would prepare Cristiano's shrimp, Sarita and her daughters would coax Luca into conjuring up his grandmother's tomato sauce. She found it quite entertaining when he used his majicks. And Angela…she wondered what delicious confection her favorite pastry chef would bake. Jane would set out plates and cutlery, Cynthia would pour the wine, and for the first time in over sixty years, Rosemary would dine aboard too, a seat of honor at their table, basking in their love, just as she herself was.

That was the truth of it. She, the grandest of *Queens*, did indeed love the women. She loved their whole ménage. For, wherever they'd been born, however they'd started out, however young or old they were, they were as dauntless and invincible as she.

Even so, not a one of them would be here forever. Many who'd sailed with her had gone, no matter how fearless, no matter how cherished. All ships and all people have a time limit, she knew, and there would come a day when they must depart.

But for the women and the *Queen*, that day was still far away. They would remain, right where they were, for a long and happy time.

AUTHOR'S NOTE

When it became apparent to me that Sarita Taylor's Vodou priestess grandmother, who'd been mentioned in Books I and II, had her heart set on being one of my featured characters in Book III, I was nervous about obliging her. With so much talk about cultural appropriation, was it seemly for me, a white woman, who knew little about the Creole culture or the Vodou religion, to write about her?

It's true that writers of all stripes have written characters of all colors and creeds. And certainly neither am I like Jane, the English chemistry professor, or Rohini, the Indian herbalist, or Cynthia, the Brazilian socialite-slash-cocktail waitress. The closest I come to mirroring one of the characters in these novels would be Angela, who is an Italian-American from New York, just as I am. But that's where our similarities end.

Even with these arguments in favor, I decided to do what Jane did in this story, and "err on the side of caution." I went directly to the source, and that's how I found myself in New Orleans, interviewing a true Vodou practitioner, Priestess Miriam of the Voodoo Spiritual Temple.

She talked to us for quite some time, and at one point she asked me, "Why did you choose to write about this character?"

I thought about how to answer, and decided I should tell my truth, which is that it was more the character wanted me to write about her. All the characters in these three novels had somehow made their way into my mind and spirit. They had their stories, and for some reason, they wanted me to be the one who told them.

The priestess's response was, "Then I think you should. And if you're worried about getting it wrong, remember this: I'm a woman first, before I'm a priestess."

A woman, *first*. That's when I stopped worrying about offending anyone, and wrote Rosemary the way I wrote Rohini, Jane, Angela, Cynthia, and Sarita—with my woman's heart, with the common denominator that beneath any of our other labels, they, and I, are all women.

At the same time, it was sobering to walk in Rosemary's shoes. There were so many things she was unable to do, so many dangers she faced during that time period in American history. Most of us know this on an intellectual level, but it was quite different to experience the limitations society put on her life, as I was writing her. I had to stop more than once to think, "Wait a minute—was she allowed to do this back then?"

I owe a great debt to the Vodou community of New Orleans. I garnered much from those meetings with the priestess, and also from Houngan Toby of Voodoo Authentica, who took the time to consult on the rituals I describe in this novel. I've taken a number of liberties with how they were described to me—a Vodou cleansing has yet to occur in the propeller box of the *Queen Mary*, for example. And there is no talking during a cleansing, whereas in the story, the women never stop talking, naturally. But I hope I've conveyed the spirit of the religion. If I had to describe it in one word, that word would be 'hopeful.'

The most important thing I discovered is also the saddest for us all, which is that Hollywood's portrayal of Vodou does a disservice to it that is criminal. In its goal to entertain, the religion has been sensationalized, portrayed on screen as satanic, and nothing, absolutely *nothing*, could be further from the truth. In fact, film and small screen portrayals are complicit in perpetuating racist mindsets, to my mind. Vodou is one of the most culturally-rich expressions of worship, and one of the most inclusive. I hope if this novel does nothing else, it encourages people to discover the truth and beauty behind this slice of human history, for it is courageous, creative, and unique. There are some excellent resources, videos, and links in our interactive Readers Guide, which is free on my website.

Here are a few other things about this story you might like to know:

» I named Rosemary after the real-life wife of the real-life Antoine Dominique Domino Jr. You might know Antoine as 'Fats Domino,' an American pianist and singer-songwriter, who was of Creole extraction. One of the pioneers of rock and roll music, Mr. Domino sold more than sixty-five million records, five of them gold, and had eleven Top Ten Hits within four years' time. While researching New Orleans, I learned that Fats and his wife, Rosemary, were pretty much the love story of the century. She was his one spouse, and they were together until her death. They had eight children. When Hurricane Katrina struck, Mr. Domino was seventy-seven years old. He refused to leave the area because Rosemary was in ill-health. They were rescued, but they lost everything. Eventually, their home was rebuilt, and Mr. Domino's gold records were replaced by his former record company. I chose 'Rosemary' and 'Antoine' as character names, but it was only later that I learned that rosemary, the herb, is used in Vodou rituals to ward off evil. To me, this was more than coincidence.

» Fats Domino isn't the only performer recognized in this novel. Little Maria Miceli's choice of song, "We'll Meet Again," is a tribute to Vera Lynn, and was written into the story by request of the dozens of *Queen Mary* aficionados I communicated with online while I was writing these novels. A number of them were stationed, or had loved ones stationed, aboard the *Queen Mary* during her years of war service,

and I wanted to commemorate that. Vera Lynn made the song syn-
onymous with the war effort by singing it to Allied troops. She was
known as "The Forces' Sweetheart" for giving outdoor concerts for
the troops in Egypt, India, and Burma during World War Two. Held
in great affection by veterans of that war and their families to this day,
in 2000, she was named the Briton who best exemplified the spirit
of the 20th century. As of this writing, Vera Lynn is still living, having celebrated 102 years of life in March of 2019. There's much more
about her in our Readers Guide, and I highly recommend you visit
the YouTube link we included to her interview with Sir David Frost.
It offers not only a fascinating history lesson, but an inspiring tale of
her courage and determination. "We'll Meet Again" was composed
by Vera Lynn, Hugh Charles, and Ross Parker.

» Another name of significance in the novel is Joy Nettelbeck the surly
chef, whose surname is an homage to Sandra Nettelbeck, the author
of *Mostly Martha*, the tale of a very headstrong chef. But her first name
is a different sort of reference, entirely. I'd asked anyone who wished
to participate to put forth the name of the most reprehensible person
they'd ever encountered, and to tell what made the person so ugly
in spirit to them. This was an online query, so first names only, of
course. The unknown Joy who persecuted one of my readers hatched
such a nefarious plot to break up her marriage and steal her husband,
she was voted "Most Awful" by everyone, hands down. And who
doesn't appreciate the irony that someone named 'Joy' made everyone in the kitchen so miserable?

The names of Sarita and Luca's daughters, Alexandra and Maria, are
the names of two of my dear writer friends and supporters. Niki is
named for one of my favorite former students, and the real Alana,

like her namesake in the novel, is a truly special young woman in real-life. (She knows who she is, and I'm waving to her right now.)

And then there is Avi, one of the heroes of Book III who made a cameo appearance in Book II. He was named in salute to the real-life Avi, manager of Chelsea's Chowder House aboard the *RMS Queen Mary*. Is he a secret superhero in real life, working against the forces of evil? I can't say. But he is force of good, one of my biggest supporters of these novels, and one of the loveliest people I've met on my visits to the *Queen Mary*. When you're at the ship, be sure to stop by Chelsea's, take a photo with him, and say hello to him, from me. Do try the clam chowder while you're there. It's famous for a reason.

And my final mention of names to note are those of Captain Sorell and Captain Fasting, who served as Captains of the *Queen Mary* during the time periods stated in the story.

» I'd also like to note here that further research and communication with the very supportive *Queen Mary* community made me aware of an error I made in Book I, concerning the death of a young crewman named John Pedder, an error I would like to take the opportunity to address now. John was an eighteen-year-old ship fireman who lost his life tragically by being caught in a watertight door when the ship encountered fog in the early morning hours on July 10, 1966. I was wildly misinformed on the circumstances of his death. I now know that the incident had no reported eye witnesses, and claims of his playing games and violating safety rules were fabricated. It's so important for me to correct this, because whether one believes in ghosts or otherwise, John was a living person, a human being who had a life, a career, and a family who love and miss him still. To pass on distortions about the circumstances of his death, in particular circumstances that malign his character, is terrible, and I regret that I did not think to check this information before adding it to my novel. It should also be noted that no one insisted I add this note. I chose to do so when I learned of my mistake, because it's the right thing to do, and I hope it serves as a reminder to us, writers and researchers in particular, to double check our sources. Rest in peace, John, and the next time I visit the *Queen Mary* Engine Room, I will whisper an apology to you. If you are indeed there, as many say, I hope you'll hear me.

» Speaking of fabrications, some are written into these novels deliberately, in order to serve the stories. One such invention is in regard to the staterooms utilized by The Secret Spice Café crew. I've gotten many emails about this, and I'm sorry to disappoint, but as much fun as it would be, there are no suites or staterooms aboard the modern-day *Queen Mary* that are permanent living quarters to any of the restaurant owners or other crew who work there. Everyone who works for the ship goes home when their shift is over. But you *can* rent the suites and staterooms for overnight stays, or just see them while on one of the tours. They are just as Art Deco-beautiful as I describe. The Windsor Suite in particular is not to be missed, but if you can't make it to the *Queen Mary*, you can see a virtual tour of that suite in our Readers Guide. As for why the characters' suites are "upstairs" in the novels, when all the real suites are situated on the lower decks, I wrote it that way on purpose as a subtle message that they're not real. However, I recently learned while the recipient of two remarkable personal tours, that there actually were First Class suites on the upper levels of the ship while she was still sailing. During her conversion to a permanently-docked hotel, those were remodeled into smaller rooms to accommodate more guests.

» Other points that might be of interest: The historical events mentioned in the novel which include the details of Queen Mary and King George's christening of the ship, the description of Queen Mary's clothing, including her coronation gown which I have her wearing when she appears to Rosemary in a vision, the dates and locales of major events during the Civil Rights Movement, the *RMS Queen Mary's* berth in New York, the information about garment workers in Harlem, are all historically accurate to the best of my knowledge. And by the way, there was indeed freakish cold in New York City in March of 1958, and a nor'easter that dumped over eleven inches of snow. Also, there really will be a "thirteenth moon" on October 31, 2020. If you read this before that date, wait for it, and let me know if anything magical happens. If you read this after that date, you can look it up.

» There does exist a book, *The New I Do: Reshaping Marriage for Skeptics, Realists and Rebels,* and it's written by therapist Susan Pease Gadoua and journalist Vicki Larson. I had to make mention of it because it's a wonderful book for those who, like the women in my novel, dare to define their lives by their own standards. I have read that book from cover to cover, and I recommend it. Vicki and Susan are indeed California authors, by the way, and this is my shout out of love to all the California authors and writing groups who've embraced me, a New York transplant. By all means, Gwyneth should definitely put *The New I Do* on her reading list.

» If you want to know the significance of the number '13' in the novels, if you want links to recipes, additional reading, fantastic videos, games and questions for your book club, a glossary, and so much more, I encourage you to check out the interactive Readers Guides we created for this novel, and the other two in the trilogy. I won't say I worked as hard on them as I did on the books, but almost, and I do think you'll find them valuable.

What a spiritual and educational journey writing this trilogy has been, but this book in particular took me way beyond. How do I close a trilogy that has meant so much to me? Novels that brought me new friends, new knowledge, sparked a whole new level of imagination and creativity? How do I say good-bye to all that, good-bye to the glorious *Queen Mary*, a ship that will live forever in my heart?

I think the words have already been said. They are words I pay homage to in the last paragraph of this novel, and they were spoken by Captain John Treasure Jones, the last Captain of the *RMS Queen Mary*. It was his bittersweet task to sail her to Long Beach, California, where she has now resided for over fifty years. Here's what he had to say after performing that final duty to her, and though it's not the same at all, at the completion of this trilogy, I understand how he felt:

> "I don't think I'd like to command another ship after having had this ship. I'd rather finish with this one, and go out with her in all her glory. ...I'm always very sorry to see a very nice ship end its days, but it's inevitable, of course. Both ships and we have a time limit, and the day must come when we go. I'm very proud to be Captain of her on this last voyage, and to have been Captain of her for the last two years, but naturally, we're all a little sad here that this is the end of her, as far as we're concerned...all my crew who have been here for so long. You get attached to a ship if you've been with her for some time, particularly if she's a happy ship, and this one has been."

> —*Captain John Treasure Jones*

AUTHOR BIO

Patricia V. Davis is the author of *The Secret Spice Cafe Trilogy*, and other works of fiction and non-fiction. For a number of years, she was a high school English teacher, teaching in Queens, New York, and Athens, Greece. She is an advocate for human rights, and all her writing encourages female dynamism. To that end, she founded The Women's PowerStrategy™ Conference, a conference to benefit Girls Inc. Patricia lives with her husband, who is both a poker player and a rice farmer, and the couple divides their time between Southern Nevada and Northern California. For more information about the author, visit her Wikipedia page. For news on upcoming works, book tours, and more, visit: www.TheDivaDoctrine.com

GLOSSARY OF TERMS
The Secret Spice Café

amada mía: (Spanish) My love

ason: (Haitian Vodou) "sacred tongue of Dan" (Danbala); rattle used to conduct services in Rada Vodou rites; symbol of authority of the Houngan and Manbo; gourd rattle

astral: a spirit that travels out of its body, under the control of black magic

bairn: (Scottish / Northern English) baby

Ballater: a place in Scotland from which Queen Mary and King George took a train to Glasgow

Baron Samedi: one of the loa of Haitian Vodou. Samedi is a loa of the dead

barrelmen: help to distract the bull at a rodeo

bebe: (Creole) baby

amou: (Creole) my love

Bixby Hills: a place in Long Beach, California where Vincenzo Perotta and Douglas Rigby live

bokur: a male Vodou practitioner who serves the loa "with both hands," meaning for both good and evil

Bondye: (Haitian Creole) Supreme Creator which translates in French into "Good God

briquette-entre-poteaux: a construction method for walls using brick as infill between heavy timber posts. In the USA, the architecture is found primarily in Louisiana

Burt Lancaster: an American actor, popular in the 1940s through 1960s

cagna schifosa: (Italian slang) filthy dog

Camels: a brand of cigarette

caplata: a female Vodou practitioner who serves the loa "with both hands," meaning for both good and evil

cariña: (Spanish) dear

cher: (sha) Cajun and Creole slang, derived from the French. A term of affection meaning sweetheart.

chica: (Spanish) my girl

Cintia Bianka di Azevedo: Cynthia's full given name, which she hates to use

Clydebank: shipbuilding and munition-making town in Scotland

Danbala: (Haitian Creole spelling) is one of the most important of all the loa, spirits in the Haitian Vodou and Louisiana Voodoo traditions. Danbala is believed to be the Sky Father and the primordial creator of all life. He rules the mind, intellect, and cosmic equilibrium. Also spelled Damballa and Damballah

Èrzulie Dantòr: (also Ezilí Dantor or Erzulie Dantó is the main loa or senior spirit of the Petro family in Haitian Vodou

Glasgow: a port city on the River Clyde in Scotland's western Lowlands, famed for its trade and shipbuilding.

granmè: (Haitian Creole) Grandma

gris-gris: (grē ı grē) Vodou charm to ward off evil

Guitar Slim: a New Orleans blues guitarist in the 1940s and 1950s, best known for the million-selling song "The Things That I Used to Do"

heave up Jonah: (southern USA slang) vomit

houngan: a male priest in Haitian Vodou

Hull No. 534: the ship, RMS Queen Mary, before it was christened

hunsi: devotees that have gone through the rite of fire, abide by the orders of the mambo and are qualified to assist with ritual activities

It's no mither: (Manchester England slang) It's no bother

Loa: (also lwa) are the spirits of Haitian Vodou and Louisiana Voodoo, who are intermediaries for, and dependent on, a distant Bondye.(God)

Los Feliz: a hamlet in Southern California where Luca and Sarita live

Lowcountry: geographic and cultural region along South Carolina's coast, including the Sea Islands

Mamãe/Mãe: (Portuguese) mama, mom

mambo asogwe: (also manbo) is a female high priestess in the Haitian Vodou religion

mambo sur point: (also manbo) is a female junior priestess in the Haitian Vodou religion.

Mambo/Manbo: term of respect when addressing a Vodou priestess, like 'Doctor' Jones

manman: (Creole) mother

menina: (Spanish) little one, dear little one

padoca: (Portuguese) a type of local restaurant for which São Paulo is famous

Rohini: (Roh-hee-nee) a partner and chef at The Secret Spice Café, who is also an herbalist

sangre de mi corazón: (Spanish) blood of my heart, a very romantic phrase used by Cristiano for his wife, Rohini

São Paulo: city in Brazil where Cynthia and Raul have a house.

Stalybridge: a town in Manchester, England, where Lester Taylor is from. (in honor of Ralph Rushton, former crew member of the Queen Mary, who was also born in Stalybridge.

tcha-tcha rattles: a type of rattle or maraca used in Haitian music

ti bon ange: in Vodou belief, the soul is made of two parts. The ti bon ange, "little good angel," is the part of the soul that contains the individual qualities of a person

tignon: a piece of cloth worn as a turban headdress adorned by free and slave Creole women of African ancestry in Louisiana in 1786. The Tignon Law was meant as a means to regulate the style of dress and appearance for people of color. Black women abided by the rule and turned it into fashion. Tignon Law eventually went out of effect in the 1800's yet, black women worldwide continue to use head wraps as wardrobe staples paying homage to their culture. A tignon worn during Vodou ceremonies is most often white, and is wrapped around the head after hair has been washed

Veve: (also spelled vèvè or vevè) is a religious symbol commonly used in different branches of Vodun such as Haitian Vodou. The veve acts as a beacon for the loa.

Vodouist: practitioner of Vodou (also spelled Voodoo)